PARTY WINE

A SOFI & CENZO MYSTERY

D. R. RANSDELL

Other Titles by D.R. Ransdell

Fiction:

Campanello Travels

Amirosian Nights
Thai Twist
Carillon Chase

Andy Veracruz Mysteries

Mariachi Meddler
Island Casualty
Dizzy in Durango
Substitute Soloist
Brotherly Love

Non-Fiction:

Secrets of a Mariachi Violinist

PARTY WINE

A SOFI & CENZO MYSTERY

D. R. RANSDELL

Author's Note:
Any resemblance to real persons is coincidental.

Acknowledgements

Many thanks to early readers including Sandra Ransdell, Elise Ransdell, John Boland, Annie Bomke, Debra Borchert, Veronica Rossi, Brenda Windberg, Lorin Oberweger, Don Maass, Chris Mandeville, Denise Ganley, and especially David Loeb.

Thanks also to all my wonderful friends and relatives in Piemonte, who really do own balmetti and make their own red wine.

To the Bessos:
Giovanni, Gabriella,
Alessandro, and Andrea,
the best Italian cousins ever

Chapter One

It was late afternoon when I rattled my way towards the *balmetti*, the village of party houses near Monteleone. The unique structures huddled together as a medieval ghost town, their uneven stone rows cutting into the mountain. The sensation was like entering the 1880s, never mind that I was arriving by car. I parked my borrowed Fiat in the adjoining piazza. It felt wrong to visit the balmetti in the dead of summer when no one else was there. Younger villagers were at work or school while the retirees were napping, but I wouldn't be staying myself. I was dropping off supplies.

Despite the quiet, my head was full of voices: "Sofi, the villagers love a party!" "Sofi, you need to pay back all the favors you owe!" The only words I embraced had come from Ivano, my cousin-in-law. "I'll pour them wine until they drop!" he promised. This was precisely what I wanted to hear. I needed a way to unload excess wine. While my parents and I had been living peacefully in Boston, my cousins had loaded the space with each year's surplus. The result was an obstacle course so packed I didn't have room to de-clutter it. The most I could do was serpentine my way from side to side.

I loaded myself with grocery bags and headed up the steep incline. Never mind the private courtyards for summer picnics or the upper rooms for winter festivities. The balmetti were important for their cellars. Thanks to the natural fissures in the rocks, the dark, damp spaces did a perfect job of protecting the homemade reds and whites. I couldn't appreciate the phenomenon. Although I never admitted it to the locals, I couldn't stand the taste of wine.

I continued past landmarks. During the last weeks Ivano had brought me to parties at a dozen balmetti. Over pasta and pastries, I'd ignored the hearty reds and concentrated on the local dialect. Piemontese was a mix of Italian, which I'd learned at home, and French, which I'd learned at school. When I caught whole sentences, I cheered.

As I climbed to the second row of structures, I imagined my four great-grandparents along this same path. They had sworn by the precious vines that provided a meager livelihood. Then they'd chanced a one-way ocean voyage. I'd grown up hearing glowing stories of the Old Country, but even after a summer in Monteleone, I wasn't sure I was Italian. Among other faults, I never cooked. Then again, even in English, I always talked with my hands.

My only loyal companion, a gray cat, meowed as I approached. As usual, he was perched on the wall that divided my property from my neighbor's. He'd meowed at me all summer but rarely left his favorite spot. I understood why. He was half on one property, half on another just as I thought half in English and half in Italian, felt half at home in Italy and half homesick for the East Coast. I loved being in Piemonte, but I didn't belong. Not really. I was too impatient. I was too straightforward. And I didn't like wine.

I flipped on the electricity box I shared with the neighbors and unhooked the high gate leading into my yard. At least the area was safe. Given the constant comings and goings of all the workers, I'd stopped locking the gate weeks before, yet the tools never disappeared. Forgotten cell phones lay right where the owners had left them. Bottles were returned, empty but washed.

Stepping inside the yard, I allowed myself a moment of satisfaction. The outside wall no longer crumbled. The electricity no longer crackled. The stairs were patched, and the cobwebs and snakes had been swept away. The weeds had been meticulously pulled, by me, one stubborn plant at a time.

For tonight's event, borrowed picnic tables crowded the yard. Plastic silverware and paper napkins filled a basket. A pot waited near the portable burner. Aunt Maria promised to make the best Bolognese sauce ever, and I could already taste the roasted garlic she would throw inside. The woman was a godsend. The guests would need as much food as possible to help soak up all that wine.

As I descended the three steps to the cellar, I extracted the key from my purse. The metal monster measured half a foot long and weighed as much as a bread knife. It was also weighted with history. My great-grandfather had made six copies of the master key: one for each of his children. Had he awarded them keys on their eighteenth birthdays? When they married? As soon as they reached puberty?

They would have been proud that their father had built such a fine party house for the family jewels—the fruit of their vines. The older teens would have filled long summer nights with friends and drinking and clandestine trysts. How many of my relatives had been conceived on the spot? My dad's father, Nonno Luigi, was the jolliest of all. He'd retired at sixty-two and moved to Florida to spend the rest of his life at leisure. Certainly, he was a candidate.

I was about to insert the key into the lock when I realized the door was ajar. This was not unreasonable. Ivano and Cousin Renato had promised to stop by during the afternoon. Either might have been careless with the door. Using my shoulder, I pushed open the wooden slab. I turned on the light switch, but after I turned around, I dropped the sacks of breadsticks, which crunched as they hit. Then I screamed.

Ivano lay on his back on the dirt floor. His gardening shorts were fresh, but his blue T-shirt was splotched with dots of burgundy. His eyes were open, so I swooped down and rocked his shoulders as if to wake him from a hallucinogenic nap, but I was way too late.

Clutching my stomach, I ran out into the sunshine and doubled over. I was dreaming. I was mistaken. Something was wrong with my eyes or my senses or my brain. I had not just seen a dead man, and the dead man was not my cousin-in-law. It wasn't possible.

I collapsed onto the nearest picnic bench, but the hot planks shot me back to my feet. I sank into the grass, hoping Ivano had died so fast he never felt it. Heart attack? Stroke? Aneurysm? Ivano hadn't hit fifty, but he was no longer thin and only exercised when he danced. At every party, he lapped up plenty of wine.

I fumbled for my cell phone, but it was too late to call a doctor. My cousin Grazia, Ivano's wife, was in nearby Aosta visiting a sick friend. Her mother, Aunt Maria, would be between grocery stores, but she might pick up.

Except that my cell phone was down to three percent.

On my way downhill to the piazza, I stumbled past the other party houses nestled into the rock fissures. I could barely see through the tears. Ivano had always been kind to me. He'd made me feel at home. He'd treated me like his own relative. How could he be gone?

I killed my aunt's Fiat's twice before starting it. I bounced over the cobblestones. Where to go? The nearest hospital was in Ivrea, nearly ten kilometres to the south. As I reached the paved road, I remembered the municipal police station between Monteleone and Cafreddo. The towns along the river were so small that one office served several of them. I strained the brakes for a quick U-turn and doubled back. A police officer would be able to help me. Surely.

Chapter Two

I pulled into the one-story station and parked next to the white Fiat Panda. I dashed through the empty lobby to reach the main office. The man behind the desk seemed a few years older than me, perhaps mid-thirties. A sharp nose aligned with a strong chin. Instead of a uniform, a blue dress shirt set off black hair.

He looked up from his paperwork. *"Sì?"*

He seemed too nonchalant to be in charge, but no one else was around.

"Lei è il capitano?"

The man yawned. "Yes, I'm the police captain." His English was fluent, but his accent shouted U.K. "You're American. East Coast?"

He was a regular Henry Higgins in more casual clothes, but his accurate appraisal took me off guard. "I have an Italian passport, too. But you're pretty right."

"Stolen purse? Lost dog?" His wedding ring caught the sunlight as he waved his hands. His imitation of a music conductor made him typically Italian.

"My cousin-in-law died in my balmetto."

He cocked his head. "Why didn't you call an ambulance?"

"Dead battery."

"Ha! Good play on words."

He scooted back and plopped his feet on the desk. If he'd had a superior, I might have complained about his informality, but from the looks of things, he was also his own secretary. Maybe even the janitor. Village life was almost always peaceful. "Can't you help me?"

"Think I bring people back to life?" Since his eyes twinkled, I imagined he was gauging my breaking point. He had no reason to suspect that I had once taught middle school and didn't rattle easily.

"If you're too busy—"

He leaned forward and offered me his hand, which was as coarse as any farmer's. "Vicenzo Bot. Call me Cenzo. CHEN-zo. Everybody else does. And you are Miss—"

"Sofi Francese."

"Francese is a typical family name around here."

"My great-grandfather on my father's side—"

"Save the history. Know how many people die in the balmetti?" He conducted a few more imaginary notes. "They're deathtraps. Who needs a village of party houses? They don't even have running water. You get the old buzzards in there drinking all night, and they die in their sleep. Let me guess. Last night you had a killer party. Get it?"

I ignored the lame joke but gave him the benefit of the doubt. He didn't quite believe me. "The party would have been tonight. That's why I went by. To leave supplies."

The man's eyebrows rose and fell, but after he grinned, he gave into a yawn. He might have been a student in my morning French class.

"Should I come back after you take a nap?"

He shook his head but didn't seem embarrassed. "You don't understand. I was up all night. He opened the top drawer and took out a packet of chocolates. "Pocket Coffee?"

Of course. In Italy, you ignored someone and then offered food. I accepted his peace offering, a rectangle of milk chocolate surrounding a burst of caffeine. I knew the treats well. I'd relied on them for all the early morning renovations.

Cenzo opened a side drawer and took out a form. He smiled as he wrote my name at the top. Progress. "When did you find this body?"

How could I think of Ivano as a body?

"Sofi?"

Snapping to attention, I shook my head. "Half an hour ago."

"You went to your balmetto and found a dead man in your courtyard."

"No. He was in the cellar."

"Locked inside?"

"The door wasn't locked."

"Why not?" He clicked his pen several times as if the sound would annoy me into a confession of negligence, but I was immune to that middle school trick too.

"There have been a lot of people coming and going."

"So you're a party girl. Nice."

Nice try. It must have been a slow week or maybe a slow summer. "No parties. Just renovations."

He scribbled something he would never be able to read. "Happen to know the identity of your dead pal?"

I shuddered at "dead pal." Ivano had been Grazia's husband, a cousin-in-law, an ally, an escort—

"You don't know the name?" Cenzo waved his pen through the air. "Perhaps he invited himself to the party? It wouldn't be the first time."

"Ivano Visconti."

Cenzo dropped the pen. It rolled across the desk, fell, and continued rolling across the floor. It came to a stop after bouncing off the wall. *"Porca mattina."*

"Pig morning" was a mild curse. When people were really upset, they used *porca Madonna* instead.

"I'm not sure I heard you right," Cenzo said.

7

I nearly smiled. "Which part didn't you get, Ivano or Visconti?"

Cenzo came around to the front of the desk. He sat on one corner of it, sending three envelopes to the floor. He didn't seem to notice. Nor did he seem to notice that I automatically backed away. Otherwise, I knew what would come next. He would spit vowels at me. In Piemonte it happened all the time.

Cenzo genuflected so vigorously I heard his fingers pound against his forehead and his chest. "The mayor of Monteleone is lying dead in your balmetto? Why didn't you tell me?"

"Had you been listening, you would have known fifteen minutes ago."

Cenzo grinned. "I don't care where you grew up. You're more Italian than American. But Ivano—never mind. We all die in the end. But maybe you wouldn't mind showing me?"

I headed for the door. "Thought you'd never ask."

Once we reached my balmetto, we slid inside the gate. I pointed to the cellar door and let Cenzo push it open. For a moment he did a doubletake. Then he slowly approached Ivano.

"Porca miseria." What a shame. Cenzo muttered the phrase over and over as he crouched near the body.

I cringed and turned away. The night before, as usual on a Sunday, while Grazia went out with her old friends from high school, Ivano escorted me to the bocce ball courts across the river in Lungofiume. While he chatted with everyone in sight, his friends allowed me to help them lose each game. I'd never toss another ball without thinking of him.

"Heart attack?" I asked.

"Probably." He sniffed the shirt. "Did Ivano often come here to drink mid-day?"

8

"No?" Ivano had a lot of friends, and he often took long lunches. The *balmetti* afforded a quiet hideout, but I'd never known him to drink alone.

Cenzo pointed to the biggest splotch. "The stains look fresh, but I don't see a used glass. Do you?"

I shook my head. As Cenzo stood, he regarded the obstacle course that had once been an orderly cellar, probably before I was born. The biggest feature of the rectangular crypt was the trio of giant wooden barrels at the back. They lay on their sides as silent sentinels, their lids stretching four feet across. Vines laden with bunches of ripe grapes decorated their sides. Another six medium-sized barrels stood upright, but they were arranged haphazardly. Their dusty lids hadn't been touched for decades.

Shelves stretched across the long side walls. Most were crammed with odd assortments of bottles, but the whole space was a booby trap. Wine was everywhere: in plastic six-packs, milk crates, crumbling boxes, and plastic bags. A few solitary bottles even dotted the ground.

Cenzo approached the closest shelf, where columns of short clean glasses were stacked on top of one another. "No used glasses."

"Or open bottles."

As Cenzo ran his finger along the shelf, he made a trail in the dust. "Are any containers out of place?"

"The whole cellar is out of place."

"I thought you were renovating."

"That doesn't mean I'd also gotten around to any organizing."

He nodded, mostly with his thick black eyebrows. "Notice anything unusual?"

I took a quick survey. "Not right off." I looked at the stain on Ivano's shirt. "You think some of my wine triggered a stroke? I'll throw it all out. Every single bottle." How was I going to explain Ivano's death to my cousin?

Cenzo tested the dust level on another shelf, with equal results. "Ivano would not have drunk sour wine, but a mayor naturally has enemies."

"Everybody loved Ivano!"

"Maybe not everybody."

"This is Monteleone, not Milano." Cities had crime. Villages did not. Everybody knew that. Even Cenzo.

He circled the body. "No politician is perfect."

I shook my fist at the ground. "If you think someone hurt him, then why are you trampling over evidence?"

"What do you think this is, American TV? Do you see any footprints?"

Of course not. The ground was way too hard.

I rubbed my freezing limbs. "Can we get out of here?"

Cenzo followed me back outside where the late afternoon sun was still hot. Shadows stretched into the courtyard, so I sat at the first shaded picnic table.

Cenzo sped-dialed a number but spoke so quickly in Piemontese that I didn't catch a word. Then he sat uncomfortably close and gave me a hard look. "You failed to mention why the mayor of Monteleone might be in your balmetto."

My shoulders drooped. "He probably stopped by because his wife told him to."

"Wife? Gold-digger, maybe. Twenty years between them."

"Eighteen."

"Last summer the whole town laughed through their wedding. They say she used to get around. Can't think of her name. Gabriella, is it?"

"Grazia. Daughter of my aunt, Maria Francese."

For the first time ever, I saw someone's mouth drop open.

"She's your cousin," Cenzo said quietly.

"She is. And if you think she's a gold-digger, I don't want to hear it."

Cenzo took a comb from his back pocket and ran it through his hair, but the straight black strands returned to their exact same position. "I didn't mean to offend you."

I shrugged.

"I meant no disrespect to your cousin."

I shrugged. I might have held out for a full apology if I hadn't known for a fact how much my cousin had gotten around. Grazia was a couple of years younger than I was, but when I'd visited Monteleone as a teen, she'd entertained me with stories of sexual escapades, stories that thrilled me because I hadn't yet had any adventures of my own.

"You think he was poisoned?" I asked.

"*Boh.* Who knows? Who was angry at him?"

"No one."

"Give me one possibility. The first that comes to you."

"I don't know! I've only been here since mid-May."

"Try."

In the last weeks I'd often accompanied my cousin and her husband to dances or dinners or balmetto parties where Ivano always received a hundred hugs and lots of free food. I couldn't imagine a villager hurting him with anything stronger than a handshake.

"No idea."

"A rival?"

Ivano had easily won his seat as a mayor, but that's where his political ambitions stopped. He'd explained this to me repeatedly. He was content serving a community that was small enough for him to manage. "Not that I know of."

Cenzo pointed towards the cellar. "Besides you, who has a key?"

"Renato, for one."

"That's Grazia's brother?"

"Our cousin."

Cenzo nodded. "He owns the metal shop?"

"Right."

"Why give him a key?"

"He's had one for years. So has Grazia. They look after the place. That's why I have so much wine. Whenever there's a surplus, they bring their extra bottles over here." The problem was that they were lazy about it. While a few carried labels such as "2017, alcohol level 13," most had been stored haphazardly without any indications.

"So we have three keys and an open door." Cenzo pointed to the garden wall where patches of fresh concrete highlighted trouble spots. "You probably haven't been here for every minute of the restorations. One of the workers might have made a copy."

"I doubt it." I handed Cenzo my heirloom.

Cenzo studied the key from both sides. "I've seen these before."

I would have explained, but it only took him a few seconds to find the indentation that released the lever and allowed the key to slide into the lock.

"I love these old things," he continued. "If you want to see craftsmanship, you don't have to look farther than the balmetti. The owners poured their hearts into making them."

"All for the love of wine."

"Yes. They would lock up their reds and whites more carefully than their houses. Most of the old farts would have parted with their wives sooner than with their bottles. You'd be surprised how slightly I'm exaggerating."

I knew enough about Piemontesi not to be surprised, but as I turned back to Ivano, my eyes filled. "How long—" I couldn't spit out the whole sentence.

While Cenzo waited, I took a few breaths. "How long do you think he's been lying here?"

He shrugged. *"Boh."*

"Could we—" I stopped mid-sentence.

"What?"

I was torn between decorum and practicality. "Could we see if Ivano had a key?"

"Good idea."

We returned to the tomb. Cenzo knelt beside the body. Awkwardly he felt along the front pocket. "Coins." He felt along the other side. "Nothing." He eased a wallet out of Ivano's back pocket and peered inside. "Did he ever carry cash?"

"He didn't like credit cards. He usually carried a couple hundred euros."

Cenzo counted the bills. "There's a hundred and forty here, which makes robbery a poor motive." He handed me the wallet. "You might as well keep this. Your cousin will need it. By the way, why haven't you contacted her?"

"My phone's dead. We went through this already."

"Right, right. Why did you come to me instead of her?"

"She went to Aosta. She didn't even take her car."

"Right. Speaking of which, where is Ivano's?"

"I don't know. When I reached the piazza, it was deserted."

"He arrived somehow. Unless he came with a killer." He paused. "Or you."

"Me!" I made fists without trying to. "What's wrong with you? If you think—"

I stopped because I heard voices. If the two paramedics recognized the mayor, they pretended not to. They matter-of-factly went back to their ambulance for a stretcher, briefly conferred, and asked Cenzo a few questions. Then they gingerly lifted Ivano onto the stretcher. Cenzo assisted them as they went outside.

I looked down at the spot where Ivano had breathed his last. He'd been snatched from life inside my own wine cellar. He'd come to do me a favor and paid for it with his life. Who needed the stuff anyway? I took the nearest bottle and flung it at the wall. It burst into pieces, throwing streaks of maroon everywhere.

"What happened?" Cenzo shouted as he rushed inside. "I heard a crash!"

I pointed to the dirt wall. A ray of sunshine that crept in from the door highlighted the smear dripping its way down.

Cenzo looked from the wall to me and back again. "You did that?"

"My balmetto killed Ivano. I'll never be able to come here again."

"Sofi—"

"All summer long I worked on this place. All for nothing."

"It's natural to be upset."

"Ivano was the nicest man I knew in Monteleone!"

He winked. "You hadn't met me yet."

I reached for another bottle, but Cenzo rushed me outside. "Sofi, I know it's a shock. But there's an explanation, and we'll find it."

"Ivano came here to help me. Wait until I tell my parents we've spent our money on a death trap!"

He snapped his fingers. "Focus. Why did your cousin leave town?"

"She's visiting a sick friend. Kristine something. Aunt Maria could tell you."

"Come on, then." He signaled for my key and locked the balmetto for me as if I couldn't do it for myself. He might have been right. "Let's go talk to Grazia's mother."

I shook my head.

"You don't know where she is either?"

"We might as well wait. She's probably on her way here."

"She's telepathic?"

I indicated the picnic tables that filled the courtyard. "I told you already. I was supposed to host a dinner party tonight. To thank everybody." And to help me clear out the cellar.

"Tonight?"

I pointed to Aunt Maria's giant pot that stood sentinel next to the portable burner.

"I'll cancel, of course. But I'll have to sit here until everybody arrives so that I can tell them to go home."

"Who's coming?"

"Everyone who helped me with repairs. Masons, carpenters, friends, their friends, their friends' friends."

"Everyone except for your cousin."

"She dropped everything and headed up to Courmayeur."

"Without Ivano?"

"She even forgot her cell phone. She left it at Aunt Maria's."

Cenzo's eyes widened. "How do you know that?"

"When I called Grazia this morning, my aunt answered."

Cenzo nodded. "Nice touch. But you expected Ivano to come to the party?"

"He promised to pour wine nonstop and stock every table with extra bottles. Don't worry. I'll gladly call it off."

"You won't cancel. Or mention anything to Aunt Maria."

I waved my arms as an airport marshal directing a runaway plane. "Won't mention—Ivano? You want me to pretend he's not dead?"

"Exactly."

"That's crazy. I can't do it."

"You can and you will."

I was not about to take orders. "What if I call the police headquarters in Torino and say, hey, your man out here in Monteleone has gone crazy and won't properly investigate the crime scene?"

"This is Monteleone, not the capital of Piemonte. In a community as small as this one, I have some leeway."

"What about the paramedics? You don't think they recognized the mayor?"

"They understand that I need a few hours before the news breaks. Trust me."

"I can't hold a party tonight. I refuse. I need time to process. I need time to be alone. I need time to cry!"

Cenzo held up his hand like a stop sign. "You don't understand. Ivano might have drunk poison. Is there any chance he was suicidal?"

Ivano was one of the happiest, most carefree people I'd ever met. He took partying—and my cousin—much more seriously than any job. Although he didn't throw it around, he seemed to have plenty of money, partly from an inheritance. From the way he catered to my cousin, cheerfully satisfying every whim, I was convinced he was deeply in love with her.

I shook my head. "He had no reason to commit suicide."

"He didn't strike me as the type. It's relatively uncommon for Northern Italians of his age group. But if someone handed him a glass of poisoned wine, he might have drunk it in a single gulp."

I closed my eyes and winced. "I still don't know who—"

"He also might have died of natural causes. Point well taken. But if he didn't, if someone had a hand in his death, you'd want to find out who it was, wouldn't you?"

"Of course I would. He was Grazia's husband. He treated me like his own sister!"

"Sofi, calm down."

"How can I calm down if there's a murderer loose?"

"That's why you need to have the party."

I waved both hands. "To give the murderer another chance?"

"With dozens of witnesses around? No. You don't understand. A party is the perfect opportunity for gathering information."

"How am I supposed to do that?"

"Not you. Me."

I finally caught on. In fact, the idea was brilliant. The Monteleonesi were talkers. They had lengthy conversations at the grocery store, the bank, the park, and on the street. They never spoke softly, even when attending mass, nor did they hold back from venting or praising. They shared so much and so often they might have been the model for social media.

At a party with lots of free wine, they would be especially garrulous. They would speak freely about anything that came to mind. At some point, they wouldn't be able to contain themselves. They would start gossiping about my cousin and her husband.

Cenzo and I would hang on every word. I would miss nuances. I wouldn't be fast enough to catch the Piemontese, but my buddy wouldn't miss a thing.

I would make sure he told me everything he learned.

Chapter Three

I expected my guests to arrive as a gentle wave. They came as a stampede. They rushed the picnic tables while shouting greetings to me and to one another. I struggled with the names of spouses and offspring while reminding myself to learn what I could about Ivano.

I was so busy greeting guests that I barely noticed Cenzo's arrival. He rode the tail of the herd, planting himself next to me at a crowded center table as Aunt Maria sent around a plate of *prosciutti*. I wasn't sure if I appreciated his attention or not. He seemed attentive, but maybe he suspected me of something. I couldn't discount him, either. He was also my only shield. Although acquaintances surrounded me, he was the only one who knew how awful I felt inside.

Cenzo simplified the scenario for me by putting on a show. He gushed into small talk so easily that not even the most skeptical attendee would have suspected an agenda. He joked and poured wine, easily switching between Italian and Piemontese as if he'd forgotten why he'd come. As a plate of fried cauliflower florets came around, however, he used the excuse of reaching for a breadstick to lean over me and whisper in English: "Who's the woman at the end of this table?"

I was careful not to turn abruptly, but the woman in question was too busy devouring a stuffed mushroom to notice. She had the kind of red hair that makes it ludicrous to wear any colors besides green or brown. Her hair clashed so fiercely with her blouse that I fought the urge to call a firetruck. "She came with one of the electricians."

"Do you remember which one?"

"No." The electricians sat together with a few other men. I wasn't even sure which had worked on the property and which were tagalongs.

"I'll find out." He served himself two deviled eggs and headed for the other end of the table.

I'd always seen the villagers as harmless. They gossiped nonstop, but they were spirited and fun-loving. They raised their kids or their kids' kids, threw dinner parties, and played bocce ball. I never once heard them discuss literature or film. They lived their lives in genuine, productive ways. I admired their lifestyle, meaning their ability to embrace family and friends over the morning's news or the latest fads. But now I needed to look at each one as a potential criminal.

My cousin Renato, who was sitting on my other side, tapped my shoulder. "What possessed you to invite Cenzo Bot to this party?" He was partly joking, but he'd invited a trio of bachelor friends he wanted me to meet. Luckily, they were ensconced at another table, intent on drinking rather than flirting.

"You might say he invited himself," I said, following Cenzo's script. "He stopped me for speeding this afternoon, so he says, and when I explained that I was hurrying to set up for a party, he hinted that he didn't have plans for the evening."

Renato laughed. "Then you must have been going awfully fast."

I played along. "Why's that?"

"He drives like a madman."

"What a hypocrite!"

"Not really. He rarely gives out tickets." Renato winked. "You can't blame him for taking advantage of an opportunity."

I liked my cousin. He was a tall, lanky fellow who ambled through life with a generous sense of humor as well as a broad view of the human experience. He'd never been to the States and would probably never go there, but he always listened to my views and gave thought to them. I trusted his basic, uncomplicated understandings, and what I wanted more than anything else was to explain what I had witnessed in the cellar.

Instead I tackled the next best subject. "Would you say that Cenzo is good at what he does?"

Renato reached for another slice of salami. Since he had generously provided the homemade slabs himself, this was only fair. "Maybe we didn't get a chance to tell you, but last year Aunt Maria's place was broken into twice."

"No!" The image of my aunt confronting burglars was shocking, especially in a small town where the population was thirty-six hundred during the winter and half that during the summer when the locals took turns flocking to the beach.

Renato snapped a breadstick in half. "Monteleone has its share of petty crime. Immigrants come hoping to find work, and when they can't, they get desperate."

Immigrants would not have come after Ivano. He had often supported their causes with services and sometimes cash. If he'd been murdered, it was by an Italian well acquainted with the balmetti. A foreigner would have never found the place.

"Tell me about the burglaries," I said. "She never mentioned it."

"Probably doesn't want you to worry about staying at my folks' place by yourself. Anyway, she slept through the first incident. Didn't realize anything was wrong until she went to make coffee the next morning and noticed that the furniture had moved around. The second time, she was at a concert with some friends. When she arrived home, the front door was wide open."

"How awful for her!" The woman was seventy-nine. She'd lived on her own since Grazia moved in with Ivano even though she had a standing invitation to live with them. Aunt Maria claimed she didn't want to intrude, but she also didn't want to give up her cute bungalow conveniently located across the street from one of the town's two grocery stores.

"Did the burglars take much?"

"They were looking for electronics, so I'm sure they were disappointed. The first set took some utensils but nothing too valuable. The second set went through all her drawers and left everything a mess. They took some jewelry, but really what they stole was her peace of mind."

"I'm sure!"

"She was so rattled that Cenzo sat up half the night talking to her. He didn't leave until she was too tired to keep her eyes open."

"Where was Grazia?"

"Traveling with Ivano. It was a month before the wedding. Laura and I were in Ventimiglia with her folks or Aunt Maria would have called us. As soon as we heard what happened we rushed back home, but by then Cenzo had installed a burglar alarm and taught Aunt Maria how to use it. You could say that's going the extra mile."

Indeed it was. I would make a point to thank him for it.

I would have pumped my cousin for more information, but Cenzo rushed to sit beside me as the steaming pot of pasta came our way. He proceeded to scoop out an exaggerated portion. He seemed wiry for an Italian man past thirty, so I assumed he cooked about as well as I did. This meant he could make a salad.

He waited until Renato was deep into a long conversation with his neighbors, who were comparing fertilizers. "Did he ask about Ivano?"

"Several times."

"What did you say?" he asked

"That I expected him at any minute."

Cenzo nodded. "Did Renato seem suspicious?"

"Not at all. Ivano is—was—almost always late."

Cenzo loaded his fork. "Convenient, eh?"

"What do you mean?"

"If you're always late, people don't expect you on time. They don't ask embarrassing questions. In the meantime, you do anything you want to."

He continued eating as if this were a normal dinner conversation, but the insinuation carried a punch I didn't like. Cenzo suspected the mayor of some kind of wrongdoing, and what if he were right? When pressed, most people had something to hide even if it was a tax bill they forgot to pay or a business transaction they'd taken advantage of. Ivano might have done something underhanded. Embezzled a few euros from public funds, for example. Supported a mistress who lived in Milano. Fathered a child or two. I didn't know much about his history. I wasn't sure I wanted to. Before the wedding, I heard he'd gotten around too.

My feeble appetite withered to nothing, so I pushed the *farfalle* around on my plate to keep up appearances. I'd developed the useful strategy earlier in the summer because if I failed to gobble down tons of pasta, I earned the third degree: Are you sick? Are you upset? Are you pregnant?

Cenzo somehow read my mind. "Ivano was hiding something. You can be sure of it."

"You didn't like him." I spoke softly though I didn't need to. The question of the best fertilizer had morphed into a loud debate.

Cenzo swallowed another enormous bite as if he might not have a chance to eat for a few more weeks. "Ivano was all right. He was also a good talker. As a politician, he knew how to play things."

"Isn't that part of the job description?"

Cenzo stretched to reach a piece of bread, which he used to clean leftover sauce from the plate. "Maybe so. But let's consider his personal life. He went through a long list of lovers before he started with your cousin. Do you know who he was seeing before Grazia?"

For a moment the words stung. I didn't like thinking about Ivano or Grazia with other partners because they'd seemed so right for one another. "She told me, but I don't remember."

"What was your own impression of Ivano?" Cenzo asked.

"He was a great guy. I never stopped to analyze him per se."

That was not true. I'd met Ivano when he and Grazia had driven all the way to Malpensa, the international airport near Milano, to retrieve me. Grazia had rushed up and given me the traditional Italian bear hug; Ivano had surprised me by doing the same. For a non-relative, he seemed overly friendly. His hug was a little too tight, his smile a little too broad. My initial impression was that he was too smooth to be a man I should like. But during the ninety-minute drive from the airport back to Monteleone, I completely changed my mind.

Ivano asked me about the long flight, commiserated with me about leg cramps, and kept me awake with Pocket Coffees. If I stumbled over a colloquial phrase, Ivano patiently supplied it. Best of all, he'd stocked my borrowed refrigerator at Aunt Angela's with enough food for a week and talked Uncle Felice into loaning me the couple's extra car. By the time we pulled into

Monteleone that afternoon, I felt as if I were related to Ivano instead of to Grazia.

"What was your gut reaction?" Cenzo continued.

I sighed. I disliked being interrogated, but at least it was for the right reason; any aspect of Ivano's behavior might provide a useful clue. "Ivano may have had his fair share of women in the past, and like most politicians, he changed his mind frequently, but he was devoted to my cousin and supremely nice to me."

"Anything else?"

"He did not deserve to die. Not at his age. And not alone on the floor of a balmetto."

While Cenzo circulated to interrogate other diners, the feast continued despite me. Dishes were passed, plates were dirtied, and, more importantly, wine glasses were emptied by everyone except for children and me. Conversations bubbled up like shoots of water in a fountain, and they passed over me without spilling any drops.

I wasn't ready to dive in. I needed to backtrack and catch myself, but instead I was dazed. I played with food I couldn't stomach and laughed at jokes I hadn't listened to.

When I wasn't busy worrying that a murderer sat among us, I silently rehearsed the conversation I would have with Grazia to inform her that Ivano was dead. Since Cenzo would do so with the grace of rhino who had been starved for three days, the messenger would have to be me.

♠ ♦ ♠

I was taking orders for after-dinner coffees when Renato beckoned me to the gate. Three men and a woman waited to make my acquaintance.

"*Ben-ëvni*," I said, cringing at the realization that I'd mixed the Italian *benvenuti* with the Piemontese *bin-ëvnù*, thus creating a word for "welcome" that was wrong in both languages.

The newcomers ignored my mistake. They shook my hand vigorously and gave their names while Renato ushered them into the yard. Evidently my ears were off; all three men introduced themselves as Roberto. A decade or so older than I, they had the relaxed air of people who were out for the evening without any worries about the time. The men wore old shorts and tank tops as if they'd come in from gardening, meaning they matched half the guests.

Carmela, who was married to one of the men, was dressed for an outing. She wore black capris and a white blouse with a ruffled collar. She'd draped a black sweater over her shoulders European-style so that her hands were free. She smiled so impishly that I liked her immediately. After such a horrible day, I welcomed any distraction.

As I led Carmela through the courtyard, she linked her arm through mine. "Renato told me all about your renovations. Congratulations!"

Condolences, I thought. But I hadn't forgotten the evening's original mission. "Can I offer you some wine?"

The woman's curly auburn strands bounced beside her cheeks. "Only a little. We had two bottles at dinner, so you can guess how we're feeling!"

While my new guests squeezed into a row of picnic tables, I brought over clean glasses and a fresh, unopened bottle. No matter what Carmela said, I knew she and her companions could polish off another litre if they set their minds to it. I sat with them to make sure they received their fair share.

Mid-sentence, Carmela's husband changed gears. His curly hair bopped over his forehead as his fair skin reflected light. "Where's your glass?"

How had he noticed? I waved vaguely in Cenzo's direction. "Over there."

He shook his gray locks as if advertising for a shampoo commercial. "You can't have a fun party that way!" He reached for a glass that was either clean or empty and filled it for me.

"I've probably drunk enough for one night."

He handed me the glass with a flourish. "Nonsense! A little wine can't kill you!"

The words knocked around in my ears. I wanted to rewind to the afternoon and show Roberto how wrong he was. No. I wanted to rewind to yesterday. Instead I meekly accept the glass.

"*Salute!*" The latecomers cheered.

I shuddered involuntarily. My mouth was so dry I could hardly open it. "I'm not thirsty."

"That doesn't matter!" Roberto cried.

"Never mind about the wine," Carmela laughed. "Tell us about your renovations. Last year at this time the property was filled with weeds as tall as you are!"

She wasn't exaggerating. Ivano had shown me pictures. Then he'd hired a gardener. "I've been pulling weeds non-stop since I got here. I'm praying it doesn't rain anymore."

"Don't do that! Otherwise the vines will shrivel up, the men will have fits, and we won't have any peace at all." Carmela pointed to the balmetto's second floor. "Have you also worked on the upstairs room?"

The staircase beckoned as a ladder dangling from a rescue helicopter. "If you can stand a mess, I'll show you." I stood quickly in case she wasn't as interested as she pretended to be.

We crossed over and ascended the narrow stairs. The balcony was only a dozen feet high, but it offered a view of the sea of tables below. The party had reached its zenith. Wine bottles dotted every table. People had been arriving all evening, and so far, nobody had left. Now that the guests were well fed, they chatted all at once. This was wonderful. While spilling their stories, they would empty more bottles. The irony was that they looked joyous. What if one of them was a murderer?

"If I remember right, this balmetto belongs to your father and his brother," Carmela said.

I was stunned she had any idea. What else did the villagers know about me? And what did they know about Ivano? "Right. I've been told that our balmetto is one of the oldest. From the amount of dust, I believe it."

"It's old all right," Carmela said. "I've been in here before. Your great-grandfather and my grandfather were drinking partners."

Of course. All the villagers were connected. Invisible strings tied them to one another. They rarely moved from the region because they were part of a spider web of history and alliances.

"I've been wanting to restore the balmetto for some time now. We knew it needed work, but we didn't know how much. I've been here over a month already."

"A lot can happen in a few weeks' time!"

Yes, I thought. You can meet a cousin-in-law and think he's the best person in the world, and the next moment you learn there were such big skeletons in his closet that he wound up a skeleton himself way before his time. I blinked away a tear.

"Are you all right?" Carmela asked.

"It's a lot," I stammered. "All the renovations. I didn't realize what a big project it was or how much effort it would be." Or that it would be for nothing since I would never enjoy the damned thing.

"Why didn't your parents come over to give you a hand?" Carmela asked.

I couldn't tell her the truth, so I walked around the edges. "They're busy enjoying their retirement. Their big goal is to move to Florida before winter hits."

"I'm glad you had the energy to come yourself. The balmetti are worth the time. Of course, the traditions make renovations difficult."

I nodded. Since the balmetti represented cultural heritage, repairs still had to be done the old way. Modernization was not allowed. Hence I had a swell party house with lots of wine and no bathroom.

"Will you stay in Monteleone until the end of the summer?" Carmela asked.

Given the last few hours, I didn't want to stay another day. I could already imagine myself halfway to Milan as I searched the Internet for the next trans-Atlantic flight. "I hadn't planned to stay this long, but I won't be teaching until the fall."

"What do you teach?"

"I'm certified for French and Italian. Fingers crossed I can find a full-time job."

As Carmela shrugged, her blouse wrinkled. "We've barely hit July. Who knows? You might decide you like Monteleone so much that you never want to leave!"

I wanted to leave right that minute. I wanted to hand over the balmetto keys to Grazia and never come back. I never wanted to think about wine cellars or dead cousins-in-law. I wanted to move forward.

I faked a smile. "I've had a great time so far. Everyone has been so sweet."

"It's a friendly town, but it's full of gossip! For example, I hear that you're staying at Renato's parents' house."

"I'm housesitting. Angela and Felice are spending the summer in Calabria."

"Of course they are!"

"I suppose you already knew that?"

Carmela looked away, but not before she betrayed herself with another impish grin. "Here's something I don't know. Do you play any band instruments?"

"I play trumpet for the Cambridge Symphony Orchestra."

"Trumpet!"

"It's a community group. We don't get paid." We also weren't very good, but that was unimportant. We had fun playing together, and we were more friends than musicians.

"They don't pay here either, but my husband is the band director. Be careful or you'll get drafted! He's conducting a big concert for the balmetto festival next weekend, but lots of the musicians are on vacation."

"There's a band in Monteleone?"

Carmela pointed to the friends who had accompanied her and her husband. She pointed to the one with unruly hair. "He plays the saxophone." She pointed to the shorter one, who had little hair left. "He plays the French horn."

"Isn't Monteleone too small to have a whole band?"

"Some of the musicians live nearby. Our first clarinet player comes from Cafreddo. The percussionists both live in Lungofiume."

"That's wonderful."

"Ivano is one of the band's biggest supporters. He's helped a lot with the fundraising."

"He hadn't mentioned it."

"He must know every musician personally. He's involved with lots of projects, of course, but he's particularly fond of the band. The people around here love music. Also, we don't have any cinemas!"

As I laughed, Cenzo looked up. He spotted me and winked.

"My! You're quite the hostess. How did you convince Cenzo Bot to come to a party?"

"I wasn't trying to. He invited himself."

Carmela laughed so hard her body shook. "It's nice to see him out and about. He's been depressed lately."

The thought surprised me. He didn't seem like the kind to give himself over to a single emotion. "His work would be stressful," I said tentatively.

"Ho, ho! This is Monteleone. Once in a while we have a robbery. Once in a while someone speeds down from Aosta and runs the stoplight in front of the train station. Never mind Cenzo's work. His wife left him a few months ago. She went back to England with the kids."

"England?"

"Sarah. She's British."

Finding out basic facts surprised me. "He didn't mention kids or a wife either."

"Lately he avoids talking about them."

By now Cenzo was waving his arms in an animated conversation with Renato and his friends. The police captain had a full glass of wine in front of him, and I'd already witnessed how much he'd enjoyed Aunt Maria's cooking. All evening he'd blended in as the perfect guest.

"I suppose she had her reasons for leaving?" The Piemontese spirit was stronger in my blood than I thought. At the hint of scandal, I was poised to listen.

Carmela ran her hand along the railing. "She told people that he hit her, but I don't think it's true."

I couldn't imagine a darker side, yet.

Just then Cenzo made the Italian sign of giving someone the finger by wrapping his right hand around his upper left arm and drawing back his left forearm as he made a fist. The villagers laughed; the gesture was part of the story.

Carmela laughed too. "He does know how to make a point! Shall we?" She started down the stairs, tripped on an uneven step, and lost her footing. She bounced against the railing. Although it held her weight, the metal rattled precariously.

As she worked to regain her balance, I steadied her. "Are you all right?"

"Ho, ho! That's one more repair you can put on your list."

"Not another one!" I tested the handrail myself. Given that Carmela was a small, slender woman, the problem was significant. "I'll tell the masons next week. They're probably disgusted with me. I claimed my balmetto would be a small job, but they worked on it for over a week."

"One more day won't kill them!"

As I continued down the stairs, I turned towards the cellar involuntarily and gulped. Carmela was right. One more day of work wouldn't kill the masons. For that, all they needed was to drink the wrong wine. But I had an important new lead. If I sat in with the band, I could overhear gossip. Lots of it. Maybe even the right kind.

Chapter Four

After I waved goodbye to the last partiers and watched them stumble down the road, I started collecting empty bottles. Even if I hadn't learned much about Ivano, the guests had made a good dent on the wine. After a few more parties, I could hazard organizing the cellar.

Cenzo helped stack used paper plates. "You spent a long time with Carmela." To my surprise he wasn't the least bit drunk, and he was more awake than I was.

I placed six empty bottles in a milk carton. "We didn't discuss the mayor. Don't tell me that makes her a suspect."

Cenzo laughed. "Not a chance. If Monteleone had an angel, she would qualify. She treats everyone like a favorite relative and does more for the band than Roberto."

The appraisal didn't surprise me. I might have guessed the same. I gathered six empties from the next table. "Roberto invited me to a band rehearsal. Some of his regulars have skipped out to go to the beach."

Cenzo dumped half-full sacks of breadsticks into a picnic basket. "Italians! They love to rush to the seaside to do nothing."

"Believe me, lounging on the sand sounds perfect right now."

Cenzo wrapped a throwaway tablecloth into a tight ball and aimed for the garbage can. "You said you were invited to a rehearsal. You're a musician?"

"A language teacher. Music is a hobby."

I went over to the corner and fished my mouthpiece from my purse. I blew through the metal a couple of times, sending slow whole tones into the dark quiet.

Cenzo viewed me quizzically. "You carry that thing around?"

I touched my index finger to my lips. "If I want to keep playing, I have to keep in shape."

He whistled softly. "I'll bet you do."

For the time being, I deflated the obvious flirtation. "You don't play an instrument yourself?"

"I never took the time."

We finished gathering the trash and sat across from one another at a picnic table. Cenzo stretched out his legs. I drew mine back when he accidentally made contact. I was glad that he seemed too concentrated to notice.

"What did you observe tonight?" he asked.

"Me? You're the professional."

His shoulders slumped. I thought about his wife and advised myself to be nicer. I'd had three painful breakups. Even though I'd instigated two of them, they were never easy. "I'm sorry. I feel bad that I don't have anything concrete to report."

"Tell me everything you can. You're an outsider. You see things differently. "

I set my elbows on the table decisively. "People in this town love to talk. The guests had lengthy conversations and didn't get up from the table for long periods of time. Though most had come with spouses, they rarely sat with them."

"Very good."

"At a party in the U.S. you would commonly find the men talking to the men and the women talking to the women, but here people sat randomly. There were multiple conversations going on at any given time. The longer people talked, the more animated they became. Or maybe it was the wine."

"Or the grappa."

The pomace brandy was the strongest after-dinner drink I'd ever tasted. I couldn't help thinking it would be more useful as cleaner fluid. "I hear it's good for digestion. Three people gave me bottles of the stuff."

"That's a friendly gesture. Who brought them?"

"The electrician with the redhead and one of Ivano's friends. The other bottle simply appeared."

Cenzo laughed. "Maybe a contractor felt bad for overcharging you!"

I felt that everyone had overcharged me, but I'd also expected some 75% fewer repairs. "Is grappa that special?"

Cenzo clicked his lips as if tasting a sample. "It's expensive. Many of the locals make it, so they appreciate it even more than fine wine."

"They make grappa?"

An owl hooted in the distance as if it were chiming in on the conversation. Cenzo briefly turned towards the mountains. "It's illegal, but they do it anyway. But go on. Tell me what else you observed."

"After people claimed they had to leave, they spent an hour saying goodbye. Since no one was in a hurry, that didn't matter. The guests were so reluctant to go home I was surprised they didn't request sleeping bags."

"Every good party around here ends the same way. What did people think of your balmetto repairs?"

"Half drooled. The other half offered to buy the place."

Cenzo laughed. "Only half?"

"Renato cut them off by saying that, even though I wasn't selling, I would sell to him before anyone else, so they could just forget it."

"Renato needs a balmetto?"

"Evidently everyone does. You too, I suppose."

I was hoping to get a rise, but Cenzo took my comment at face value. "By default I already have one, but that's another story."

"I suppose some are more valuable than others."

"The ones closer to the parking lot have a more prestigious location. Roberto and Carmela's is on the first rung, for example, which saves the older folks a steep climb. I've also heard that some of the balmetti are connected through underground passageways, but I've never seen evidence of it. So do you own this place yourself?"

"On paper it belongs to my dad and his brother Luigi. Since they've put off renovations for years, you could say that the balmetto is mine by default."

"But you wanted it."

I'd been questioning myself since the first difficult repair. "It's a visible tie to Italy. My way of maintaining a strong connection."

"But you have relatives."

"Yes. But by owning property, I feel like more than a guest. I feel legitimate, somehow. Or I did until today. You must think that sounds crazy."

Cenzo leaned back. "No. It sounds Piemontese. The people here love to own property. Once they do, they rarely give it up. That's why the balmetti are a rare commodity. There's a limited number."

"Why don't people build more?"

"The angle of the mountain is crucial. Everything changes if you move too far over. There are a few balmetti over in Liguria, but ours maintain a more constant temperature. But don't tell me you're planning to live in Monteleone permanently. People move out, but they rarely move in."

"This was supposed to be a summer haven. I just finished my teaching degree, so my grand plan was to spend part of every summer around here."

"Good plan. Your parents didn't come themselves because they're not well?" He spoke softly as if the topic might be painful.

I appreciated his delicacy but choked up a laugh all the way from my gut. "They moved to Florida this spring so they can play *Scarta Quaranta* all night with Uncle Luigi and Aunt Elena."

Cenzo nodded. "Discard Forty is a pretty good card game."

"They think so! Anyway, they're too busy to be interested in the place themselves."

Across the fields, a big truck rumbled past as if to remind me of reality.

"And now—" I gestured at the cellar. "I'll never want to be near the place."

"Things will get easier."

I must have frowned.

"They will, but you'll have to give it time." He paused. "Who all asked about Ivano?"

"Almost everyone, but when I mentioned Grazia's sick friend in Aosta, they assumed he'd gone with her and switched topics."

"Nice work."

I wished my mind could switch off as easily. Instead it flashed images of having dinner with Ivano and Grazia in their cozy kitchen, partying with them around town, and finding Ivano on my hard cold floor. "Unfortunately, people kept wanting me to show them the cellar, and I nearly cried every time. I shoved them off on Renato as often as possible."

Cenzo nodded approval. His eyes felt heavy on me as if he were mentally summing me up, but I couldn't decide on which levels. After such a noisy evening, it was a relief to talk to only one person at a time. If he noticed moisture in my eyes, at least I didn't have to explain about it.

"Did you learn anything useful tonight?" I asked softly.

He took a big whiff from his wine glass, which he had somehow hung onto. "You don't like wine." He grinned so broadly that I didn't bother to deny it.

"Was I so obvious?"

"Remember? I'm trained."

"I try to be subtle."

"You sat beside me for three hours without tasting a drop. When you were sitting with Carmela, Roberto poured you a glass of wine, and you took a single sip. You switched your full glass with his as soon as you had a chance."

I felt the hairs on the back of my neck bristle. I wasn't sure I should be flattered by Cenzo's close observation after all, especially since I'd switched glasses with him at least twice. "Never mind about me. What did you learn about Ivano?"

"I didn't know that he prevented a plumbers' strike last winter. It happened while I was out of town."

"That speaks well of him."

"Does it?" He waved his arms. "The group bargained for an hourly increase and got what they wanted right away. Your masons told me that Ivano took a kickback of at least three thousand euros to support their cause."

I sat up straight. "I doubt that very much!" I wouldn't believe such a thing until somebody showed me the numbers. It was easy to make up stories about people, and usually the tales became more exaggerated with each telling. A hundred euros, maybe. Three thousand? No.

"Most politicians have crooked sides," Cenzo said matter-of-factly. "That's not the issue. It comes with the drive to get elected. You're from the States. You've seen it often enough."

"But Ivano—"

"Let me finish. The problem is that while Ivano intervened for the plumbers, he hadn't done the same for the carpenters when they went on strike the year before. They lost so much business that they finally retracted their demands. They went back to work for the same salary after losing three months' wages. You can imagine the effect something like that would have."

"How would it be Ivano's fault?"

"Maybe it wasn't." Cenzo ran his comb through his hair, but it looked exactly the same afterwards.

"If the workers were mad enough to kill him, why wouldn't they have done so months ago?"

"I'm not saying they were desperate. I'm rounding out the picture. How about this: Did you know Monteleone had a bid from an electric company that wanted to build a power plant on the riverbank? The company would have created a wealth of jobs and created growth for the whole area, but Ivano turned the offer down."

Several owls hooted in unison. I'd never noticed them until tonight. At the balmetti I'd always been concentrated on the dozens of conversations flitting past me as dandelion seeds in the wind. As I wiped away a single tear, I concentrated on the sounds.

"Ivano said that an ugly plant at the entrance to the town would ruin the view," I said as soon as I felt more composed. "I completely agreed. I love Monteleone just the way it is."

"Many of the townspeople agree with your view, but growth means progress. Maybe he was waiting for a better offer. Or a better bribe."

Since I felt Cenzo was trying to trick me, I suddenly felt hostile myself. "Sure, that's easy. Make all the accusations you want while Ivano isn't here to defend himself."

"Would you like to hear a list of Ivano's lovers?"

Now I felt even more uncomfortable. If Cenzo wanted to push my buttons, he was about to find the best ones: unwarranted accusations. "Not really. Is there a law against sleeping around?" To have the excuse to stand up, I retrieved a container of Aunt Maria's blueberry tarts from the picnic basket.

Despite the great quantity of food he'd already eaten, Cenzo readily accepted a tart, but he picked up right where he'd left off. "It's dangerous to sleep with other men's wives."

I let blueberry filling drip on the grass. "Surely not all his lovers were married."

"No, just Stefani, Alicia, and Marta. I'm not sure about Teresa."

"Grazia knew about his past. At least most of it."

Cenzo nabbed a second tart. "That's probably why she turned him down so many times. At least that's what Renato told me."

"You were pumping Renato too?"

"Do you know how much Grazia stands to inherit from her husband?"

I handed him the whole container. "She quit working after the wedding, so I figured they were doing all right. We never discussed it."

"Ivano's net worth is probably over five million euros."

I whistled. I assumed he was well off, not a multi-millionaire. "Impressive. You're sure?"

"I sat next to his lawyer for twenty minutes. When your lawyer is jealous, you have it made. Five million euros! Of course your cousin quit her job. Why do you think she married the old fart anyway?"

"He wasn't so old. And she married him for love."

"Your cousin didn't do badly for a few months' work."

I chomped into another tart so forcefully that I bit my tongue. I focused on the sky until the pain subsided enough that I could mask it.

"Do you have a key to your cousin's house?" Cenzo continued.

"Why do you ask?"

"Tomorrow morning I'll be there with a search warrant. Either you let me in, or I'll break down the door." Cenzo took another tart himself as if we were somehow in competition.

"Grazia wasn't in town. You can't think she would have murdered her husband!"

"You think she wasn't in town, and you're probably right. But she wouldn't have done it herself. She would have paid to have it done. She'll get the money back soon enough."

How had Cenzo leapt from investigating villagers to accusing my closest relative? Either he was taking himself too seriously, or he didn't know what he was doing after all. "That's the stupidest thing I've heard all night."

Cenzo raised his hands and dropped them. "She had everything to gain."

I banged my fist on the table. "Don't be so dramatic. I'm sure there are multiple candidates for gaining from the death of a mayor."

"Your cousin leads the race by several million laps."

To be stubborn, I pretended numbers meant nothing to me. In truth I'd wondered why my cousin had settled on an older man. She was pretty enough to attract lots of attention. After I met Ivano, I stopped wondering. "You don't know her as well as I do."

"How well is that?"

"She's been taking me around all summer. She and Ivano. Invited me on outings. Introduced me to their friends."

"They avoided spending time alone?"

"That's not what I'm saying."

"Ah. They were a madly loving couple."

I stared Cenzo straight on. The light from the streetlight beyond the gate painted his face with a hint of blue. I wished I'd met him at a party instead of at a police station so that we could have started as equals.

"People do lots of strange things." I pointed to his left hand. "For example, why are you wearing a wedding ring?"

He yanked at the ring so hard he might have broken his finger. I winced without trying to.

"Can't get the damned thing off," he said. "You didn't answer my question."

"Don't you realize I have to tell Grazia her husband is dead? How fun is that?"

"It's beside the point. You either have a key or you don't."

"As a matter of fact, I do. If it means clearing my cousin from your empty list of suspects, I don't mind using it."

Grazia a killer? Ridiculous. I could hardly wait for the morning to show Cenzo how wrong he was.

Chapter Five

I strode over to the mayor's two-story upscale riverside residence a few minutes early. If Cenzo were determined to snoop around, I wanted him to finish well before Grazia returned and blew up at the invasion of privacy. Even though the house was Ivano's, Grazia had coddled it as much as a new mom protects a newborn. She didn't allow dirt or disorder, nor would she have allowed Cenzo without a fight.

The house sat on a wide plot at the edge of the Dora Bàltea River. The front door separated the picture window on the right from the two-and-a-half-car garage on the left. The grass needed cutting, but the roses crawling up the trellises suggested a standard, carefree household with an above-average income. Ivano's passing had ruined everything.

Cenzo pulled into the driveway and cut the engine. "You beat me!" The dimple in his right cheek deepened when he smiled, disarming me. He greeted me in the traditional hug-kiss-kiss style of the region as if to emphasize that I was not alone. I couldn't match his cheer, but he embodied a reminder that, like the river, life went right on. I would have to do the same.

"Front door?" he asked.

"I always go in through the garage." I led him around to the side where Magru, the next-door neighbor's son, polished a Fiat sedan in the shade between houses. The thin twenty-something wore baggy jeans that showed way too much of his backside whenever he leaned over to work on a car, which was most of the time, including now.

"Ciao, Magru," Cenzo said.

Magrulino had a real name, Antonio, but I'd always heard him referred to by the abbreviation of the nickname that meant "skinny." He glanced up long enough to recognize us and grunt before returning his attention to the vehicle.

Cenzo snickered as I led him through the unlocked side door. "Friendly guy. Then again, I keep giving him speeding tickets. Not that he has anywhere to go."

The rectangular windows inside the garage gave us enough light to make our way between the two cars and the jumble of boxes surrounding them. Tools reached out like hungry weeds from every available shelf. Carefully sidestepping the garbage bins, we gravitated towards the door that led into the house.

"That guy pretends I'm contagious," I said. "He ignores Grazia too, but his mother seems nice enough."

"Magru is twenty-two. He hasn't figured out that the world doesn't revolve around him, and his mother hasn't informed him otherwise. I've detained him more often than anyone else in the village. When he's not pretending to be a Formula One driver, he gets into fights."

I stepped over a basket of apples, careful not to fall inside. "Isn't he too old to live with his mother?"

Cenzo copied my maneuvers. "Where else would he go? He's never had a girlfriend for more than a week at a time."

I fumbled to dig the house key from my purse. "If I were his mom, I'd scheme to get rid of him."

"Monteleone is not so progressive. Magru is young, and his mom is a widow. It probably hasn't occurred to either of them that he might live somewhere else."

Cenzo was probably right. Conversely, after college it had never occurred to me to return home to live with my parents. We'd all felt it was time for me to move on.

Cenzo rapped on the hood of the red Fiat 500L. "Isn't this Ivano's car?"

I nodded and pointed to the other vehicle. "Grazia usually drives the Panda."

"Would Ivano have walked to the balmetto?"

"Not yesterday. He would have been carting around too many supplies."

As I reached for my keys, I realized the door was already ajar. "Cenzo?"

"I see it."

We stared at the wood as if it could talk.

"They often forgot to lock the door," I said quietly. "They joked about it all the time."

"Let me go in alone."

I was sure the unlocked door was an oversight, but I was glad to let Cenzo take over. He slowly opened the door and entered a black hole. The room's sole illumination came from the digital green clock that shone out from the stove.

Cenzo took out his cell phone and selected the flashlight app. I stayed in the doorway as he silently moved through the kitchen and made a soundless round of the downstairs rooms. I heard the weight of his steps on the stairs but lost him once he reached the second floor.

He returned a few minutes later and flicked on the kitchen light. "Come in. I'm sure we're alone. You say Ivano and Grazia often left the door unlocked?"

"They didn't mean to, but it wasn't something they kept track of."

"Most people around here don't. No wonder we're plagued with transients."

We each cranked open a blind, revealing a comfortable, modern kitchen where everything had its own place. Sets of ladles and funnels hung from the wall while pots paraded above the double marble sink.

Wooden cabinets stretched to the ceiling. An island in the middle of the room gave Grazia ample workspace no matter the number of ingredients in her recipes.

I'd spent many pleasant hours in Grazia's kitchen. Usually I perched on one of the bar stools that hugged the island. While I asked her about current slang, she sashayed around the sink.

On days she didn't cook, I often suggested that we sit outside, but Grazia never humored me. She adored her kitchen so much I sometimes wondered if she'd moved in with Ivano to take advantage of it. She liked the rest of the house, the living room with the light blue couch, the master bedroom with the walk-in closet, the bathroom with the fancy tub topped by swan fixtures, but she didn't enjoy any of the other rooms the same way.

"I'll start my investigation in here," Cenzo said. "You can watch, but don't try to help." He opened the closest cabinet.

"I would think pawing through other people's houses would be fascinating," I said over his shoulder.

Cenzo snapped around. "Pawing? You think that's what I'm doing? You think I enjoy it?"

I jumped automatically. I hadn't meant to strike a nerve, and I was embarrassed that I hadn't thought before speaking. "I'm not. I meant exactly what I said. Everybody's so different. You could search every house in Monteleone and never find two the same. I would find that interesting."

I wasn't sure whether or not he believed me, but he stopped scowling. "It is. For example, Grazia's water glasses are in perfect rows, and the plates are in even stacks, suggesting she has time on her hands."

"She does. Plus she adores her kitchen."

"Does Grazia still keep things at her mother's?"

"I think so. Why?"

"Why hide a murder weapon in your own house when you can hide it more safely somewhere else?"

I backed another few feet away. I had reason to be angry myself. "Why do you insist my cousin is guilty?"

"The most obvious solutions are usually correct."

"She didn't have any reason to kill Ivano."

"She had several million of them."

I knew that spouses were the first suspects in a murder, but I'd never heard Grazia complain about Ivano except to mention his occasional snoring. While Cenzo opened the next cabinet, I sat on a bar stool, wondering how I could prove her innocence.

Cenzo read my mind. "You'd be surprised how often spouses kill one another."

"I suppose they have their reasons." I raised my eyebrows so he would know I was joking.

The ruse worked. He smiled as well. "Some of them do."

Given Carmela's hints from the night before, I assumed Cenzo had fantasized about killing off his spouse at least once. I opted to keep the mood light rather than hostile, so I pointed to a CD player on the counter. "Do you mind?"

"Go ahead."

Ivano had lots of music I liked, mostly pop tunes by Italian singers. I pressed "play" without checking to see which CD was in the machine. Within seconds Eros Ramazzotti made claims about the wonders of romantic love. I immediately turned down the volume. For once I didn't trust my favorite Italian singer. The very idea of love was suspect.

Cenzo ignored me, working with single-minded efficiency. He tried drawers and checked inside pots. He opened cookbooks, shaking them to make sure nothing fell out and cursing when loose recipes floated to the floor. He went through each shelf so thoroughly and put things back so carefully that I was sorry he hadn't become a housecleaner instead of a policeman; I would have hired him. For now I needed him to be satisfied there was nothing to find so that we could move on.

"Sofi, would you mind making coffee?"

I hesitated momentarily. I wasn't the maid, but Cenzo wasn't necessarily an enemy, the request was reasonable given my familiarity with the premises, and, anyway, we'd be stuck spending the morning together. I took the Bialetti off the drying rack and fired it up.

"Sugar or milk?"

"Neither."

I prepared demitasse cups while furtively watching Cenzo. He appealed to me, but why? Yes, he was lithe. Maybe he exercised. Maybe he gardened as the other villagers did. He took his work seriously, a quality I admired in anyone. In contrast to most of the men I'd met in Monteleone, he might soon be single.

But he was also quick-tempered. He'd made wild accusations about my cousin despite my protests. I didn't know where he stood, which made him a question mark. While he opened and closed drawers, I imagined his British companion, no doubt a blond bombshell. I wondered how they'd met and how someone as Piemontese as Cenzo could marry an outsider. An English socialite wouldn't fit into Monteleone any easier than Cenzo would fit into a London apartment. He wouldn't have room to wave his arms when he talked.

After the coffeemaker stopped gurgling, I poured Cenzo a coffee and handed it to him. He thanked me before draining it, Italian-style, in a single gulp.

"I drink too much caffeine," he complained. "Boh. I have to get through the day somehow. But then of course I can't sleep at night."

47

Bad sleep didn't excuse his accusations, but I credited him with a thorough job. While he tackled the pantry, I savored my espresso. "How long have you had trouble sleeping?"

"Since I received a copy of the divorce papers."

I hadn't expected such a raw and honest admission. "Sorry to hear it."

"Boh. I was working so hard we rarely saw each other, and when we did, we fought. Still, the paperwork bothers me. I'm not sure why. Of course, I would have reacted more reasonably if I'd seen it coming." He finished one shelf and started in on the next one. "You don't have to sit and watch me if you'd rather come back later."

It didn't feel right leaving him alone in the house, but I didn't want him to think I was worried. "What's the rush? I'll go out to the balcony for some fresh air."

I traipsed up to the master bedroom. I'd always admired the cheerful room with blue walls and light-colored maple furniture, but the giant wedding portrait of Ivano and Grazia stopped me cold. I knew the photo well because Grazia had sent me a miniature version a month after the wedding. Wearing a black tux with a satin lapel, Ivano smiled brightly. His left arm circled Grazia's waist; his right hand held hers. Between expensive lace and professional makeup, Grazia looked more radiant than usual. She smiled at the camera as if she commanded everything in her world.

The room made me shudder. I hurried through it and wrenched open the door to the balcony. Below, flowers swayed in the wind while blades of grass reflected golden rays. The homey scene called for infinitely patient mothers and children who brought home stray dogs. It should have been a beautiful summer day. Instead, all the positive things reminded me of Ivano, which depressed me all over again.

I blew dust off a plastic chair and took a seat. For long moments I stared at the clear blue sky as I practiced the dreaded message: *Grazia, I have terrible news. Grazia, I have to tell you something. Grazia, I'm so, so sorry.* There was no decent way to soften a message about a dead spouse.

Cenzo joined me on the balcony.

"Yes?"

"Do you know where your cousin keeps rags? I knocked over a glass in the living room. I think it was white wine."

Grazia was particular about her carpeting. I raced Cenzo to the kitchen cabinet and reached for the clear plastic bottle that Grazia had labeled "white vinegar." I handed it over to Cenzo. "This stuff will clean anything."

I grabbed three rags and ran into the living room; in this case, seconds mattered. While Cenzo knelt beside me, I poured a small amount of liquid onto a cloth and started blotting. "Wow. Vinegar back home must be a lot stronger. I can't even smell this stuff."

"Can I see that?"

I assumed he would blot the carpet more rigorously than I had. Instead he sniffed the rag.

"What's the matter?"

Cenzo took a pair of plastic gloves from his pocket and stretched them over his hands before picking up the bottle and shaking it. "This isn't vinegar."

"What is it?"

"Pesticide? Weed killer? I'm not sure."

Fine granules sifted through the liquid before settling on the bottom.

"Congratulations, Sofi. Looks like you found the murder weapon."

No way. There couldn't have been a murder weapon in the house, and I couldn't have found it.

"This is much too easy," I protested as Cenzo hurried back out through the garage. "You can't think my cousin would be stupid enough to concoct something lethal and hide it in her kitchen."

I veered too closely to the recycling bin and knocked it over. The clang might have been heard in Geneva. *"Porca Madonna!"* I slammed crushed cans back into their container.

Cenzo bent over to help me. "Congratulations, Sofi. We're both clumsy."

"Thanks."

"Don't take it so hard," he said. "It's not every day you catch a killer."

"My cousin did not kill her husband! You don't even know for sure that Ivano was poisoned!"

"You weren't listening when I said that the most obvious solution is usually the right one."

I stamped my feet as a teenager who hated gym class. Then I hurried after Cenzo as he continued through the garage and out to his car. I had to keep my eyes on him before he accused my cousin of something even bigger, such as poisoning the world.

"Grazia is innocent."

"We'll see."

I'd had enough. "Blaming my cousin is the most convenient solution. Eliminates your workload."

Cenzo stopped so short that I ran into him, and he was so solid that I ricocheted off. He didn't try to steady me. I caught my balance by reaching out and bracing myself against the car. This was a mistake because the metal had been broiling in the sun, and my hand stung as I pulled it back.

"Porca mattina!"

Cenzo ignored my plight. "I'm well aware that I have many defects. If you talked to Sarah or any of her friends, you could have a whole list of them. A whole notebook. But I am not lazy. I do not jail random citizens to lessen my workload."

I stared into his eyes, which shone between blue and green. "So now what?"

He opened his car door. "Now I talk to Maria to find out where your cousin is staying."

I got in the passenger side.

"What do you think you're doing?"

"Coming with you."

"Why would you do that?"

So that I could break the news to Grazia myself. Soften the blow. Witness any wrongdoing.

"You'll probably need me to find Kristine's place."

"I doubt that very much."

I fastened my seatbelt. "Or to find Aunt Maria."

"You think I don't know where she lives?"

"I think you don't know where she does her shopping on Tuesday mornings."

I stared straight ahead. For a moment Cenzo did nothing. Then he started up the car. "If you know what's best for you, you'll let me do the talking."

I knew what was best for me: complying with Cenzo until he realized he was wrong. Certainly I had enough patience for that.

♠ ♣ ♠

We caught Aunt Maria as she walked home from the bread store with a fresh loaf in her cloth sack. When Cenzo rattled off some nonsense about needing information from Grazia, Aunt Maria invited us inside. She wrote out Kristine's address, which was in Courmayeur, the west end of Aosta, nearly ninety kilometers away.

Cenzo thanked her and directed me back to the car. He accelerated through the remaining five blocks of Monteleone, shot past his office, and sped north, zigzagging along the narrow village roads. I was thankful we had the road to ourselves, but when he fumbled for the radio switch, I gave in.

"Let me," I said.

"I'd rather have a conversation, but I can't stand the silent treatment."

"Isn't that a shame for you." I scrambled to find a station. "I stood there like a dummy while you lied to my aunt about my cousin."

"Do you think I enjoy lying?"

"You might."

"You know nothing! Nothing at all."

Cenzo screeched into the recess of a gas station so that he could turn all his attention to the radio. To my satisfaction, he couldn't find a station with a clear signal either.

"If Grazia is as innocent as you claim, we're doing her a favor." Cenzo flipped off the radio and zoomed back onto the highway. "If she's involved in Ivano's death, running won't help. The quicker we unravel the facts, the quicker the issues are resolved. Don't you think Aunt Maria would rather have a small scandal than a huge one?"

I rolled down the window so that the force of the wind would help me keep my big mouth shut.

"Don't you care enough about Ivano to want to find his killer?"

If there even was one. I pretended not to hear.

"*Porca miseria,*" Cenzo said under his breath.

When I was a toddler, my dad's mother babysat me. She was a severe woman who blew up if I displaced a box of Kleenex, let alone broke a dish or spilled a drink. When she chided me, my stomach churned so much that I couldn't eat the food she'd prepared, which made her even angrier. I was probably the only kindergartener in my class who was ecstatic to have to spend the afternoon at school.

Over the years, I avoided making people angry at all costs, but Cenzo had turned me back into a naughty five-year-old. I naturally wanted to protect my family. Possibly Cenzo was trying to protect it as well, but I couldn't be sure.

As if to prove the point I hadn't articulated, Cenzo picked up the pace as soon as we hit a flat stretch. Vehicles blasted past as if we were on a racetrack. Fields blurred. I wanted to protest that I didn't have a death wish. Ironically, Cenzo began to relax. Each time he made a risky pass on the two-lane highway, he grew more satisfied. When he squeezed in between two trucks with seconds to spare, he grinned.

To distract myself from the queasiness, I noted the towns we passed: Verrès, Saint-Vincent, Saint-Pierre. We were heading towards Italy's northwest corner, the region closest to France. If we crashed into someone, I could complain about my driver in flawless French.

Cenzo kept his eyes on the road and his hands on the wheel. He didn't speak until we saw signs advertising the tourist attractions of Courmayeur. "I know you don't accept my methods." By now his tone had calmed. I no longer thought he was trying to kill me with his reckless driving although I hadn't ruled out the possibility of his killing both of us together.

"I appreciate that you've been cooperative," he continued. "But after all, it's in your best interest to do as I ask. The man was found dead on your property. Unless it's proven that he died of natural causes, a certain amount of suspicion naturally falls your way."

He whizzed by another car, entering the right lane as a baseball player sliding onto third.

I didn't speak until I could catch my breath. "Great. Now I'm under suspicion along with everybody else."

"No. That's why I'm keeping an eye on you. Mostly." He gave a shade of a smile.

"Are you trying to be funny?"

"No. I was trying to be cute."

"It's not working."

"Lighten up. If you're nice to me, I can help you out."

Right. I always sought help from delusional racecar drivers. "How could you do that?"

"By letting your cousin think that I'm the one who found the poison."

I turned so he wouldn't see me roll my eyes. That didn't change the fact that my cousin was still a prime suspect. To clear her name, I would have to play along.

Chapter Six

I secretly cheered when we reached Aosta. As we left the highway to enter the alpine getaway of Courmayeur, sharp turns slowed Cenzo to a reasonable pace. That gave me a chance to catch my breath and observe. In winter tourists flocked to the town's nearby slopes for skiing, in summer for hiking. The houses were so neatly arranged and the streets so clean that it felt like a different country, one that was more precise, more Germanic.

Cenzo's outdated GPS sent us to an empty field, so we doubled back to the main square. On the third try, Cenzo found somebody who could give us directions to Dolfino Street. The Boccio house melted into the block because it was exactly the same as its neighbors with one exception: all the curtains were closed.

"Yes?" Grazia herself opened the door. I'd never seen her so subdued. Her eyes were puffy, and her nose was red. Instead of her usual fashionable clothing, she wore baggy sweatpants. A tissue loomed from a T-shirt pocket. "Sofi, what are you doing here?"

I indicated the police captain.

"My mother!"

"She's fine," Cenzo said. "But you need to return to Monteleone. Please get your things. I'll explain along the way."

I looked past Grazia to the living room, where a dozen people sat in a circle, speaking softly.

"Kristine?" I hadn't met the woman because she'd been in chemo ever since I arrived in Monteleone, but Grazia had often recounted trips with her high school friend.

"She passed this morning," Grazia whispered. "We weren't surprised, but it still hit hard."

"I'm so sorry," I said.

"Maybe it's better. Who knows?"

"Please," Cenzo said. "I'll help you gather your things."

"I can't leave now."

"You can and you will. Sofi, would you mind waiting outside?"

I was happy to. The air was much cooler in Courmayeur, but sunlight bathed the village. I leaned against the hood of the car, wishing it were a normal day and cursing the rays for being so bright. Somehow I expected them to commiserate, to ease the burden of talking to Grazia. Instead the rooftops made fun of me by twinkling in the sunlight.

Grazia, your husband is dead. No. *Grazia, we have terrible news.* No. *You won't believe this, but ....* No. There was no good way.

I didn't wipe away tears. I let them stream down my face how they wanted to.

By the time Cenzo and Grazia emerged, my cousin had changed into jeans and a blouse. She carried her purse and a small grocery sack while Cenzo followed behind her with a duffel bag. Angry, she marched towards me. "I'm not getting into this car until you tell me what happened."

He folded down the driver's seat and pointed Grazia to the backseat. "Get in."

"Tell me now!"

"Get in."

"You have no right to order me around. You give me one good reason—"

"Ivano's dead," Cenzo said.

For a half second she smiled as if the words didn't register. Then she noticed my face; I assume my eyes were red. Her own widened. "That's impossible!"

Cenzo pointed to the backseat. "Please."

"A car accident?"

Cenzo placed his hands on her shoulders and pushed.

Grazia scrambled to keep her balance. "Tell me!"

Cenzo shook his head and got into the driver's seat. I took the passenger seat without saying a word. With a jolt that nearly tossed me into the trunk, he started the engine and sped to the nearest corner.

Cenzo watched Grazia through the rearview mirror. "Where were you yesterday?"

"At Kristine's, of course."

"Alone?"

"Her aunt and uncle stopped by in the evening."

"Otherwise you were alone?"

"Kristine was too sick to want much company."

"See what I mean?" Cenzo told me. "That's not good enough."

"What are you talking about?" Grazia shouted.

Cenzo pulled up against a curb and turned off the motor. Then he twisted around to face Grazia straight on. "You're under arrest for the murder of your husband. Don't make me get out the handcuffs, although I will if I need to."

"What in the hell is wrong with you, Cenzo?"

He restarted the car. "If you think something is wrong with me, you ought to take a good look at Ivano."

I opened my mouth to protest such a crass comment, but I caught myself in time. I didn't need to be reminded that Ivano had been found on my own property, and I wasn't sure of a logical next step. Renato and Grazia had tons of friends, but as far as I knew, not one was a lawyer, and I was afraid I might need one.

"You don't know what you're talking about," Grazia said.

Cenzo responded with silence. I didn't mind following his lead. I watched the road without saying a thing, but I was listening more carefully than a doctor through a stethoscope.

Teardrops may have run down Grazia's cheeks, but I never once heard her cry.

♠ ♥ ♠

I followed Grazia into the office while Cenzo rummaged around for the correct forms in the adjoining room.

"I can't believe he's dead," Grazia said.

"He is," I whispered.

"Murdered?"

"Maybe."

"And I was supposed to have killed him at the same time I was watching Kristine die? What in God's name is going on?"

"Yesterday I found Ivano dead in my balmetto," I said.

She straightened up, her voice rising with every word. "Yesterday? Why didn't you come for me last night? What's wrong with you? And why involve the police?"

"Grazia, listen to yourself! The man was dead! What else was I supposed to do?"

"Not call Cenzo."

"What?" I stamped my feet. "I should have left Ivano in the cellar? How was I supposed to find you when you took off without telling me?"

She shook her finger. "You found me easily enough today."

Although I wasn't surprised by it, she'd stood me up for lunch. I'd sat around for long minutes before stomping off for a walk. Then I'd bought breadsticks and driven to my balmetto.

For a moment we glared at one another like two schoolkids in a playground standoff.

"Then what happened?" she asked.

"Before the party or afterwards?"

"You had a party even though my husband was dead?"

I'd never heard Grazia raise her voice so loud before. Italian or not, shouting didn't suit her. I had a flicker of doubt before gathering my senses. "How dare you have a husband who died on my property? Don't blame me for finding him. And do you think I wanted to have a party? Cenzo wouldn't let me cancel it."

"That's the rudest thing I've ever heard!"

"Maybe, maybe not. He planted himself amidst the guests and asked trick questions all night."

"He didn't find out anything important, did he?"

"If he did, he didn't share. But this morning, he found something weird in your kitchen. Your bottle labeled 'vinegar?' Not vinegar. How do you explain that?"

"What was that man doing in my kitchen?" she yelled.

I strode to the window to stay as far away from Grazia as possible. "I feel horrible about Ivano. But if somebody killed him, I want to help find out who it was."

"I'll bet you do."

I leaned against the wall. My shoulders were tight, and my knees felt weak. I wanted to wake up and learn it was the day before so that I would never have to find Ivano dead or meet Cenzo Bot. I pretended not to listen as my cousin repeated obscenities, including several directed at me. I tried to put myself in the terrible shoes of someone who learned about a dead spouse while mourning a dead friend. Maybe Grazia couldn't help what she was saying. Maybe it was a necessary form of self-defense.

As if she'd flipped a switch, Grazia quieted down. "What was it like to find him?"

"Like a nightmare."

"He didn't have a single enemy. Not a serious one."

"I know."

"My mother knows he's dead?"

I shook my head.

"Cenzo is a jerk."

"He jumped to conclusions."

"If you found poison in my house, somebody planted it. Someone who was jealous of us. Plenty of people were. Take Sanalto. He was the mayor for two decades before he lost his seat to Ivano."

"Sanalto must have had a lot of supporters."

"Every businessman in town."

"Anyone in particular?"

"Not that I can think of."

Cenzo announced his return with a fake cough. I assumed he'd been listening from behind the wall in case we said anything incriminating. Clever.

"I would never have hurt my husband," Grazia barked. "You have no right to accuse me."

"I have every right. Your tax money pays me to do so."

"So I have to sit here with you all afternoon?"

"Until you tell me what happened."

"I don't know!"

Cenzo sat on top of his desk and leaned towards Grazia. "You haven't done a lot since marrying, have you? It hasn't been such a bad life compared to the long hours you worked at the bank." He leaned back and crossed his arms. "But you don't have the nerve to kill anyone."

"Thank you."

"You would have used your husband's resources to pay someone to do it for you."

"That's nonsense!"

"Leaving your house unlocked was smart planning, by the way."

"Cenzo!" Grazia yelled.

The man herded me into the adjoining office. "Let's see if a little time for reflection jogs Sra. Ivano Visconti's memory."

"If there's nothing to jog?"

He blinked, dislodging the wrinkles in the bags under his eyes. "That's where you're wrong. There's always something."

He was wrong about Grazia, but I couldn't expect him to take my word for it. I would have to prove it to him.

Chapter Seven

While Cenzo buried himself in paperwork, I raced over to Renato's fast enough to warrant a speeding ticket. I parked in front of the shop and breathed in metals.

My cousin sold iron products and associated tools. He had a workshop in the back room where he built projects for customers. Spiral staircases were his specialty, but he also made fancy balcony railings. He loved every aspect of such projects. During my first days in Italy, he'd taken me on a walking tour and showed me every balcony he'd constructed within the confines of Monteleone. He was often called to nearby towns, in which case Laura would take over the shop, managing as best she could with their two-year-old, their four-year-old, and all of their customers.

As I barged in, Renato tallied handwritten receipts behind the cash register. He was so engrossed in the numbers that it took him half a minute to notice me.

"Sofi!" he smiled as he slid his pen behind his ear. "Can I get you something? A light bulb? A hammer?"

The most I could do was shake my head.

"Don't tell me that toilet is acting up again?"

If a broken toilet were my only problem, I would be ready to throw another balmetto party. I felt my chest tighten. I wanted to be strong, but each second was harder than the last.

"Fender bender? Don't worry. It's an old car."

Tears formed at the corner of my eyes. I breathed deeply, fighting for control. "Car's fine."

He set down his receipts and hugged me.

"Tell me what happened. We were having such a fine time last night. Did—Oh, God. Don't tell me that Cenzo got too friendly. I'll kill the bastard."

"No." I buried my head in my cousin's chest and gave in to sobs.

He walked me to his workbench, sat me down, and wiped away teardrops as they fell.

"Something back home?" he finally asked.

I shook my head.

"Are you hurt?"

I waited until I could catch my breath. "Ivano's dead and Cenzo thinks Grazia did it!"

"What?"

It took me several tries to explain the whole story.

Renato looked deep into my eyes. "We have to tell Aunt Maria."

"That's why I came here first. I can't do it by myself."

He pulled me to his chest. "You shouldn't have to. How much time do we have?"

"What do you mean?"

"Cenzo can't keep Ivano's death quiet indefinitely."

"I don't know. We didn't talk about it."

"It's smart to delay as long as possible. When the information gets out, the town will go crazy."

Renato put a "*Torno subito*" sign on his door and escorted me to his pickup. The truck was a good fifteen years old and so full of dust I immediately started sneezing. Renato didn't notice. He whizzed through town so fast two teens on bicycles had to veer out of the way.

I didn't mind. For the first time since Ivano's death, I didn't feel helpless. However, I was sorry to return to Aunt Maria's on such a dark mission. From my first hours in Monteleone, she'd treated me as a starving stray dog and drawn me into the bosom of the family.

She insisted I attend family dinners and sent me home with enough leftovers for a family of six. She kept my counters stocked with fresh fruit and vegetables from her garden. She did everything for me that she could, but I hadn't done a single thing to stand up for her daughter.

We heard Aunt Maria plod towards us. After she pulled back the edge of the curtain to see who we were, she hustled us inside with some explanation of a neighbor she was avoiding. She led us to her living room where she'd been glued to a Mexican soap opera. I felt terrible about interrupting her favorite kind of afternoon.

When Renato explained that Ivano was dead, Aunt Maria crossed herself three times and asked if he'd had a heart attack. She didn't start yelling until we explained that he might have been murdered and that Grazia was the prime suspect.

For the next half hour, *porca mattinas* flew left and right across the room. Each one made me feel better.

Finally my aunt switched from cursing to analyzing and opened her address book. She ran her index finger down each page, muttering names out loud and shaking her head as she discounted them. No leads. Next she took out a wedding album, a miniature of the extravagant volume I'd viewed several times at Grazia's house.

While Renato and I huddled over her shoulders, Aunt Maria looked through the pictures, skipping ones of the happy couple and scouring group photos where multiple faces were scrunched into four by six squares.

She pointed at a pale face. "There's the one who died. Kristine and Grazia went to grade school together. That's why they were so close."

Aunt Maria turned the page. "Her!" She pointed triumphantly to a woman who stood at the edge of the crowd. The other women wore dresses with long sleeves, but this woman wore a skimpy sleeveless model that barely covered her panties. "Teresa. You can't trust that one."

Grazia often complained about the friend who'd scoffed at her for dating Ivano right up to the moment the couple got engaged. Then Teresa made a play for Ivano herself.

Aunt Maria closed the book but went over to the cabinet. "I have more pictures here somewhere." She brought out an envelope with loose shots. Most were out of focus or overexposed.

Aunt Maria handed Renato a photo. "That's the secretary. What's her name?"

"Pia."

"Pia! She ached to get her claws into Ivano."

"Was he interested?" I asked.

"Have you ever seen that poor woman? She has a man's nose and the body of a walrus, which might be tolerable if she didn't have the personality of a turnip."

"Can you think of anyone else?" Renato asked.

"His maid, for one. A Romanian. They come to Italy by the score. She would have done anything to have a permanent place to live and no worries about money. But Grazia got rid of her right away."

"Do you remember her name?" Renato asked.

"Antonella might know."

"Who's that?" I asked.

"The mechanic's mother," Renato said.

"Antonella has lived next to Ivano for years," Aunt Maria said. "In a town this small, the neighbors know almost everything."

Better yet, they were almost always willing to share.

"Feeling better?" Renato asked as we headed back to the shop.

"A little."

"Stay for dinner?" His house was above the shop.

Half of me wanted time to process. The other half craved company. Alone in an empty house, I'd feel depressed right away. "Love to."

When Renato escorted me into his kitchen a few minutes later, Laura stopped tearing apart the lettuce long enough to let him kiss her. "You make me work half the afternoon in the store, and then you bring a guest to dinner. How am I supposed to get along?" She winked as she tore more pieces of green.

At her house, I had a standing invitation. An extra diner was no problem because, just as all the other women I'd met in this town, Laura was a medalist in the kitchen. She juggled the tasks of boiling pasta and simmering sauce and chopping up salad as if she were an octopus. Wearing an apron on top of a miniskirt, she looked sexy and fresh, as if homemaking were so easy she could be ready for her husband whenever he was ready for her. Such wonder women made me feel particularly un-Italian. At home I rarely had friends over for dinner. We sampled local restaurants instead.

Laura was a supermom as well. Eduardo sang to himself in his playpen in the living room while his big sister Daniella played nearby. Laura had the household and her life firmly under control. She turned away from her lettuce long enough to face me. "Sofi, I heard five people offer to buy your balmetto last night. Remember that if you ever want to sell, we're first in line. All right?"

"Sure, sure."

She picked up a final lettuce leaf and tore it savagely. "I mean, not that you would ever want to sell even though you live so far away and hardly ever come here!"

"Uh huh." This was the point I kept making to my parents.

"It's almost like the balmetto is ours anyway. We've used it a hundred times more often than you have."

My cousins were the reason my cellar was full of unidentified wine. They stored their leftover reds indiscriminately.

Renato took a serrated knife and sliced half a loaf of fresh bread. "Never mind about wine cellars right now. I need your opinion as an outside observer. My cousin's marriage to Ivano—"

"The one you were so opposed to?" Laura asked.

"Right."

"Don't you feel silly now? You saw them at the dance last Saturday. I'd say they're completely in love." She handed her husband the silverware and me the water pitcher. In Italy, news took second place to dinnertime.

"Laura, I need you to concentrate," said Renato.

She turned on the faucet to protect the pipes from the scalding water and poured the linguini into a strainer, jiggling it as she did so. Then she added the noodles to the large saucepan and tossed everything together. "I am concentrating."

"Who was the most opposed to the wedding?"

"Besides you?"

"I was only worried that Ivano wasn't right for Grazia."

Laura mouthed Renato a kiss as she pushed past her husband to set the pasta on the table. "I know. And I love you for it. You had a right to be concerned. Ivano has a reputation. Maybe he's earned it. But you know how people like to exaggerate, especially around here."

"Was Grazia nervous before the wedding?" I asked.

"She had the usual butterflies. Who doesn't?" Laura took the bowl of grated Parmesan cheese from the refrigerator and set it on the table. "I didn't sleep the night before our wedding either. After the reception, I fell asleep right away. Renato couldn't wake me up." She paused long enough to share a grin with Renato. "Luckily, we had more fun the second night. Please, sit."

"Thanks, Laura. I'm not hungry, so—"

As usual, she served me a huge portion of pasta.

I breathed in the roasted garlic. "Laura, you know Grazia's friends. Were any jealous of her getting married?"

"Only half a dozen. She lost friends over it. Well, you could argue they weren't real friends. Take Gizelle, for example. She and Grazia had gone to high school together. Gizelle kept saying, 'Ivano's too old for you, too experienced, too everything,' and guess who was in the process of getting a divorce? Gizelle had her own best interests in mind."

"She wanted to date Ivano herself?" I asked.

"Why not? Do you think Gizelle has ever worked? Not since before she married. She doesn't want to start now." Laura served herself a modest amount of pasta. "Then there's Teresa. She had her eye on Ivano too, but when he asked her out, she turned him down. As soon as Grazia started dating him, Teresa realized she'd lost out. His secretary, Pia, didn't take the marriage well either. Not that she had a chance. Forget about the fact that she's a few years older than he, because Ivano doesn't much care about age, but with a body like hers? How can you expect to entice a man when your stomach stretches from the chair to the table?" Laura might have been writing the town history.

"Can't you think of anyone else?" I asked.

"Ivano was always going around with someone or other. Come to think of it, we ran into him with

Antonella at Lake Viverone one time. Remember that, Renato?"

Renato paused in between bites. "Vaguely."

Laura twisted her fork around the linguini. "They didn't seem 'together together,' though. You can assume they're fast friends. I admire that about Ivano. He's a good listener."

Renato twisted his fork as well. "Let's turn the tables. Weren't a few ex-boyfriends jealous of Ivano too?"

"Honey, I know she's your cousin, but honestly, where have you been for the last few years?"

"You're saying several people were jealous?" I asked.

"Start with Dario. Grazia invited him to the wedding to be polite, but what else can you do when you're marrying the mayor? You can't ignore people who are mad because you'd have no guests. So Dario was at the wedding, knowing he'd lost out. When I passed him right after the mass, he had a tear in his eye." She shook her fork at me. "You're not eating. What's the matter?"

"Are you kidding? I ate two days' worth."

"Don't think you can avoid dessert, either," she laughed. "You can tell an American right away. You're not trained to eat hearty dinners."

"Dario," Renato continued. "Who else?"

"Every man except you. Didn't you notice Fabio Sanalto? That old scumbag was a lousy mayor anyway. But there he was, leering over Grazia as if he'd be next in line. At the reception he was watching Ivano and Grazia dance, and guess what he was doing? Touching his private parts. I swear to God. He didn't think anybody noticed, but I noticed plenty."

I shook the ugly image from my head. "Any other political enemies?"

Laura brought over the braised beef slices and served Renato and me several. "You can pick between Fabio, who almost had a heart attack when he didn't get reelected, and his buddy Baruzzo Senior."

"The guy who owns property along the riverfront?"

"Yes," Laura said. "He was anxious to sell to developers, and Ivano wouldn't let them buy it. Then there are the carpenters, who lost money last year, and the staff at the Medical Recovery Center."

"What's that?" I asked.

Laura took a single bite. "It's a mini-hospital for post-surgery."

"How was Ivano involved?"

"The center wanted to double prices, and Ivano threatened a tax increase."

"I thought Ivano was popular."

Laura popped up to add olive oil to the salad and proceeded to toss it. "You can't please everyone. But Ivano prevented the plumbers' strike. He found money to fix potholes. He started an after-school program for the elementary grades. He created a cultural exchange. Yes, he's made mistakes. He's also made decisions that were in his own best interest. That's human nature. I don't know why people expect their politicians to be saints."

She plopped salad on Renato's plate and my own. Suddenly I understood how she stayed so slim after two kids and thousands of home-cooked meals: She talked instead of eating. "But tell me. Why so much interest in Ivano? Did he and Grazia have a big fight? I'm sure it will blow over."

"Ivano had a fight, all right," Renato said, "but it wasn't with my cousin." He checked his watch before turning on the TV.

"Shocking news," said the anchor for the nightly *Piemontese Report*. "In the normally quiet town of

Monteleone, tragedy has struck. The town mayor was found dead, perhaps by the hand of foul play."

Laura gasped. Then she cried out. Then she ran over to Renato and sobbed. While I hated to see her in pain, I was thankful for one thing. I was convinced she had nothing to do with Ivano's demise. Renato either.

Two suspects down. One village to go. Boh!

Chapter Eight

On Thursday nights, the Municipal Band of Monteleone rehearsed in the basement of the elementary school. I'd promised Roberto I would show up, but I wasn't going as a musician. I was going as a spy.

The room bustled. Half the musicians arranged the chairs into a big semi-circle. The rest armed their instruments or checked pitches. A red-headed boy who looked too young to play an instrument stood on tiptoes to prop open a window. A roly-poly clarinet player sauntered in, greeting the others with traditional embraces. The two men who had accompanied the maestro and his wife to my balmetto party strolled in together, nearly late but unhurried.

I strained to listen. Despite rapid-fire sentences, I caught the word "mayor" in two separate conversations. I tried to follow along, but the speakers were drowned out in the jumble of other greetings. But the word was out. In an enclave such as this one, news spread more quickly than spilled soda over a laptop. I put my ears on high alert. Just as Cenzo had crashed my dinner party, I was crashing the band rehearsal. I hoped for better results.

The maestro sat on the left side of the room before a huge wooden table loaded with sheet music. As he called out the names of instruments, corresponding players rushed over to collect parts. Roberto was in too much of a hurry to make eye contact.

I stood quietly until Roberto finished giving out the sheets.

"Sofi! Forgive me. I didn't see you."

He dug out another trumpet part from the stack. Then he escorted me to the outer semicircle, which was still forming, and dragged over an extra chair. "We'll put you on the same stand with Marco. If Bartoleo shows up tonight, which I doubt, you can move over."

"I hope I can keep up. Last season I only played a couple of concerts."

"Boh! No better time to start than now. You read music, no? Tonight, play what you can. You can study the parts next week."

"Roberto, I don't know if Carmela mentioned it, but I have a small problem."

"Oh, yes! You need a trumpet! Follow me."

Roberto hurried me into a crowded office. He shook his head as he plowed through the clutter. Boxes of clarinet reeds topped a photocopier while a stack of chairs cradled a mangled tuba. Programs from previous concerts dotted the floor like peanut shells while photos on the wall celebrated the band's accomplishments. The conductor pawed through the miscellany until he found a trumpet case.

He blew the dust off the top. "This is only a student model, but it's not too bad."

After making do with a mouthpiece all summer, a borrowed trumpet was a welcome luxury. I quickly took my seat and assembled the horn.

"Places, everyone!" Roberto stepped onto a low wooden platform and lifted his baton while band members scrambled to ready their instruments. "Let's give the new piece a twirl. One, two, three, four!"

The talent of the local volunteer musicians astonished me. Given the area's population, at best I expected a ten-piece band of beginners. Instead the group numbered over forty strong. The first measures sounded sturdy if uninspired. Then the young redhead, who was the timpanist, entered two beats late.

"No!" Roberto roared as he pointed at the youth. "From the top!"

On our next attempt, we reached the tenth measure.

"No!" Roberto pointed to his friend, the French horn player. "You don't come in until Letter A!"

The stakes were higher than I'd realized. To avoid making egregious mistakes myself, I kept my eyes on the first trumpeter, a rotund middle-aged man with a hairline that had receded to the top of his head. A seasoned musician, his timing was impeccable. The second trumpeter, a blond woman a decade or so my senior, played precisely but had a tinny sound. Since she looked at me with mild disapproval, I ignored her. Marco, the little old man next to me, disregarded me altogether. He wore such thick glasses that I suspected he couldn't read through them. He skipped as many notes as he played.

Roberto stopped us a dozen more times before we waded through the first page. The maestro was exactly as Carmela described him. He was so excited he could barely conduct us, yet his passion made him impatient. He expected perfection.

He didn't get it. As we continued to Copeland's *Rodeo*, which I'd performed in Boston, Roberto stopped us over and over. Marco was the only player Roberto spared from criticism. The others didn't crumble, however. They carried right on. Then we reached the *Hoe-Down*. At the entrance for the brass, I was the only one who came in.

"Hai sentito!" shouted the maestro. "Did you hear that?" He pointed at me. "Why are you making this so hard? Follow the American!"

I'd gained instant status as a member of the club.

After we reached the end of a treacherous Milt Jackson piece, the maestro told us to study the parts for the next rehearsal. The musicians collected music, disarmed instruments, shouted across the room, and whipped out cell phones. Carmela hurried down the stairs carrying a huge bag. When she spotted me, she waved and disappeared down the hall.

I wiggled the mouthpiece from the trumpet and wiped it off. The instrument was an American-made Windsor, not unlike the instrument I had at home, with a reasonable tone and quick valve movements. At least I'd played enough to blow the dust out. A dent on the bell suggested at least one hard fall, probably on the practice room's cement floor.

I approached the maestro, but band members had clustered around him, bidding him goodnight or shouting questions. I stood to one side. People had smiled at me in friendly ways, but I hadn't talked to anyone, not even Marco. I hadn't wanted to interfere with his concentration.

"You did very well," Roberto said. "You've had a lot of band experience."

"I enjoyed sitting in with you."

"Sitting in? We need you for the concert. You can take Marco's music folder home with you. He never practices."

"That'll be great. I promise to practice. Have a good night!"

"Where are you going?" Roberto pointed to the French horn player. "It's Roberto's birthday. Since three of us are named Roberto, we celebrate together. It's a tradition."

When I looked behind me, I was nonplussed. Indeed, a few band members had left, but others assembled makeshift picnic tables by placing long boards over two-by-fours. Two players welcomed spouses who had just arrived. The principal flautist, a forty-something woman, brought out a paper tablecloth from a back room and rolled it across the tables.

Carmela appeared with loaves of bread that she placed at opposite ends.

"Sofi!" Carmela beckoned me towards a back room where a kitchen sink was flanked by enticing casseroles. "Glad you could come. I hope Roberto didn't yell too often?"

"Only a few dozen times."

The second clarinetist passed by with slices of sausage on a cutting board.

"You can't leave," Carmela said. "I've prepared a delicious pasta."

"I hate to barge in."

"*Non scherzare!* Don't kid me! You've suffered an entire rehearsal. You deserve linguini, at least."

The invitation was so genuine that I didn't dare turn it down, never mind that Laura had stuffed me silly three hours earlier. "I'm sorry I didn't bring any food, but how can I help out?"

"This isn't my first band dinner! I have everything under control."

The French horn player swept past us brandishing a red plastic carrier that held four bottles of wine. He nodded as he passed.

"We call him Roberto Two." She pointed to the saxophone player, who was struggling with a huge sheet cake. "We call him Roberto Three. Since my husband is Roberto One, we don't bother using the number!"

I wasn't crazy after all. There really were three Robertos. "I won't bother to learn anyone's name. I'll call everyone Roberto, even the women."

"There's a Roberta, but she didn't show up tonight!" Carmela said gleefully.

Despite the cheerful chaos, Carmela convinced everyone to sit down, including her husband, who saved me a spot between them. Moments later, plates of salami made the rounds.

The conductor cut a huge slice and put it on my plate. "Good stuff. Comes from Roberto Two's farm. They have the best year after year."

I refrained from confessing my lack of hunger. As Roberto opened a two-litre bottle of wine and poured me the first glass, I also refrained from admitting my attitude towards wine.

"This is the best I've made in years," Roberto told me as he filled several other glasses. "Drink up! Don't think that we'll run out."

"Run out of wine at the Annual Roberto Party?" cried Roberto Three. "Impossible!" He held up his glass for a toast, and everyone joined in.

I politely took a small sip. I was more enthusiastic about the aroma of roasted garlic. Carmela served me an exaggerated portion of pasta, but I pardoned myself for the unneeded calories. I was part of a carefree crowd where the most dramatic action was snagging slices of bread before they disappeared. Carmela introduced me all around, and I was greeted with smiles and mouths full of food.

While Carmela passed around the cheese plate, her husband called the partiers to attention. I picked up my glass for the inevitable birthday toast.

"Quiet, everyone," said the maestro. "Some of you may not have heard the bad news about one of the band's biggest supports, but Ivano Visconti is dead."

Roberto Three attacked the pecorino. "Of course we heard. Everybody did."

"He was pretty old," said the redhead.

"A heart attack," said the clarinet player.

"Stroke," said the female trumpet player.

Marco raised his wine glass. "I heard he drank bad wine."

"Face it," said an elderly female clarinet player. "He was murdered."

Several gasped.

"Why would anyone murder him?" asked Roberto Two.

For a moment, none of us spoke. Then everyone chimed in at once:

"Because of elections!"

"Skimming off the top!"

"Wrong place, wrong time!"

"A jealous husband!"

Ideas pinged back and forth as a badminton birdie punished by eager opponents.

The trombone player calmly poured himself another glass of wine. "Maybe his wife paid to have him taken out so she could spend all his money with a younger lover."

"You call Grazia a wife?" asked the flautist. "They ate at Ristorante Polipazzo at least once a week because she was too lazy to cook."

"Lots of people eat out," said Carmela.

"Newlyweds stay in," said the clarinet player. "That way they can get straight to bed for dessert."

Roberto Three took another huge piece of pecorino. "At least that woman is good for something."

Carmela silenced us with a flick of her hand. "Stop sticking your feet in your mouths." She patted my shoulder. "Grazia is Sofi's cousin."

Everyone in the room turned and stared as if I were holding a bottle of poisoned wine.

The clarinet player broke the ice. "Where did you study music?"

"When I was a fifth grader —"

"Does Cenzo have any leads?"

"Did you know Ivano well?"

"Did Ivano receive any death threats?"

"What does Grazia think about the murder?"

For several minutes, theories flew. Then, as if he were back in elementary school, Marco stood to get our attention. "Now that there has been a death on the property, will you be selling your balmetto?"

"I'll buy it!" cried the trombone player.

"I want it!" shouted Roberto Two.

"I want it more!" insisted Roberto Three.

I shook my head. "No sales. Sorry."

Twenty people sighed. Then Carmela calmly took orders for coffee. By the time she served the plastic demitasses, the musicians resumed their simultaneous conversations. I watched them without making any useful observations. They may have been excellent chatterboxes, but I was a failure as a spy.

After the party, I followed Carmela out to the parking lot because she wouldn't hear of my walking the three blocks home by myself. I felt adopted.

Carmela buckled herself in. "No wonder Cenzo was at your party. He was gathering information, wasn't he?"

Not adopted. Imprisoned. I didn't have time to react.

"I knew he was there for a reason," Carmela continued. "Is he sure of the cause of death?"

I'd been lulled by the cheerful setting of the band rehearsal, but now Carmela had total control. I answered her questions as if taking a lie detector test in a police station. "He ordered an autopsy."

"Do you know who found him? The news report didn't say."

I looked out over the quiet street. By now we had it to ourselves.

"Oh, no. You found him, didn't you?"

I brushed away a hint of moisture.

Carmela pulled over, cut the engine, and demanded details. What could I do? I told her the whole story as far as I knew it myself.

"Are you all right?" she asked.

"I'm not sure. Cenzo thinks Grazia did it. He won't listen to reason!"

Carmela started the engine again. "Cenzo will be more reasonable once his deputy returns to work. Stefano's mother had a hip operation last week, so he had to take time off."

Never mind the rest of the band. The only person I needed to talk to was Carmela. She knew everything.

"Cenzo doesn't have the right to jump to conclusions."

"His exterior is an act. Tell me. Don't you think he's handsome?"

No innocent questions were asked in Monteleone. Since I'd confessed quite enough for one night, I toned down my thoughts. "He's all right."

"He's been unhappy."

"His wife left him. So what? That happens to a lot of people."

"He worked as a detective in Milano for several years, but everyone in town knew she was cheating on him before he did. That would hurt."

Porca miseria! Didn't these people do anything but sleep with one another?

Carmela squeezed the steering wheel. "If she hadn't taken the boys to London with her, he wouldn't feel so bad."

"How can a cheating mother get custody of her children?"

"By dragging them away while Cenzo was out of town. He could take her to court, but they'd have an expensive cross-country battle that he would lose anyway."

"Are the kids better off with her?"

Carmela rolled her eyes. "Sarah will make sure their jackets are warm enough and that they do their homework, but she'll fill their heads with her petty complaints. She loves to be unhappy."

"Great role model."

"The worst of it is that both kids are budding musicians. One plays the sax, the other the clarinet. They're gifted, Roberto says. But who knows what will happen? Never mind that for now. Did you enjoy meeting your fellow musicians?"

"Very friendly. Half of them offered to buy my balmetto."

"Whatever you do, don't tell them it's for sale until after the band concert. Otherwise they'd hurt one another arm wrestling and wouldn't be able to play!"

"I'm probably not interested in selling, though."

"Of course not. It's family history. But all the musicians will keep asking you. Don't pay attention."

"On the other hand, I don't even live here."

Carmela's eyes twinkled as she pulled up outside my aunt's house. "One day you might."

I thanked Carmela for the lovely evening and waved as she drove off. Live in Monteleone? Ridiculous. Too small. Too dramatic. Too Italian.

The answering machine in the kitchen blinked red. I rushed to hit "play," sure I would hear good news about Grazia. Instead my mother had called. I hadn't answered my cell, and she wanted details about my dinner party.

I was glad there were no other messages.

Too wide awake to consider sleeping, I scooted a chair onto the balcony overlooking Via Guido Rossa. Before Ivano's death, I'd spent odd moments on the balcony pleasantly fantasizing about summers to come. Whenever Aunt Angela didn't need me to housesit, I would stay with Aunt Maria or Grazia or Renato. I wouldn't care about where I slept because I'd spend long hours at my balmetto hosting parties night after night. Now my plans sounded stupid. So far, I'd spent my happiest hours in Monteleone with Ivano and Grazia. I couldn't imagine one without the other. I'd have to dive into Ivano's past and bring everything back out of it: women, stray family members, politicians, townspeople.

Somewhere there were some loose ends. If I wanted to regain my peace of mind, I needed to find the loosest one.

Chapter Nine

The cell phone woke me from a sound sleep. I reached for the device, prepared to yell at the annoying early caller. Then I noticed it was ten-thirty.

"Your cousin needs a change of clothes," Cenzo said. "We don't do laundry."

"Good morning to you too." I cursed myself for answering.

"It's not my fault if I'm in a bad mood. Last night the phone rang every few minutes. Reporters and newscasters wanted tidbits while every citizen in Monteleone wanted to share theories about who hated Ivano enough to kill him."

I relented because I could imagine the circus. The region was normally quiet. A suspicious death would provide enough gossip for a decade. "All right, already. I'll bring a change of clothes. Should I bring breakfast? I suppose you're not a restaurant, either."

"She says she's not hungry. But as a personal favor to me, you might bring some coffee."

"Haven't learned how to make it yet?"

"No, I mean, I ran out a couple of hours ago."

"Is that why you're so cranky?"

"That's only half of it."

I envisioned Cenzo as a store owner shooing away unwanted customers even though the waves kept coming. Since I was doing him a favor, however, I saw no reason to hurry. He sounded so angry that I knew he was wide awake whether he realized it or not.

The police station's small parking lot was so jammed that I had to park along the highway a hundred yards away. A couple of camera crews blocked the entrance to the station, but Cenzo magically appeared at the doorway and pulled me through the crowd before I had to answer any questions.

He led me straight to his office.

"What a mess outside," I said.

"That's what I was trying to tell you. It's been like this since the newscast went out last night."

"Didn't you expect this kind of reaction?"

"I didn't expect it would be this bad. You brought coffee?"

I handed him a nearly full container of Lavazza Rosso.

"Thanks. Now go talk to your cousin."

I held up a small laundry bag. "Do you want to make sure I haven't brought a steak knife?"

He shook his head without answering.

I went through Cenzo's office to the detention room where Grazia combed her hair. As I sat in an adjacent chair and handed her the bag, I noticed my eyes were puffier than hers were.

"Hi, Cuz! Thanks for coming." As she smiled, she seemed relaxed and well rested. "I could have managed without the clothes, but I wanted to see how Cenzo would react," she whispered. "He called you right away. I finally calmed down, but we had a shouting match a few hours ago."

"What about?"

"His accusations. He's an idiot, but of course he's too stupid to see that."

Once again my cousin surprised me. She hadn't done a 360 from the day before; it was more like a 540. Despite a night in the police station with Cenzo, she seemed perfectly controlled.

"You've drawn quite a crowd."

"I ought to be pleased that people care about my husband, but God! The reporters are vultures. They didn't let poor Cenzo sleep more than an hour or two."

"Poor nothing. Did you forget he's the one who locked you up?"

Grazia shrugged. "He's a peon who thinks he's doing his job. In a way I can understand. Murders don't happen in Monteleone."

"It's not clear Ivano was murdered."

"No, but it looks that way. By now the townspeople are so wound up they can't think straight."

"I'm so sorry about Ivano."

"I cried all night until I got cried out. He's gone and won't be back. The only thing I can do for my husband is to cooperate with Cenzo so that he can figure out what happened." She spoke so smoothly that I wondered if she had practiced.

"Have you heard from Ivano's relatives?"

"They'll be swarming over here soon enough, hoping they can inherit something."

"I thought in Italy the estate always went to the immediate family."

"For the most part that's the case, but there can be small exceptions."

"Did Ivano have any children?"

"Not that I'm aware of."

Given what I'd learned about the Monteleonesi lately, I had a sudden flash of a funeral in which five screaming children appeared from nowhere and ran to the coffin calling out *"Papi! Papi!"*

"Am I interrupting girl talk?" Cenzo asked as he entered the room.

"Nothing that we can't continue later." Grazia spoke so sweetly that we might have been at a luncheon.

I was glad I hadn't been too stubborn to bring coffee. Cenzo's mood had noticeably improved. Maybe he realized that since Grazia was innocent, he might be nicer to her. He pulled up a chair. "The team from Torino should be here soon. They're more official than I am." He turned to me. "When it comes to murder, I'm required to request backup help."

"There's no rush," Grazia beamed. "At least here you can protect me from the press. I won't be able to go anywhere in Monteleone for months. I'll have to let Sofi do all my shopping."

I had an image of being at Grazia's beck and call doing needless errands. I didn't like the picture. Usually Ivano had been roped into that kind of stuff.

"Grazia, we need to think of other angles to investigate. What can you tell me about Ivano's views on politics?" Cenzo asked.

"You're out of luck. Ivano talked about politics all the time, but honestly, I never listened."

That much I believed. She tuned out anything that didn't concern her directly, which was why I'd attended several social functions with Ivano.

"Tell me this much," Cenzo said. "What was the relationship like between the former mayor and your husband?"

"So-so. Fabio couldn't believe he'd lost the election. He did everything he could to make the transition difficult."

"Do you think he was bitter enough to harm your husband?"

Grazia paused so long I thought she'd spaced out. "No. His pride was hurt. Fabio enjoyed having a reason to be angry, nothing more."

"What about the other opponent from the last election? What was his name?"

"Patrizio Farmacio. No. He was relieved rather than disappointed. He didn't want the job, but friends had pressured him into running. He probably didn't even vote for himself."

"We're not getting anywhere," Cenzo said. "I need more to go on. Ivano wasn't a random victim. He was a public figure."

Grazia sighed. "Politics is the area of Ivano's life I knew the least about, but he kept important papers at home rather than at the office. You might try looking through them."

"If the Torino Investigative Unit finds that you are unsupervised, I'll be out of a job."

I stood. "The TIU won't care if I'm here or not."

"So?" Cenzo asked.

"I don't exactly have a full schedule today."

Cenzo brightened. "Of course. Do go look around."

"I'll start with the desk." Usually it was stacked with folders.

Grazia frowned, probably because she didn't like the idea of anyone snooping around her house, but she couldn't say anything. Whether she admitted it or not, she knew I was trying to help. Granted, I had an ulterior motive. If I could uncover bona fide enemies, I would stop having the nagging sensation that somehow I was at fault.

The house was so dark and sad that I went around opening the shutters to let in natural light and fresh air. Standing before the living room window, I saw that the grass was too high and that weeds threatened to overtake the flower beds. The roses were doomed because Grazia would be no help in the garden. Ivano had taken pride in the lush greenery of his manicured yard and spent countless hours working on it, but Grazia never noticed.

For a crazy half-moment I thought about offering to mow the yard. After all, my cousin had lots of things to think about. Then again, it was her yard, she wouldn't be appreciative, and I'd never used a power mower. If I successfully managed the task a first time, Grazia would assume I would be willing to do it a second and third and so on. I'd be better off waiting to perform favors she explicitly asked for. I was sure there would be plenty.

Next door, the flowers in Antonella's yard grew haphazardly, and the grass was nearly a foot high. Why didn't she ask Magru to do some yardwork? If the blades got much longer, they'd have to be cut with a machete rather than a lawn mower. Maybe Magru refused to work on anything as clean as vegetation; he preferred car grease.

The grass itself served as a cruel reminder of time marching by. Since I couldn't push back the clock, I sifted through my memory trying to unlock what had gone wrong. If Ivano had violent enemies, wouldn't he have recognized signs of danger? Grazia was intuitive about people. Wouldn't she have sensed such enemies herself?

Resigned, I dragged myself into Ivano's office. Flanked by wooden bookcases, a large desk and wooden chair faced the door while a metal filing cabinet took up the corner. Two chairs, almost touching, held court by the window. Renoir prints of smiley, pudgy women in rich dresses supervised us from their featured spot on the wall. Grazia had often told me how much she disliked the prints; Ivano had vetoed their removal.

I sat at the desk, feeling awkward as I invaded a dead man's space. Ivano had practiced real estate law and spent most mornings working from home. He had an office in the municipal building to attend to the business of Monteleone, but he kept truly sensitive materials at home to prevent the janitor from helping himself to information. Mornings at home also gave him more time with his wife. They might have a long lunch before he went into town. Grazia had boasted that more than once, he hadn't made it to work at all.

Nor had he wasted time organizing. An unread newspaper lay on the floor while a jacket haphazardly covered a chair. The wastebasket brimmed with crumpled papers. The desk was decorated with notes on scrap paper held down by Venetian paperweights. The stack of documents was unremarkable: car registration, utility bills, memos from town hall meetings, a proposal for a children's playground, a complaint about a broken streetlight.

Not a single folder graced the desk. The top drawer held the regular jumble of desk materials. The drawers on the right-hand side held lists of household finances, paper-clipped stacks of paid bills, and tax files. The drawers on the left side contained election materials such as brochures and sample artwork. A notebook listed the election expenses in neat blue script.

Ivano had no reason to have deadly enemies. If he were murdered randomly, it was a matter of timing. If I'd arrive earlier, I might have been killed on my very own property.

Something banged against the living room window. The sound might have been a pebble, but why would it have made contact with the glass?

I rushed downstairs. I hurried straight into the living room before chiding myself that my actions were foolish. Or maybe they were arbitrary. Nothing seemed unusual or out of place. As far as I could tell, not even Aunt Maria had come around within the last day or so. I ran up to the picture window and looked out on the lawn, but nothing had changed.

I chalked the noise up to my excess nerves. With Ivano gone, the world was out of whack. Strange noises were to be expected. Maybe they were in my head. I couldn't even remember what I'd been thinking about. The best thing I could do was to cut my active imagination some slack. I hadn't slept soundly because I'd been considering all my connections to Ivano. No wonder I was on edge.

The obvious solution was to fill a small plate with the delicious butter cookies. I arranged several on a plate and carried them back upstairs. They were a tangible reward for tackling the filing cabinet.

Ivano's black metal rectangle broke the harmony of an otherwise peaceful room. Worse, each of its drawers was stuffed so tightly that I accidentally tore the first folder I pulled out. I was supposed to find something worthwhile in all this? Perhaps if I had a few spare years.

I stood back and bit into a cookie. I wasn't sure which kind of folder to look for. Then I heard a *thump* from downstairs as if someone had knocked against the fridge.

Porca miseria!

I froze with sugary dough in my mouth. I didn't imagine noise; someone else was in the house. I felt for the house key, which was in my pocket. I couldn't remember whether or not I'd locked the door. Normally I wouldn't have. An intruder could have waltzed right in.

I went to the hallway and listened. The locals had learned that Ivano was dead, so if they knew Grazia was at the police station, they would have assumed the house was empty. I tried to remember if there was anything valuable on the first floor other than the new TV, which would be hard to detach from the wall and awkward to carry down the block. The robbery would be child's play: crystal, glassware, kitchen appliances.

I remained motionless, torn between impulses to hide in a closet or face a criminal. My heart thumped louder than a timer. Someone was still in the kitchen. I heard the gradual creaks as he—I assumed—opened and closed cabinets. Two glasses clinked together.

Anyone searching for valuables would soon tackle the second floor. I decided action trumped inaction. I tiptoed back to Ivano's office and grabbed three heavy law books from the middle bookshelf. I held them over the staircase and dropped them like a bomb to the floor below.

The result simulated an earthquake. I heard footsteps milliseconds before I heard a door slam. By the time I made it downstairs, no one was in sight. Without thinking, I ran outside. I circled the entire house, but I was too late. I went back to the kitchen where a single cabinet hung open. I put the first rows of glasses in a plastic bag and headed back to the police station.

In the sleepy burgs of the area, robberies happened at night when people were out at lengthy dinner parties. Whoever entered the house had done so quickly, expertly, and brazenly. That meant one thing. The intruder was someone who knew the property inside out. A relative. A neighbor. A carpenter. A friend.

I rushed to Cenzo's office and entered, breathless. Instead of fending off reporters or investigating, Cenzo was enjoying a peaceful and abundant lunch with Grazia and her mother in the detention room. Miffed that I'd been doing more work than they, I noted they were roughing it by eating without the usual obligatory tablecloth.

"Are you a free woman," I asked, "or does Cenzo always dine with his prisoners?"

"Both things at once," my cousin grinned. "We were preparing for lunch when they called from Torino."

"Sit," said Aunt Maria. "Have some prosciutto." She thrust me a plate. I recognized the flowered print from the dishware in her kitchen. She passed me the cold cuts before offering an additional selection of olives and cheese. A wine bottle reigned over the table, and three used, empty glasses indicated that I'd missed the first round. Only in Piemonte.

I reached past Cenzo for the bottle of *frizzante*. "Let me guess. Grazia's fingerprints were not on the bottle."

He tried to look contrite, but his mouth was too full.

"The most they found were smudges," Grazia said cheerfully. "Yet the lab team is convinced the contents are deadly. The assistants are running extra tests, but obviously I've been framed by someone who had access to the house."

"The door was unlocked," I said slowly.

"Exactly. So it could have been anyone. Anyone at all." She smiled as if a murderer had played into her hands.

Aunt Maria cut herself a thick piece of pecorino. "I always tell her to lock the door. Does she listen? No."

"Everyone had access to my house," Grazia said. "How simple is that? Yet how can Cenzo hope to interview everyone?"

She seemed a little too happy. And it wasn't really her house. She'd moved in after the wedding, but Ivano had bought it some years before.

Cenzo shook his head. "I'm sure you can help me narrow down the list. But if someone poisoned Ivano, the act wasn't random. It was a personal vendetta."

"That's what I told you yesterday," I said.

Cenzo swallowed two olives at once. "I remember."

Aunt Maria cut a piece of bread and handed it to me. "It's crazy. Everybody loved Ivano."

Not everybody, I thought, remembering Cenzo's words.

"Did you bring the folders?" Grazia asked as casually as if we were discussing taxes.

I chewed my bread a long time. I wasn't sure whether or not to be honest. "I didn't find any."

"They were right on top of the desk," Grazia said.

"No."

Aunt Maria indicated the food items. "Renato's coming for me because I must visit your Aunt Luisa before the clinic closes. Grazia, can I leave you here with this mess?"

"Go ahead, Mom. Sofi can take me home. I know my aunt is dying to have some company."

"Luisa is ninety-eight," said my aunt. "She's merely dying. Yet she clings on. Maybe I will, too." Her cell phone rang, and after a stream of *"Sì, sì, sì,"* she snapped it closed. "Renato's outside." She hugged her daughter. "I'll visit you afterwards."

"Thanks for lunch," said Cenzo.

"Stop wasting your time flattering me and find that killer!"

"My mother," Grazia laughed as the woman left the room. "She can go from one situation to another without blinking: daughter detained, sister-in-law in hospital. By evening who knows what crisis we'll have!"

"We won't have to wait that long," I said quietly. "While I was at your house, I had a visitor."

Cenzo chided me for potentially putting myself at risk. Then he asked for every last detail. He didn't say so, but I guessed that we were thinking along the same lines: whoever had planted the poison had come back.

I would have to learn to lock doors.

Chapter Ten

An hour later, I listened to Grazia while swiveling around on a kitchen barstool. For someone who had been detained the night before, she seemed too cheerful.

"Brace yourself. This came on hour ago." She pushed "play" on the message machine.

"You can't be expected to know this," said a crinkly female voice, "but the family cemetery is in Fiume. The caretaker's name is Sigilla."

With a flourish, Grazia erased the message. "Know who that was?"

"A busybody."

"That was Ivano's Aunt Elena. As if I needed her help! I've already made arrangements. Ivano wanted to be cremated." She reached into the cabinet for cups.

"I thought everyone around here was Catholic." I was too, in the Christmas-Easter sort of way.

"His relatives are. I hope to offend each one. They might have offered condolences."

"Maybe they don't know he's gone."

She prepared the two-cup Bialetti, screwing the metal components together with quick jerks. "They know. They dropped their dishtowels in their sinks so they could hurry and spread the news. Buzzards. They want Ivano buried quickly so they can start fighting over the will. Since we hadn't been married long, they'll argue that I don't count."

I swiveled in a full circle, barely catching myself instead of flying to the floor. "Are they crazy or optimistic?"

She turned on the burner and adjusted the heat. "Greedy. They didn't pay attention to Ivano when he was alive, so I'm immune to their opinions."

"Why would Elena care where Ivano is buried?"

She added sugar to our demitasse cups. "She enjoys being difficult. It's so amusing to give me a hard time."

I knew a lot of people like that. They existed in a lot more places than Monteleone. "I suppose she was a real joy at the wedding."

"Boh! She wore a floral dress so bright I needed sunglasses."

The doorbell sounded three times in a row.

"Wow, Cenzo already." I started for the living room. "That was fast."

"Wait!" Grazia whispered as she turned off the burner. She pointed to the staircase and hurried up the stairs. I followed behind her to the master bedroom where we peered out the window.

On the front doorstep, a wizened lady leaned over a cane. A young girl steadied her.

"Elena and one of the nieces," Grazia whispered. "*Cazzo!* I can't deal with them today. I refuse!"

My cousin had referred vulgarly to an aspect of male anatomy.

"Don't open," I said. "Pretend you're not here."

"Elena might have heard voices."

"She's so old that she's probably deaf."

While Elena rang the bell a few more times, I pulled my cousin to the floor. "Don't let her see us."

"Good thinking," Grazia whispered. "Do you often practice hiding from people?"

"Only from ex-boyfriends. Hiding from nosy old ladies is much more fun." I was kidding, but I was enjoying myself.

The woman rang the bell again and again as if the noise might raise Ivano from the dead.

"How is she related, exactly?" I whispered.

"The old bag is Ivano's mother's brother's wife. She's the only living relative of that generation." Grazia peered out the window again. "She's thinking about leaving, but believe me, she'll be back."

I hazarded a quick look myself. Cenzo pulled up in front of the house as Elena hobbled away from it. Cenzo asked cordially if anyone were home.

"Why would I be outside if someone were home, young man?"

"That's strange. Grazia was supposed to meet me here."

"A whore is a whore. She's probably out searching for a new man by now, someone she can spend Ivano's money with!"

I was so surprised at the colorful vocabulary that I grinned.

My cousin did not. *"Stronza!"* Grazia stood up straight as she called the woman an' "idiot." "How dare she!"

I latched onto my cousin's arm and pulled her back down to the floor. "Leave it."

"How can I leave a thing like that? That's not how it was at all! And quite frankly, before our marriage, Ivano got around much more than I did!"

Grazia started to get up again, but I stopped her. "Never mind," I said.

My cousin sat against the wall and pouted. "I knew there was a good reason I didn't like Elena. From the first time Ivano took me to meet her, I put up my guard."

We heard Cenzo say goodbye and get back in his car.

Grazia shook her fists. "Great! Now Cenzo will think I'm running away."

I wrestled Cenzo's bent business card from my pocket. Then I slipped into the study and dialed his number. He answered on the first ring

"What do you want?" he barked.

"If you'd rather, I'll call back when you're in a better mood, but you've already had too much coffee."

"Sorry. Grazia was supposed to be waiting for me at her house."

"Relax. That's where we are. We were avoiding that senior menace you encountered. Drive around the block, and as long as you don't act like a cranky old lady, we'll let you in."

♠ ♣ ♠

Minutes later, I admitted Cenzo. He marched to the center of the room and plunked three plastic bags on the kitchen counter. "Where's your cousin?"

"Upstairs calming down. She wanted to kill Aunt Elena, but I talked her out of it."

"That woman does have a mouth, but if you worry about what everyone says, you won't have any free time."

"She called Grazia a whore!"

"Elena didn't think your cousin was listening. Don't take her too seriously." Cenzo opened the first bag and took out an electronic device.

"Are you preparing to guard Fort Knox?" I asked.

"What's that?"

"A place in Kentucky where they stash Federal gold. Surely you're not that worried?"

He took more devices from the sack. "I'm not sure which one will work. The equipment is pretty old."

"We could have given you money for a new alarm."

"No. This is compliments of the local government. Given the circumstances, they should be able to do that much." He picked up a device and started tinkering with it. "Did Grazia find any important documents?"

"She hasn't looked."

"She should. We have to settle this case before something else happens."

"Like what?"

"Like a scandal."

"Ivano's death isn't scandal enough?"

"Sofi, you've been here long enough to realize that gossiping is a favorite sport. Usually the people mean well. Not always."

"But they do interfere."

"That's what happens here. People get wrapped up in one another's lives without trying to. I've watched it happen over and over."

"I thought I'd like living in a small community. Now I'm not sure." I'd grown up in West Roxbury and moved the short distance to Chestnut Hill, but I rarely encountered people I knew.

He took wiring out of the next bag. "You have to balance the pros with the cons. Believe me. You never get to a point where it's all pros. I keep trying, though."

I helped him unroll the wire. "I feel bad for Grazia. Not only has she lost Ivano, but her sex life is the biggest topic in town."

"For now it will stay that way. But watch and see. Things will calm down as soon as the Monteleonesi have something new to gossip about."

"Wait until they start arguing over the will," Grazia snapped as she entered the room.

"That woman is an old widow," said Cenzo. "She craves entertainment."

Grazia banged her fist into her hand. "Ivano could barely put up with her for five minutes."

"You only have to be civil a while longer. Then you can ignore her. But speaking of Ivano, what about those folders?"

"No one was mad at Ivano over business or anything else. His murder was accidental."

Cenzo slapped his hands on the table. "You're saying he was poisoned for no reason? In Milano? Perhaps. There are a lot of deviants. In Torino? Farfetched but still possible. In a balmetto outside Monteleone? That's crazy!" He waved both arms as a frantic traffic cop. "Sift through Ivano's papers and give me something to work with."

Grazia shook a finger at Cenzo. "You think Ivano was a crook!"

"I didn't say that."

"You implied it."

Cenzo faced Grazia straight on. "I need facts. I do not have a hidden agenda."

"You think Ivano did something wrong and then wound up paying for it!"

Cenzo connected a wire to a small timepiece. "Grazia, calm down."

"I am calm!"

She marched around the room before slamming her hands on the kitchen sink. She stared out the window so we couldn't see her tear up. I didn't blame her. I might have done the same. One minute her life was picture perfect and neatly figured out: beautiful house, comfortable existence, social status, doting partner. Now the only thing that hadn't changed was her kitchen. To be at peace, we would have to dig into Ivano's past. I worried it might not be a pleasant process, but when Cenzo announced he was going to city hall, I offered to go along. Neither of us knew what to look for, but I had a better chance of knowing when I saw it.

I couldn't bring Ivano back. Finding his murderer wouldn't be much help either, but I at least had to try.

♠ ♥ ♠

When Cenzo and I strode in the front door, the secretary looked up from her monitor as if we were interrupting her afternoon soap opera. Maybe we were.

"Pia, we need to get into Ivano's office." He held out his hands for the key.

"I can't let you in without permission." As she waved her head, curled ringlets bobbed in her face. She'd missed a strand, which now hung limp against her left cheek.

Cenzo rapped on the desk. "Whose permission would you like to ask? Ivano's? Too late for that. The TIU's? Be my guest. I can give you the number." Cenzo took out his phone and started scrolling. "Where's Daniella? Didn't anybody tell her she's the acting mayor now?"

Pia pursed rust-colored lips. "Daniella couldn't come in today because she couldn't find a babysitter, and I don't want to get in trouble. We're all upset. People don't get murdered in Monteleone."

Cenzo nodded. "Not until now."

She reached into her desk and pulled out a set of keys labeled with a white tag.

"Thank you, Pia," Cenzo said as he snatched up the keys. "Remember that you're helping the mayor."

She pursed her lips before speaking. "There's nothing we can do to help him now."

I knew how she felt. The loss was personal.

Cenzo and I scooted down the hall. A few other office workers emerged when they heard footsteps, waving sheepishly at Cenzo after they recognized him.

"Was Ivano a good mayor?" I asked as we stopped in front of his office.

"He was competent and straightforward." Cenzo tried the first key, which didn't work. "He told people what he thought, and he was charismatic enough that if they didn't agree with him, he convinced them to change their minds. Usually."

The second key opened the door. I followed Cenzo into a dark room. As I flicked on the light, the stale air made me cough. I rolled open the shutters, and natural light cascaded over a large metal desk and a wall of filing cabinets. Six chairs surrounded a round conference table. Over the last weeks, I'd often stopped by to say hello. Even when he was surrounded with paperwork, Ivano had always taken the time to listen to my latest balmetto snafus.

"Do you suspect that someone broke into his office?" I asked.

Cenzo rubbed his neck. "This building is too close to the center of town. The entrances are so exposed that a criminal would be running a risk even at two a.m. Tell me again why Ivano went to your balmetto that afternoon."

"He was bringing stuff for the party. Cenzo?"

"What?"

I didn't care to share my deepest thoughts, but keeping them inside wasn't pretty either. "Do you think Ivano's death had to do with me? I haven't been in town long enough to make enemies that I know of."

Cenzo sat on the desk. "The Piemontesi love it when Americans return to their roots. You speak reasonable Italian and even understand some dialect. No, I don't think you could have riled anyone enough to cause trouble."

"Every villager is eying my balmetto."

"Yes, but you haven't promised it to anyone, have you?"

"No. I've never even hinted that I might sell it."

"Therefore you couldn't have made any enemies." He winked. "I suppose it's just as well that you haven't snagged any of the local hotties."

I laughed inadvertently. Despite Ivano's best efforts, that plan hadn't worked out in the least. "I haven't been tempted."

Cenzo smirked and then tried to hide the reaction by turning sideways. "The local women don't know you think this. They'd be angry if you spirited away one of their possibilities."

"I'll keep that in mind."

Cenzo smiled broadly, but I pretended not to notice. He had to know he was attractive, and technically he was still married. I could imagine gently running my hand down his shirt to explore the chest below. *What was I thinking?* I wasn't sure I could trust him. And he lived a long way from Boston.

I rapped on the nearest filing cabinet. "What are we looking for?"

"I don't know. Whenever Ivano wanted to do something to improve Monteleone, he magically found funding for it."

"Maybe the funding came from his own pocket." The comment seemed silly even as I said it.

"That's one explanation."

"What are we looking for, then?"

"I'm hoping we'll know when we see it."

I dove in. The first files were all about tax laws. Then came strategies on crop rotation. Next, research on grapevines. Not useful.

The next drawer wasn't any better. Proposals. Complaints. Unfinished business from the previous mayor. Nothing that stood out, nothing that represented substantial sums of money.

Why be mayor at all if the job were tedious? Because of all the fun social functions. The dinners. The balmetto parties. Ivano had known nearly everyone in Monteleone. Walking through town with him was like being in a pinball machine. We never managed a straight line. Instead we crisscrossed the street so he could greet people. And he remembered details. How was the sick dog that had spent the night at the vet's? When was the nephew coming from the States? His list of information about the villagers could have filled a book.

If anything, that was the one we needed to find.

"Have you ever heard the phrase 'looking for a needle in a haystack'?" I asked after I gave up hiding yawns.

Cenzo continued with his own row of files. "I know something's here. I can feel it."

"Have you found a single thing?"

"There are a suspicious number of correspondences with Bernardo Baruzzo."

"Regarding?"

"Inquiries about plans for another plant."

"Baruzzo wanted to build, but Ivano wouldn't give the permit. Sounds routine."

"Maybe. The problem is that we need to get ahead of the TIU. They should be here by tomorrow, at least. After that the investigation will be out of my hands."

"Yesterday you said they'd be here today. Maybe the Torino squad isn't so interested in local politics after all."

"It's a power play. Dangle me along, let me do the detail work, and then steal the investigation. It wouldn't be the first time or the second either."

"If they irritate you so much, maybe you should join them."

"There's bad blood between us."

"Professional rivalry?"

"You might say." He tapped the file drawer. "Choose a haystack and dig in as deeply as you can. That's the best we can hope for."

I didn't last very long, probably because I didn't believe in the cause. After I studied the diplomas and photographs that adorned the walls, I turned to Ivano's box of music tapes, which was on the floor near the cabinets.

I'd often poked through the box. At Ivano's invitation, every time I dropped by, I borrowed different music. Thanks to his extensive collection, I'd sampled the most famous groups of the last thirty years.

When I picked up the box, the bottom fell out. Tapes cascaded to the floor in such a noisy chorus I was surprised Pia hadn't come running. Cenzo tried not to laugh as I bent to pick them up. A few were in pristine cases, but most were already scuffed or cracked. "Drinking Songs for Lake Como" read one cover. "Sanremo 1975" read another. Then I found a tape that might have been home recorded. The cover had no markings at all, but the strip of adhesive was labeled I.V.

Ivano Visconti.

"Cenzo."

"If you don't stop destroying Ivano's personal effects, his secretary will have us arrested."

"Cenzo."

"She won't hesitate. She'll panic and call Torino and then we'll spend the rest of the night explaining ourselves after we're beaten a few times with tree branches."

"Cenzo!"

He crossed the room to peer over my shoulder. "What's that?"

I held up the homemade tape. "I may have found a needle."

Chapter Eleven

I unlocked the backdoor and ushered Cenzo into the kitchen.

"You have the house to yourself?"

I nodded. The cozy area had light blue walls and white, handmade curtains with frilly edges. A large window over the sink gave me a perfect view of the neighbors' fence. During the day, light streamed into the room.

"Aunt Angela and Uncle Felice spend the summer down south. They were delighted to have a house sitter."

They might have changed their minds had they seen their kitchen. My sweaters were piled on the table. Empty grocery sacks vied for counter space among the army of soda cans awaiting a trip to the recycling center. The organic garbage bin smelled of rotten pears.

I made no apologies. I hadn't expected company.

By the time I retrieved the ancient tape recorder from the living room, Cenzo was pawing around in the cupboards. "Have any decaf?"

"You might as well drink water."

"Never mind. How about a coffee?"

"Fridge. Top shelf." I cleared room on the table and plugged in the Sony. "What's your hang-up with coffee?"

He spooned coffee into the Bialetti. "What are you talking about?"

"You've had half a dozen cups today that I know of. No wonder you're jumpy."

He sat across from me. "My hang-up is smoking. Every time I crave a cigarette, I have a coffee instead. To tell you the truth, I'm not sure if I'm helping myself or not."

"Maybe you should switch to water. Or tea."

"I tried that. Believe me, it's not as satisfying." He slipped the tape in the slot and pressed "play."

We waited tersely for several seconds. The tape gyrated, but nothing had been recorded on it. Cenzo fast-forwarded and checked again. Nothing. Then he tried another three times.

"Try the other side," I suggested.

After he rewound the tape, we waited, breathless. Nothing.

I played with the volume to no effect. "Maybe Ivano thought he'd recorded something but hadn't. I've done that before."

"Could be. This was the only non-commercial tape in the box, am I right?"

I hadn't found a needle after all, and I was terribly disappointed about it. "Looks like we're back to square one."

"We don't even have a game board." The coffeemaker started hissing, and before I could get up, Cenzo was at the sink helping himself to a demitasse. "Want some?"

"Why not? There should be another cup up there somewhere."

Cenzo opened the cupboards two at a time without waiting for instructions.

"Ah." From the back of the shelf, he extracted a second cup and saucer. "Sugar?"

He brought the jar to the table while I fetched a spoon. Italian-style, he polished off his coffee in one gulp. "Sofi, tell me more about your experiences with Ivano."

I wanted to stick to unimportant questions about coffee.

"I told you everything already," I said softly.

"Are you sure?"

I took a small sip. My eyes felt moist as I imagined Ivano sitting right where Cenzo was. He might drop by for five minutes in the morning with extra bread or an evening's invitation. He'd come over immediately when I'd jammed the garbage disposal. He was always on my side.

Cenzo slid into the bench across from me. "What was going on between you two?"

"What? Between me and Ivano? Nothing."

"You seem awfully upset."

Ivano had been my friend even more than my relative. Of course I was upset. "It's sounds like you're on a fishing expedition."

He kept quiet for a moment. "You know that I have to investigate."

I pounded the table. "He was my friend!"

My saucer slid toward the edge of the table. Cenzo noticed at the same time I did, and our hands met as we tried to prevent broken porcelain.

"Sorry," I mumbled.

"It's all right." He took the lucky cup and saucer over to the sink, well out of my reach.

"I'm just upset."

"I know."

"He died in my balmetto."

"I remember."

"Yet everyone wants to buy the place anyway."

"Drinkers are not superstitious."

Cenzo sat again, and this time I let my eyes slowly meet his. "I've never been through anything like this," I said. "Not since my grandmother died. And she was old. And not murdered."

"We can't be sure about Ivano yet, but if Grazia thought Ivano was fooling around, she would have reason to kill him."

"She was out of town, remember?"

"Or have him killed."

"You have it so wrong you'll never find who did it."

Cenzo tapped the table. "Try to remember your last conversation with Ivano."

I wanted to tell Cenzo to go away, but it was easier to play along. "On our way back from bocce ball, we discussed which cheap wine glasses I should buy at Carrefour."

"Okay, give me the second-to-last conversation."

That wasn't any use either. Ivano had taken Grazia and me to a cookout at his friends' house in Quassolo where we'd had a typical killer dinner followed by rounds of toasts. On the way back to Monteleone, Ivano and I had been so giddy that we started singing. Grazia asked us to stop, but we didn't listen.

Ivano's fun-loving nature is what I had appreciated the most. His profession hardly mattered because he would have been the same guy whether he'd been a businessman or a farmer or an artist. He liked being with people and interacting with them. He helped people when it was in his power to do so. He made sure that I felt comfortable in Monteleone and introduced me to as many of his single friends as possible. He cheerfully listened to my endless complaints about balmetto restorations and facilitated the process by signing permission slips or making phone calls on my behalf. Without him, Monteleone wouldn't be as wonderful for me or anyone else.

"You ought to know more about Ivano's enemies than I do," I said.

Cenzo took a deep breath. "Maybe we should start with who gained and who lost when Ivano was elected mayor. He no doubt found jobs for some friends. Found a way to profit as a middleman."

"You're accusing Ivano of using his position to line his own pockets."

"I wouldn't say 'line.' Beef up, maybe. It's almost expected."

"Seven, one, six, five, six" boomed Ivano's voice. Without thinking about it, we'd left the machine rolling.

Startled, I spilled the rest of my coffee, which oozed over the table.

"Two, two, two, eight, four, cypress," continued Ivano.

Back to silence.

For several seconds we stared at one another. The voice of a ghost had even unnerved Cenzo.

"One, eight, five, four, three," the voice continued. "Six, eight, zero, one, nine, cypress. Eight, seven, eight, two, four. Nine, seven, two, three, zero, cypress."

Cenzo and I stared at one another as if waiting for a tornado to hit, but that was the end of it.

"An ingenious way to hide information," Cenzo finally said. "If you hadn't offered me a coffee, we'd have never noticed."

So I'd found a needle after all. Finally.

I threw down my pen on top of the piles of scratch paper. "I give up."

We'd arranged the numbers a dozen different ways without finding anything concrete. A safe combination? An address? A bank account? We'd played the entire tape again without hearing anything new.

"There have to be cypress trees around here somewhere," I said.

"Here and there. Of course, up in Biella we have a whole park full."

Cenzo stretched his neck, which made an alarming crackling sound. "Ivano could have been talking about the country."

"Cyprus? Near Turkey?"

"He might have had a business deal. It's not too far from here. Do you know if he ever visited the island?"

"I'll ask Grazia tomorrow."

He spun the cheese knife that lay mid-table. "Let's keep it to ourselves for now. She has enough on her mind."

Cenzo was lying to me. He didn't want me to say anything to Grazia because he didn't trust her. As much as that annoyed me, it also made me wonder why he trusted me. Or maybe he didn't.

I cut off a sliver of pecorino. "The numbers could be from a bank account on Cyprus."

"Maybe. Try getting onto Ivano's home computer tomorrow. Think you can find the password?"

"I used his computer lots of times because he has a good Internet connection. I know the password."

"Great. Try looking for electronic files with those numbers."

"You mean snoop through Ivano's computer."

Cenzo cut another slice of provolone. "Maybe we could call it browsing. It's in service of tracking down a killer. Can you manage it tomorrow?"

"Some friends are coming over to say the rosary. Since there's a bathroom upstairs next to the office, it would be easy for me to slip off. Anything else?"

Cenzo shrugged. "Keep Grazia talking. She's bound to know important information, but she might not recognize what it is. That's usually what happens."

"There were some topics she and Ivano had agreed not to discuss."

"Such as former partners?"

I nodded. "Grazia felt old history should be left well enough alone. I'm sure Ivano agreed."

"Right. Maybe she sensed the skeletons in the closet would have rattled too much dust. She's shrewd, your cousin."

Shrewd was a harsh word. IRS inspectors were shrewd. Professors who suspected students of cheating. Criminals.

And now, my cousin. I couldn't protest because part of me agreed. "Maybe she's practical."

Cenzo glanced around the kitchen. "Have anything else to drink?"

I pointed to the refrigerator. "Help yourself."

Cenzo retrieved the bottle of red wine I'd opened to kill insomnia the night before. Drinking the stuff was a sacrifice, but the trick usually worked.

"Can I pour you a little?" Cenzo asked.

I emptied my water glass. "A drop." I could tell another restless night was coming right up.

Cenzo's drop was closer to a slug. Gamely I took a sip, but I couldn't help grimacing as I swallowed.

Cenzo laughed broadly. "It's that bad?"

"I keep trying to like wine, but so far no luck." I tapped the bottle. "The quality probably doesn't help."

Cenzo shook his head. "It's a decent house red. Renato did a fine job."

"He and his friends make a new batch every year, but they never drink it all. That's why my balmetto is so full."

"With grapes you never know when you're going to have a bad season, so you make all you can."

"Isn't that expensive?"

"Not really. Wine made for personal consumption doesn't have to follow any regulations."

"Why bother to go to all that work when the SuperDì is full of the stuff?"

Cenzo laughed until the dimple in his cheek risked getting stuck in a permanent groove. "You pretend to be Piemontese, but you won't fool anyone."

"Are you telling me you make your own wine too?"

"I'm too busy. I used to make grappa, though."

"I thought that was illegal."

"When I was young, I didn't mind taking the risk. The townspeople see it as simple tax evasion rather than a crime."

"Why not tax wine production instead?"

"Wine is considered a necessity! Like food. Grappa is a luxury item. I know the system is arbitrary."

"Doesn't grappa come from grapes too?"

"It's more refined because it takes more steps. That's why it's so expensive."

On more than one occasion, Ivano had coerced me into drinking grappa. His excuse was that it aided digestion. I never considered it an improvement over wine, but at least no one ever poured me more than a few drops at a time.

I forced myself to brave another sip. "Here's the irony. I probably won't learn to like wine until I'm on my way back to the States."

"Already thinking of leaving?" He sounded concerned, which seemed like a compliment.

"Yes. No. I'm not sure. I have a ticket for the end of next week. I was going to apply to some jobs around Northern Italy, but then I got wrapped up in the renovations."

In the back of my mind, the idea of working in Italy seemed like a romantic way to step out of my comfort zone. In reality I wasn't sure I was ready for it. I was so comfortable in Boston that living anywhere else would be a challenge. At the moment I had plenty of challenges just thinking about Ivano, so the idea was less attractive than ever.

"Why not apply now?"

"I might." I'd put it on my To Do list a dozen times. "I was so caught up with the balmetto that it took over."

"Speaking of your balmetto—"

"Yes. I agree exactly."

"With what?"

I wasn't sure I wanted to admit that I was thinking along the same lines as Cenzo. What did it mean if we were sharing wavelengths? Would we be sharing something else as well? "We missed something. We need to go back and take another look."

"Yes. I'm glad you agree."

I wanted nothing less than to return to the horrible space where Ivano had died. But unless his murder were committed by a roving intruder who was now three thousand miles away, somebody needed to pay.

Chapter Twelve

By the time we reached the piazza, we had to squeeze into the last available spot. Since it was a typical summer evening with pleasant temperatures and clear skies, the balmetti hummed with activity. Every fourth or fifth party house boasted rambunctious gatherings. As we passed the balmetto for the carpenters' union, several partiers invited Cenzo for a toast. He waved and smiled as if we were out for an aimless evening stroll. I wished I could put on an act as easily as he could.

"Oh!" cried a female voice. "Where do you think you're going without saying hello?"

Carmela peered at us over her gate before swinging it open. She ushered us into her yard before we could protest. I wouldn't have anyway; I was glad to see her.

"Sofi! I thought you'd be home practicing the trumpet instead of out entertaining young men. Come in!"

I was delighted to see such a welcome familiar face, and Carmela's easy humor lifted my spirits. I felt at home without trying to, and I needed the gentle sensation of being among friends. Better yet, her balmetto was a perfect setting for hearing gossip. The property was typical: The cellar hugged the mountain, the upstairs room offered shelter from rain and cold, and on a lovely summer night such as this one, the guests crowded the courtyard. They huddled around a long table that stretched from one side of the property to the other.

Aside from Carmela and Roberto, I recognized the clarinet player, Marco, Roberto Two, and his wife Luisa. Another woman accompanied them, but I didn't recognize her.

Roberto handed us glasses. "Have a drink!"

The others scooted over so we could squeeze onto the bench right next to Roberto and Carmela. The table was crowded with salami, cheese, bread, breadsticks, cookies, salad, and fruit. Several empty wine bottles had been placed on the ground out of the way.

"White or red?" Roberto asked, holding up a fresh bottle of each.

"Red," said my companion.

"Have any *frizzante*?" I asked.

"Fizzy water?" cried Roberto. "Who needs that?" The partiers laughed merrily. I did too, until Roberto ignored my request by pouring me a full glass of red.

"Here's to our new trumpet player!" Roberto said while the others raised their glasses.

Cenzo drained half his glass in a gulp. "What? No audition?"

"She was on time for every entrance. Not like that one." Roberto rolled his eyes at Marco.

The trumpet player winked away embarrassment. The wine had washed away any seriousness several bottles earlier.

Cenzo reached over me to fork a slice of salami. "You're more a part of this town than I am." He ate the whole piece in one bite. "Delicious!" he said with his mouth full. "Try one."

While I munched on breadsticks and slices of cheese, I relaxed into the playful atmosphere. I listened haphazardly to the most burning questions: Would the grapes get enough rain? Would Juventus win against AC Milan? Since the deputy mayor had refused the job, who would become the new mayor?

Cenzo waited for a moment when all the others were engaged in conversation to whisper, "Once they'd spotted us, we couldn't avoid them."

"That's the story of my life in Italy. Always getting stuck at one party or another!" It was one of the things I liked the best.

"You don't mind being stuck here with me?" Cenzo asked. "I'll ruin your reputation."

I handed Cenzo a plate of roasted eggplant. "Is your luck with women really so bad?"

"It depends on what they've heard about my marriage."

"So far, all my friends have claimed it's her fault."

"In that case, you have the right friends!"

I winked back, but I didn't want to give him too much encouragement. Besides, I was digesting the ridiculous number of ties among the diners: Marco's son was married to Carmela's daughter, Roberto Two's daughter lived with the clarinet player, and Roberto rented half his garden to Luisa and her husband. Those were merely tangible surface connections, but they underscored a truism about the villagers. They had deep connections because they couldn't avoid each other. Nor could they avoid conflicts. They were like a large family living in a double wide trailer. Occasionally somebody got mad and kicked the window out.

Roberto Two cleared his throat twice before he addressed me. "Sofi, your balmetto renovations are wonderful. You must have spent a lot of money."

"My parents did. My investment was time."

"Are you planning on moving to Monteleone?" he asked gently.

Despite the polite façade, I knew where he was heading. "Let me guess. You're wondering if I might sell my balmetto?"

Sensing that he had been caught red-tongued, Roberto Two nodded nervously. "I've tried to buy one for years. A balmetto came up last season, but an anonymous buyer gave it to the carpenters' union."

"Boh," said Roberto. "You don't need a balmetto. You always drink here with us!"

"Someday my kids will want one. They're starting to bug me about it."

"They're only teenagers."

"That's my point. They're already teenagers!"

"You have plenty of time," said Roberto. He topped off his friend's glass before prying open another bottle and pouring again. Over my protests, he reached for my glass.

"Enough!" I cried when he'd added a drop.

"Nonsense! Do you have to work in the morning?"

"No."

"So drink up!"

I couldn't fight Roberto. He enjoyed hosting parties as much as he enjoyed conducting the band. When Cenzo's wine glass was nearly empty, though, I switched his for mine. Since he didn't seem to notice, I repeated the switch another three times. My main efforts were thwarted, however. I didn't learn a single thing about Ivano.

♠ ♥ ♠

After we said goodnights, Cenzo and I started up the path towards my balmetto. By now most of the parties had broken up, so we had the ziggety path to ourselves. The cobblestones were so uneven that I had to plan each step. How did all those drunken townspeople get around? Practice.

The night air was cool enough to suggest a sweater, but the wind tickled our shoulders without biting down. After an evening of struggling to follow simultaneous conversations in dialect, I appreciated the quiet. I also appreciated Cenzo. Not only was it pleasant to have an escort for a change, but his air of nonchalant confidence was a reminder that everything would be all right, eventually.

Cenzo missed a step and stumbled for two or three, narrowly catching his balance before tumbling to the ground.

"We can come back tomorrow," I said.

"I'm fine, I'm fine! We're almost there."

I doubted Cenzo was alert enough to notice anything important, but I was glad to spend time alone with him. His presence gave me a sense of security, no matter how false, and I was too wide awake to return to an empty house.

Before I could pull out the key to the gate, Cenzo stopped me. "Wait." He shook the metal, testing its strength. The eight-foot structure included a series of spikes topped by curlicues. Cenzo checked all the surrounding walls for loose stones.

"Don't trust my masonry?" I was flirting, but Cenzo was too concentrated to notice.

"People usually hide keys outside somewhere. Then they can stop by the balmetto at the last minute even if they weren't planning on it."

"In that case, why bother with a gate at all?"

"It's a small deterrent," he said. "Sometimes that's enough."

I found multiple dead bugs but no loose stones. Cenzo fared no better. He rattled the metal. "Let's pretend we forgot the key." Despite the wine, he easily scaled the gate.

"All right," he called from the other side. "That part's easy."

I unlocked the gate and walked into my courtyard. "I see your point, but there's still no way to get into the cellar without one of those old-fashioned keys."

Cenzo fingered the solid brass lock. "Maybe not. But what if the door were already open?"

"You think the killer walked in and surprised Ivano?"

"Boh."

The streetlight illuminated the empty courtyard, making the stone walls shine. Although the masons had done solid work, the new cement was so white it stood out.

Cenzo pointed around the yard. "This is a top-rate balmetto."

"That's what Renato says too."

"The stonework is harmonious, which isn't always the case."

I'd walked past the stone walls dozens of times without thinking about aesthetics. Instead I'd focused on the three hundred and thirty euros I'd paid to repair a small section.

"A person could spend every free evening here — relaxing, dining with friends, philosophizing," Cenzo continued. "That's the whole idea, of course. Leave behind your workaday world and come here to escape. Great plan in theory."

"Until you find a dead body."

He cocked his head to one side. "I realize that Ivano's death has colored your thinking. Give yourself some time. People have the same problem when their relatives pass at home. They keep thinking, I can't go in the room where granny died, and so on. Sooner or later they run out of rooms."

As if I were a spectator for my own video, I imagined finding Ivano all over again. Then I looked at Cenzo. "Death doesn't faze you."

"I'm desensitized. When I worked in Milano, we investigated one murder after the other." Cenzo indicated the cellar door. "Mind if we go inside?"

As we entered, cold air oozed out.

"Ah," Cenzo said. "The perfect temperature for wine."

I crisscrossed my arms across my chest. "Way too cold."

"Not if you're wine. Or dead. You said the door was ajar when you arrived. How wide?"

I held my fingers an inch apart. "I didn't notice until I reached for the lock."

Cenzo opened and closed the door several times. It was too heavy to be swayed by the wind.

"What are you calculating?"

"How hard it would be to transport a body from a car to this spot." He shined a flashlight on the ground around the entrance, but the dirt was too packed to hold a print. "Unless you had a wheel barrel, of course. Which nearly everyone does."

I shuddered. "You think Ivano was killed elsewhere and brought here like a sack of cement?"

"I think it's unlikely. I merely want to consider all the possibilities."

Cenzo entered the cellar, but I retreated to the picnic table, glad for my own privileged life. Boyfriends had come and gone, sometimes with harsh words or insults, but never in a coffin. I'd lost elderly relatives, but none whose death was an unnatural tragedy. I lived in a city ripe with crime, yet this was the only time I'd encountered violence that hit me on a gut level.

An owl hooted as Cenzo emerged again. "Any luck?" I asked.

"No. I'm sure I'm missing something."

I nodded. "You'll find it."

"Eventually." Even though all the picnic tables were at his disposal, Cenzo sat inches away from me. I wondered if he always overdid the aftershave or whether he'd done so in my honor. "So what are you thinking?"

I forced myself back on track. "I'm worried about Grazia. How can you bounce back from losing your husband to a killer?"

"She'll be okay. She's young enough to have another life. That will help. So will the money."

Even though I knew Cenzo was right, for the moment I couldn't imagine it. But at least Grazia wouldn't be poor. She wouldn't even have to go back to work if she chose not to.

Cenzo regarded me carefully. "Can I tell you something without your getting mad at me?"

I'd already heard that Grazia was a slut, a whore, and an opportunist. It couldn't get much worse. "Try me."

"Your cousin wasn't in love with her husband."

I was wrong. That was much, much worse. For a moment I listened to the owl that retreated into the black of the night. Then I thought about the beautiful wedding portrait above the couple's bed. "Proof?" I asked softly.

"When she was out with Ivano, she eyed other men the way a dog eyes a bone. I realize that's not specific."

I knew that look. I'd seen it often, but I told myself that my cousin was merely alert. Cenzo's explanation was more logical.

He looked down at his hands. "I'm not saying a partner has to be the center of your existence. It's probably better for you if she's not. But I always had the sense that for Grazia, her husband was arbitrary. That might or might not have been good for Ivano, but it will make getting over him a lot easier."

Surely Grazia had loved Ivano in her own way, but I was no longer sure what way that was. "You're saying she married for money."

"Not necessarily. Maybe what she wanted was companionship. Security."

I thought about Kristine and the shopping trips. Ivano's money would have helped with that. "You think my cousin had an agenda."

Cenzo suddenly snapped at a mosquito. He checked his hands: no blood. "Do you?"

I felt naïve. I'd never thought to question Grazia's relationship with Ivano. "I don't know."

"Do you think she has a lover up in Aosta?"

I bit a hangnail. She'd gone up to Aosta twice before, for the day, but she'd come back sad and distant. "No. What she loved was her kitchen. I know how bad that sounds."

"Who's to say?" he asked. "Relationships are hard to understand. Maybe impossible. You start out thinking they'll last forever. A decade or a year or a week later, you realize how fragile they are."

Suddenly the air was heavy. I'd wanted to ask about his marriage, but not a single time had been right. "Do you ever talk to your ex-wife?"

He paused. I wondered if he were gauging how much to say and how much to hold back or how much he didn't even tell himself. "I don't talk to her if I can avoid it. The kids tell me what I need to know."

"And what's that?"

"When she'll let me have them. It's been a constant battle."

I didn't have any close friends with kids, let alone friends in custody battles. But since we already had so much unpleasantness on the table, I risked my other question. "Have you been dating?"

"*Mio Dio,* that's the last thing I need."

"After years of marriage, I suppose it's hard to start over with someone new."

Cenzo blinked so many times I wondered if he had tears in his eyes. "It's far better to have a fresh start than to spend every day wishing you'd never met your spouse. What I mind is thinking that I never knew her."

"Did you try, really try, to listen?"

"I'm not sure."

The thought was as devastating as it was honest. It was also familiar. I'd lost at least one boyfriend because I'd been too wrapped up in my studies. Between teaching classes and finishing a dissertation, I hadn't often put Keith first. I'd intended to do so as soon as I graduated, but he'd left me long before that. I couldn't blame him.

I hadn't mourned the relationship either. Too many differences. He wasn't interested in travel. Didn't understand why I wasted time going to the French conversation group or had loud conversations with all my Italian relatives. I was sad that he broke up with me but hadn't tried to talk him out of it, and I hadn't missed our usual weekends together. They'd quickly filled with chores or job applications. He'd been extraneous.

Grazia might have seen Ivano the same way. He was useful to her. A willing escort. Someone to give into her whims if she wanted a new chair or a pretty shawl. She'd played the game so seamlessly I hadn't seen it.

Maybe I hadn't known either of them. On the surface, things were perfect. I never knew what went on late at night or early in the morning. I knew about Ivano's successes in the community but not his failures. He hadn't talked about them, and neither had Grazia. Why would they? But somewhere along the line, he'd failed. He'd angered someone who held an eternal grudge. Someone determined enough to take risks.

That was the person we had to find.

Chapter Thirteen

The first visitors for the saying of the rosary arrived twenty minutes early. When I yanked open the door, Aunt Elena stood before me with the girl who had accompanied her the day before. Both wore heavy black clothing. Aunt Elena's smelled of stale closets.

"I suppose you are the maid. Romanian?"

I looked as Italian as Elena did, but what better way to infer that I was a poor foreigner? I hadn't even introduced myself, but I already wanted to kill her.

"I'm Sofi Francese, the American cousin."

She pushed me aside before I had the chance to get out of the way. The young girl was about twelve. She gave me a plaintive look that said she didn't have a choice. I was glad I wouldn't have to trade places with her.

Aunt Elena marched to the living room. Grazia and I had gathered all the chairs in the house and borrowed five folding chairs from Antonella next door, but Aunt Elena placed herself in the middle of the biggest couch.

"Where is the widow? Or she didn't have time to come?"

Upstairs I heard the hair dryer, so I knew I was stuck. "My cousin has been awfully upset. She's freshening up."

"She's fresh all right. Every day of her life."

"A soda?" I asked the girl.

"Carolina does not drink soda!" shouted Aunt Elena. "Vile stuff." She patted her stomach, which was flat. "Hurts you."

The girl frowned. I could tell we were both in for a dreadful evening.

"Sparkling water, cold," said Aunt Elena. "We will both have some."

I jumped, delighted to leave the room. No wonder Ivano hadn't introduced me to any of his relatives. I stalled so that I wouldn't have to return to the living room one second earlier than necessary. I couldn't remember the lineage—Ivano's mother's side? He'd come to Monteleone from Chivasso, on the outskirts of Torino, and now I understood why. If his other relatives were one bit similar, I would have escaped as soon as possible. If necessary, I would have changed my name.

The doorbell rescued me. I deposited the glasses of sparkling water with Ivano's relatives and nearly tripped myself running to the front door. Three elderly women wearing headpieces and veils were on the doorstep. They smelled of garlic, but I accepted their hugs graciously. Any barrier between me and Aunt Elena was welcome. The nuns immediately consoled the woman for her loss as they settled across the room in the remaining comfortable chairs.

As other visitors arrived, I stationed myself at the door and herded people inside. Grazia had expected a crowd, but instead we were overrun by a deluge. As soon as Renato and Laura appeared, I sent them off to bring more chairs. When Antonella came, I didn't have to ask; she immediately returned home to scrounge up a couple of stools.

Aunt Elena was the only party pooper in the room. Everyone else had come for a social event. I strained to hear gossip about Ivano, but instead it was all about the above average temperatures we were having, deathly hot, and the butcher's wife who had been sent to the hospital in Ivrea for an emergency hysterectomy. When Grazia finally joined us, hardly anyone noticed.

Conversations flew like flies around a watermelon. I was surprised the nuns began saying the rosary at all.

They'd only managed the first few lines of prayer when Grazia's friend Teresa made a grand entrance. She squeezed between me and Grazia on the love seat; I moved to the floor across from them so that I could continue breathing. The newcomer clung to Grazia's side. My cousin didn't pull away, but neither did she show emotion.

She was probably too drained. She'd spent the afternoon with the special lab unit from Torino that had been dispatched to Monteleone because a murdered mayor was an unacceptably high-profile case. The trio of investigators had interviewed Grazia and me, read Cenzo's notes and made copies, dusted the balmetto for fingerprints, and taken a dozen wine samples. An hour later they packed up and took off because they were needed back in Torino for an even higher-profile drug runner case. They told Cenzo to keep investigating and promised to hurry with the lab results.

Even though the Torino detectives were polite and professional, the experience was degrading. They went over the same ground Cenzo had but without understanding it. They collected data in an organized fashion, but they knew nothing of Monteleone and its people. When Grazia explained that Ivano had been a popular mayor, they were skeptical.

No wonder Grazia had an air of bewilderment. During the whole prayer session, Teresa protected her like support pantyhose and whispered in her ear more often than a sports announcer commenting on a soccer match. Gizelle, Grazia's other childhood friend, was more compassionate. She recited along with the nuns, often drawing a tissue to her eyes or leaning her shoulder into the man beside her who was quietly respectful.

Even though the sisters were mumbling, I could have caught onto the Italian version of the rosary and chimed in with the best of them. Instead I watched every participant in turn. Not a single one seemed suspicious. Ivano would be missed, but life would go on because it had to. Tomorrow evening the nuns would pray for someone else. The others would chat on the bocce ball courts.

After the prayers finally ended, I stood back so the guests could stampede their way to the kitchen. Many of the women had brought dishes: I counted five pasta casseroles, four salads, and several trays of salamis and cheeses. Others had brought cakes or plates of cookies. Thank goodness they'd brought donations; they'd also brought huge appetites.

They chatted noisily as they formed a line into the kitchen. I took a safe place on the carpeted stairs leading up to the second floor. It was dangerous to be around a buffet when this many people anticipated a feast; had I been trampled, no one would have noticed.

"May I join you?" Antonella asked. The graceful, forty-something sat beside me on the steps. She wore a modest black dress that nonetheless outlined robust curves in appropriate places. "I'm so sorry about Ivano."

"Me too."

"I came back from Cinque Terre as soon as I heard."

"I still can't believe it."

She patted my hand. "Ivano was one of the nicest men I've ever known. Not everybody understood his tactics, but he worked in the best interest of as many people as possible. Sometimes that made him seem two-faced, but he wasn't."

Finally I found someone as fond of Ivano as I was. "Did you know him well?"

"Years ago Ivano represented my husband in a dispute over land, and when Michele died, Ivano helped me with the legal proceedings. Ivano was very, very kind. He came to my rescue at a time when I was lost. I couldn't thank him enough for that. He even helped me purchase my house."

"As a neighbor, I guess you saw one another often."

"We couldn't avoid each other! I was always glad to see him. I was happy he married your cousin because I'd never seen him as excited as on the day of his wedding."

I nodded, thinking back to the scads of joyful wedding pictures. What would Grazia do with them now that each would be a painful reminder of a happy marriage cut short?

Antonella toyed with a ring on her wedding finger. "Most men are too scared to enjoy their own ceremonies, but Ivano wasn't worried at all. He was delighted to be marrying Grazia. She brought out the best in him."

"I still can't believe he's gone."

"I was married to my husband for seventeen years before he passed, and it took me several years to accept that he was dead. At least I'd lived a life with him by the time he died. Grazia is young, of course. She'll move on."

Herded by Teresa, Grazia passed by.

"Is she doing all right?" Antonella whispered. "Is she eating?"

Leave it to an Italian mother to worry about food. I wouldn't have thought about it. "She pretends to be holding up, but I think it's a façade."

"Do they have any idea what happened?"

"Not really."

"When I learned that Ivano was dead, I assumed he'd suffered a heart attack. But murder?"

"They're not sure yet."

"No. Someone targeted him, someone cruel or sick. There's no other explanation. Ivano was a brave man."

 She wiped away a tear. "I know we all have to go eventually, but this was not the way. Not for Ivano. But what can you do?" Her eyes drifted to the people passing by with heaping plates. "Shall we have a bite?"

Only in Italy. Coming from someone as gentle as Antonella, the segue wasn't awkward. I accompanied her to the kitchen table and tried to decide among pasta dishes. The baked lasagne looked as tasty as the stuffed mostaciolli or the spinach ravioli, but I only took small spoonfuls of each. I wasn't in the mood to enjoy anything.

"Do you know if Ivano ever went to Cyprus?" I asked.

Antonella reached for some salad. "What makes you ask?"

"Grazia and I ran across some postcards," I lied. "As far as Grazia knew, he'd never been there."

Antonella forked several spears of grilled broccoli. "Ivano traveled all over. Cyprus, Turkey, Malta, Greece. He loved going to new places." She pointed to a casserole that had nearly been decimated. "Do take some of the stuffed zucchini. I made them this afternoon."

Before I could ask any more questions, Antonella was spirited away by friends. Instead of joining other conversations, I slipped up to Ivano's office. I had the number sequences in my pocket, but I didn't find anything that corresponded to them on Ivano's computer. Finally I gave up and answered a few emails of my own to avoid the crowd downstairs. The big news from Florida? There wasn't any. My dad had sent three jokes. Wasn't I having a wonderful summer? I finally decided I might mention Ivano's passing, but I did so by stressing that he'd had heart problems. After all, he was a lot older than my cousin, I wrote in the final line. I was pretty sure my parents wouldn't read into it, and that's exactly what I wanted. Otherwise they would have called incessantly about a situation they couldn't change.

♠ ♦ ♠

Many dirty plates later, the guests finally trickled out. I saw the last ones to the door myself. Then I collapsed on the living room couch with Grazia, Aunt Maria, and Cenzo, who had arrived late but seemingly appointed himself one of the family. We embraced pauses in the conversation while finishing off various bottles of wine. In the spirit of tidying up, I had a few sips myself.

"It wasn't as bad as I expected," Grazia said. "At least Aunt Elena didn't spend the night talking my ear off."

"That's because Teresa barely let go of you," Aunt Maria said. "What did she want, anyway?"

"She was trying to help. Ever since her mother died, she thinks she knows about grief."

"That was two years ago."

"She's had that long to practice."

"I'm sorry, but I don't like her," said Aunt Maria. "Even when she was a little girl, she was irritating."

"She can be, but I let her talk." Grazia turned to Cenzo. "Speaking of talking, did you hear from TUI? They should have run some poison tests or whatever."

"It's TIU, Torino Investigative Unit. The test is called a tox screen."

"Well, what did it tell us?"

Cenzo pulled a note from his pocket. "They found zinc, bromethalin, cholecalciferol, and bromadiolone."

"Does that mean anything?" I asked.

"It depends on what you're looking for."

"I nearly flunked high school chemistry," I said. "Can you break it down for us?"

"Those are common ingredients for rat poison."

"What?" Grazia exclaimed. "Are you saying my husband was killed like a rat?"

Cenzo folded up the note and returned it to his pocket. "I wouldn't think of it that way."

"I'm not sure there's another way to think of it."

I wasn't either.

"Learn anything tonight?" Cenzo asked softly.

I shrugged. "Everybody I talked to was full of respect for Ivano and sorry he was gone."

"You didn't talk to any of his relatives," said Aunt Maria. "They were gleeful. They envied his successes, and that includes his marriage."

Grazia frowned. "They'll do everything they can to get their hands on his money."

"They can try," Cenzo said, "but Ivano knew the law. I'm sure he knew how to protect his wife."

His wife stared straight ahead. I couldn't tell whether she agreed or not. She was too wrapped up in memory—and perhaps regret—to conceive of a next step. I would have to find one for her.

My mother had left a message on the house phone. She thanked me for my email but wanted me to phone as soon as possible. Instead of calling, I kicked around the house wasting time. I reviewed the evening in my mind, but I couldn't think of anything useful. Nothing had triggered my suspicions or Cenzo's either.

When my mother called again, I gave in and picked up. I hoped for a mild conversation about the weather, but she grilled me about the news from Monteleone. Why hadn't Ivano taken more precautions? Had he overexerted himself to keep a young woman happy? I fudged my way through, hoping to remember what I said.

"I'm beat," I lied. "I better ring off. I have to attend the funeral tomorrow morning." I neglected to say that, actually, mass would be said at noon.

"Oh, wait! You had a piece of mail I wanted to tell you about."

I had to wait another couple of minutes while she rummaged through items she'd been saving for me.

"It was forwarded from the French Cultural Center. Should I open it?"

Yes! I'd been working for them part-time for the past three years, but they'd promised a full-time job as soon as I finished my degree.

"Oh, dear."

"What?"

"I can read it to you later."

"Mom!"

"Who needs bad news at this time of day?"

"Mom!"

She hung up. I called her back and she didn't answer. I called another three times before she picked up. "Go ahead, Mom. It's better if I know, and I promise not to shoot the messenger."

"Well, this is what it says: 'The job search has been cancelled due to funding. We're cutting classes for next year and won't be able to hire you back in the foreseeable future.' I'm sorry, honey."

The French Cultural Center! And they'd promised!

I hadn't relied on their coming through. I'd applied at Bunker Hill Community College as well as RoLa Languages. Unfortunately, I didn't have personal contacts anywhere. I could imagine each school's response. Budget cuts. Overhead. Fewer students. Who studied French these days when Spanish was more practical, and Mandarin was the new Spanish?

"I'll find something else."

"Rent in the Boston area is expensive, you know. You could move to Coral Gables."

Follow my parents to a retirement mecca? That was high on my list of ways to commit social suicide without even trying. "I'll think about it."

"Or Monteleone."

"Right."

"I'm serious."

"Me too." Given my Italian passport, I could be hired easily without expensive or time-consuming paperwork, but I'd already scoped out jobs in the immediate area. Even if I could find a position, I'd be making a lot less than I had back home. Salaries were higher in Torino, but the commute would take over an hour each way.

"Honey, maybe you could try to get a job teaching Italian instead of French."

Great idea. In the U.S., Italian was even less marketable than French. Besides which, I hadn't taken enough upper-level division classes to qualify. Being a native speaker didn't count. But employment was the least of my immediate problems, and I already knew how quickly I could sell the family balmetto if I really needed the cash. For the moment, none of that mattered. A killer was loose in the village, and I had to help Cenzo find him.

Chapter Fourteen

"Thus we know our Brother Ivano has gone to a better place. In heaven there is no crime. In heaven there is no hunger. In heaven—"

I closed my eyes to block out the rest of the sermon. The priest seemed so pleased to extol the virtues of death that he seemed to be batting for the other team. Maybe the awkwardness wasn't entirely his fault. Normally the priest would have said a few words at the house before leading the walk to the cemetery, but Cenzo hadn't been allowed to release the body because the TIU had ordered more tests. Not only was there no coffin and no urn, but with the exception of a decade-old photo, also no Ivano.

Afterwards all the family and most of the friends brought their best casseroles to Grazia's for yet another feast. While the starving guests rushed the loaded table, Renato and Grazia and I migrated to the living room couch. Grazia had circles under her eyes and had confessed to a sleepless night. She wore a black skirt that was at least one size too tight, and she kept tugging at her blouse so it wouldn't pull apart.

"I'll be so glad when this is over!" Grazia feigned a smile. "I'm going to kill the next person who asks about Ivano's mysterious death. The town is crawling with amateur journalists."

Renato slouched against a pillow. All morning he'd facilitated the proceedings, which meant explaining why we weren't going to the cemetery. On the surface he'd managed with friendly ease, but the effort drained him.

"You're good gossip," Renato said. "The mayor of Monteleone murdered? It'll be news for decades."

"There's still no proof he was murdered," Grazia snapped.

"There's no proof he had a heart attack either," Renato said. "At some point you have to face facts."

She glared at her cousin. "When there are facts, I'll face them. But do you know how many meddlers have called over the last couple of days? They pretend to offer condolences and then they want to know details."

"Things will calm down," I said. "A lot of people didn't know what happened."

"You'd have to live in a cave to avoid this story," said Grazia.

"Or be on vacation," said Renato. "National news hasn't covered Ivano yet."

"Let's pray things stay that way."

A man in a crumpled gray suit came over. He was about my age or perhaps a bit younger, but his long face didn't fit the rest of his body; it deserved a bigger frame. His skin was pale, meaning he hadn't spent a moment of the summer outdoors. He sat on the arm of the couch next to Grazia in such a familiar way that I was ready to jump up and defend her, but neither Grazia nor Renato seemed concerned.

"Cousin Gerardo, meet our cousin from Boston," Grazia said. "Gerardo Baruzzo, Sofi Francese."

The name rang a definite bell. "My cousin too?" I asked.

"Dad's side of the family. Dad's great-grandmother and Gerardo's father's grandmother were sisters. Or something like that. What does that make us, Gerardo, second cousins? Third?"

"Third cousins, twice removed, I think." He shook my hand. "Grazia told me you were coming for the summer, but I've been tied up with business travel. Have you been enjoying Monteleone?"

I'm not sure who gave him the sternest look—me, Renato, or Grazia.

Gerardo lowered his voice. "Up until this tragedy, of course."

If I said what I really felt, that Monteleone would never be the same without Ivano, I feared Cousin Gerardo might get the wrong idea. Instead I rewound my tape to a couple of days earlier. "I love it here. Monteleone is a wonderful town."

"I suppose you've never been before?"

"We visited a couple of times when I was growing up, but I haven't been here lately." A gap of some fifteen years stretched the definition of "lately," but sensing a mild reprimand, I withheld details.

"I'd like to visit the Boston area. It's interesting geographically." Gerardo proceeded to tell me what he knew about my city. Grazia tuned out immediately, but I listened politely. Usually the townspeople had so many misconceptions about the U.S. that I had to work to keep a straight face, but at least Gerardo's intel about Boston's origins was accurate.

I smiled weakly. "You're a walking geography book."

Gerardo shrugged. "I pick up a bit about this and that."

"I was thinking about taking a trip to Cyprus," I said. "Can you tell me anything about the place?"

Grazia sat up sharply but moderated her voice. "You never mentioned Cyprus to me."

"I haven't made firm plans," I said. "Maybe we could go together. It's supposed to be scenic."

I watched for more of an acknowledgment, but Grazia seemed to take the words at face value. Since I usually asked for advice, perhaps she was stunned that I mentioned travel plans she didn't know about. I didn't have more of a chance to gauge her reaction, however, because once Gerardo took the floor, he kept it. He editorialized for so long about the Greek-Turk conflict dividing the island that I eventually I tuned out myself.

"You could get a fair market price this year," Gerardo said.

I nodded without having any idea what the man was talking about.

"I'm not sure she wants to sell," Renato said. "Anyway, I asked first."

"Asked about what?"

"Your balmetto," Gerardo said. "You'll be selling it, won't you?"

I might as well have been wearing a neon sign that announced Balmetto for Sale. The sign was invisible to me, yet it blinked for every inhabitant of Monteleone. "I haven't decided what to do with the property," I said slowly. "It would be a family decision."

"You own it with your other American cousins?" Gerardo asked.

I nodded to avoid going through the whole story.

Gerardo pulled at his chin. "Obviously you don't need an entire wine cellar. I'll stop by and review the improvements you've made. When you're ready to sell, I can get you cash for it."

"I can too," Renato said. "Anyway, Gerardo, your dad has a swell balmetto. Why would you want another one?"

"Not for me, for a friend. Sofi, I can get you a fair price. My friend is desperate."

"Desperate?" Renato asked. This was the first time I'd heard him make a sarcastic comment.

"The usual thing. He wants to propose, but he needs a way to impress the in-laws. Can't you help a guy out?"

"I doubt it, but thanks for the tip," I said. "I'll keep you in the loop."

Renato pointed to his chest and mouthed *sell it to me.*

"More wine?" Grazia asked.

Gerardo and Renato rose simultaneously.

"That man is such a bore!" Grazia didn't bother to lower her voice.

I laughed. "He doesn't realize it."

"That's probably why his wife left him. She couldn't stand his constant flow of information."

"Surely there was something more than that."

"That would have been enough."

Cenzo motioned to me from across the room until I rose and joined him.

"I need Grazia to circulate," he whispered. He escorted me to the dining room, where we sat down with Carmela.

While she scrutinized my appearance, a single jewel from the cross on her silver necklace caught the light. "You look tired. How are you?"

"So-so. It's bad enough going to the funeral for a ninety-year-old. When it's someone who died before his time, it's awful."

"That's why I encouraged Roberto to stay at home," Carmela said. "After a gathering such as this, he can be depressed for days."

"Let me guess," Cenzo said. "He's at home working on a musical arrangement."

She nodded. "He's transcribing a movie tune he wants the band to play. The house could catch on fire and he wouldn't notice."

He nodded. "But you notice everything. Who are the three men seated by the living room window?"

It took her a minute to isolate the men from the others in the crowd. They looked to be in their thirties, which made them younger than most of the others, and they wore sport coats, which made them more formal that the rest of us. None seemed the least bit sad.

"They're developers," said Carmela. "They wanted to build a paper mill on that triangle of land by the riverbank. Ivano rejected their proposals."

"They're working with Baruzzo?" Cenzo asked.

"Hoping to. Up until now Ivano stood in their way, but they assume the next mayor will be a little more sympathetic."

"By 'sympathetic,' do you mean easier to bribe?" asked Cenzo.

"Of course," laughed Carmela. "That's exactly what I mean."

Cenzo asked her about other guests, but by then I was concentrating on the jovial trio.

"We need to talk to them," Cenzo said as soon as Carmela was whisked away by other friends.

"About what?"

"I don't know what we need to know. That's why I'm sending you."

I wasn't good at introducing myself. "Wouldn't it be rude to barge in?"

"Walk around with a wine bottle and offer refills. They'll think the conversation is accidental."

Easier said than done. The first bottle went so fast that I didn't get halfway around the room. With the second, I was more careful. I zigzagged from group to group until I reached the trio. As I approached, they were discussing government investments.

"More wine?"

The closest one stood. "Don't tell me the Italians are hiring Americans to do their menial jobs these days!" he joked.

"No," I said, "they're drafting family members. It's more economical."

"I'm Emilio," said the man.

"Daniele," said the next one in line.

"Rinaldo," said the third.

Emilio grinned. "And you would be?"

"Sofi Francese."

"That's right! I heard about you, though I don't remember who told me. Maybe Ivano's secretary."

"That woman keeps track of everything," I said.

"It's an act," Emilio said. "Pia forgets as much as she remembers, and her stories change every time she tells them. Still, she's friendly, so what can I say?"

"Be careful what you tell her," I laughed. "If you have any secrets, she'll weasel them out of you."

"Ivano used to complain about the same thing," Emilio said.

Daniele and Rinaldo spotted Teresa and went off to speak with her, leaving me with Emilio. He towered above me, but we sized each other up simultaneously.

"I feel bad about Ivano," Emilio said. "I can't believe someone murdered him."

"When you're the mayor, I guess you should expect trouble."

"Not here. In Monteleone, what's at stake?"

"There's the riverfront property, for example."

He drew back several inches. "You don't mince words."

"The river was something Ivano talked about," I improvised. "He felt protective of it."

"After months of work on our part, Ivano finally seemed open to a contract. Now we'll have to start the process from scratch."

"I suppose a paper mill would be a good industry for Monteleone."

He shrugged. "In theory you always work in the name of progress, but sometimes you go backwards. A new plant would bring business, but if a town grows too fast, it loses its center."

Ivano had told me nearly the same thing. He also said the last thing Monteleone needed was an ugly paper mill that greeted its visitors. But I wanted to see how much information I could draw out of Emilio. "I suppose there are always pros and cons, but I never understood why Ivano was so opposed to letting go of the land."

"I do. Haven't you ever been there?"

I shook my head.

"The sunset from the edge of the river is striking. You go down by the old bridge where you can hear the quick pull of the water and watch the sun disappear behind the mountains. Ivano was afraid we'd ruin the natural beauty of the spot, and he was right. We'd have to tear down the old bridge and block the view."

"It's the most beautiful spot in Monteleone," Gerardo said, barging in. "Why should we ruin it?"

"I'm sure you don't ask your dad that question!" I laughed.

Gerardo quickly surveyed the room, checking to see who was within earshot. "Not too often."

Emilio and Gerardo embarked on a long discussion about harnessing the river's power. I was about to slide away when Gerardo lightly put his hand on my arm.

"The spot is truly beautiful," Gerardo insisted. "I'm surprised you've never been there."

"Ivano explained how to get there, but I've been tied up in repairs."

"It's a sight you shouldn't miss, especially at this time of year. If you're not busy this evening, I'll take you."

Aunt Maria had hinted the family might have dinner together, but I'd already eaten enough for a week.

"Thanks, Gerardo. That sounds lovely."

He whipped out his cell phone so we could exchange numbers. I might have preferred solitude, but having an escort would be useful. I wouldn't be focused on the view, however. I'd be too busy pondering what the view told me about Ivano.

♠ ♥ ♠

Gerardo's white sedan rattled so much I worried it might fall apart and leave us in the street. The interior smelled musty, and I couldn't decide whether the lemony air freshener made things better or worse.

My companion concentrated on shifting gears as he headed west towards the river. He was fresh in summer shorts, a lightweight shirt, and a smile that suggested a relaxing day rather than mourning. "I didn't get much work done this afternoon. Funeral services make me pensive."

"Me too."

He slowed down for a stop sign and then rolled through it. "Services are helpful in the long run, but they make everyone feel bad."

"I've had plenty of practice at feeling bad lately."

"You're lucky you don't know everybody yet. I've lived here all my life, so I'm always going to somebody's parent's funeral. It's one long stream of social events after another."

"My cousins live up and down the East Coast. I try to make the weddings, but I can avoid everything else."

"I don't get a break unless I'm out of the country for business." As we passed an intersection, he pointed right. "My aunt lives down there." He pointed left. "My dad's mom lives over there." We turned onto the bridge that spanned the river. "If we kept going straight, we'd reach my cousins' place. I have to go to every event: baptisms, funerals, First Communions, weddings, even name-day parties."

"You have a lot of excuses to socialize."

"Always with the same boring people."

No wonder he'd snatched the chance to talk to me. At least I hadn't heard any of his stories and vice versa. In a burg as small as Monteleone, any newcomer meant fresh ears.

He pulled into the gas station at the edge of town. "This will just take a moment. Prices are supposed to go up, so I wanted to throw in an extra ten euros."

"I'll get it." As I exited the car, I pulled cash out of my pocket.

Gerardo shook his head and held up his wallet. "Plastic is always faster."

I stood by as he topped off the tank. "I hate to say it, but your car might need a tune-up."

"You're probably right," he said. "I'll add that to my list."

"You're pretty busy, I imagine."

"Not too busy to help you." He fumbled with the lid for the gas tank. "We're cousins, sort of. If you need anything, don't hesitate to let me know. You have my number."

Once we were off again, Gerardo drove a kilometer before rumbling off the main road to park along a grassy ledge. We walked to a clearing where the path terminated along a handrail. The river ran below us, hurrying over its stone bed, while the houses of Monteleone peeked at us from the other side.

The spot was beautiful. No wonder Ivano had revered it. He'd made plenty of pragmatic decisions for the town, but he'd thought about beauty, too.

Gerardo leaned against the rail. "I love the sound of the water. When I was growing up, I used to bike here every summer night to hear the current." He studied the flow as if answers to the world's largest problems lurked beneath.

"Back home I'm surrounded by water," I said, "but I don't take time to ponder it." I was too busy taking things for granted: nice apartment, nice job, nice life.

"Funerals force you to step back and put things into perspective. Shall we walk a bit?"

Absolutely. If I kept my body active, my mind could coast. That way I might be able to push past the dreary funeral mass, the famished guests, and the loud hullabaloo Ivano would have enjoyed being a part of.

I followed Gerardo onto a path that led between the riverbank and forest. Hiking boots and tennis shoes had left prints in the mud. A bicycle track wove in and out among them. The townspeople appreciated this area, and Ivano had been right to protect it.

"I don't tell my dad this," Gerardo said as we went along, "but I've never been in favor of developing here. Most people approach Monteleone from the south or the north. From the north, you have a huge metal works plant. Why not preserve this southern entry? For the last two hundred years, this piece of land has offered unobstructed views of the city. It would be a shame to change things."

"People assume that change makes things better."

Gerardo alerted me to a patch of uneven ground. "But it doesn't, does it?"

"Not usually."

"Have you been enjoying having your own balmetto?"

"So-so. Does your family own one?"

"My father couldn't survive otherwise. He does love his wine."

We climbed high enough to have the best possible view. Monteleone unfolded to our left while forested hills stretched up to the right. Far below, we could still hear the river.

"Wonderful, isn't it?" Gerardo asked.

I felt teary again. "Ivano's town. Even if he's not here to enjoy it."

The best I could do was imagine that he was watching me, happy to know that I cared about his town. Nobody had noticed how hard he worked to defend it until he was gone.

"Did you know Ivano well?" I finally asked.

"Around here, everybody knows everybody. They can't help it." Gerardo took a deep breath. "Can you keep a secret?"

I indicated the trees surrounding us. "Who am I going to tell?"

"I voted for him for mayor," he said softly.

"Instead of voting for your father's buddy?"

Gerardo's eyes grew wider. "Don't get me wrong. I respect my father, but Fabio Sanalto is too old to be effective. He ran out of new ideas years ago, but in a town this size, you need action. Not that I mentioned this to my father."

I was tickled that he was confessing to such a minor charge. "Parents don't need to know everything."

"No, they don't. Anyway, I came to know Ivano better when we took a trip together a couple of summers ago."

"Just the two of you?"

"Oh, no. It was a cultural exchange to Nicosia."

Ivano would have fit in perfectly. No matter the environment, he knew how to make friends.

"This was before Ivano became mayor," Gerardo continued, "but you could see where he was heading. He always thought Monteleone should have more outside contact, and he was right. He set up an exchange, but he couldn't round up enough participants."

"Why not?" I would have jumped at the chance, especially if I'd been stuck in a spot as tiny as this one.

"They came up with all kinds of excuses — suddenly their relatives were sick, and the European airports were full of terrorists. Ivano had to beg for participants. That's how Margarita — my ex-wife — and I got involved."

"Did you enjoy the trip?"

Gerardo tore a cracked branch off an oak and proceeded to pull it apart leaf by leaf. "Margarita and Ivano did."

The words rang loud. For the first time, Ivano disappointed me. It was one thing that he played around as a bachelor. Pursuing married women was a different matter, especially if their husbands were anywhere in the vicinity.

Which meant that Gerardo certainly had motive. Which meant I was traipsing around with a potential murderer.

I tried to remember everything Grazia had said about Gerardo, but she'd discounted him the moment he was out of range. He bored people and he talked a lot. He wasn't a man of action, and he was related to Grazia. Would he have killed her husband? I chided my imagination for getting carried away. Gerardo wouldn't have had the gumption to kill my cousin-in-law. To talk him to death, maybe.

To be on the safe side, though, I wanted to get Ivano clear out of Gerardo's head. I chatted about Boston as if paid by the word, recounting every aspect of the city that I could think of. I worked so hard to keep talking that before I knew it, I had told Gerardo more than I meant to about my rent and even my tax bracket. Then I switched to details about the balmetto renovations and how my dollars were holding out against the euro. I didn't ask any questions because I was afraid he'd get back to his wife's relationship with Ivano.

By the time we started our descent, I made the mistake of taking a breath.

"I don't want you to think that Ivano caused our divorce," Gerardo said. "If it hadn't been him, it would have been someone else. But naturally I've never thought of Ivano in the same way."

"Of course not. You couldn't have." I didn't blame him. Gerardo was boring, but his ex-wife would have realized that before the end of their first date.

"While the rest of us went to archaeological sites, Ivano and Margarita said they were too hot or too tired or too thirsty. Worse, it took me all week to catch on."

"I'm sure that happens to a lot of people." I didn't believe my words. Most spouses would have noticed more quickly because they wouldn't have been busy talking.

Gerardo stopped as abruptly as if someone had slapped him. "Forgive me. I didn't drag you here to complain about my ex-wife."

I swatted a mosquito. "It's probably therapeutic."

"Maybe. But it doesn't help."

I'd lost at least one ex-boyfriend to a meddling girlfriend, but that was back in high school, and I would have never married the guy anyway. I felt sorry for Gerardo, but I couldn't pretend to understand how he felt. Nor did I want to. The situation was too painful. On our way back to town I thanked him for the excursion, but I vowed not to repeat the experience any time soon.

To find out more about Ivano, I'd look somewhere else.

Instead of going home to an empty house, I asked Gerardo to drop me at Grazia's. She and her mother were in the kitchen drinking Negroni Sbagliati: Negroni with sparkling wine. A pile of used Kleenex lay between them.

Grazia rubbed her eyes. "We were wondering about you. Did you have band practice again?"

"Not until tomorrow. I was out with Gerardo. He was showing me the sunset." That explanation was easier than discussing land rights, and my relatives were too absorbed in grief to question me.

"Now there's a poor man," said Aunt Maria. "His wife treated him like a book on a shelf, and his father dictates every decision he makes. He's a year older than you, right, Grazia?"

"A year and a half. Remember? We took piano lessons together."

Grazia left her perch long enough to find me a shot glass and make me a drink. I wasn't fond of Negroni, but, as with grappa, I was never expected to drink much of it. It was easier to accept the drink than spend ten minutes protesting why I didn't want it.

"Margarita has always been a wild one," Aunt Maria said. "I'm surprised she stayed married as long as she did."

Grazia kicked back what I assumed was a second drink. "I'm surprised she lasted a month. The man won't stop talking. You should have heard him go on and on about Boston today, and he hasn't even been there."

"He's a better talker than a listener," I said. "He did offer to help if I needed anything."

Grazia tapped her ear. "He needs someone to listen to his pathetic little stories."

"His problem is confidence," said Aunt Maria. "He hasn't been the same since Margarita left."

I fingered my glass. "I'm always amazed at how everybody's connected around here."

Grazia laughed. "Usually in nine different ways."

"How can I put this delicately?" I asked. "That's why I'm surprised so many people run around."

"Like Margarita?" Grazia asked. "She had one lover after another. You're forgetting that having affairs is the national pastime."

"Don't the partners ever retaliate?" I thought of the final scenes of *Divorzio all'italiana, Divorce, Italian Style*, the old classic in which Marcello Mastroianni schemes to get his wife together with a lover so he'll have the excuse to shoot her and suffer little jailtime for it. I was surprised I hadn't thought of the film earlier except that Gerardo was a thousand-kilometre cry from the charismatic actor.

"If jealous partners murdered their lovers, there wouldn't be any Italians left," Grazia said. "People have to do something for fun."

The glib summary surprised me. "They can't stay at home and watch TV like we do back home?"

Aunt Maria shook her head. "That might work in the winter. In the summer there are too many reruns!"

What a country! Even my elderly aunt could joke about affairs.

Careful not to drop the glass, I tasted the dark concoction. Tonight was the perfect occasion for something strong enough to knock me to the street. "I can understand having an affair in Florence or Rome, but in Monteleone people are bound to get caught. Mathematically they can't avoid it."

Grazia made herself another drink. "All the better. What's the point of doing something wrong if you don't get credit for it? You can't build a reputation playing bocce ball every night."

I wondered if Grazia were subtly making fun of me, but those evenings had been among my favorite. The bocce ball courts buzzed alive in the evening as friends challenged one another to toss their balls closest to the mark. The game called for a good eye and the ability to calculate distance times force times the weight of the

D.R. Ransdell

ball. I was a miserable player, but no one seemed to care who won, not even the winners. The games were an excuse to socialize on a carefree summer night. I loved every minute.

"Gerardo was fortunate," Aunt Maria said. "They didn't have any kids, and Margarita was working. Otherwise Gerardo would be expected to pay alimony."

"I thought she was the one who had the affair."

Grazia and Aunt Maria launched into a complaint session about current laws. I got lost in their legalese, so I concentrated on my drink as I remembered the ridiculous antics of Fefè, the Mastroianni character.

"In the end, keeping a man happy is the same as keeping a woman happy," Aunt Maria said. "Give them what they want, or they'll look for it someplace else. Life is that simple."

"Does Margarita live around here?" I asked. "I didn't want to ask Gerardo."

"No," said Aunt Maria. "She lives way over in Quassolo. That's nearly three kilometers."

"She lives with one of Gerardo's older cousins," Grazia said. "That's the other side of the family. The side I'm not related to."

"They're roommates?"

My cousin laughed so loudly Antonella could have heard her next door. "*Che scema!* Honestly, Sofi! You are so stupid. They're way past that."

If "stupid" was a strong slur in English, the Italian "SHAY-ma" was a slap in the face with a calzone. My bad angel wanted to say, "How do you know?" Just in time, my good angel told me to shut up.

"Grazia! That's no way to talk to your cousin."

"Lay off, Mother. I buried my husband today, so to speak."

"You don't have to be rude."

150

Although I agreed with Aunt Maria, I tried to put myself in Grazia's position. She was mourning a husband whose cause of death was presumed but not confirmed. She was forced to hold his funeral without a body. Every day brought the chance for her to learn more than she wanted to know about Ivano's exploits.

Monteleone. It really was an amazing place. The more I knew, the more I needed to find out. Now that I realized I was living atop an iceberg, it was time to chisel my way down through the surface. Somehow, there would be more bodies along the way. As I walked home through the blessedly silent streets, I wondered where they were.

Chapter Fifteen

I'd almost reached my front door when I heard a whistle. For a moment I was startled, but I reminded myself that I wasn't back in Boston. When someone whistled at you in Monteleone, it was someone you knew.

Cenzo was sitting in his car across the street from my house. For a moment I was torn between being irritated and being flattered; flattery won. I went over and bent down to his window. "I didn't know I was a flight risk."

He winked. "I didn't know you were a socialite."

"I've been gathering information."

"I suppose Gerardo was full of news. After all, his father is the biggest employer in the area."

I took a step back. "How did you know I was with Gerardo?"

"How's Grazia holding up?"

I made a mental note to look over my shoulder at all times. Maybe I would have to make a habit of walking backwards. "Have you been following me all night?"

He smiled. "I saw you with Gerardo as you passed through town earlier this evening. He would have escorted you home. Since you came from the south right now rather than the north, I assumed you walked here from Grazia's."

Good answer. Anonymity was impossible in such a small town, and I was pleased to see Cenzo. He was way better company than Gerardo. "Are you here to check on my time schedule or to invite yourself for coffee?"

He pushed open the passenger door. "I was hoping for an accomplice."

I joined him. He looked fresh in a black Polo shirt, and he wore jean shorts that were popular amongst the farmer-gardeners. To complete the casual look, he wore sandals. He'd shaved within the last hour and was wearing a trace of Acqua di Giò, an Armani product also favored by Renato. The result was effective; I wanted to get closer for a better whiff.

"You wouldn't have in mind doing something outside the scope of legal police business, would you?"

"Barely outside."

I couldn't complain. I wanted information too. "If you get caught, do you detain yourself?"

He winked. "I never get caught." He started the car, which hissed once before turning over. "Have you guessed where we're going?"

I shook my head as he headed for the main drag. "I'll let you surprise me."

He beamed, satisfied, but my ego wasn't prepared to stroke his as much as that.

"Or maybe we're going to the Baruzzo plant."

"Why would you guess that?"

"Because you don't seem at all bothered that I spent half the evening with his son. You think I might have learned something useful."

Although he kept his eyes on the road, he broke into a grin. "If you're so clever, tell me why we're going now and not some other night."

I rolled down the window as if fresh air were the cure for a dumb question. "The bocce ball tournament in Lungofiume. Besides us, everyone will be there."

He smoothed his lips with his fingers, hiding his expression. I'd impressed him, and he didn't want me to know it. "You're good. I might be able to hire you sometime."

I leaned back against the seat and stretched my arms above my head. "You probably can't afford me." I didn't have to look over to know that he was smiling.

The Baruzzo plant was a couple of kilometers outside town, tucked into a narrow space behind the river and the highway. From a distance, the buildings snaked above the fields like a sea of periscopes.

We crossed the railroad tracks and traveled on a bumpy two-lane road that curved past several vineyards before reaching the parking lot. A lone motor scooter was the only other vehicle, but lights on tall poles illuminated the grounds, casting exaggerated shadows in every direction.

The night was so still that our steps rang out as we traversed the lot. The main building, an old-fashioned one-story structure, was marked by a large sign, a shallow porch, and a welcome mat. Cenzo tried the metal door, which was firmly locked. I was only slightly surprised when he reached into his pocket and pulled out a set of master keys. I acted nonchalant as he tried various ones. It was fun to be doing something vaguely wrong, no matter that it was for the right reason.

He seemed to sense what I was thinking. "Lots of businesses use the same locksmith from Aosta."

"I see."

"It turns out that Enrico, the locksmith, had especially bad luck. The worker who had been stealing from him was also a nephew of the police chief up there. I helped Enrico catch the man red-handed."

"He gave you a set of master keys?'

"'Gave' might be too strong. I think he forgot I have them." He tried another key, and the door gave way.

Dim emergency lights ran the length of the corridor. To the right was an office for visitors. To the left were several closed doors, all labeled with various managers' names.

Walking briskly, Cenzo made a right turn down a smaller hallway.

"You've been here before," I said.

He put a finger to his lips. "There's a night watchman," he whispered. "I'm sure he's asleep somewhere. But yes, I've been here several times. Baruzzo always has some complaint or another."

Cenzo only needed a few moments to unlock the door. We entered cautiously as light trickled in from the hallway. Nestled among filing cabinets, an old desk dominated the room.

He handed me a pocket flashlight and turned on his own. "Be discreet. Don't get anything out of place."

I headed to the desk, where papers crowded a large computer screen. I glanced through the documents on top, but they all seemed like normal business correspondence. Bernardo Baruzzo had signed them in tall, curvy letters.

Cenzo opened a filing cabinet. "Try the computer?" he whispered.

The Dell desktop was old, but it wasn't ancient.

"It'll have a password."

"It might be 'Gerardo.' I was looking over Baruzzo's shoulder the last time I was here, and I thought that's what he typed."

"I'll try."

The desktop hummed to life, but "Gerardo" didn't get me inside.

"Try 'Lucrezia,'" Cenzo said. "That's his wife."

"Wrong again."

I frowned. "Is Baruzzo the cautious type?"

"He's a successful businessman because he makes conservative decisions."

I rummaged through desk drawers. "Cautious people keep backup drives."

He opened the next drawer of the filing cabinet. "Good thinking."

The desk didn't hold any electronic components, so I went for the floor. The system had been set up haphazardly, with wires in spaghetti strips, but I located a backup drive. I was trying to unhook it when a loud sound rang throughout the building. It was so deafening that I put hands over my ears as I stood. "Fire?"

Cenzo shook his head. "Unlikely. Stay here."

He opened the door and ventured into the hall.

How had I let him talk me into this? I went to the window, which easily opened. I had one leg outside when Cenzo returned.

"You're so anxious to get away from me?"

"It's so—" The ringing stopped. "—loud!"

The dead might have heard my last word. Cenzo motioned for me to continue out the window. He followed right behind.

Even though the building only had one story, the windowsill was high enough off the ground that I hung from the sill and carefully angled my body before I let myself drop.

Cenzo came right after me, but in his hurry, he dropped incautiously.

"Ow!" He rolled on the ground, cradling his foot.

I bent to the ground. "Are you okay?"

He stopped rolling long enough to take off his sandal and massage his ankle. "I think so."

The light switched on in the office. We looked to one another in panic before backing ourselves along the wall.

From inside the office we heard loud footsteps as the security guard neared the window. *"Van cool post!"* He shut the window, latched it, and retraced his steps.

Cenzo put both hands over his mouth. He managed to contain himself for several seconds before laughing out loud.

"That was Piemontese, wasn't it?" I asked. "What did he say?"

"Go to hell!"

Funny indeed. I felt like a ten-year-old on a cookie hunt. I pointed to the locked window. "Now what?"

"Do we need anything from inside the office?"

"There was a backup drive on the floor. It's a black box about six inches wide."

"You think we need it?"

"Think you can get it?"

He grinned. "I'll tell the guard someone called in about the noise."

"And make an excuse to walk right through the building."

I gave him my hand as he struggled to his feet. "You're good at this."

"Not really. Trying to keep up with you."

I wouldn't want him to think I was merely along for the ride.

An hour later I was sitting at Cenzo's desk reading through useless information while Cenzo returned the contraband. So far I'd found Excel sheets that outlined the company's expenditures, information on clients, proposals for an additional building, and copies of correspondence. There were no references to Ivano or any of Baruzzo's family or anything out of the ordinary. Worse, I was too sleepy to care.

Then I found a file of older correspondence, some of which was personal. I started reading through letters, complaints, proposals, and even thank-yous.

Under a fifth sub-level of a file innocently labeled *vecchio*, meaning "old," I spotted a folder labeled "gra."

Inside the folder was a single pdf file labeled "*anticipo*" or "advance."

In November, my cousin Grazia had signed a receipt for a check for ten thousand euros. I sat up so fast that I knocked the stapler off the desk. While there could be a thousand explanations, right off I couldn't think of any I approved of. Of course, I didn't have proof that she'd cashed it.

"Still awake?" Cenzo asked as he entered the office. "It's about time I took you home so that you can rest up for tomorrow."

I wasn't absolutely sure I wanted Cenzo to know about the money. He would jump to conclusions. Hence I faked a yawn. "You were gone a while. Have any trouble?"

He shook his head. "I had to lie to the security guard, but he let me take another look around. Then we had a long conversation about vagrants." Suddenly Cenzo's eyes narrowed. "What did you find?"

"Nothing much."

He sat on top of the desk, invading my space.

"Tell me."

For a split second I struggled. It was one thing to have spent the morning at a funeral. It was another to have my cousin's use of the word "stupid" ringing in my ears. As I showed him the receipt, I was relieved I hadn't been clever enough to lie.

Chapter Sixteen

As I walked the short distance to Aunt Maria's the next morning, I thought of ways I could corner Grazia during our traditional Sunday meal. The problem was that the dinner was a joyful, frenetic event where everyone spoke at once—even while they were eating.

Today, however, Renato and Laura were as somber as Aunt Maria and Grazia. While the children played in the living room, the rest of us went through motions. Between his joking and his joviality, Ivano had been such a presence at every dinner that we didn't know how to proceed without him. Everything we did felt strained and awkward, and no matter how lovingly Aunt Maria had prepared the *agnoletti* with the creamiest ricotta cheese, pasta squares stuck to my throat until I drank enough water to coax them down.

In between bites, I studied Grazia. During the entire meal, her thoughts were elsewhere. More than once she was staring so far off into space that she hadn't heard questions addressed to her. The others would have attributed these lapses to normal mourning, but I couldn't make the leap. The image of Baruzzo's receipt circled through my mind as a gerbil running on a wheel.

Normally when Grazia cleared the table, I rushed to help her. After she hand-washed the pots that wouldn't fit into the dishwasher, I would dry them and put them away. Today I didn't offer assistance until she prompted me to do so. I too pretended to be lost in thought. In truth I didn't trust my reactions. Even if Baruzzo had nothing to do with Ivano's death, I now had ten thousand reasons to suspect Grazia of something.

She attacked the frying pan with a soapy sponge. "You didn't elaborate about your date with Gerardo last night. Did you have a good time?"

Since Grazia normally focused on herself, I was first surprised and then suspicious that she bothered to ask. "I wouldn't call it a date."

"Given his track record, I'm sure he thought it was."

I had that sensation myself but didn't care to say so. "He does lack social skills."

She handed me a wet pan. "Gerardo is a busybody. Did he ask weird questions about your income and such?"

I used the pan to hide my expression. Her comment was a computer virus asking for a social security number. All she needed was a little more information to fill in the pieces of the puzzle. A few days earlier I would have answered her question as a matter of course. Now I protected each word. "We talked about the river. He gave me the whole history of Monteleone. Why would he ask weird questions?"

"No reason," she said quickly over the noise from the faucet.

I stretched my praise of the beautiful summer weather over the process of drying the remaining pots and returned to the dining room table before she could manage another question. If she wanted to play the interrogation game, I could play dodge ball.

Yet I was hardly safe in the dining room either. Renato slashed into a kiwi. "What progress has Cenzo made on the case?"

I wanted to trust Renato, but by now I knew to be wary. Behind his helpfulness, his eyes were glued to my balmetto. I took a kiwi myself, but I cut it rather than attacking it. "Cenzo is still looking into leads. He doesn't have any new information."

Renato ate a juicy bite. "Here's what I don't understand. Our tax money goes to Torino, but when we need the Torino Investigate Unit, where are they?"

"They told Cenzo they were about to crack a big drug case."

"They're always working on a drug case," said Renato. "What happened here is different."

"How could a drug dealer be more important than a town mayor?" asked Aunt Maria. "The Torinesi have no sense. Narcos are like termites. They hide underground for a while but then they resurface. You never get rid of them."

"What about that bottle of poison?" Renato asked.

I didn't remember mentioning it to him. Were my cousins scheming against me? Somehow they shared unseen communication lines that an outsider couldn't perceive. The safest ploy was for me to cut my losses. Sell the balmetto. Then I'd be done with the damned thing, and I could forget all about bad red wine.

Stalling, I bit into a kiwi section. "The bottle didn't contain suspicious prints."

"I'm not surprised. Whoever did this knew what he was doing," Renato said.

"What makes you sure it was a 'he'?" asked Laura.

Grazia stood and threw her napkin into her plate. "My husband is dead! Stop asking all your stupid questions!"

She marched through the dining room and out the front door, which she slammed behind her. She revved her engine several times before blasting off.

"My poor daughter," said Aunt Maria. "It's too much stress. She's not herself."

This was true. She was somebody new I didn't recognize.

"We have to be patient with her," said Laura. "And with ourselves. We've suffered a big loss."

"I've been too depressed to do any housework," Aunt Maria said. "The dust bunnies will start having parties under the kitchen table."

"We could go for a drive this afternoon," said Renato. "That would be a decent distraction."

Aunt Maria frowned. "I would love to, but Francesco might come over to give me an estimate on the broken shower tiles."

"On a Sunday?" I asked.

My aunt nodded. "When you're in business for yourself, you work weekends, evenings, and holidays."

My aunt loved nothing better than an excursion, and I longed to be alone in a house where Grazia used to live. "I have a heavy date with my trumpet this afternoon. I'm practicing for the balmetto concert. Since the principal trumpet player has to go to Calabria for a wedding, Roberto asked me to play a solo. Why don't I practice here? If Francesco comes, I can let him in."

Aunt Maria didn't hesitate. "You wouldn't mind?"

"Of course not. Just give me ten minutes to fetch my horn."

Aunt Maria seemed so delighted about the prospect of getting out of Monteleone for a few hours that I neglected to mention that I could almost never hear the doorbell over the sound of my trumpet. Then again, I wasn't sure I would spend any time practicing.

♠ ♣ ♠

As soon as everyone left, I skipped through the living room full of knickknacks and photos of Aunt Maria's long-deceased husband and went straight up to Grazia's old bedroom. I set the trumpet case on the bed and took out the instrument on the off-chance Grazia came around and caught me off guard. While I didn't expect her, I couldn't outguess her, either.

For long moments I studied the room. The bubblegum pink rectangle had windows on two walls.

Wedding presents, mostly cookware, covered the small bed. Why hadn't she returned stuff? Maybe this was her re-gifting repository. She wouldn't have wanted the presents anyway. They wouldn't have suited her unless she'd chosen them herself.

I looked over the mementos on her desk. On the surface they represented typical family trips: a bell from Austria and a teddy bear bobby from England. A picture showed Grazia with her parents on a beach, maybe in Southern France. I wondered if Grazia had forgiven her father for passing when she was still in grade school and how close Ivano had come as a replacement.

The top drawer held pens and pencils along with several unused wedding invitations. Somewhere in my apartment in Boston I had an identical invitation boasting curly silver letters flanked by pink roses with delicate green leaves. I wondered if my cousin had picked out the cards on her own or whether Ivano had helped her. On second thought, she would have marched into the stationery store, made a quick order, and never looked back.

The way she wasn't looking back now.

The next drawer held an extension cord, an empty box, blank index cards, old hard candies. The third drawer stuck. When I pulled, it refused to open. When I gave the drawer a yank, it flew from the desk, spilling papers everywhere.

Perfect. I needed to examine each item. Several letters dated back to Grazia's employment at the bank. One was a long letter from Kristine describing a long-lost summer at boarding school. One was a deposit slip for the sum of ten thousand euros. *Cazzo!*

My suspicions had played out. Grazia had cashed Baruzzo's check and kept the receipt where Ivano wouldn't find it. A business deal, but what kind? A bribe so that she could put a bug in Ivano's head? A project he wouldn't have approved of? A foreign holding? While I played long notes, I tried to imagine the most likely possibilities.

What bride started married life by harboring a ten-thousand-euro secret? Ivano was the mayor of the smallest possible community. Maybe in politics there was no escape. Villagers complained to you day and night, family members urged you to do special favors twenty-four seven, and even your spouse profited from you behind your back.

I hated to think it, but maybe good old Aunt Elena wasn't so far off after all. I could hardly wait to find out one way or the other.

Chapter Seventeen

Even if I hadn't considered myself a village spy, I would have been delighted to spend the evening at Carmela and Roberto's balmetto party. When I arrived, the musicians cheered. They'd started drinking in the late afternoon, so by early evening they cheered at the mention of almost anything. As they welcomed me, they scooted closer together so that I could squeeze in between Marco and Roberto Two.

Roberto the maestro handed me a glass and poured red wine, spilling a few drops because he no longer held a bottle steadily. The others chided him for his wastefulness. Carmela giggled, interrupted her work of stirring pasta over the gas mini-stove, and handed me an empty plate. A full spread of appetizers filled the table: salami, pickled cabbage, chicken salad, stuffed eggplant, and my favorite local breadsticks. I'd already pondered how many packages I'd be able to stuff into my suitcase for the trip home.

While busily munching, I listened to various conversations, dismissing them as soon as I was sure they had nothing to do with Ivano. Meanwhile Carmela teased us with the aromas of roasted olive oil and fresh tomatoes. After the huge pasta pot went around the table, we stopped talking. Hot linguini trumped everything.

I'd only managed a few forkfuls before a disaster occurred. As Roberto attempted to open the next bottle of wine, the corkscrew broke into pieces.

"Cazzo!" Roberto cried.

"The one time I don't carry one on my keychain!" cried Marco.

"And I brought the wrong purse," cried the wife of Roberto Two.

The trombone player was already on his feet. "I have one in my car. Give me two seconds."

Roberto and Roberto Three disappeared into the cellar to look for an extra. They emerged minutes later with clammy skin and empty hands. Carmela checked upstairs where she kept the winter kitchenware. Nothing. Even the trombonist returned with bad news.

I stood. "I have at least three in my balmetto. I'll be right back."

"Eat first!" cried Roberto.

I squeezed off the bench and wrestled my keys from my shoulder bag. "It won't take a minute." I didn't want poor Roberto to hurt his hands trying to strangle the bottle. More importantly, if I took a break mid-meal, I wouldn't have a chance to tempt myself with seconds and thirds because the pasta would be gone by the time I returned.

I skipped towards my balmetto. We'd reached the height of summer, and the temperature was perfect. A gentle breeze served as a natural air conditioner, and the mosquitos were only out in half force. I still felt awful about Ivano, but making new friends eased the pain.

I flipped on the electricity and unlocked my gate. Inside my courtyard, I opened the fancy old lock. Leaving the key in the door, I pushed my way into the cellar and switched on the light. The single bulb cast shadows while stacks of wine bottles grinned at me from dark corners. I still had a lot of sorting to do, but it would wait. Perhaps indefinitely.

I located a six-bottle carrier and blew dust off the handle. Given the way their friends were guzzling supplies, Roberto and Carmela could surely use more wine. I chose four reds and two whites. I was reaching for my best corkscrew when I heard a small sound behind me.

I whirled around, but I didn't see anything. I could have sworn I'd heard a noise. The wind, maybe. I marched outside, but my picnic area was deserted. I traipsed up to my winter party room, but the door was firmly locked. Strange.

Reentering the cellar, I chided myself for being jumpy. Mice were frequent culprits in the balmetti. Where was that gray cat when I needed him? I stood in the middle of the room, listening. Then the door slammed shut, and the key turned in the lock.

"Hey!"

Cazzo. I was in the cold, in the dark, and if my friends had already rustled up another corkscrew, they might never miss me. Naturally, my cell phone was in my purse back at Carmela and Roberto's.

"Aiuto!" I yelled for help even though no passerby would hear me through such thick walls. I was stuck. It was the ultimate insult, like being drowned in your own sink or electrocuted with your own computer cords. I leaned against a wine barrel, knocking over an empty bottle in the process. I listened while it hit the dirt and rolled.

I was already cold. Sixty degrees might have been a fine temperature in winter, but it was a miserable shock on a hot summer's night. After a few minutes of rubbing my arms, I felt my way around to the shelf where I kept an old jacket. I shook out the dust and slipped it on. Then I did jumping jacks.

Carmela would be the first to notice my absence, but she would merely assume I'd fallen victim to the most common reason people were late all over Monteleone: because they ran into someone they had to talk to.

The temperature forced me to focus. I hadn't been locked inside my property because of the wind or even a mere troublemaker. If someone had wanted to murder me, they would have already done so. Instead they were sending a message. Sell the balmetto and get the hell out of town. The messenger might have been an employee, a relative, a band member, or someone I hadn't even met.

Boh. To kill time, I started counting seconds but lost track between eight and nine hundred. I felt my way around to the side of the balmetto where a ledge held various samples of wine and a ten-pack of orange-flavored Crodini, a gentle, non-alcoholic, aperitif. By placing my hands gently on the ledge, I felt around until I found a bottle opener. After several tries, I pried the lid off a Crodino. The metal cap rolled after it hit the ground.

I took a small taste and concentrated on the sweet carbonated beverage. I sipped slowly, making the drink last, telling myself that when I got back to the States, this would be a great adventure I could describe to my U.S. cousins. They would pretend to commiserate, but I was the only member of the younger generation who had visited Italy. They wouldn't be able to envision the situation.

But I wouldn't be able to forget it. If someone were bullheaded enough to lock me into my own balmetto as a way to convince me to sell the damned thing, that person was dead wrong. I wouldn't be scared off my own property, and I certainly would not sell.

I wasn't being stubborn. I was merely being Piemontese. We were property owners. We couldn't help it.

I jogged in place while cursing everyone I could think of, including Ivano. He knew all the dirt about Monteleone and its inhabitants. He knew the town's lovers as well as its never-do-wells. How dare he ruin everything by letting a killer take him by surprise?

I stopped doing arm circles when I thought I heard a voice. "Speak up!"

"Sofi?" Cenzo's voice was muffled, but I clearly heard my name.

"Get me out of here!" It felt like hours later even though it had only been twenty-seven long minutes.

"How?"

"First turn on the electricity!"

The light had a psychological effect. Despite its dim quality, I imagined that I felt warmer.

Cenzo hollered at me through the keyhole. "What happened? Did you lock yourself in?"

Maybe I didn't feel like hugging him after all. "Of course not! Somebody trapped me inside!"

"Where are your keys?"

"I left them in the door!"

"They're gone."

"Go get a key from Renato or Grazia before I get bronchitis AND pneumonia!"

"There should be some way you can open the door from the inside."

"You don't think I've been trying?"

"Sofi, maybe if you —"

"I'm freezing! Call Renato! He drives faster."

I rattled off the phone number. Renato answered on the first ring and promised to hurry.

"Sofi, are you all right?" Cenzo had the audacity to ask.

"I'm freezing in this stupid place! I hate it in here!"

Even the talky Cenzo was at a loss for a moment. "Let's play a game," he said slowly. "You tell me about things you're looking at, and I'll try to guess what they are."

"What? You're telepathic?" And stupid.

"Or, I know. Count the number of bottles of wine along the east wall, and —"

"How am I supposed to know which way is east?"

Oh, I was the stupid one. He was trying to keep my mind off the cold, or maybe he was afraid I would panic. I appreciated the gesture. I was still cold, but I was too mad to panic. But I vowed to write a list of nasty retorts I could make to anyone who offered to buy the place. Tradition! Custom! *Che schemo!*

"How many bottles?" Cenzo asked.

"Twenty on the first shelf," I shouted without trying to count at all. I made up a few more numbers, but the only ones I cared about were the number of minutes Renato needed to reach me.

Eleven, as it turned out. He loved the excuse to drive fast.

Renato yanked open the door and bear-hugged me. "Cuz! How did you get locked inside?"

He warmed me up by rubbing my arms until I protested that he was taking my skin off. He sat with Cenzo at the picnic table in the courtyard while I explained. I was too wired to sit down, and I was still cold. I waved my hands, punctuating my explanations.

Cenzo shook his head as he heard the last details. "You didn't hear anyone come up behind you?"

"I heard a noise close by. Maybe he was behind me."

"You're sure it was a guy?"

"No."

"You would have noticed if someone else were here," Renato said.

I waved my hands. "Not if someone was in the courtyard crouched down behind a picnic table." As I demonstrated, I saw a piece of metal shining in the light.

My key hadn't traveled far away after all. I reached to grab it.

"Don't!" Cenzo yelled. He shone his pocket flashlight on the key, and then carefully turned it over and examined the other side, but it was wiped clean.

Whoever had locked me in was as devious as he—or she—was careful.

Renato stood and wrapped his long arms around me. "I'm beginning to think Italy is the wrong place for you."

"I've been thinking the same thing. I guess it could have been worse." Especially if they wanted to harm me rather than give me a silly scare. "Cenzo, how did you know to come looking for me?"

"I stopped by Roberto and Carmela's to say hello. They were starting to wonder."

"I'm surprised they noticed."

"They still needed the corkscrew!"

I started to go back inside my cellar. "I forgot all about it."

"Never mind. Roberto Three called his wife, who came and brought one."

"First Ivano and now this," Renato said. "Sofi, you don't have any idea who was here?"

"I thought I was alone until the door locked behind me. I don't suppose the thing is haunted?"

"Not that I know of," Renato laughed.

"Cenzo, didn't you tell me that some of the balmetti are connected through secret passages?"

"Ghosts are more likely," said Renato. "I mean, it's ridiculous."

"Bats?"

"No," Renato replied. "But there has to be some explanation."

"Speaking of which, we better get back before Carmela sends out a search party," I said. "By now she'll imagine we got sucked into the mountain."

We started down the path towards Roberto and Carmela's. At my insistence, both Renato and Cenzo carried a six-pack for me. Those musicians were certainly thirsty from all that talking.

We were only a dozen feet away when Cenzo calmly stopped and said, "I think it's best not to mention what happened."

I immediately saw through Cenzo's game. He didn't want Renato to think too deeply about the situation.

Renato shrugged. "Why not?"

"If some kid thought he was being funny, why alarm our friends?" Cenzo asked.

I carefully picked my way among the stones. "Besides, I would never live down being stuck in my own wine cellar."

Renato patted my shoulder. "You're right. Who would even believe it?"

I burst into Roberto and Carmela's balmetto, faking laughter as I scrutinized for guilty faces. The partiers greeted us happily as they waved us inside; the only thing they were guilty of was drinking a lot of wine.

"Sorry to take so long," I said. "I ran into Renato, and we started talking. Then we ran into some of his friends and couldn't get away."

"You play the trumpet a lot better than you fetch corkscrews!" Roberto quipped as he popped open one of my reds. "And don't think I'll forget it."

Roberto was kidding, but I wasn't going to forget being trapped in my balmetto anytime soon. Nor would I let it happen a second time.

Two hours later Cenzo walked me to my car, but after the other partiers drove off, he pointed up to the balmetti. "Sofi, do you mind if —"

"I know. You want to take another look at my balmetto without Renato around. I do too." I hardly thought Renato would work against me, but he was keen on owning the balmetto, and he'd made sure everyone in Monteleone knew it.

"Is there anything else you can tell me?" Cenzo asked as we climbed the hill.

"I thought I heard a noise. I sensed something was wrong. I couldn't tell what."

"You didn't have a reason to be suspicious. You're sure you can't remember anything else?"

I'd told him my story several times. What I remembered the most was the cold. "I'm sure."

After I unlocked the door to the cellar, brisk air rushed out to slap me. Determined, I shadowed Cenzo as he slowly examined the room.

"I don't see anything unusual," I finally said.

He started around the room a second time. "I don't either. We're missing something."

All I saw were wine barrels and bottles. As soon as I started shivering, I went back outside and sat on top of a picnic table. My mind raced around faster than a car at Formula Uno. Who would be mean enough to sabotage me? What made them think that a little scare would convince me to sell my property? Why wouldn't they confront me instead of playing games?

Cenzo emerged a while later. "There's not enough light for me to do a careful job. We can try tomorrow morning when there's a bit of daylight."

"That might help."

He sat beside me. "Renato dismissed the idea of an underground passageway, but he might not know."

"Or he might not want us to."

"Either is possible," Cenzo said.

"Maybe mine is connected to its neighbor as well. I've never checked."

"Some of your older relatives might know the history."

"It's not a family property. I've only owned it for a decade."

"How did you manage it if they're so hard to buy? And why would you want one?"

"You might say I acquired the property by accident. A guy I knew was desperate for a loan. The balmetto was collateral."

"He never paid you back?"

Cenzo leaned back on his elbows. "He died. They say the tumor in his head was the size of a cabbage. Anyway, I got the better deal."

As if on cue, a church bell rang in the distance.

"Do you use your balmetto at all?" I asked.

"I don't have much of a social life. Thanks to my ex-wife, everyone thinks I'm a jerk."

I winked. "Carmela says you're not so bad."

"She doesn't count. She likes everybody." Cenzo pointed to the cellar. "You said most of the wine belongs to Renato?"

"Who can tell? Me, Aunt Maria, her sister Angela, Renato, Grazia! But wine has a shelf life, right?"

"Unless it has special preservatives, most wine is only good for a couple of years. It's drinkable for a while after that, but eventually it turns to vinegar."

I laughed. "Are you sure it doesn't start out that way?"

He scooted a bit closer. "I love the way your face puckers up right before you take a sip."

"That can't seem polite. I better learn to control myself."

He slid his leg next to mine. "Losing control can be a good thing."

"You're sure about that?"

When he leaned in, I didn't back away. We kissed for long moments while our tongues explored. I could have kissed him all night, but when his hands reached for my blouse buttons, I gently edged out of reach.

He immediately backed off. "This is a bad idea, isn't it?"

I wanted to tell him that I didn't care whether it was a bad idea or not, that one night of fun or passion or lust or whatever would have done me some good. But I didn't want a one-night stand, nor did I want a long-distance relationship. "I'm sure we've both made worse decisions. Call it a night?"

Fortunately, we were driving separate cars. He didn't hear me giggle myself silly on the short ride back to town. Who was to say we shouldn't enjoy one another? That wouldn't be more wrong than anything else that had been going on around Monteleone. It seemed Cenzo was as attracted to me as I was to him. Yes, he was investigating Ivano's death, but so what? He'd been so surprised that I was sure he wasn't involved in the murder himself. Some fun would do us both good.

The next time we had the occasion, I wouldn't back away.

Chapter Eighteen

"Here, kitty!" I'd called to the stray all morning, but he wasn't ready to make friends yet. He was content supervising me. I was a supervisor myself, taking intermittent sunbaths while Cenzo examined my balmetto. Given the previous evening's incarceration, I wasn't keen on going inside.

When Cenzo emerged from the cellar, the cat scampered off. He returned his flashlight to his pocket as he joined me outside. "For now I give up."

I was hyper aware that he chose to sit beside me exactly the same way he had the night before. It was too early in the day for serious flirting, but I chose not to move away. I liked being close enough to smell his aftershave. I also liked looking at him in the morning light. The sun played with the black in his hair, giving him a softer look. We hadn't found what we'd come for, but we'd enjoyed the interlude.

"Aren't you supposed to be in your office in case there's an emergency?"

Mentally I replayed our kiss, wondering whether I'd been prudent or crazy to pass up such an opportunity to finally experience some romance in Monteleone.

"His mother is stable now, so Stefano is back on duty. To tell you the truth, the towns around here are so sleepy that we spend most mornings philosophizing." In Monteleone, Cenzo was a lion stuck in a birdcage. Pieces of him kept pushing out of one side or another.

"Your talents are wasted here," I said. "Wouldn't you find it more interesting to work in Torino?"

"More interesting than sitting here with you, pretending to be working? No, Sofi, the job I have now is perfect."

"Couldn't you make more of a difference working in a city?"

"No, damn it!"

I shrank back, wondering how I'd pushed a button.

"Sorry," he said. "I didn't mean to bark."

"I didn't mean to pry." I hadn't been prying. I didn't know the buttons.

He leaned back against the table. "Here's the thing. If you're in a big city, the work never stops. It's constant. Calls in the middle of the night. Every case urgent. Newspaper reporters in your face. Nights off that suddenly become nights on again. You earn more money, make more of a difference, and ruin your life at the same time. It's not recommended."

"Right."

"I might as well tell you. That's what happened to me before. I was assigned to a special investigative unit in Milano because they needed a fluent English speaker."

"That's a long way from here."

"An hour and a half on a Sunday afternoon. On a weekday, it's double."

"Double?"

"On a good day. It's a crowded motorway."

"Don't tell me you drove to Milano every day."

"No. I drove back and forth twice a week. I had a small flat, so I would go over Monday morning, drive home on Wednesday, return to Milano on Thursday morning, and come back to Monteleone Friday night."

I couldn't imagine the tension caused by that much commuting. "That's a terrible schedule."

He ran his fingers across his brow as if that would help him remember. "At the time, I was too busy to notice. I like driving, so I didn't mind being on the road. However, there were personal consequences."

"You had an accident?"

"My then-wife started sleeping around."

What was it with these people? Something in the wine? The town was full of sex maniacs. I wondered if I would become one if I stayed long enough. "I'm sorry to hear it."

Cenzo flicked a beetle off his arm. "Although it's tempting, I can't entirely blame the job. Sarah is a woman who needs constant attention. Don't think I'm opposed to giving a woman attention. That's one of life's greatest pleasures. But she shouldn't need it all the time. A man has to sleep sometimes. Or be by himself."

"I understand exactly." I'd had boyfriends who were similar. When they started clinging, I ran.

"Maybe Sarah was irritated that she was always stuck taking care of the boys while I was off doing something more dramatic. Who knows what a woman thinks, eh?"

He was trying to make a joke, but I didn't want to give him too much leeway. "It's hard to know what any partner thinks," I said.

"It helps if both people are trying to communicate."

Communication. Nothing was more crucial. In a place such as Italy where people loved to talk, it should have been easier. It wasn't. I stared at the wall beside us, the one that divided my property from my neighbor's.

Then I pointed wildly. "What idiots we are!"

"Why?" Even as he questioned me, he caught on. Together we carried the bench to the wall.

Before he could think to stop me, I scaled the eight-foot wall, dangling from the other side before dropping down into the next courtyard. The weeds were high enough to suggest that no one had entered the property all summer, but the space was a mirror reflection of my own. The red-plated roofs were the same, and each was missing about the same number of tiles. A wooden bench was surrounded by a host of stools. The only immediate difference was that the adjoining yard had aloes while mine had marigolds.

Cenzo peered at me from over the wall. "What are you doing? Besides trespassing, I mean. Who owns this place, anyway?"

"In all the time I've spent remodeling, I've never noticed anyone over here. Know what I'm thinking?"

He held out his hand; it took me a couple of tries to find a foothold in the wall, grasp his hand, and make it back over.

"We've been wasting our time," Cenzo said. "The passageway isn't in your balmetto. It's in this one."

"There's no other explanation. That's why I thought I heard someone the other night."

"And you did. Someone jumped over the wall, as you did just now, and shut you in. Now we're getting somewhere."

I nodded as I blew the dirt off my hands. It was about time we learned something useful.

The next morning I headed to Grazia's to see if I could worm out some information. My good angel whispered "traitor" in my ear for thinking so badly of my own cousin. My bad angel whispered, "Remember, you almost froze in your own balmetto."

I started up the walkway to her front door. "Grazia!"

Normally she would stick her head out of the closest window and beckon me inside. Today she didn't answer.

I couldn't think where she might have gone. The only business open on Monday morning was the

SuperDì grocery store, but Grazia had a houseful of food.

"You're a good two hours late," said Magru as he straightened up alongside a sedan.

I was startled because I hadn't noticed him, yet no doubt he'd been watching me. Behind that mechanic's gaze was a silent critic. What, my pants were too long or too short? Bad hair day? Worn sandals? I might have said the same about him since he always wore ripped, grungy clothes filled with grease. For his mom's sake, I hoped he changed as soon as he went back inside the house.

"Two hours, huh?"

"She was out of here by eight. Took off like she was chasing a tornado. He patted the bumper. "I suppose you recognize this car."

I stared at the sedan that resembled three-fourths of the vehicles in Monteleone.

"Take a closer look."

I wasn't in the mood to play guessing games with an ornery neighbor. Then I noticed the air cleaner dangling from the mirror.

"Gerardo Baruzzo's."

"*Esatto!*" Exactly.

Everyone in this town was more observant than I was. "You saw us driving around yesterday."

"No. Gerardo told me all about your date when he brought in the car."

I was irritated twice over: at Gerardo for saying we'd been on a date together and at Magru for holding it over me. "Did he tell you anything else interesting?"

"He didn't mention where you went after leaving the river."

I started walking off. "You'll have to put that on your list of things to wonder about."

"Like where your cousin went so early this morning?"

"Esatto."

I left as quickly as possible, more perplexed than irritated. Not only did Grazia rarely shop for groceries, but she made a point never to leave her house before ten. I needed to find out where she'd gone—and why.

As I walked off, my bad angel laughed.

I puttered around the house, but by early afternoon I felt antsy. The house was stuffy, and I was tired of walking in circles. I had a car at my disposal, and I needed relief from the confines of Monteleone. I automatically drove towards the balmetti. Then I remembered the feeling of being locked in. I turned around and headed for Ivrea. The community of twenty-three thousand was the closest town nearby. I'd come several times with Grazia for shopping. A walk along Dora Bàltea would offer a Zen-space.

The midday shoppers had taken up every free parking spot. Why should I have to pay to take a short walk? I completed the regular circle around the city, which was one-way, and came to the north entrance again.

I circled again, more slowly. I could have gone off the main path, but since the narrow medieval-sized streets were haphazard, it was easy to get confused. Boh.

I exited town and returned towards Monteleone. I considered heading to Biella instead, which was double the size of Ivrea, but I didn't relish the mountainous road to get there. I might have traveled further north towards Aosta, but where exactly would I go?

Instead I settled on the balmetti after all. How could the area be dangerous in the middle of the day? I would be the only one there. The heat alone would have driven everyone else away.

I parked in the empty piazza and headed towards my property. Occasionally I heard the chirp of a bird or the buzz of a fly, but I didn't detect anything human. Even the cats that prowled among the party houses at night were sleeping off their latest feast. I had the world to myself.

Once inside my courtyard, I sat at the shadiest of the picnic tables. A leaf fluttered down from the trellis above my head. Vines were starting to stretch into a canopy that would shield the picnic area from the final weeks of summer sun. For now, the leaves made speckled patterns of shade on the weeds.

The leaves were a reminder that time was slipping away. I needed to make practical decisions and kick into high gear. It was already July, meaning that school administrators would start getting serious about staffing classes. I'd sent follow-up emails to promising schools in the Boston area, but I didn't expect any nibbles. Hence that morning I'd also applied at language schools in Bologna and Florence. Such popular cities would attract lots of competition. Milano was closer, but I hadn't found any ads for French teachers or English teachers either.

I was torn anyway. I didn't want to move from Boston, but I needed a real job. If I couldn't find one in the area, I might as well be flexible. The logistics of taking a position in Europe would be daunting, but I would have the added benefit of practicing language skills on a daily basis. Anytime I had a three-day weekend, I could visit a new town or even a new country.

Cenzo loomed on the horizon. He was a piece of the jigsaw puzzle that belonged in a different box. I wouldn't want to make decisions based on a flirtation, but what if he turned out to be more than that?

I opened the door to my balmetto as wide as it would go and propped it open with a stack of six full milk crates. If anyone wanted to lock me in, they would make a lot of racket first. That would give me plenty of time to grab the closest wine bottle and fling it in their direction.

To achieve a vague sense of accomplishment, I sorted dusty wine bottles from less dusty ones. I reasoned that I could donate an inordinate number for post-rehearsal parties. I had an additional strategy. During the festival, balmetto owners threw open their doors so that villagers could come and socialize. I would herd people inside and fill their glasses to the top. If Renato wasn't paying attention, I would send them on their way with complimentary bottles.

By the time I went up to my balcony to warm up, the gray cat was perched on the wall between my property and the neighbors.' When it meowed, I reached out my hand. As it scooted away, I moved closer.

"Kitty, kitty." I leaned over the railing but couldn't quite reach. I pulled my cell from my pocket and clicked on the camera app. I was finally close to my target. If I moved a little closer, I could catch him artistically, half in the shadows and half in the sun. As I took my first shot, the cat looked away. For the second, my hand jerked, and I photographed a blur. The cat moved a little farther off, so I compensated by stretching another few inches.

As I framed the perfect shot, the railing squeaked as it started to pull from the wall. I was too stunned to react before it gave way. The phone flew from my hands and landed behind me as I cascaded into the adjoining yard. I broke the fall with my right foot but immediately crashed to the ground. Luckily, the broken railing hadn't hit me or the cat. Instead the metal landed with a big bang a few feet away.

The cat had been smarter than I. By the time I hit the ground, the animal had vanished.

I tried to stand but immediately sat back down. Lightning bolts shot through my right ankle, and I clutched the flesh above it, trying to muffle the sensation. Using my arms and my left leg, I scooted towards the bench. Without putting any weight on my damaged foot, I hoisted myself off the ground.

It took me long minutes to catch my breath. So much for successfully finishing my renovations. Now I'd probably have to repair the whole balcony. And buy crutches.

I briefly weighed the pros and cons of scaling the wall or, for the second time in two days, being locked up where I didn't want to be. I opted for freedom. I dragged a chair next to the wall, balanced on my left leg, and hoisted myself over. I lowered myself with my hands as far as I could and then let go, trying to land on my good foot and crashing down to the ground on both.

I'd landed on stones that dug into every muscle. I scooted on my butt to reach the phone.

Grazia didn't answer. Nor did Cenzo, Aunt Maria, or Laura. Carmela didn't answer, but she would have been at the music school with Roberto. Renato answered, but he was working in Castellamonte, which was a half an hour southwest of Ivrea.

I considered options. I might have attempted driving a stick-shift with one foot. I might have waited a while and retried my friends' numbers. Neither choice was appealing, so I did something more desperate. I called Gerardo.

Chapter Nineteen

I hate being sick. It's boring to need extra rest, especially when your illness is something as mundane as a cold. But physical injuries are even more annoying. If someone plows into you with a car, at least it's not your fault. But when you fall off a balcony that you knew was unsteady, it's hard to convince yourself that you're not an idiot.

I was still cursing myself when Gerardo reached me.

To his credit, he ran to my side. "What happened?"

"The normal. I was taking a picture when the balcony gave way."

He eyed the damage and whistled. "You're lucky you didn't land on the other side!"

I said nothing. Gerardo didn't need to know everything, and I didn't want to admit to trespassing if I didn't have to.

He walked to the wall to survey the damage. "The balmetti are over a century old, you know. These kinds of accidents are common."

I could imagine they were. I didn't usually consider myself clumsy, and I wasn't drunk. How did the rest of the clan manage?

Gerardo tested some of the stonework with his fingers. "Loose." He pulled apart a piece of stone and threw it alongside the other rocks.

"Loose."

He repeated his action. The next several stones were secure.

He crossed back over to me. "When people need structural repairs for their homes, they don't delay, or at least not as much. But when it comes to spending money on a party house, people think twice. It's a luxury, so that's a totally different thing."

It was indeed. I cursed my parents for thinking otherwise. I wouldn't even have the satisfaction of complaining. If I told them about the accident, they'd worry without being able to help me.

"Think you can stand?"

I could. But I had to allow, even request, for Gerardo to support me the whole way down to his car. As an additional insult, I had to let him practically carry me up the stairs into the house. By the time he deposited me on the sofa, I felt like a newborn.

"Painkillers?"

"Upstairs bathroom. There's a bottle labeled Tylenol."

"Where, exactly? I don't want to go through all your stuff."

"Above the sink. But don't worry. There's nothing personal."

And there wasn't. I didn't take any medications, and I didn't have much jewelry. Unfortunately, I also wasn't sure if I had any more Tylenol.

"Found it!" Gerardo bounded back down the stairs, setting the plastic vial before me. "Let me get you some water."

While he left for the kitchen, I checked the bottle. I had three pills left.

After Gerardo returned triumphantly with a glass, he arranged a cushion on the coffee table and helped me prop up my ankle. "It's pretty swollen. You should see a doctor."

My ankle looked ready to burst from its skin. "Think it's broken?"

"I've always heard that when you break something, you know it."

Gingerly, I made an impression with my index finger. Either the pain had lessened, or I was getting used to it. "Maybe it's a sprain."

"If your ankle is broken, it's better to see a doctor immediately. The hospital in Ivrea is only twenty minutes away."

"Let's wait."

Gerardo smiled, at which point I realized there was a gap between his two front teeth. The effect made him look childlike. "What's the matter? Afraid of doctors?"

"I'm afraid of sitting all afternoon in a waiting room to find out that nothing is wrong. When that happens, you wind up feeling like a perfect dummy for not knowing your own body."

He nodded as if he'd had the experience. I wondered if he were a hypochondriac. "Let me bring you some ice at least."

"Good idea. If you look under the sink, you'll find a plastic bag."

He hurried off to the kitchen. "Found it!"

A minute later he returned with a makeshift icepack.

"Thanks. That might help."

He scrutinized me as if I might not know what to do with the ice. "I need to run a few errands. Why don't I stop by afterwards? I'll either take you to the hospital or to a restaurant."

"I told Grazia I'd have dinner with her. Aunt Maria and I don't want her to be alone."

"Then I'll invite both of you. How's that?"

I wasn't in a position to argue. "Perfect."

He glanced around the room. "Can I bring you anything else? A book or something that you want within easy reach?"

"See the magazines by the TV? Bring me those. And the TV control. Maybe I'll catch up on my soap operas."

"Which ones do you watch?"

"None so far. I have a lot of catching up to do."

I was thankful that Gerardo had rescued me, but I was happier when he left. Granted, I'd had plenty of distractions, but the accident was my own dumb fault. I should have asked Renato to review the ironwork immediately after the party. I closed my eyes and considered the logistics. I should have remembered the railing was loose, and I should have heeded the two-second warning. Had someone rigged the balcony on purpose? Unlikely. No one would know I'd be stupid enough to risk my life chasing after a cat.

To distract myself from my foot, I mentally reviewed employment options. First I allowed some self-pity. It was heart-wrenching to think I'd finished a doctoral program for nothing. To be fair, I hadn't applied outside the Boston area. Now I would need to. I'd also contact Kathy and Brett, friends from the Center, to see if they'd suffered the same fate.

I could look for translation jobs, but the most lucrative consisted of dry legal documents. They took forever to finish because they inevitably put me to sleep. Court systems sometimes needed translators, but the certification was time-consuming and costly.

The Tylenol helped me pick my best solution. I would live illegally in my toilet-free balmetto, forgo taking showers, and survive on bad red wine.

I needed better drugs. Then I needed a better plan.

Since I was still ensconced in the couch, I heard Gerardo moments before he reached the front door. "It's open."

He entered slowly. "How are you?"

"I'm not sure yet."

"Should I come back later?"

I shuffled around to a sitting position, carefully swinging my legs around to the coffee table. "No. Give me a minute. Naps make me tired, and I was too zonked out to get off the couch."

"I tried to call, but you didn't answer your cell phone."

"I didn't hear it."

He sat beside me. "Your foot doesn't look any worse than it did earlier. It doesn't look much better either."

"I haven't moved since earlier."

"Are you hungry?"

I wasn't awake enough to know. Regardless, I wanted to leave the house. "Getting there."

"Is Grazia coming with us?"

"She hasn't texted me back." Maybe she napped as deeply as I did. "Would you mind if we stopped by?"

"Not at all."

Using Gerardo as a crutch, I hobbled to the car. Either my ankle was so numb I couldn't feel the pain, or it was doing better. I was grateful either way.

He drove the short blocks to Grazia's and parked in front of a silent house. He cut the motor. "Should I try the doorbell?"

"If you don't mind."

I slouched down on the seat and closed my eyes. When I felt someone breathing in my face, I sat up so quickly that I bumped my foot. "Ow!"

"Are you always so jumpy?" Magru asked. He was dressed in raggedy work clothes, but the smell of sweat overpowered the car grease.

"Only when I'm in a bad mood, which these days is most of the time."

"No sign of your cousin. Seems like she's taking the mourning thing seriously."

"I'm sure she is."

"Sofi!" Antonella called from her front door. Her flowing, violet dress fluttered behind her as she crossed the yard and joined her son. "How have you been?"

"Holding up."

"Grazia?"

"So-so."

"I feel so bad about Ivano," she said.

"He was a politician," said Magru. "They're all the same."

"That's not fair," said his mother. "Ivano did his best."

"He was still a politician."

"Sofi twisted her ankle," Gerardo said as he joined us. "Do you have any strong bandages? Or maybe some crutches?"

While silently cursing Gerardo for broadcasting so much information, I explained the incident. Magru melted off, bored by my small problems, but Antonella listened carefully and took a close look at my right ankle. She agreed that I probably hadn't broken anything. She brought out three elastic bandages and loaned me all of them. Then Antonella and Gerardo switched to Piemontese and traded admonitions about using those crazy old balmetti.

I knew I was making progress. Despite the dialect, I caught every word.

♠ ♠ ♠

When Gerardo and I pulled up to Pizzeria La Dolce Vita, I hid a frown. The last time I'd gone out to eat with Grazia and Ivano, we'd come to the same spot.

Gerardo read my expression as a slam against pizza. "We could go somewhere else if you'd rather."

As in most of Italy, around Monteleone you could go to a pizzeria and pay a modest price, or you could go to a restaurant and spend a fortune. To me such high prices were distracting, especially since every single pizza I'd had in Italy was five times better than anything I ever cooked myself.

"Gerardo, thanks for asking, but I love pizza. It's just the darned ankle. Would you mind helping me out of the car?"

We hobbled into the bustle of a successful night at a favorite locale. Two thirds of the tables were taken, and rousing conversations ensued in all directions. The air smelled pleasantly of roasted garlic and olive oil.

I was grateful when the waiter led us to an unromantic table for four in the middle of the room. No matter how uncouth it might have been, I sat across from Gerardo and propped up my foot on the extra chair between us. Given the generous tablecloth, I hoped no one would notice. I hoped even more that none of the waiters would knock into me.

The middle-aged waiter appeared immediately. *"Vino?"* He didn't make it sound like a question.

"We'll take a litre of the house white," Gerardo said.

"I'm not thirsty," I said quickly.

Gerardo lowered his voice as if the waiter couldn't hear. "It's a much better deal."

Not really, since the only drinker would also be the only driver. "I don't think we actually need — "

The smart waiter scurried off before I could attempt to change Gerardo's mind, not that the man needed to worry.

My companion perused the menu. "This place has the best pizza in Piemonte. If you're not too hungry, go for the Margherita since it doesn't have anything extra on it. If you're indecisive, then go for the *Quattro Stagione*, because you get four different choices wrapped up in one. If you'd rather try something exotic, The Hawaiiana has ham and pineapple — "

I stopped listening. The man made a poor date. He continued explaining about the different styles of pizza as if I couldn't read the menu myself, but I'd decided on a *Quattro Formaggi*, Four-Cheese Pizza, before leaving the house.

Gerardo chose *Pizza Arrabbiata*, but Angry Pizza wasn't at all hot. The recipe called for crushed pepper leaves, but the amount of bite was disappointing if you hoped for anything vaguely Mexican—I'd already tried a few weeks earlier.

"So how long are you planning to stay in Italy?" Gerardo asked.

"School starts back in the fall," I said vaguely. I hardly wanted to confess to job failures on top of walking issues.

"No boyfriend who can't wait to see you?"

I didn't need to confess in that area either. I would have been content to have a pleasant, unmemorable dinner, but I could only hope to survive by mirroring my inquisitor. "No boyfriend at the moment. But what about you? How long have you been divorced?"

"Not that long."

"Do you like working for your father? I know about family business and all that, but wouldn't you rather branch out?"

"I've considered it, but Dad would struggle without me. He doesn't know how to modernize, so without me, the whole company would fall into the Dark Ages."

"Are you satisfied living in Monteleone?"

"People are friendly here. The pace is relaxed. I have a whole town of friends at my fingertips. If I want to talk to somebody, all I have to do is walk across the street or maybe next door."

"But are you satisfied?"

Finally I threw a question that lassoed him. Gerardo spoke loudly, but he needed to convince himself more than he needed to convince me. Point by point he lost his own argument. His eyes flickered when he talked about the summer in Paris and the month in Munich that he spent doing university internships. He wasn't a flight risk, but he'd tasted the outside world and was ready for a second course. I wondered what would happen in the long run if he didn't get it. Moving to a small town was one thing. Being stuck there was different.

"I'm sorry Grazia couldn't come with us tonight," he said during a rare pause. "I was hoping we could make her feel better."

I didn't believe him. I was certain he was happy to be alone with me. "I guess she found something to take her mind off Ivano."

"I wonder where she went," Gerardo continued. "You must have some idea."

"She might have gone to visit Kristine's family. Her best friend passed within hours of Ivano."

I should have thought of it hours earlier. A hurried trip to Aosta would have been logical, and Grazia wouldn't have bothered to tell me.

By the time I tuned back in, Gerardo was offering a diatribe on the medical profession. He continued with a diatribe about modern life. When I started yawning, I mentally kicked myself. If I ever needed a sleeping aid, I knew who to call.

"Gerardo!" shouted a woman entering the restaurant.

"Patrizia!" Gerardo shouted back.

I recognized her from band practice, but I couldn't remember if she played the flute or the clarinet. She was with two other women who took a table several feet away.

Our assailant hurried over, greeting Gerardo with an awkward hug as he tried to rise from his chair. They locked right into small talk. Where had Gerardo been hiding himself? When were they going to have the coffee date that he had promised her?

If I'd been on a normal date, I would have been annoyed at the interruption. Instead I relished the break. By wiggling her chest when she spoke, Patrizia broadcast her availability. She announced it so loudly that Gerardo might have reached for earplugs.

"And how are you doing tonight?" Patrizia asked as if she'd suddenly noticed Gerardo was not alone.

"I'm fine."

"She's hurt!" Gerardo pointed to my foot. "She might have broken her ankle!"

"That's terrible!"

"I'm sure I'll be fine," I said.

"Let me see."

"Patrizia is a nurse," Gerardo explained. "She's helped me out lots of times."

But right now I was in a restaurant where, thanks to Patrizia's loud voice, everyone present also knew I needed help. I was surprised a doctor didn't emerge from the corner of the room, determined to operate, perhaps in the kitchen.

"I'm sure by tomorrow—"

"Nonsense!"

By then a waiter had procured an extra chair for Patrizia. She immediately pulled readers from her purse and examined my foot by first observing, then touching, then poking, then prodding.

"How much does that hurt?"

"Some," I said as an understatement. My ankle hurt generally, not because she was attacking it.

Then she wrapped both hands around my ankle. Despite the fact that I felt like a display item in a clothing store, her touch comforted me.

"Patrizia has been a nurse for over twenty years," Gerardo told me confidently.

"Shh!" Patrizia laughed. "People will think I've already reached forty!"

I was sure she was past forty-five, but in Piemonte, people frequently joked about their age. Since the inhabitants had known each other since birth, they couldn't hide their years, let alone anything else.

Patrizia patted my leg softly. "I don't think you broke anything."

"Thanks. That's what I had concluded myself, but I wasn't sure."

"Stay off your foot for the next three days and keep icing it. If you can't put weight on it then, go straight to the hospital."

"I will."

"Patrizia!" called one of her friends.

She stood. "I better order before my friends order without me." She placed her hand on my shoulder as if she owned me. "I hear you have a balmetto for sale. Have you decided on a price?"

The town was full of balmetto vultures. How had my parents never noticed this? Maybe their Italian wasn't as strong as I had assumed. "I haven't decided to sell."

"She will," Gerardo said.

"When you do, let me know, okay? Gerardo has my email and telephone number."

"Thanks. I'll remember that." I ordered myself to forget as quickly as possible. I was thankful her friends had called her away.

"What shall we drink to?" Gerardo asked as he raised his glass.

Much more weakly, I raised my own. "Let's drink to Grazia."

"*Salute!* It must be rough for her to lose two people at the same time. Last spring two of my classmates died. One had a tumor. The other had a heart attack. They were in their mid-thirties! There's a message in that."

"Which is?"

"I always conclude that I should take more time off, but instead I go right back to work."

The waiter brought steaming pizzas.

"Grazia thought she had her life all worked out," I said as I wafted the smell of roasted olive oil towards my nose. "Look what happened."

"My poor cousin. She's had a tough time all right." But instead of sincerely commiserating, Gerardo filled his mouth with melted cheese. I was glad Grazia wasn't around to see him.

♠ ♦ ♠

By the time Gerardo brought me home, my car was in the driveway. This was not magic. I'd called Renato in the afternoon and asked if he and Laura could retrieve it for me.

Gerardo didn't seem to notice. He was too bent on helping me to my front door. "I can come in if you want."

"I'm fine, really." I really couldn't stand another minute.

"I can set everything within reach."

"Thanks to all you did this afternoon, I'm set. Really." I drooped my shoulders as if I were so tired I could hardly fish my keys from my purse.

"I could make sure that—"

"Thank you. I mean it. And for the lovely evening. But I'm fine."

He put his arm on the doorway as if determined to keep me from walking through it. "You're in no shape to cook. You'll be hungry again tomorrow, so how about if we—"

Oh, no. Not another "date" with someone who talked as much as he did. Besides, I was hoping for a better invitation, namely one from Carmela.

"Gerardo, I'm so exhausted that I can't possibly think about tomorrow. Again, I thank you, but I need to rest." I handed him the keys so that he could make a chivalrous show of opening the door for me. Before he could do anything else, I grabbed them back again. I hobbled through the door—I would have gladly crawled, if necessary—and locked the door behind me.

As soon as I sank into my couch, however, I realized I was much too awake to relax. I turned on the TV, but every channel was broadcasting boring news reports. I'd had more than enough information for one evening, so I switched off the TV and picked up my cell. I needed to text Renato a "thank you" for rescuing the car.

Then I noticed that Cenzo had left three messages.

Instead of wasting time with texts, I called his number. "Still working?"

"Why didn't you answer earlier?" he asked angrily. "You left a strange message about being stuck at your balmetto."

His irritation was a bit sweet. At least he'd paid attention. "I probably slept through your calls."

"In the middle of the afternoon? What's wrong with you?"

I smiled at his terrible bedside manners. The world was lucky he hadn't chosen medicine. "I might have taken too many painkillers. But that was only because my ankle turned into a melon."

"A melon!"

I briefly explained my fall.

"How's your ankle now?"

"Big and ugly. I think it's turning purple. Maybe it will become an eggplant."

197

"You'll be glad to know I've had First Aid classes. I have a certificate."

I could have taken his comment as simple information, but instead I read the flirt right into it. "Does that mean you're willing to offer your services?"

"Thank goodness. For a moment I thought I would have to invite myself over for no reason at all. See you in a few."

"Good job, Sofi," I said out loud. Mentally I also patted myself on the back. I would have bet my balmetto that a late-night tête-à-tête with a law officer would be a lot more fun than watching the news.

Chapter Twenty

By the time I hobbled to the kitchen and propped my ankle up on an extra chair, Cenzo was knocking at the backdoor.

"Hello?"

"Come in," I called out as loudly as I could.

Cenzo strode through the house. By his grimace, I could tell my ankle was worse than he anticipated. He pulled up a chair and gently touched the discolored skin.

"Hurt?"

"A little." By now I couldn't feel the pain, but I could see it.

"Do you want my professional opinion?"

"Any old opinion will do."

He continued fingering my ankle, but I assumed he was trying to comfort me rather than perform a full investigation. "It's a bad sprain."

"That's what Patrizia said."

"The nurse? Ha. That busybody loves nothing more than an injury as long as it's not hers. You went to the hospital?"

"I ran into her when I went out to dinner with Gerardo."

Cenzo tried hard not to smirk. "Have fun?"

I pointed to my leaky faucet. "That kitchen sink has more charm than Gerardo."

He laughed, but he might have been trying to humor me. "Gerardo did manage to get married. Then again, Margarita was anxious to leave her parents' house."

D.R. Ransdell

Cenzo glanced around. Since I didn't cook, the counter was spotless, and all the dishes were clean. "Mind if I make coffee?" I started to rise, but he shooed me back down. "Let me."

I pointed to the cabinet by the sink, where I kept coffee and sugar. The espresso maker was on the drying rack, where I had set it hours before.

"Want some?"

"No thanks. I'm drowning my pain in Amaretto." I filled another demitasse. After all, I wasn't driving anywhere.

I watched as Cenzo carefully filled the espresso maker. Then I waited for him to sit down and give me his full attention. "I learned something interesting. Ivano and Gerardo and Margarita went on a trip together. Something about a community exchange."

"Right. I forgot about that. My son wanted to go, but his mother vetoed it."

"Evidently Ivano and Margarita spent quality time together."

Cenzo fiddled with the burner. "Margarita got around. She didn't waste too much time with Gerardo."

"You're not surprised?"

He turned up the flame. "I know Gerardo."

I wished I hadn't spent the last two hours learning more about him. "Gerardo is like a student who doesn't do any work yet complains when the teacher doesn't compliment him."

"In other words, he gripes about working for his dad even though he continues to do so."

"Exactly."

Cenzo shrugged. "A lot of people fall into the family business. They can't seem to help themselves." He went to the stove to wait for the Bialetti to start gurgling.

I liked the intimacy of watching him work in the kitchen. I also imagined feeling his butt through the tight jeans. "Your father was a law officer?"

"A farmer. Something must have gone wrong with me because farming never crossed my mind."

"Your father didn't push you to emulate him?"

"He could tell I didn't have a green thumb. When I was a kid, my mother would put plants in my room, and they'd die straight away. I don't know what it was. Maybe I didn't talk to them enough."

"I had the opposite problem. My parents, who were high school teachers, advised me not to go into teaching."

"Why not?"

"Hard work, low pay. Working with adults or college students is different. Instead of worrying about discipline, you worry about funding." I explained my current dilemma.

"You could stay in Monteleone," Cenzo suggested.

"I wrote some language schools near here, but most places choose their candidates ahead of time. They go through the motions of having interviews, and then they hire their friends."

Cenzo poured himself a coffee. "*Tutto il mondo è paese*. The world is all the same."

"Right. It's full of opportunists." I felt like one myself, but in the best possible way. Here I had an attractive man at my house late at night. He'd come over to make himself useful, and thanks to the coffee he wouldn't be falling asleep any time soon. "Do you have any news for me?"

Cenzo downed his coffee in one gulp. "Ivano's banking records are in order. I didn't find any suspicious transactions."

Five points for Ivano, I thought. He needed them.

"I found out who owns the balmetto next to yours. Does the name Quacchia mean anything to you?"

I shook my head. "It sounds like a duck."

"Yes, I suppose it does! Sofi, you always have a cheerful way of looking at things. Gerardo's mother is a Quacchia, and she's the official owner."

"Excuse me?"

"Gerardo's mother's family owns the balmetto next to yours. They're probably hoping to buy you out so they can expand."

I hit the table with my fist. "What? I spend two hours with Gerardo, and he doesn't mention his mother's balmetto!"

Cenzo poured himself another coffee. "I've never seen Gerardo at that balmetto or any other one."

"What else can you tell me?"

"The property was probably built over a hundred years ago by the Quacchia family. You might even be distant cousins."

"Grazia would have known this, of course. And Renato. But why would Gerardo's family want to expand if they don't use what they have now?"

"The locals are property owners. They love owning things even if they don't use them."

"Gerardo wasn't taking me out to dinner. He was snooping."

"I hope he didn't expect you to pay half."

"I offered, but he whipped out his credit card before I could reach my purse."

"He can afford a couple of pizzas! But his dad has probably lusted over your balmetto for years. Maybe Ivano was in on it."

"Ivano would not have tried to trick me!"

"Not trick you, maybe. He may have been hoping to negotiate a price."

I didn't want to believe it. I wouldn't, not without proof.

"Maybe he wanted to do Baruzzo a favor or return one," Cenzo continued.

I didn't like that idea any better, but it made more sense. As mayor, Ivano had been constantly working angles and building goodwill. It was part of a game that he enjoyed playing. He always made it look easy. He made every move seem like a win-win situation.

"I'm confused. If Ivano wanted me to sell the stupid thing, why let me work on it all summer?"

"Boh. I can't make the connections, but Gerardo takes you out, and his mother owns the property next to yours. I don't like it. Here's something else no one explained to you: If somebody owns property but doesn't claim it for twenty years, other people, or the state, can claim it instead. When is the last time your parents visited Italy?"

"Maybe seventeen years ago. Maybe nineteen. I don't remember exactly."

"Renato and Grazia may have been hoping to claim the balmetto and sell it legally."

I wanted to stand up so that I could kick something. Instead the best I could do was wave my arms from my seat. *"Porca miseria!* All this time, my own relatives have been waiting for the right moment to cheat me!"

"It's possible."

I hit the table again. "This is unbelievable."

"There's more. I suspect Gerardo locked you in your balmetto the other night."

"Gerardo? How would he have found me?"

"You parked in the piazza, right? Gerardo would have made an educated guess."

"Lots of cars were parked there. "

Cenzo scrunched up his lips as a doctor concealing bad news, but I was starting to catch on. Gerardo had been following me. Good old Grazia might have been helping him.

I was ready to kill both of them. But first, I poured myself more Amaretto. "Guess what Gerardo asked me about. How much I make an hour. How much I pay for healthcare. What an idiot I was!"

Cenzo tapped the table with his little coffee spoon. "Not at all."

"I should have seen right through that bozo!"

"We might be wrong about Gerardo."

"Wrong how? You don't think he would commit a crime of passion?"

"I'm not sure he's ambitious enough. If he wanted revenge for being cuckolded, he'd have to kill half the males in Monteleone."

I gasped. "You're expecting more murders!?"

Cenzo shook his head. "No, no. Margarita had several lovers that even I knew about. I sense that something bigger is at stake. Something more dramatic."

Knowing your lover was sleeping with someone else seemed dramatic to me, but maybe the Monteleonesi were used to it. "You don't have anything concrete, do you?"

"No. What I don't understand is the balcony. Surely the crew who fixed the wall noticed the railing was a hazard."

"Renato should have noticed. Ironwork is his business." Silly me. I had trusted Renato implicitly. And Ivano. And Grazia.

"You hired Jacobo and his brother, right?" Cenzo asked.

"On Renato's recommendation. They were at the party."

"Usually that pair does good work, but Baruzzo might have paid them off."

"You think the balcony was rigged?"

"Don't you?"

I felt as naïve as a child eyeing lollipops while the nurse prepares a shot. I'd babied my ankle all afternoon thinking I'd had a simple accident, but the balcony shouldn't have given way, not that quickly.

"Cenzo, the balcony is so low that a fall wouldn't have killed me. So why bother?"

"Maybe Gerardo is hoping you'll get fed up with the damned place. Figure it's bad luck. Make a quick profit and go away."

"He assumed an American wouldn't care about an old Italian tradition."

"Exactly."

I could think of other traditions I approved of as well. And after such a bad day, I deserved to treat myself.

Cenzo smiled as if trying to cheer me up. "What are you thinking?"

I was thinking Cenzo was supposed to be the authority figure. I was thinking it was time to have fun. Above all, I was thinking that I hadn't shaved my legs for a week. Maybe longer. "I've done enough thinking for one day."

"Shall I leave?"

"I have a much better idea."

"Oh?"

"You can help me upstairs."

Cenzo raised his eyebrows. Then he smiled. Then the smile turned into a grin. He immediately rose from his chair.

I silently applauded. It had taken a month, but I was finally thinking as a local.

Chapter Twenty-One

I awoke well after dawn, more aware of him than of myself. As I lay across his chest, I felt the rhythm of his heartbeat. I wondered what was supposed to happen next.

"I was snoring?" he asked suddenly.

"Not that I know of."

"But you couldn't sleep."

I sat up, drawing the sheet around me. "I slept most of the night. Then my ankle started throbbing again."

His eyes bored into me. "I hope I did all right."

I grinned. "Yes."

"When your wife leaves you, you always wonder."

I ran my finger down his cheek. "Even when you know she had ulterior motives?"

"Guys assume every problem stems from inadequacy in bed."

"You're kidding, right?"

"Guys never kid about feeling inadequate."

I responded by hugging him tightly and settling back onto his chest. The lovemaking had been fine. Rushed, perhaps. A bit awkward given my leg. But after a summer of abstinence? It was great. I didn't have to admit how low my standards were.

"Are you sure—" he started to ask.

"Shhh. Let me lie here and feel you."

"My ex-wife—"

"I don't care. Keep her out of the bedroom."

He took the hint, hugging me gently for sweet long minutes.

Then he shifted so that he could face me. "Never mind about me. It's my sons who are stranded. That's something I can't forgive myself for. They won't forgive me either."

I stroked his hair. I didn't have any experience with having children or feeling responsible about them, so for once I was wise enough not to say anything.

"Do you realize that—"

The phone started ringing. I had no intention of answering, but when the message machine kicked on, I automatically strained to identify the speaker.

"You don't know me, but I'm Margarita Giraudo. You might have heard my name as Margarita Baruzzo. Never mind. I hear you have a balmetto for sale. I'll be glad to help you with that. And since I'm a tax accessor, I can help you with the necessary paperwork. As an American, you'll never be able to wade through the paperwork! I can barely manage, and it's my profession! Give me a call as soon as you can, and we can get started."

Margarita left her number. She might have divorced Gerardo, but they still had a suspiciously close connection. I was surprised it took her a whole twelve hours to call.

Cenzo sat up. "Interesting. I didn't remember that she was a tax accessor. She would have worked with Ivano."

I lightly punched his side. "You didn't sleep with me for sex. It was for my balmetto. I know it!"

"I already have a balmetto that I don't use."

I tapped his forehead with my finger. "But you need five or six to be like all the other villagers. Tell me the truth!"

He pulled me to his side. "I want your balmetto! It's your only asset!"

"Don't think you'll get it by marrying me!" As soon as I heard my words, I wanted to kick myself. We'd spent all of one night together! It didn't necessarily mean anything, and I didn't want Cenzo to suspect I might think otherwise.

Before I could get worked up with my analysis, the phone rang again.

"It is always like this around here?" Cenzo asked.

I put the sheet over my head, but I kept listening.

"Sofi, Sofi, wake up!" This was the first time Aunt Maria had ever sounded disoriented. "Call me right away. Grazia didn't come home last night! She's disappeared!"

Slowly I pulled back the sheet as Cenzo's eyes met mine. "You know what this means, don't you?" I asked.

"We have to get out of bed."

"I was afraid you were going to say that." I flexed my ankle. Some of the swelling had gone down, but bending it was painful.

Cenzo checked under the chair for his briefs. "Aunt Maria wouldn't panic for no reason, would she?"

I swung my legs around to the side of the bed. "She didn't panic when you threw her daughter in jail."

"How would she know Grazia hadn't gone home?"

I shook wrinkles out of the sleeveless shirt that had landed in a heap on the floor. "She would have stopped by the house."

"It's barely nine-thirty. Grazia might still be in bed."

"Aunt Maria has a key. She would have gone inside."

"Do you know anyone Grazia might have spent the night with?"

"Boh." An overnight visit to grieving relatives in Courmayeur no longer fit with the image of a cousin who probably wanted to trick me out of my property.

"Do you think we should be concerned?" Cenzo asked.

"By now I have no idea what to think."

I watched as he slid into his jeans, thinking it was a shame to watch his body disappear into clothes.

He caught me when he reeled around. "I hope you're admiring rather than criticizing."

"I liked last night." It was an understatement, but I didn't want him to get cocky.

He stopped mid-zipper. "I did too, but I hadn't planned for it. If your foot hadn't been sore, I wouldn't have had an excuse to get into your bedroom without a fight."

I raised an eyebrow. "Who says it would have been a fight?"

He kissed the top of my head. "How is your foot?"

"Better."

"Do you want to see a doctor?"

"One crisis at a time. Let's go to Aunt Maria's. At the very least, we can calm her down."

"Do you think we should arrive together?"

"Worried about your reputation?"

He smiled until his dimples twinkled. "According to my reputation, I'm difficult and cranky. Worried about yours?"

"I'm an American. I can get away with anything."

Even though I could have managed on my own, I let him carry me downstairs.

Aunt Maria opened the door as I reached for the buzzer. She didn't seem surprised that Cenzo and I were together. "Something terrible has happened!"

Usually she noticed a crooked collar from across the room, but today she ushered us into the living room without realizing that Cenzo assisted me over to the sofa.

"Did you call the hospital?" I asked.

"Ivrea and Courmayeur. Neither admitted a Grazia. She must have run off the road somewhere in between! She could be lying in a ravine!"

Aunt Maria gestured for us to sit but continued pacing until Cenzo led her to the easy chair and sat her down. He sat nearby. "I know you're upset, but you need to tell me what you know."

"Last night I tried to call, but Grazia didn't answer. I thought she might be taking a shower, so I waited and called again later. I left a message for her to please call me, but I was so tired that I fell asleep."

"Maybe she tried to call during the night but didn't leave a message?" I suggested.

"I would have heard the ring."

Cenzo glanced towards the backdoor. "You never stepped outside, not even for a breath of air?"

"Too many mosquitoes."

"No messages this morning either?"

"That's the whole problem! She always calls between nine and nine-fifteen. Today she didn't call at all. As soon as I dressed, I went to her house. The shutters were never closed. That's a sure sign she didn't spend the night in her own bed!"

"Who are her close girlfriends?" Cenzo asked. "She might have overdone it on the wine and not wanted to drive home."

A tuft of hair had escaped from Aunt Maria's bun and fallen into her face, but she didn't notice. "Grazia would not have done that!"

Cenzo tapped his fingertips together. "When people are under a lot of stress, they sometimes act out of character."

"She's hurt! She might be dead!"

No. She was up to something. I could feel it.

Cenzo patted her hand. "Grazia probably arrived home late and left early this morning.

Aunt Maria blew into a wet handkerchief. "My poor daughter is not the kind to get up and go somewhere in the morning. She always calls me between nine and nine-fifteen. She always does. Sofi, can't you think where she might be?"

"Do any of her friends like to camp?"

"She's never camped in her whole life."

No, of course not. She might have ruined her shoes.

Cenzo stood, and I copied him. "Maria, we all know your daughter is intelligent. I'm sure there's an easy explanation, but we haven't been able to follow her thinking. For now I must return to the office."

Aunt Maria stood, blocking our path. "There's nothing you can do?"

"I can find out if her car has been in an accident. That's the place to start."

"Wait a moment." Aunt Maria marched down the hall and disappeared into a back room.

"What do you think?" Cenzo whispered.

I shrugged. "I tried to call Grazia myself yesterday, but she never answered. What's the usual reasoning in cases like this? I'm sure people disappear from time to time."

"In Torino, they do. In Monteleone, this would be a first."

Aunt Maria emerged from the hall with a blank piece of paper and a pencil. "Teresa has a *baita*. Maybe Grazia headed there."

Cenzo snapped his fingers. "A perfect place to get away, plus there's no phone service. Where's it at?"

"Along the road to Biò. I'll draw you a map."

"What's a *baita*?" I asked.

"A summer house," Cenzo replied. "In the mountains."

D.R. Ransdell

A perfect place indeed. Especially for someone who didn't like to camp. I watched with full attention while Aunt Maria scrawled us a map.

♠ ♥ ♠

We buzzed into Cenzo's parking lot as a tall man carefully extricated himself from a Panda. Cenzo pulled alongside. "Let me introduce you to Stefano."

As soon as we got out of the car, the two men embraced, heartily slapping one another on the back.

"I'm glad your mother is better," Cenzo said.

The man was younger than Cenzo but towered above him. "We had a big scare, but she has the constitution of an ox." He held out his hand. "You're Grazia's cousin?"

I nodded. "Sofi Francese."

"Stefano Rossi." He had a hearty grasp and a kind, tanned face. "Pleased to meet you. I'm sorry to hear about Ivano. I really liked him."

"We have a new problem," said Cenzo. "Grazia appears to be missing."

Stefano raised his eyebrows.

"Her mother has begged us to search for her," Cenzo said.

Stefano locked his car with a click of the remote. "It's hard to find people who don't want to be found."

Cenzo nodded. "It's harder to refuse the requests of little old ladies."

"When did you become such a softie?" Stefano pretended to give me the once over. "Oh. Now I get it. You're trying to impress the new girl in town. But she can barely walk. What did you do, take her out dancing and stomp all over her feet?"

Both men laughed. I appreciated their easy solidarity.

"Whenever I'm bored, I make it a point to fall off a balcony," I said.

"Nice," Stefano said. "That way you always need to be rescued!"

I liked Stefano immediately. Within two minutes he'd put me at ease, and he had the same effect on my companion.

"Get this," Cenzo said. "Baruzzo's wife owns the balmetto next to Sofi's."

"Baruzzo's an old buzzard. Do you know how many balmetti his family owns? At least five. What are the rest of us supposed to do? My brother's been trying to buy one for years, but they never come up for sale."

"I know of one that might," I said. "But who needs multiple party houses? You can only celebrate in one place at a time."

"How do you know Baruzzo has five balmetti?" asked Cenzo.

"I get all my information from Pasquale Minaccio."

I nodded. "That name sounds familiar."

"He's the geezer who owns the balmetto at the end of the first row. He knows everything."

"He badgered me into trying his wine the other day," I said. "I made the mistake of stopping to talk to him."

"How was the wine?" asked Stefano.

"Awful."

"Don't listen to her," Cenzo said. "She has no taste. Would Pasquale help us with some information?"

"Sure," Stefano said. "As long as you pretend to enjoy his wine."

I'd been pretending to enjoy wine all summer. For Ivano's sake, one more glass couldn't hurt.

Chapter Twenty-Two

I braced myself as Cenzo lunged into another hairpin turn. "You say people come up here for fun?" I kept my eyes glued to the road, which was his remedy against carsickness.

Cenzo took another sharp curve as if he relished such challenges. "Piemontesi go to the mountains the way Romans go to the beach."

"They come up here to stay in huts?"

"More like small houses."

"So they're not roughing it?"

"They're getting away. After all, this region is the *'pie di monte,'* the foot of the mountain. People naturally develop an affinity for heights."

I didn't share the feeling myself. I felt an affinity for parks, for restaurants, and for art museums, things that were tamer and more urban. I wasn't impressed that the Alps were only a short drive away. Boh! Perhaps I wasn't Piemontese after all.

We continued the vertical climb, ascending via a series of sharp curves. I was grateful I wasn't driving. The two-lane road was so narrow that anytime we came across another car, we had to negotiate who would go first.

When Cenzo suddenly hit the brakes, I slammed my hands across the dash.

"Afraid of heights?"

"I prefer them from an airplane."

"When we went up to Aosta the other day, I thought it was the company you were allergic to."

"You were doing the tough guy act. It doesn't suit you."

He stepped on his brakes to give right-of-way to a cyclist. "I have to wear different hats for different situations. In your case, I had to rule you out."

"You thought I might have killed Ivano."

"It crossed my mind."

"Then why would I have reported it?"

Cenzo honked at a dog, which scurried into a patch of grass beyond the road. "Maybe you didn't have a way to get rid of the body. Maybe you assumed I'd think you were too naïve to be involved. I told you already. People do all kinds of things that you'd never expect."

"When did you rule me out?"

"What makes you think I have?" He put his hand around my kneecap and squeezed hard enough to make me squirm.

"Ow!"

"Sorry," he grinned.

"So I've been seducing you to take your mind off the murder."

"Exactly. No wonder I can't concentrate."

I pointed to the road ahead. "Don't you dare flirt with me on a dangerous mountain road. Wait until we get to Monteleone."

He reached for my kneecap, but I shifted my legs out of his grasp. "If you say so."

Cenzo slowed a tiny bit but stopped along an overhang where we could park and appreciate the view. He tried to hug me, but I wrestled away. I took my cell phone and hobbled the three steps to the guardrail.

The valley lay beneath us like a scenic picture puzzle. Rooftops huddled in lush greens twinkled as they caught the sun. Squares of green gave way to sets of dark yellow fields. Birds chirped so loudly they drowned out traffic.

Monteleone skirted the far edge of the valley, its church steeple a gray pinhead.

I took a series of shots so that I could remember the whole panoramic view.

"Take your picture?" Cenzo asked.

"Please." I posed against the rail. "Kathy said that if I sent another balmetto picture, she wouldn't open the attachment."

"You haven't had much time for tourism."

I turned back towards the valley. "Not half as much as I expected. I don't mind about that because I was so busy the whole time, but this is beautiful."

"From the bottom, all you can see are the firs. From the top, you see everything, or you think you do. That's why people like to come here. By the time they climb this high, they've set aside their troubles long enough to feel peace."

It wasn't working. No matter how idyllic the scene below, I was only viewing the surface. I didn't have enough facts to guess at the missing pieces. I couldn't be at rest until I understood more about Ivano.

♠ ♠ ♠

We continued around a few more curves until part of the road forked off onto a smaller path. We followed along until we reached a wooden gate secured with a padlock. Cenzo put the car in neutral and fished a set of keys from the glove compartment. After he exited the car and unchained the fence, he drove us past it and chained it back up again.

"Private property?"

"Communal. A dozen or so people have access."

"You have property up here?"

"Stefano does. A few years back he gave me a copy of his key."

I indicated the trees on either side of the road. "What good is a key to the forest?"

"Have you ever heard of truffles?"

"Vaguely," I lied. Chocolate?

"They're a kind of fungus. They're also a prized delicacy in any local kitchen. A few times during the summer, Stefano and I come up to hunt for them ourselves."

"You come all the way up here for mushrooms?"

Cenzo frowned. "If you'd ever had proper truffles in your pasta, you'd know why they're precious."

I pretended to agree.

We continued another few miles until the road gave way to grass. Then we bumped along until we came upon a small, brick mountain house. The construction looked recent.

Cenzo consulted Aunt Maria's hand-drawn map. "This should be it."

The structure presided over a wide piece of land surrounded by trees. The soft, wild grass was laced with wildflowers in bright yellows and purples. Cenzo walked me through them carefully until we reached the front door.

"Hello? Hello?" He knocked several times on the wood.

Nobody answered. We circled the hut, Cenzo supporting me as we went around. We peered through the bare windows into two bedrooms with double beds and a living room/kitchen with a few chairs and little else. There was no hint of recent visitors.

Cenzo and I settled down among the flowers where we could view the fields below.

"We could bust into the house, but I don't see much point to it," Cenzo said. "No one's been here for days."

"I can see why Aunt Maria wanted us to check," I said. "If Grazia wanted to get away from everybody, this would have been the place for it."

Cenzo plucked a yellow flower and stuffed the stem into the top of my blouse. "Absolutely. You get up here, and you're completely alone."

As soon as he started kissing me, we lay back on the grass. He fingered my shoulders while sunlight danced on my face. "What do you think?"

"I'm glad we didn't make the trip all the way up here for nothing."

"Funny," he said, kissing my cheek. "I was thinking the same thing."

For the first time, I made love in nature. I opened myself up not only to Cenzo, but to the whole sky.

I was still breathing heavily as we bumped over the grassy driveway and caught the road that led back to town. "It's a good thing your work schedule is flexible."

Cenzo readjusted the rearview mirror. "Don't you know? That's why I chose this profession in the first place. Long lunches followed by long drives to nowhere."

I rolled down my window to smell the pines. Saplings rose on either side of us. They were surrounded by tall trees that stretched out of sight. It was a beautiful view. Maybe a mountain house was a good idea after all. Back home I never found an easy way to get away. "How did you explain your work schedule to your wife?"

"My ex-wife. I don't remember. We didn't talk much, and when we did, she did most of the talking." He patted my leg. "If I'm not careful, you'll get the wrong idea. The truth is that I never cheated on Sarah although I might have stayed saner that way. Ironically, Sarah claimed that I was the one sleeping around."

"Convenient story."

"Not really. When no one seemed impressed, she claimed I'd been slapping her."

I could imagine someone exaggerating, but making up stories wholesale was alarming. "Was she really that angry?"

Cenzo slowed for a pothole. "She didn't want people to think she was a horrible mother for breaking up a family, so she had to justify herself."

"She went back to England. Why would she care what anybody in Monteleone thought?"

His face clouded over. "She didn't move right away. She tortured me by walking out without warning and living in Quassolo for a few weeks. When she left for London earlier this year, she took the kids along. No warning for that either. My sons! Can you imagine how that felt?"

I couldn't. My only friends with children were happy enough in their marriages.

"Deandre is fifteen. Kenzie is twelve. That's a terrible age for your parents to split up, don't you think?"

I thought no time was optimal, but I didn't say so. Instead I waited for the air to clear. "You talk to them, right?"

"Only when I'm not working and their mother isn't home. You can guess how often that is. Once they go back to school, we'll connect more easily. She won't be able to keep track of their schedules. Of course, neither will I."

Cenzo saw the next pothole too late, and we bounced uncomfortably. He didn't slow down until we reached the edge of the private road. There Cenzo repeated the rigmarole of unlocking the gate, driving through, and locking it behind us. A car zoomed past, the first we'd seen since leaving the main road an hour earlier. Two cargo trucks followed behind. Then we had the road to ourselves.

"What makes me angry about Sarah is that I never saw the breakup coming," Cenzo said as we continued our descent. "I never realized that she was so unhappy. Now I question whether I knew her."

"If it's any consolation, I thought Grazia loved Ivano. Now I'm not sure." For weeks I'd thought I was in the presence of happy newlyweds. Ivano had doted on his bride, and from Grazia's actions, I assumed she'd doted on him as well. Evidently, Ivano and I had both been deceived.

"Maybe Grazia didn't know how she felt herself."

He was trying to be kind, but the truth smashed my head like a hammer. I was pretty sure Grazia always knew exactly how she felt.

As we rounded another curve, Cenzo's cell phone started ringing. While he drove one-handed, Cenzo fumbled with the device, tiny in his hands.

"Want me to do that?"

"I've got it, I've got it. Yes?"

"Cenzo! I need you to come right now!" The woman was shouting so loudly I would have heard her in the next car, one going in the opposite direction.

"Who is this?"

"It's Daniella Labrese! I'm at town hall. They came to threaten me! How fast can you get here?"

To my chagrin, Cenzo accelerated. "We'll see."

Chapter Twenty-Three

Cenzo ran up the town hall steps while I toiled behind him. Daniella was sitting in Pia's office crying, and Pia was handing her tissues. I had met Daniella on several occasions. She was a happy-go-lucky housewife who was glad to help out as long as community projects didn't intrude too much on family time. She was a decade older than I, a little plumper, and, usually, a whole lot more cheerful.

As soon as she saw us, Daniella ran to hug Cenzo. "It was horrible!"

"Who threatened you?"

"They were from the electric company," said Pia. "I think one was the owner. There were four of them!"

"How did they threaten you?"

"They said they'd ruin the community if I didn't sign over permission for the electrical plant!" Daniella cried. "They said it was all set up, and Ivano had already received the paperwork and promised to sign. They brought this stack of papers and kept telling me the deal was already agreed upon. I didn't know what to do!"

"Did you sign anything?" Cenzo asked.

"She did not," Pia said proudly, her arms crossed over her chest. "I kicked them out. Then we called you."

"We might have overlooked a pending contract," I said. "Should I take another look at Ivano's desk?"

Cenzo nodded. "You might as well."

To my surprise, Pia handed over the keys without protesting.

Ivano's office was even mustier than when we'd come before. I opened the shutters and the windows. My ankle was too sore for me to stumble around mindlessly, so I sat at Ivano's desk and tried to channel his thought pattern. Where would he have stashed the most important documents? Then I tried to channel Cenzo. He'd looked through the desk, so what would he have missed?

I didn't believe that Ivano had agreed to any contracts, but he might have taken notes or drawn up a compromise. I took the first set of folders from the drawer and opened the top one. Wedding photos. A mess of four by sixes and five by sevens. Several depicted Grazia by herself. I flipped those right over. Then I reached shots of the couple.

It hurt to see Ivano's bright face. At least he'd enjoyed his last year on earth. That was the only consolation I could think of, and it didn't help me enough to prevent me from tearing up. Who could have been so mad at him? Business deals were made and broken all the time. How could they have been worth a life?

I started crying before I reached the end of the photos. Behind them was a receipt for the hall, which had been loaned to Ivano for a slight charge. A receipt for the photographer. A copy of the wedding invitation. A list of guests, with names checked or crossed off, no doubt the list of people who had promised to come or sent regrets. I started counting the guests. I'd reached two hundred and sixty when I turned over the page.

Then I lost count. The next sheet had a list of expenses for the caterers and so forth. Behind it was a handwritten spreadsheet with sets of numbers in two columns. The spindly handwriting was neither Ivano's nor Grazia's, but the sets were in groups of fives, just like the numbers Ivano had recorded on the tape.

"Ready to go?" Cenzo hollered as he approached the room.

Instinctively I snapped the folder shut.

"We have a visit to pay," Cenzo said. "Now."

I tapped the folder. "Wedding photos. Might as well take these to Grazia, don't you think?"

"Might as well. Come on."

I hugged the folder to my chest. I didn't like the possible implications. Maybe Ivano was involved in something I didn't want anyone else to know about. The last thing he needed to pay for posthumously were unimportant mistakes. As much as I'd enjoyed my previous night with Cenzo, I wasn't willing to share my findings with him, at least not yet.

Cenzo zipped us through Monteleone so quickly we might have been in a space shuttle.

"Fill me in?" I asked.

He headed northwest towards Lungofiume. "Dario Sanalto manages the electric plant for Cafreddo and San Stefano. He has Daniella so scared she's about to have a heart attack. Then we'd have no mayor at all."

"Dario sounds like a winner."

"Guess who sent them to the office? Renato."

"My cousin?" I might have a heart attack too.

"He stands to profit. If Sanalto puts in a big electric plant, he'll need specialized ironwork. He's a shrewd one. Both of your cousins are shrewd, as it turns out. I'm glad neither had siblings."

Renato. He always pretended that he had quite a lot of work, but he never discussed his exact income. The store had a steady stream of customers, but half of them came to buy a bag of nails for a couple of euros.

"Nice guy, huh?" Cenzo asked.

"Wonderful."

"Renato called this morning and asked her to meet with a couple of so-called businessmen who might offer beneficial developments for the community. Then four men stormed her office. She would have called her husband, but he works in Torino."

We screeched to a halt outside a white one-story building at the bottom of a hill. The few windows were small and dark. Near the entrance, a billboard announced the electrical company in plain black letters.

"Now what?" I asked.

"I'm not sure yet." He slammed the car door.

I limped inside behind him. The office was a wide room with bright neon lighting. Several empty desks crowded either wall. A man I'd never met sat behind the biggest desk. His crewcut made his big ears stand out like an advertisement for hearing aids. His T-shirt touted Benetton.

Although he sat before a laptop, the man was not working. He was chatting with three men who sat in a ring around him. I'd met the trio at Ivano's funeral: Daniele, Rinaldo, and Emilio. The later looked sheepish. I couldn't read the expressions of the others.

They all stood as Cenzo and I approached.

"If it isn't the industrious police captain," Dario said. "Run out of speeders to stop today?" He turned to me. "And you must be the famous Sofi Francese." The man wrung my hand until I snatched it away. "Dario Sanalto. At your service. So to speak."

"How dare you threaten Daniella?" Cenzo asked.

"We did not threaten her," Dario said. "We stated facts. She chose to be intimidated."

"You stated that Monteleone would wither and die within a year unless she signed. You call that a fact?"

"I'm free to state my opinion. Ivano promised us a contract. Daniella is bound to honor that."

"No, she's not," Cenzo said. "Ready to call in Santini?"

"There's no need for a lawyer," Dario laughed. "It's a business deal."

"There was no deal," I said. "Ivano never promised you he'd sign the contract."

"Ha! And you would know?"

"He wasn't interested in your plan to destroy the riverfront," I said, raising my voice.

Dario winked. "You knew him well, you say? Another lover?"

"That's enough," Cenzo said in a low growl.

"Touchy, touchy." He looked between us. "Ah. So the American has the mayor first and now you. She fits right into the community. But if she really knew Ivano, she would know how crooked he was."

Cenzo punched his fist into his hand.

"That's enough!" I shouted.

Cenzo brushed me in back of him and stepped closer to Dario.

"As to Daniella, she's weak-willed." Dario held up a finger. "One more trip to the office, maybe two, and she'll bowl right over."

Cenzo took one step to reach Dario and punched his jaw so hard the man reeled back. He staggered before catching his balance. "Hey!"

"Go to the mayor's office again, and I'll hit you where it counts." Cenzo addressed the others. "He offended my girlfriend. Remember that."

The others were too startled to move. I could barely move myself, but after a few moments I hobbled after him.

He opened the car door with a jab on his key fob and slammed the door behind him as he sat. He started the car as sharply as a racecar driver while muttering to himself under his breath. His forehead was red.

He was much too angry to talk.

I was impressed he'd left Dario's office before the situation could escalate any further. Because I couldn't think what to say, I sat quietly as if studying the road.

"Are you all right?" he asked as we neared my house.

"Yes. How's your hand?"

"It hurts."

"What do you think all this has to do with Ivano's death?"

"Not a thing."

"So why would Dario threaten Daniella?"

"To take advantage of an opportunity."

I sighed. "So we learned nothing about Ivano's death?"

"I don't think so, no."

I had to agree. As uncomfortable as our encounter had been, I reasoned that Dario was too busy counting his money to commit something as personal as murder. That meant I had to find out more about the people who surrounded Ivano. In particular, I needed to find out more about my cousins. Both of them.

Chapter Twenty-Four

I asked Cenzo to drop me off at Aunt Maria's. I was about to ring the doorbell when the woman threw open her front door and herded me into her kitchen. "I was hoping you'd come by. What did you find at the baita?"

"Nothing besides wildflowers and pine trees. Can you think of any other place Grazia might have gone?"

"That's what I've been trying to do all morning."

Aunt Maria automatically took out the espresso maker, but instead of bustling around as usual, she plodded. She'd aged a decade overnight, maybe two. I wanted to comfort her and tell her everything would be all right, but what did I know? At this point it was more likely that things wouldn't turn out right at all.

"All things considered, Grazia has been holding up well," I said.

Aunt Maria sighed as she sat across from me. "That's the moment when you're the most likely to snap. When Grazia was born, I thought I would only have to worry about her for the next eighteen years. I was wrong. Keep that in mind if you get serious about a boyfriend."

If anyone could give me leads, it should be Aunt Maria. "I suppose Grazia had one or two you didn't like."

"More like most of them! Some of her beaus I wanted to run off with a kitchen knife. Every year she managed to find handsome men who were rude or demanding. The worst was that terrible Dario. He's Sanalto's son. But that's all in the past."

Sanalto. The former mayor. And the handsome son who ought to be icing his jaw. I should have guessed he wasn't a random businessman. He and Grazia went way back. He hadn't come to the funeral, so he'd sent in his troops. Clever.

"You can't think of anywhere else Grazia might have gone?" I asked.

She shook her head.

"Did you try calling Laura and Renato?"

"They're as confused as I am."

I trusted Aunt Maria to tell me what she knew. My aunt frowned so deeply her cheeks made sets of lines. "Sofi, there was a moment before Ivano when there was someone else."

"Oh?"

Aunt Maria rose to check on the coffee, which was gurgling.

"I thought Ivano came along after a lull," I said.

"That's what I thought too. And don't tell Grazia I told you about this. If I'm telling you now, it's because I think you need to know. Not that I know. Not exactly." She took out two demi-tasse cups. "Sugar?"

"Just one."

She carefully poured us each a cup. Then she brought our coffees over to the table and took her seat again. When she leaned towards me, I caught a whiff of blueberries.

"What happened?" I asked.

"Two things. Last September we went to a festival in Biò. We were about to leave when we ran into some distant cousins who invited us to their home for dessert. Grazia protested that I was too tired. That wasn't true and I said so. In the end we went over to their house, but Grazia kept quiet. She was irritated but couldn't say so."

"As if she wanted to be somewhere else?"

My aunt stirred her coffee a dozen extra times. "Exactly. We didn't get home until midnight. When we entered the living room, I noticed that the message machine was blinking, but I ran straight through to the bathroom. By the time I came out, the light was off. Grazia was sitting on the couch like the cat that blames the broken plate on the dog. 'Who called?' I asked. 'Nobody. It was a hang up.' I pretended to believe her, but I didn't."

"It wasn't a wrong number?"

She stirred the coffee a few more time. "No. She was too self-satisfied. A week later, she told me she was going to Ivrea to see a movie with Teresa. She came home late, well after the movie house was closed. But that's all right. You know, you stop to chat. Anyway, I happened to be awake when she arrived, so I asked about the film.

"She'd said she'd seen the new one with Giancarlo Giannini. 'Good?' I asked. 'Pretty good.' That's all she said." She set the spoon on the saucer but didn't taste the coffee.

I drank half of mine in one gulp. "Then what?"

"Two nights later, Teresa and Grazia were sitting right here when I came back from playing Tombola. Naturally I sat down with them. 'Did you have a nice evening?' I asked. 'We sure did,' Teresa said. 'We saw that new movie with Giancarlo Giannini.' Grazia gave her a look that could have killed. I pretended I didn't notice anything strange."

"Maybe the actor was in two new movies at once?"

She put her elbows on the table and slumped. "Not that week. I checked. She hadn't been so secretive since high school. I assume he was married. What other explanation was there?"

Right off I wasn't sure, but now I had even more reason to learn about my cousin.

♠ ♥ ♠

On my way home I stopped off at the music school hoping to track down some valve oil. Instead of finding the music director preparing for the evening's rehearsal, the only person in the building was Carmela, and she was mopping the floors.

As soon as she saw me, she put down her weapon and invited me to sit with her.

"Do you honestly do every single thing around here?" I asked.

Carmela laughed. "During the school season we have the janitor. During the summer, you're looking at her."

She wasn't doing an expert job. Somewhere in the background, I heard a leaky faucet. "I'm not sure Roberto appreciates your hard work."

"Not in the least!"

"The cook shouldn't also have to be the janitor."

"I've told Roberto that for years, but he doesn't listen!"

I patted my stomach. "You're dangerous, you know. Don't you ever run out of tasty dishes?"

"That would be the end of me. Roberto would look for another woman faster than a runaway scherzo!"

"No. He wouldn't know where to look! Anyway, I stopped by for a little valve oil. Would Roberto have some?"

Carmela nodded. "We could take a look through the trumpet cases." She led me into the office where the extra instruments were stashed.

"I love the balmetto parties," I said as I checked the first case. "But, honestly, don't you get tired of doing all the work?"

"In the beginning I did, when Roberto was starting out. Back then I made all the uniforms too! But the band is what makes Roberto happy, and the balmetto is what makes the band happy. That's a cycle I don't fight."

"Surely some of the musicians have balmetti."

"Roberto Three does. And Patrizia. But as you can guess, they're hard to come by! As long as the musicians are invited to frequent parties, they're satisfied. They donate their time to the band, and I donate my time to the parties."

"And you husband donates his time to the music."

"Yes!"

I was still amazed at the musicians' devotion. "Wouldn't the band members rather party with their own families?"

"Night after night? No! They'd rather spend time with people who share their interests. That's important. Take the carpenters, for example."

"What about them?"

"When they went on strike, Ivano placated them with a balmetto. The big one next to the piazza. Technically the donation came from the city, but Ivano orchestrated it."

Only in this area of Italy would a party house be a solution. "The carpenters were satisfied?"

She shrugged. "They lost some wages, but what they gained was far more important. That crowd parties half the night! Then again, that's what a balmetto is for."

The drip became even louder. "Carmela, did you leave the faucet running?"

"Oh, goodness, I hope not! Otherwise the water bill will be so high that Roberto will expect me to pay it myself."

I stood. "It might be a toilet that won't shut off."

"I'm no plumber. I'm just the cook, the chauffeur, and the janitor!"

I took a few steps in the direction of the sound. Then a few more. I turned on the light and entered the girls' bathroom. The row of five sinks was quiet, and the bathroom stalls were still. Then I noticed water seeping out from under the door to the boys' bathroom.

I hurried next door. Water gushed from the fourth sink. Its faucet lay on the floor nearby. "Carmela!"

I met her in the hallway. "You need to shut off the water to the whole building."

"I can't."

"Why not?"

"Superman himself wouldn't be able to turn that handle."

"Pretend to be Superwoman and give it a try? I'll see if I can get the faucet back on."

I stumbled back to the bathroom and picked up the plastic piece. It was a cheap one and might have still been serviceable. But I had a sudden brainstorm. I stomped on the piece to make sure it would never work again. Now I had a perfect excuse to investigate my cousin.

Chapter Twenty-Five

I beat Carmela out to her car, but as soon as she cranked the ignition, she shot out of the parking lot.

"I'm sure Renato has a piece that will fit," I said.

Without slowing down, Carmela took the first left, which pointed us towards Via Aosta.

"Renato's is back the other way."

"It's nearly dinnertime! I hate to bother him. We can go to the Carrefour."

"We won't make it in time. But don't worry about Renato. That's why he lives above his store! It's no trouble."

Although I felt bad for doing it, I was lying to Carmela. I knew the Carrefour schedule perfectly. Had we sped through Ivrea, we would have reached the megastore with a few minutes to spare. But I wanted to snoop around at Renato's, and I wanted him to be busy with a customer. This was the perfect moment to show up on his doorstep.

Even though she was speeding through Monteleone, Carmela took out her phone, punched in the code, and sped-dialed a number. Then she handed her cell to me. "See if you can reach Roberto! He went out to his garden."

The maestro could not be reached. By now he was probably taking a shower.

Carmela pulled up in front of Renato's. "Laura might be serving dinner. This is terrible timing."

Italians! Meals trumped almost any situation. I wondered if they trumped earthquakes too. "He's used to interruptions. Trust me."

"Renato!"

My cousin stuck his head out the kitchen window.

"Emergency at the School of Music! Give us a hand?"

He wiped his mouth with the back of his hand. "I'll be right down."

Renato hurried us into his shop. He had breadcrumbs on one cheek along with the smallest bit of tomato paste. "You say you turned the water off yourself? That's very good. Most people panic."

"This has happened before," Carmela said. "And the first time, I did panic!"

"We have rehearsal in less than an hour," I said, "so we have to fix the faucet right away."

"What do you need, exactly?"

Carmela extracted the broken piece from her purse. "This."

Renato took one glance. "I'm sure I have something that will fit. It might not match, but it will get you through the evening."

While Renato led Carmela to a shelf in the plumbing section, I hurried to the counter with the cash register. I opened the receipt book and flipped back to Thursday. I'd found Ivano around three o'clock, but he had probably died a couple of hours earlier.

The final entries were in Renato's strong, firm handwriting. His last sale was for a bunch of screws. Before that, a hammer. Before that, a small saw. I flipped backwards. If Renato had left the shop, Laura would have taken over for him. He would have only needed forty minutes to drive Ivano to the balmetto, offer him some wine, and driven back home again.

"This one should work," I heard Renato tell Carmela. "Want to give it a try?"

I flipped faster. The receipts for the entire day were in his handwriting. Renato, Renato, Renato.

"Sofi! Are you ready to take over the cash register?" Renato asked, smiling.

I let the receipt book fly out of my hand so Renato couldn't tell what I'd been doing. Then I retrieved it from the floor and quickly turned to the first empty page. "Trying to speed things up for you." I picked up a pen. "How much?"

"Never mind," he smiled. "I never charge for emergencies."

I knew the real reason. Opening the cash drawer for a two-euro purchase was not worth the trouble when hot pasta waited. We thanked him and ran.

Carmela moved so quickly that I had to limp-hop to catch up with her. As we sped back to the School of Music, however, I felt satisfied. My proof might not have been scientific. It might have been shot down in a court of law. But as far as I was concerned, Renato was cleared as a suspect. He hadn't left his premises long enough to hand Ivano any poison. That meant the real killer was still anybody's guess, and I needed to find him before he came looking for me.

I rode in Carmela's car again that evening from the rehearsal to the balmetto party that followed it. By then I deserved some party time. Roberto had led us through such a difficult band practice that my lips hurt. Since the band had the important task of opening the balmetto festival, the maestro expected a perfect performance. The problem was that he overestimated our abilities, which I assumed he did for every concert. Saint-Saëns' "Bacchanale" from *Samson and Delilah* was so intricate that we wasted half the rehearsal on it without making progress. Copeland's "Saturday Night Waltz" wasn't as hard, but I was the only person in the room who had a sense of it, and that was only because I'd performed it a decade earlier.

In typical Piemontese contradiction, however, even though Roberto had spent most of the rehearsal shouting at us to play with better timing, intonation, or dynamics, he'd forgiven us for our shortcomings by the time we arrived at his balmetto for the pre-festival activities.

As usual, Carmela and Roberto enjoyed a fine turnout. Who wouldn't want to spend the evening chatting with friends over wine and pasta? The best parties that I'd attended around Boston didn't come close to the balmetto spirit where the evenings stretched into the morning and the canteens were full of supplies. Carmela had no doubt spent quality time in the afternoon preparing yet another tasty sauce, this one with roasted peppers. When I was given the task of stirring the saucepan, the aromas were so delightful that I considered jumping inside.

Carmela had recruited helpers. Patrizia brought celery stalks with ricotta and stuffed boiled eggs with sardines. Iliana, the wife of Roberto Three, brought a salad so huge it might have fed an army of hares. Beatrice, a clarinet player, brought a pound cake. Liza, the pianist, brought *canestrelli*, small flat cookies of the region. Others brought bottles of wine from their home production or salami or grappa.

The setting was perfect. No one was in a hurry, and no one remembered what Roberto had been complaining about an hour earlier. Even the moon shone its approval. By the time we protested that we couldn't eat another bite, empty wine bottles were lined up like pins in a bowling alley. Simultaneous conversations rippled up and down the table, mostly in dialect.

"Do you know who wants to be mayor?" asked Roberto Three. "Rikki Constananza."

Guffaws boomed into the night.

"That guy's an idiot!"

"He's so stupid he can't work a cell phone!"

"Who's mayor now?" Patrizia asked.

"Daniella Labrese," several people chorused.

"But she doesn't want the job," said Roberto Three.

Patrizia refilled her own glass. "Being the mayor would be an honor."

"I don't blame Daniella a bit," said Carmela. "She has three teenagers, and each one is a handful. Ivano talked her into being his deputy by promising she wouldn't have to do anything."

"What else did Ivano talk her into, I wonder?" laughed Beatrice.

"He didn't have time for Labrese. He was too busy with Antonella!" laughed Liza.

"Who's Antonella?" asked Roberto Two.

Several people started to explain that she lived next door to Ivano. I sat at attention. I didn't want to hear any mean gossip about her, but I couldn't have stopped the flood of words with a twenty-foot wall.

Patrizia waved her breadstick as a baton. "And guess what? She was in the gyno ward not a year ago."

"Are you sure?" asked Roberto Three.

"I was her nurse. Of course I'm sure."

"Maybe she was going through the change?" asked Marco.

Several women nodded.

Patrizia waved her breadstick. "She was going through a change all right. Call it an intervention if you want."

"I didn't know she was seeing anyone," said Roberto.

"Who needs a boyfriend when you have a neighbor?" asked Iliana.

I slapped my hands on the table. Not a single person noticed.

"One with a well-deserved reputation!" added Patrizia. "No matter how it happened, that jerk got what he deserved."

I rocked the table so hard the partiers had to scramble to save their glasses. "Ivano was not a jerk! And if that's what you think, you didn't even know him!"

Because I'd threatened their drinks, I'd stunned them into silence. I finally realized that gossiping was the perfect crime. It gave the villagers the chance to feel superior with little threat of jail time. No wonder they loved it.

The awkward pause continued. I imagined that everyone was trying to think of an innocent rejoinder, but given the wine, the band members and their spouses were slower than usual. Not even Carmela was quick enough to jump in and smooth things over.

Ivano and Antonella. Since a driveway separated their houses, they had automatic access to one another. So Aunt Maria would have been wrong. There would have been at least one more jealous woman at the wedding. I thought back to the funeral services. Antonella had seemed sincere in mourning Ivano. No wonder. She might have cared about him more than anyone else in the room. And certainly more than Grazia.

"Who will have more grappa?" Roberto asked, standing up to locate empty glasses. "It can't go to waste."

Instantly the conversation returned to neutral ground. Grappa. Several of the men found room for a few more drops.

I let Roberto pour me a small amount, but I dumped it under the table when no one was looking. I needed to be sharp enough to catch the slightest innuendo. Hence while I participated in an innocent chat about beach vacations with Carmela and Liza, I strained to hear other conversations around me. I needed to arm myself by knowing everything the villagers did.

"Another party?" Cenzo opened the gate and let himself in. He'd taken time to clean up. He wore a light blue shirt I hadn't seen before over wrinkled jeans. He might have been another villager out for a stroll except that from everything I'd heard, he never partied.

I winked. "Do you crash dinners every night?"

He winked right back as he squeezed in next to me. "Every chance I get." He lowered his voice. "Also, Carmela bribed me into stopping by."

"How did she do that?"

"She assured me you were coming."

I smiled in spite of myself. No wonder Carmela had insisted on giving me a ride. She was always working behind the scenes. I would have to remember to thank her for it. And I would have to thank Cenzo too. I needed his show of support almost as much as I needed information about Ivano. I didn't want to chance explaining that while surrounded with so many eavesdroppers, though, so I played along, acting as if it were a normal night at a relaxing balmetto party. While nodding and occasionally chiming in, I tried to calculate who else might have been working behind the scenes. I knew there was somebody.

Chapter Twenty-Six

I put on my seatbelt even though Cenzo didn't bother with his own. He started the engine while looking my way. "I hope you were glad to see me."

I answered by patting his arm, but I kept my other thoughts to myself. Did my body respond to Cenzo because he was handsome or because he was a port in a gossip storm? Was I attracted to him or desperate for attention? Maybe it was everything at once, which made it doubly confusing.

Cenzo took a fast curve without noticing he'd done so. "Carmela has a master plan. She figures that if I settle down again, I can gain custody of my kids, who would then come back to Monteleone and help with the band."

"Wouldn't your kids prefer to be in Italy?"

"It doesn't matter. My ex wouldn't give me custody if she had both feet in the grave. If I took her to court, I'd wind up poor and she'd still have my sons."

He didn't sound sad; he sounded resigned. I wasn't sure how I would have reacted in his position.

He slid through the yellow light. "How did rehearsal go?"

Exasperated, Roberto had stopped us so often that I couldn't get an overall sense of the pieces. "We'll be fine as long as the audience gets drunk first."

"The band members will pull together for the performance. They always do."

I was less certain than he was, but the band was a problem for another day. I had more important matters at hand. I assumed Cenzo might fish for an invitation when he pulled up at my house, but I didn't give him the chance to load the bait. "I need you to come in."

He turned off the engine as if he were used to following orders and put on the emergency brake even though the ground was flat. "Worried about getting up the stairs?"

"I can manage. But we need to talk."

Cenzo immediately parked and walked me up the short flight of stairs to the door. The house was completely dark; I'd forgotten to leave on a light. I stumbled into the living room as Cenzo steadied me.

"Are you all right?"

I hopped to the sofa and sank into it. "Nightcap?"

"Maybe water," he said slowly. "Are you mad at me?"

"No."

His shoulders relaxed. "Are you in pain?"

I'd taken Tylenol twice that evening. The pain was manageable, but before I tried to sleep I would opt for another dose. "Not much."

"Put your foot up. I'll bring drinks."

"There's *frizzante* in the refrigerator. I opened it this afternoon."

He returned a couple of minutes later with glasses of fizzy water. He sat apart from me, but the couch was so soft that we rolled closer together.

I pushed myself a couple of inches away, but then I fell back again. "I wanted to share some information. Grazia used to date that Dario jerk."

"Do you know when?"

"An Excel sheet wouldn't be big enough to keep track of her boyfriends, so she might not remember either. But they have a connection."

Cenzo nodded. "Perhaps they still do."

"Physically, Renato didn't have time to kill his cousin-in-law." I explained about the receipts.

Cenzo nodded. "Interesting approach. I suppose it's not foolproof, but it's something to go on. What happened at the balmetto party before I arrived? Did you get another few bids for your property?"

"Several. Roberto Two seemed sincere about it. The others, I don't know, maybe they were dreaming. They'd probably love to have a balmetto as long as they didn't have to pay for it."

Cenzo stared into my eyes. He didn't have detective work on his mind. "No doubt. It's true you could make a lot of money. Whether or not you could get a fair price, I'm not sure."

"Never mind about a stupid party house. I heard some dirt about Ivano."

Cenzo kicked off his shoes and stretched his legs beside mine. I wondered what else he wanted to kick off, but I wasn't ready to find out — yet.

"Poor Ivano," Cenzo said. "There's no resting in peace for him."

"I heard something serious."

"Another married lover?"

I took a deep breath. "He got a woman pregnant."

A shadow passed over Cenzo's face. "I'm surprised he hadn't been more careful. Are you sure?"

"Would you trust a nurse?"

He paused for a second. Then he snapped his fingers. "Of course, Patrizia was in high spirits tonight. So who was Ivano's lucky woman?"

"His next-door neighbor."

Cenzo sank his shoulders into the cushions. "I thought Antonella was in her forties."

"That doesn't mean she couldn't conceive."

"Boh. I should have guessed a connection between them days ago. When did this happen?"

"A year ago last spring. Ivano proposed to Grazia shortly afterwards. No matter how you do the math, it doesn't seem right."

Cenzo sighed. "Does Grazia know about their relationship?"

"We never discussed her, so I don't think so." Had Grazia been angry, she would have explained every last detail. Unless she had a specific plan. "Will you question her?"

He nodded thoughtfully. "As soon as I figure out the best way to do so. A better question might be why Ivano wanted to marry Grazia."

"Wouldn't a wife be useful politically?"

Cenzo gently lay his foot on my leg. "For being the President of the Republic, yes. For being the mayor of a village, not so much."

His body was warm, and mine was warming up. "Right."

"The people around here are practical. They care about their gardening, their vineyards, and their children. They want everything to run smoothly."

"You're saying they didn't care about Ivano's love life?"

"Not in terms of politics."

"Only in terms of self-interest."

"Yes. For the job of mayor, a partner didn't matter."

So they married for a different reason. Rather, they each married for different reasons. Perhaps a lot of relationships were like that, but I didn't enjoy thinking about it.

Cenzo put his arm around my shoulders. "Maybe this isn't the moment, but—"

When he bent to kiss me, I closed my eyes and let the warmth run from my head down to my toes. In a perfect world we might have spent the night speculating on Ivano's love life. We might have analyzed all the participants of tonight's party in turn, ruling them out as we pulled together bits and pieces of their lives.

Instead we gave in. As soon as we came up for air, I pointed to the ceiling, and Cenzo carried me straight to the bedroom. Once we were there, I let all the worries about Ivano slip out of my mind. For one day, I'd discovered all I could. Now I wanted to discover Cenzo.

♠ ♦ ♠

I felt the mattress spring back when Cenzo left the bed. "Is it morning already?"

"It is," he said.

A few feet away, Cenzo zipped up his jeans. A better lover might have jumped up to make coffee, but instead I snuggled into the sheets. "Mind if I don't get up?"

"You're on extended vacation. You can sleep until noon."

He sat on the bed to give me a hug, and I wrapped my arms around his waist. "You're a good cushion."

"It's lucky I'm good for something," he said sharply.

"Don't be hard on yourself. It's okay to fall asleep."

"Not when you're not trying to."

I patted his right hip. "More energy for tonight." I didn't mind that he'd fallen asleep while snuggling. It had given me the chance to enjoy his presence.

He buttoned his shirt. "I'm scaring myself. Being with you is too comfortable."

"For me too. But it's always like that when you're starting something."

"True. Somehow you assume that the two of you will always agree and everything will work out." Cenzo stretched the watchband over his wrist. "I should at least show up at the office so that Stefano knows I'm alive."

I propped myself up with one elbow. "What should we do about Antonella?"

"Nothing for now. She and Ivano may have had an affair, but Patrizia is a gossip first and a nurse second. If we questioned all of Ivano's lovers, we'd have a roster full of satisfied women."

"They didn't mind being loved and lost?"

He looked in the mirror to straighten his collar. "I doubt that he made empty promises."

"They knew he wasn't serious?"

Cenzo ran his comb through his hair, but it looked the same. "My guess is that what he offered was a night of fun, a few hours of passion. You can hardly blame him for that."

"Antonella might know something useful. Especially if they spent a lot of time together."

Cenzo took my hand and squeezed it. "I'll talk to her when I can do so casually. Let me think about it first."

He kissed me lightly on the head and promised to call later in the day. I listened until the door shut behind him, but I didn't go back to sleep. I toyed with the idea of another snooze, but it seemed decadent. Instead I exercised my ankles, slowly. The swelling had gone down, but my right ankle was still tender. I promised myself to go easy on it. I was thankful I'd be playing a concert that evening rather than marching in a parade.

When I heard the doorbell, I hurried downstairs. I assumed Cenzo had forgotten something important such as his keys. I flung open the door ready to give him a hard time, but Roberto Two stood before me. He was wearing a suit and holding a hat in his hands, his head bent over.

"Roberto! Good morning."

The man strained his neck to look up. I wondered how bad the hangover was. "Sofi, I'm sorry to bother you, but I want to tell you something."

I stood aside. "Would you like to come in?"

"I'm on my way to work, so I can't stay. But I needed to talk to you when no one else was around."

Roberto Two was a decade or so older than I, and he had a wife and several children. That meant only one thing was missing from his life. "You want to buy my balmetto?"

His expression turned to a soft happiness. "How did you guess?" He pulled a piece of paper from his back pocket. "I've been doing some research. The last balmetto sold at a public auction seven years ago. The final price was—"

"Roberto, I'm not selling."

He sighed. "You might change your mind."

I was ready to change it right that moment. Why not give intense joy to a fellow musician? Because Renato would have killed me. Or maybe Grazia. And then the other musicians would have clobbered Roberto Two with the band's only tuba.

Before he had time to put it away, I took my colleague's sheet of paper. "I'll keep your information, all right? And I'll think about it. I really will. I appreciate your asking."

He frowned. "You promise?"

I sighed. As a general rule, I never lied to people. "Roberto, if I did sell, I'd have to sell to my cousins. You know that, don't you?"

"I would pay you more. I'd find a way."

I nodded as faintly as possible. Then I watched as Roberto Two dragged himself back to his car.

As soon as he was out of sight, I texted my mother. "That balmetto? I think we need to sell. Soon."

Since it was midnight Boston time, I didn't expect a response. Instead she replied almost immediately. "You wouldn't want to break your father's heart, dear. I'm sure you'll find a job. Good night."

Great. Now even the chickens made me feel guilty about the balmetto.

I shuffled to the kitchen and filled the coffeemaker. It was already the kind of day that called for extra caffeine. While I waited for the water to heat up, I took out the folder with Ivano's wedding photos and skipped to the page at the back with the numbers. Four crude columns had been made, semi-evenly, in a woman's handwriting. Antonella's?

When the Bialetti hissed, I turned off the coffee but didn't pour it. Antonella hadn't shed any light on Cyprus, but I knew who might. I called Margarita.

I was thrilled to hear the sarcastic you-know-what-to-do message. I spoke as quickly as possible. "Margarita, this is Sofi. I'm not convinced I'll sell, but maybe you could draw up some numbers for me. A rough guestimate will do."

As I reached for the sugar, I noticed a red light flashing on the answering machine.

The first message was from the school I'd contacted in Milan. They weren't hiring, but they had friends who ran an international language school in Lugano. Should they send along my file? Lugano was supposed to be beautiful, it was on a lake, and it was in the Italian-speaking part of Switzerland. It was only a couple of hours' drive from Monteleone. What could be better than that?

I was so ecstatic that I didn't hear the beginning of the second message. After I tuned in, I couldn't distinguish many words. Not only had the speaker used Piemontese, but he'd placed his mouth too close to the receiver. I didn't recognize the deep, male voice, but the harsh tone would have been clear in any language.

I pressed "replay." The second time through I distinguished a few more sounds.

By the third time I began to panic.

I called Cenzo's office. Stefano picked up on the first ring, greeting me cheerfully.

"Has Cenzo arrived yet?" I asked.

"He should be here soon. Shall I have him call you?"

"No. Tell him to come to my house as soon as he can."

Stefano's demeanor changed completely. "Is it an emergency? Are you in danger?"

"No. It's urgent, but not critical. Send him over."

By the time Cenzo bounded in the front door, I already had an interview with Lugano Internazionale for that afternoon.

"Very sneaky!" he exclaimed. "I didn't know you had it in you. Stefano bought your story without a second thought. Of course, I do need to work from time to time, but it was a perfect move."

He sat next to me and started planting kisses, but I pushed him away.

"Sofi, what's the matter?"

"Remember last night?"

He stroked my temple. "Let me make it up to you."

I wrestled free. "I mean, do you remember when we came back here, and I sat down on the couch and you went into the kitchen?"

"Yes."

"And then we went straight upstairs?"

"Is this a trick question?"

"Please try to remember. Did you notice the answering machine on the kitchen counter?"

"Should I have?"

I led him to the kitchen and played the second message. When Cenzo heard the heavy sounds, he started frowning. He placed "replay" twice, raising and lowering the volume as he listened.

"Do you know the voice?" I asked.

"Maybe. Stefano might. Did you understand the message?"

"I caught my name. And the message starts with an apology."

"Right." Cenzo pressed "play" again, pausing so that he could translate between each phrase. "'I am very sorry, Sofia, but there are no other options. Your dear cousin made us a promise. So be ready with the papers tomorrow night at ten o'clock. I'll tell you where to meet. That is, if you care about seeing your cousin again.'"

"What do you think the 'promise' is supposed to be?" I asked.

He cupped his hands. "It's the ultimate coup de grâce. You're supposed to sign over your balmetto."

"What?"

"It sounds like they've kidnapped Grazia."

Kidnapped? No. That was too dramatic for Monteleone. This was a small town with a couple of thousand people where the biggest indulgence was sleeping around and around and around. "Are you serious? Kidnapping a woman for a balmetto?"

"You know the villagers. Everyone in town wants to buy yours."

"Enough to blackmail me?"

"Why not? A balmetto is more precious than a house or a vineyard. And yours has something special. It must. We need to go back and look again."

I poured out the stale coffee and reloaded the Bialetti. This was too much thinking for so early in the morning. "What papers are they referring to? The deed must be somewhere, but I have no idea where. At my dad's? Somewhere between Boston and Florida?"

"The townspeople wouldn't know that."

"But they assume I'm willing to sacrifice my property for Grazia? For the record, I'm not."

"Mind if I unplug your message machine?"

"I wouldn't mind if you threw it against the wall."

Carefully he unplugged the black square and wrapped the electric cord around it. "We'll take it to Stefano for a second opinion. And maybe the caller was counting on a simple business transaction. At any rate, we have plenty of time to make a game plan."

"I'm not signing over my property to a bully."

Cenzo finally cracked a smile. "Of course not. But you might need to pretend that you're willing to."

"That won't work either."

"Why not?"

Living in Monteleone had taught me flexibility. Even patience. But so far, I wasn't clever enough to be in two places at once. "At ten o'clock I'll be playing a solo in the band concert."

He nodded. "Everything always leads back to the balmetti. Somehow all the answers lie there."

I snapped my fingers. "At this time of the morning, there's only one person who would be over there."

"Of course. You're thinking of Pasquale."

"He's there every morning. I think he has to escape from his wife."

That was handy. It meant he wouldn't even think of escaping from us.

Chapter Twenty-Seven

We found Pasquale in the exact same place I'd seen him the last time, atop a table right outside his cellar. He'd left the door ajar so that he could catch the stream of cool air coming out. In one hand he held a small bottle of white wine. He held a smudged glass in the other.

As I approached, I could smell the strong aroma of the wine. "Hi, Pasquale!"

"My little American friend!" He embraced me before shaking hands with Cenzo. "Why haven't you come to see me anymore?"

"I've been busy. Too many family commitments."

"Ah! Now you sound like a villager. But why hang out with this suspicious character?"

"Shh," said Cenzo. "She's not supposed to know that much."

Pasquale tottered back inside his cellar and returned with two glasses. "Join me!"

Before we could protest, he filled them both. Cenzo fell into the act, leading Pasquale through a string of pleasantries about how the nearby vines were doing and when the next rainfall was expected.

"The truth is that we have a problem," Cenzo said. "Sofi's balmetto neighbors are giving her a hard time."

Pasquale shook his head. "No one has used that adjoining space for years."

"Lucrezia Quacchia owns it. Baruzzo's wife."

"That woman doesn't give a damn about any balmetto. Won't even drink a glass of wine at a wedding."

Cenzo took a sip of the homemade concoction as if he enjoyed it, or maybe he did. "Lucrezia might not be interested, but it seems her husband is."

"Baruzzo was a jerk fifty years ago when I first worked for him, and now he's an old jerk who farts. What's he mixed up in?"

"We think he wants to acquire Sofi's property."

"What!? Don't give in to the bastard, young lady! You keep your balmetto! It will bring good luck to you, mark my words! Why, a balmetto is at the heart of the Piemontese soul! It's where life happens. It's where love happens. It's where sex happens! Don't you sell to that old bastard no matter what price he offers!"

I'd never seen the man so stirred up, and I appreciated his quick jump to my defense. "Don't worry. I don't intend to sell."

"I hope not!" Our host topped off his glass before taking a sip. "The rascal wants to acquire your balmetto so that he can own the two of them together. That way he can tear everything down and start over."

"I thought you couldn't make changes to the party houses," I said.

Pasquale pointed to his cellar's façade. "You can't make changes to the outside. You have to keep the same old-style look. On the inside, you're allowed to make some improvements."

Why did the townspeople make things so difficult? "I don't understand why he doesn't ask me about it."

"The sly dog is waiting for the end of the summer. As soon as you prepare to return to the States, he'll make you an offer. He'll pretend he's doing you a favor."

Cenzo took a step back, calculating the size of Pasquale's property. "I can understand Baruzzo wanting to combine the balmetti, but doesn't he have a big one already?"

"He does. Remodeled it a few years ago. Even put in a toilet! In a balmetto!" Pasquale topped off Cenzo's glass, shaking his finger at me when he noticed I'd barely touched mine. "Of course, you know there are passages between some of the properties."

"I'd heard that," Cenzo said, "but I'd never seen it for myself."

"There's a passageway between the Trupiano balmetto and the Varini balmetto, for example. I've been in that one. People got scared after one of the tunnels caved in a decade ago, but most of them are sturdy."

I didn't like the cold, clammy cellars anyway; I couldn't imagine an even clammier space between them. "Why build a passageway?"

"Even after Italy unified, the villagers didn't trust the government," Pasquale said. "Having a place to hide gave them a sense of security."

Cenzo wiped his lips with the back of his hand. "Do you think there might be a passageway under Sofi's part of the balmetto?"

Pasquale polished off his glass. "Of course there is. That's why Baruzzo is so anxious to get his hands on it."

We stayed with Pasquale long enough for another round. The second glass wasn't one bit better than the first. Luckily, his information was better than his wine.

With Pasquale's words still in my ears, I led Cenzo the short distance back to my property.

"I'm sorry I didn't believe you when you said someone was in the balmetto with you," Cenzo said.

"You didn't disbelieve me. You took the most logical view. But why would a passageway be important?"

"I'm not sure. But Baruzzo has probably been eyeing the place for years. He might have orchestrated a deal with Grazia, but then you showed up and ruined their plans."

I turned on the electricity from the box on the street and opened my gate. The balcony was still slouched over the wall as if it were a drunken cartoon character. I didn't know what I wanted to do about it.

"One problem at a time," Cenzo said as he followed my gaze.

"Right. That's more than enough." I went to the cellar door and wrestled with my ancient balmetto key. "Didn't you examine the floor already?" I asked as we crossed inside.

He switched on the light. "I did, but now I have a better idea what I'm looking for."

Cenzo knelt and started fingering exposed sections of the wall. When his cell phone rang, he answered before the second ring. "Yes? Interesting. Can't handle it right now. Say you can't get a hold of me and go yourself. But be careful."

He set the phone on the nearest shelf. "Guess who called. Baruzzo's manager. Says there's something strange over there at the plant."

"Think it's a legitimate call?"

"I don't know."

We reviewed every inch of the balmetto. We moved dusty boxes and blew cobwebs off empty wine bottles. We traced the floor with our fingers as we hunted for a reasonable sign of a door. Every few minutes I went outside to warm up, but then I dived back inside. If we could figure out the connection between balmetti, we might have a clue about Ivano's killer.

Cenzo called me over from across the room. "Do you know anything about these crates?"

I surveyed the stack of six milk crates. All contained sets of dusty bottles. "No. Why?"

He pointed. "All the other empty bottles are stacked along the walls."

"So?"

"They're out of place."

Two by two he moved the stacks. Then we gasped at the same time. The crates had been hiding a trapdoor with a shiny metal hinge. In contrast with the rest of my property, the trapdoor wasn't dusty.

"Clever," Cenzo said. "No wonder we were confused."

After Cenzo propped open the door, we stared at the makeshift rope ladder that led into the abyss. I couldn't believe what I was seeing. Grazia and Renato had been paid to take care of the property for years, and they'd used it liberally. Neither had mentioned a secret passage.

I took out my cell phone and turned on the flashlight attachment. Weak beams illuminated the floor.

Cenzo shook his head. "I have a better idea."

"What?"

"Wait."

While Cenzo went to the car for a bigger flashlight, I donned my spare jacket. Ordinarily I would have been ecstatic to discover such an architectural feature. I would have started thinking about secret liaisons, partisans hiding from the Nazis, children playing tricks on one another. At the moment, all I could think about was confronting my cousins. Why hadn't they mentioned this special feature?

Cenzo returned with a yellow flashlight so large he looked like a handyman. He winked, but I didn't respond. I grabbed the rope and started down.

"Don't you want me to take a look first?" Cenzo asked.

Suddenly I imagined bats or maybe spiders, but I kept going. "Follow me."

I descended into a tunnel so low I couldn't stand up straight. The walls smelled so clammy I imagined they were full of mold. "Watch out. If you don't bend a bit, you'll hit your head."

"Thanks," Cenzo said as he joined me. We took baby steps into the corridor until we reached a turn.

"I don't like it down here." The tunnel was at least five degrees colder than the cellar. I zipped my thin jacket up to my chin.

"You're not supposed to. The passageways were built as a last resort." He flashed light all around. "Too bad the ground is so hardened we can't get footprints. Hey!"

Ahead lay a stack of crates. The top one held neat rows of unmarked bottles. Cenzo picked up the first one and held it to the flashlight.

"Poison?" I asked.

He unscrewed the lid and sniffed. "Take a whiff."

The strong smell nearly knocked me over. "Grappa."

He took a quick count. "Several hundred bottles of it." He handed me the opened bottle. "Be my guest."

"You're sure it's not poison?"

He chuckled. "Not the kind you're thinking of."

Even though I only took a sip, the liquid burned in my throat, and I coughed before it went all the way down. "It's as awful as usual."

"Trust me. After a five-course dinner at a wedding celebration, it hits the spot. If grappa doesn't help you digest, you might as well head for the hospital."

I held the flashlight and watched while he took a slug himself. He swallowed with an appreciative smile.

"They did a good job."

"Why keep grappa down here? Does it need to be especially cold?"

He took another slug, screwed on the lid, and slid the bottle into his pocket. "The temperature is favorable, but you could hardly find a better hiding place."

"Oh, right. Because making grappa is illegal."

"Exactly."

I tapped a bottle. "And people pay for this stuff?"

"Twenty to thirty euros a bottle."

I regarded the stacks before me. "We're looking at a fortune."

Cenzo nodded. "This is what it's all about. The problems with your balmetto. The balcony that gave way. Getting locked in."

"Why my balmetto?"

"Easy access. A couple of guys could park at the edge of the piazza and move all this contraband within minutes as long as they had a sturdy wheelbarrow."

"A balmetto on the first row would be even better."

"Too obvious. And yours would be easier to acquire." Cenzo indicated the passage behind us. "Come on. Let's see what else we can find down here."

We trudged onward one foot at a time. A few feet later, Cenzo nearly tripped on a similar makeshift ladder. I held the flashlight while he ascended a few steps, but he still banged his head on the ceiling of the passageway.

"*Cazzo.*"

"I thought you had a hard head."

"Not that hard." Cenzo pushed on the trapdoor several times, but it wouldn't budge.

"I bet no one has come this way for years."

He climbed back down. "Maybe you have to open it from on top."

"Where do you think we are?"

"I'm not sure. I don't have a sense of how far we've come. Let's keep going."

A few more steps took us to a dead end with a low ceiling, but another trap door was overhead. "Let's try this one," Cenzo said.

Using his head as a lever, he opened the door inch by inch until he could easily swing it open. He hoisted himself into the balmetto long enough to shine his flashlight around before lowering himself back down.

"See anything up there?" I asked.

"We're alone. Go on up!"

Using Cenzo's bent knee as a step, I lifted myself into a small balmetto. The narrow rectangle had shelving along one wall and a pair of oversized wine barrels against another.

"Any idea whose this is?" I asked as Cenzo joined me.

He patted the shelves. "No, but the wood is high quality." He focused on the entryway. "Hold this. Let me see if I can open up."

He couldn't. The door locked from the outside the same way mine did.

"If we could figure out who owned this place, we'd be getting somewhere," I said.

"You won't have long to wait. The balmetto festival starts tonight."

"So?"

He flashed a light beam on the various corners. "Tomorrow people will open their balmetti to the public and offer snacks and such. With any luck, this one will be open."

"We can't wait that long! If I want to see Grazia alive, I have to sign tonight!"

"Sofi—" Cenzo stopped himself mid-sentence. Usually he said too much rather than too little. Usually he held nothing back, and as a typical Monteleonese, said far more than he should. So why wouldn't he have told me exactly what was on his mind?

Because the information was too painful. I felt a jolt as logic whipped through my brain and cracked its whip over my back. Of course she hadn't been kidnapped. She'd disappeared on purpose with her kidnapper. Or maybe she was the kidnapper.

"I could kill her myself," I said.

"I'm sorry. There's a chance I'm wrong."

He wasn't wrong. He knew the possibilities. The area. And Grazia. "Can we leave?"

Cenzo flashed his light through the room a second time. "Notice as many details as possible so that you can recognize the cellar later."

A set of beer mugs sat on a low bench. A silver tray held dirty glasses. Carvings of curvy grapevines decorated wine barrels. That would be enough to jog my memory.

"Get me out of here. I'm freezing."

We re-entered the passageway, taking the same baby steps we had before. But at some point, driven by the temperature, I grew too impatient. Just as Cenzo paused to double-check his footing, I rammed into him. The flashlight flew from his hand, hit the dirt, and conked out, leaving us in total darkness.

"Are you okay?" I asked.

"*Managgia!* Yes. You?"

"I guess." I knelt and groped at the dirt. "Where's your cell phone?"

He fumbled around, checking pockets. "In your balmetto. Yours?"

How could I have been so stupid as to rely on Cenzo? "Same."

"Did you hear where the flashlight landed?" he asked.

I felt around for the plastic lifeline. "It's not over by you?"

"I don't think so."

We felt around in the dark.

"Oh, oh," I said. "Here's a piece of it." I'd found the bulb. I felt for Cenzo and handed it to him.

"Not good."

I scooted a few inches forward, examining the ground with both hands. "The rest of it has to be around here."

"I found one of the batteries," said Cenzo. "*Cazzo*. Flashlights aren't supposed to bust apart like that."

"Here's the handle." I held out the plastic piece until he was able to grab it. We kept feeling around until we located the other bits. After several false starts, Cenzo fitted them back together.

"Finally," he said. He screwed the head to the handle and flipped the switch.

Nothing.

"Are you missing a piece?" I asked.

"Maybe."

I located the extra part a few minutes later. Feeling smug, I waited while Cenzo took his cheap flashlight apart and put it back together again. Then I heard him flip the switch.

Nothing happened.

"*Cazzo!*"

"Maybe you put the batteries in backwards."

He opened the device and fiddled around. Still nothing. "Sofi—"

"Right. No choice but to keep moving." Feeling like I was stuck in an incredibly stupid Halloween movie, I moved forward, hugging the wall as I went along in complete darkness. I kept imagining I was touching bugs. Instead clumps of dirt gave way in my hand.

"Watch out," Cenzo said. "The turn should be coming up."

"Shouldn't we be going downhill?"

"Maybe."

Party Wine

I continued until I reached the shaft. Then I stepped aside so that Cenzo could climb the several steps of the rope ladder and wrestle with the lid.

"I thought I left this darn thing loose." The lid creaked as he lifted it up and shoved it out of his way. "Wait a second and I'll go turn on the light."

He took a couple of steps before falling flat. "Boh!"

"Are you okay?" I called out.

"Perfect."

"What happened?"

"I don't know. I tripped over something. Thought I remembered where everything was."

I crawled up the ladder. As I reached the top, I spread my fingers on the floor. Instead of dirt, I felt linoleum. "Cenzo, this isn't my balmetto."

"What?" With a heavy sound, he wrestled the entry door open. Strands of sunlight greeted us. We were in a kind of mini-balmetto, a small four-by-four equipped with shelves and wine vats.

"Where the hell are we now?" he asked. He stormed outside, and I scrambled beside him. We found ourselves on the tier of balmetti above my property. While killing time during balmetto repairs, I'd walked past the spot several times.

"This is a storage space?" I asked.

Cenzo shut the door behind us. "That's it."

"Why would it be unlocked?"

"I don't know."

We both felt the same way, clueless. But once again, the balmetti had proven the test of time. Their passageways harbored more secrets than a cemetery. Now we had to start digging.

Chapter Twenty-Eight

When we entered the office, we found Stefano sitting with his chair tilted back and his feet on top of the desk. Evidently, he had so little to do that he was testing his balance.

"Glad you're working hard," Cenzo grinned as he marched in. I followed behind a bit more slowly. My ankle didn't hurt a lot, but it had swollen up again.

As Stefano struggled to sit up, he knocked a stack of loose papers on the floor. "You have dirt on your elbow. Where the heck have you been? Or don't I want to know?"

"I have dirt on my elbows, my knees, and my shoulders," Cenzo said. "I'm sure I have it in my hair and on my face. I've been exploring balmetto passageways. It's her fault."

"Of course," said Stefano merrily. "Women are always at fault. That's why we love them!"

"What I need is a shower," Cenzo continued.

"Go home for a while."

He indicated the empty chair around the room. "You can see I'm swamped."

"We need you to listen to this for us."

Cenzo set my answering machine on the table and played the blackmail message twice. "Suggestions?"

Stefano frowned. "Sofi, I think you'll need to meet with this guy. We'll be there too, of course. Should we call Torino for some backup?"

"Not so fast. I'm supposed to be in a band concert at that same time," I said. "If I don't show up, Roberto will have a cow—and then he'll shoot me. Then you'll have two murders to account for."

"What if we found out more about Sofi's balmetto neighbors?" Stefano asked. "You should be able to get the records from town hall."

"I already checked. Some records have disappeared."

Stefano shook his head. "How could that happen?"

"Nobody knows. Quite a few people had access to those files, including Ivano."

"You don't think he destroyed the records?"

Cenzo frowned. "I'm only saying he had access."

I couldn't imagine Ivano doing such a thing, but there had to be an explanation. Maybe he'd been pressured by a force much stronger than he was.

Stefano leaned forward. "There should be tax records that indicate the owners and how much they pay."

"According to the government, some of the balmetti don't exist. They're not on the books."

"And their owners haven't been paying taxes," Stefano said. "How did they manage to keep it quiet?"

"People do all kinds of things when money is at stake," said Cenzo. "You know that."

"Now what?"

I addressed Stefano. "I convinced Cenzo that we might take a ride over to Baruzzo's."

He immediately started the awkward process of getting to his feet. "To the plant?"

"To somewhere more personal," I said.

"Excellent. In that case, we're going to his house." Stefano might have looked relaxed, but underneath his demeanor hid an alligator. One with sharp teeth.

As agreed, Cenzo stopped the car along Via Andrate, an artery of Monteleone that snaked up into the hills and wound its way onto a dirt road with dense trees on either side. Each house sat on a wide plot, so there was ample space between them. "Are you sure you want to do this?"

"It was my idea, remember?" I silently told my ankle to buck up.

"If you're at all afraid —"

"I'm not." I opened the passenger door. "What's the big deal, anyway? All I have to do is look in the windows."

"I like this woman," said Stefano. "Maybe we could hire her."

"No," said Cenzo. "She would show us up, and then we'd be out of a job."

I shut the door. "I'd make you guys do the dirty work!"

They chuckled as I started up the road. Even though the town was moments away, we'd reached a secluded area protected by a sea of trees on all sides. The summer greens were out in full force and birds chirped as if in competition. I wanted to take in nature at my own pace.

Instead I considered the act of kidnapping. Usually victims were the offspring of rich parents or partners of crooked businessmen, not cousins of balmetto owners. I didn't know if the enterprise seemed ridiculous because I was American or because the sunlight filtered through the leaves in perfect rays. In contrast, balmetti were dark, clammy places. Maybe one good earthquake would shake them to the ground, and we could be done with the lot of them.

The path wound uphill, so each step was more difficult than the last. I walked slowly, enjoying the momentary silence. Not another person or house was in sight, but I thought about all the good things that had happened in this town before I arrived to mess things up. If I hadn't come, maybe Grazia and Ivano would have muddled through long enough to figure out a nice life together. They might have had children or adopted some. Grazia might have sold the balmetto out from underneath me with the excuse that it had been abandoned, and the dumb American cousin would have never known what happened.

On the off-chance she was kidnapped, I felt the smallest amount of guilt. Hence I obeyed a sudden impulse and, despite the expense, called Florida.

"Good morning," my dad said jovially. "Well, make that late afternoon for you. You must be having fun now that all the renovations are completed."

Fun. Well, in some ways. I maneuvered past small talk. "Dad, having a balmetto is great and all, but what if we sold it instead?"

"Sofi, you must be kidding. That would break your mother's heart."

What! The two were in collusion. Not fair. They hadn't provided me any siblings to help me argue my case. "What if we needed the money?"

My father ignored my every word. "You can't believe how happy your mom is. She already booked tickets for next summer."

"For what?"

"For the Italian-American Francese Family Reunion! We're going to have it in Monteleone! At our balmetto!"

"What?"

"Your aunt and uncle are coming too. Can you believe it? After all these years of thinking about going to Italy, they've finally committed to a trip. Should I buy you a ticket as well? I'm sure there's still room on our same flight. Of course, it's nearly a year away."

The Italian-American Francese Family Reunion. Lovely. I could hardly wait. As if a family reunion could possibly be a good idea. Maybe I'd have to tell them the truth about Ivano after all. They could change their plane tickets and fly to somewhere tame like Maui instead. I'd be willing to pay the extra fees myself. All of them.

"Dad, gotta go." That was easier than explaining my ambivalence.

As I reached the Baruzzo house, I fought off images of a big noisy reunion where English, Italian, and Piemontese were shouted in equal amounts. Such a party could only end in disaster. With casualties. Maybe the first casualty would be me.

The house in question lay on a wide clearing. The structure had a modern design that included generous, high windows. Carefully tended rows of flowers bordered the low picket fence and led to the front door. The neighbors' houses were out of sight, hidden behind the trees.

I headed diagonally across the lush grass towards the house. It wasn't until I'd nearly reached the building that I realized the house had been built on a platform, which set it three feet about the ground. Since I wasn't tall enough to see into any of the windows, Stefano wouldn't need to hire me after all. If the Baruzzo family were holding anyone ransom, I'd be the last to know about it.

I circled the house, listening for muffled shouting, but I didn't hear anything at all until I reached the east side. From the open window below the kitchen, I could hear Stefano and Cenzo talking to a woman, presumably Sra. Baruzzo.

The trio spent several long minutes discussing unemployment in Monteleone before moving on to the lack of rain. Then the coffee machine started hissing, and Sra. Baruzzo stopped conversing long enough to pour espressos. By the time Cenzo finally steered the woman to the matter at hand, I nearly forgot that I was spying and cheered out loud.

No, Sra. Baruzzo didn't know that the balmetto next to hers had been broken into and vandalized. She and her husband didn't use the property because it was supposed to be for Gerardo. She hadn't been there since last summer or so. It was an effort for her to walk up the sharp incline to reach the place. When she and her husband had parties, they used the balmetto she'd inherited from her mother rather than the one she'd inherited from her father. She didn't think she could help with any valuable information, but she'd certainly inform her husband and ask him to check on things.

No, she didn't want to call him right away. He never liked to be bothered at work.

When I heard Cenzo and Stefano start to make goodbyes, I returned to the road, meandering along until the guys caught up to me.

"What did you find out?" Cenzo asked as I climbed into the backseat.

"How short I am." Both men laughed.

"See, Stefano? If she were the boss, she'd have been smart enough to post one of us outside instead." Cenzo adjusted his rearview mirror so that he could see me. "You didn't notice anything at all?"

"No."

"Did anyone pass by?"

"Not even a cat. And let me guess. You didn't learn anything from Sra. Baruzzo either."

Cenzo sped up to second gear. "That old gal was as pleasant as could be. She thanked us for our concern over the supposed break-in and insisted we have coffee."

"She put out a whole plate of canestrelli," said Stefano. "I ate most of them myself."

"I don't like the ones with anise," Cenzo said. "It's not my fault I couldn't help you."

"Sra. Baruzzo didn't seem nervous enough to have someone hidden in her house?" I asked.

Stefano turned to face me. "She was friendly in every way. She wanted to make us sandwiches."

I sat back against the vinyl. "If she were hiding someone, it should have been obvious."

"Skilled criminals are good liars," Stefano continued. "They've had a lifetime to practice. Sra. Baruzzo? I don't think so."

"Me neither," said Cenzo. "She never once seemed anxious to get us out of her house. If there's been a kidnapping, she wasn't part of it."

"Now what?" I asked.

"Now we wait for tonight," Cenzo said, "and hope the blackmailer is dumb enough to go to the festival."

"Never mind tonight." I consulted my watch. "I have to start thinking in French and get home."

"Why's that?" asked Stefano.

"In thirty minutes, I have a job interview."

"Should I drop you off at your house?"

"Take me to Grazia's. Her Internet is reliable."

The last thing I needed was to miss out on a job opportunity because of a faulty connection. I needed all the ducks under my control to line up. There were plenty of geese trying to get in the way.

I launched Skype on Ivano's desktop and crossed my fingers that I could sound prepared. I hadn't bothered to explain that my balmetto was under siege or that I'd found a dead man on my property; the committee would have assumed I was a nut case. By the time the old desktop whirred to life, I had exactly one minute to ready myself.

Then nothing happened. I waited several minutes in panic before checking my email to see if they'd changed the time. They had not. They couldn't figure out how to turn on the microphone and were calling an assistant.

Since it was already seven o'clock, everyone else had gone home.

Perfect. I walked around the room, thinking up pretend answers to imaginary questions. How do you handle recalcitrant students? I find out more about them. Usually there's a reason they resist language learning. Check. How do you keep current with your language skills? Every night I watch a Netflix show in French, and I never cheat with subtitles. Check.

I increased my circles to include the hall. What did I think of all the foreign loan words infiltrating the language? I cautioned students to learn the official terms, but to understand current lingo, they needed a full vocabulary.

When a piece of fuzz between the rug and the wall caught my eye, I bent to pick it up. The gray strands were from heavy material, probably jean pants. Grazia never wore such clothes, so the fuzz was from Ivano's. Funny that she hadn't cleaned the house more thoroughly. Usually she was meticulous, but maybe she'd been too busy getting herself kidnapped.

I chided myself for the tenth time that hour. How could I have not seen through my cousin's coarse exterior? Cenzo and Stefano were right. She'd no more been kidnapped than I'd been offered a job as the university president. Now the trick was to change my whole thinking: about her, about myself, and even about Monteleone. When I heard Skype ringing, I slipped the fuzz into my shorts and went back to take the call.

I needn't have been nervous. By the time we started the interview, my interlocutors were so far behind schedule that they were more flustered than I was.

A pleasant group of three women and one man asked me typical pedagogical questions: which teaching methods did I prefer, how did I work with slow language learners, how much grammar did I incorporate into daily lesson plans? I'd answered similar questions for other job applications and felt fluid as I explained my position, at times in English, at times in French. The committee members also asked about my teaching experience, commiserating with me about the mad dashes I'd made among schools the year before.

The professors took turns asking questions, but when the chairperson asked for final comments, it was the assistant who asked how my Italian vacation was going and which cities I'd visited. I confessed that I hadn't hit a single cultural highlight because I was so immersed in balmetto renovations. Then I had to explain what a balmetto was. I wasn't surprised; the structures only existed near Monteleone and along a strip of land down in Liguria.

Strangely enough, the committee was fascinated to hear all about my wine cellar. In their hearts, they were Monteleonesi. They were probably waiting for an opportunity to buy the place.

"Isn't it hard to arrange for repairs if you don't speak the language?" asked the chairperson.

My *curriculum vitae* listed the languages I spoke fluently as English, French, and Italian. It listed the courses I'd taught, including Italian 101, 102, and 303. The committee should not have been surprised that I spoke the language, but I was hardly offended at the oversight. Search committees had to go through huge packets of materials from their candidates, and they mixed things up all the time; earlier in the season I'd received an email from a California college thanking me for my interest in Asian studies.

"I grew up speaking Italian. That's why I majored in French; Italian was too easy. But this last month has been a perfect opportunity to work on Piemontese."

"*Lei parla bene l'italiano?*" asked the man. You speak Italian well?

"*A volte mi confondo con i pronomi o mi dimentico di doppiare la consonante.*" Sometimes I confuse pronouns or forget to double the consonant.

The committee members nodded so enthusiastically that I launched into an explanation of my Italian background and subsequent interest.

For three long seconds no one spoke. I was on the verge of apologizing for what must have been embarrassing mistakes in my Italian when the chairperson cleared her throat while glancing around at her colleagues.

"Would it be all right if we Skyped you back in a few minutes?" she asked.

Since I really needed a job, instead of explaining about an imminent concert, I said "sure."

After we rang off, I alternated between worrying about how the interview had gone and how long I would have to wait to hear back. I was satisfied with the French portions. Only once had I slipped in an Italian word, but I'd caught myself and corrected it before finishing the sentence. But it was already eight o'clock, and the concert was set for nine. I needed to run home, change into black, fetch my trumpet, and hustle myself to the balmetti piazza. Since everyone else in town would be headed to the same spot, I wasn't sure about traffic.

I paced so hard I had to grab the lamp before it jumped off the desk.

Nineteen minutes later, I hit the Skype video function after the first *ding*. "We apologize for the delay," the chairperson told me, "but we needed to discuss a few details. Would you consider teaching a combination of French and Italian?"

"Oh!?" Teach my two favorite languages? I would have agreed under almost any circumstances, never mind that I would have a hard time keeping Piemontese out of both my French and my Italian. The job wouldn't be the issue. Working in Europe would be a paradigm shift. It would mean giving up an apartment in Boston, storing half my possessions at my parents' in Florida, and accepting completely new challenges. Was I ready? Why not?

The woman cleared her throat repeatedly. "One of the Italian teachers has suddenly left," she said slowly, "and we won't have time to search for anyone else before classes start. We're all going on holiday, you see."

Of course. Europeans took vacationing seriously. If I were smarter, I would have emulated them. Perhaps if they hired me, I could learn.

I took a deep breath. I needed a real job, and an excuse to stay in Europe was attractive too. And to stay near to Cenzo. "I would be delighted to teach both languages."

The committee members seemed surprised but pleased. I assumed most candidates gave them the runaround, asked for time to decide, or bargained for more money.

"Will you give us a day or so to make an official offer?" the woman asked. "We can discuss additional details at that time."

"That sounds perfect."

"Do you have any questions?"

I had plenty, but she didn't protest when I pretended I didn't. I thanked the committee and ended the session as quickly as possible. I'd just agreed to make a 180-degree shift in lifestyle and life expectations. My brain wanted the time to slow down so that I could think things through carefully, maybe drawing up lists of pros and cons. The rest of me was surprisingly unconcerned. A simple thought spun through my mind like a revolving door: If I hurried fast enough, I might make it to the band concert before the downbeat.

Chapter Twenty-Nine

I needn't have rushed. When I reached the piazza, the Robertos were still setting up the music stands. Amid noisy salutations, townspeople moseyed towards the rows of folding chairs. Since this event opened the Balmetto Festival, everyone itched for the chance to celebrate. Several of the men nipped from bottles they had brought with them. A concession stand at the back of the piazza aided those unfortunate few who hadn't come with their own supplies.

I stood next to Carmela and surveyed the scene. The band commanded nearly a fifth of the piazza even though the Robertos were trying to make more room by scrunching the music stands closer together. If I weren't careful, I'd be playing the trombone by accident.

"Good turnout, isn't it?" I scanned the crowd, not sure what I should be watching for.

Carmela laughed so whole-heartedly I thought I'd committed some kind of verbal faux pas. "Most people won't arrive until halfway through the concert!" She had a smile for everyone. She was the band's biggest fan, supporter, recruiter, assistant, secretary, chef, and janitor combined. Although I would have never admitted it to the maestro, she was more important than he was.

"Why didn't Cenzo come with you?" she winked.

She caught me off guard. I stammered nonsense about office work and how he would catch up later.

"When his sons were playing, he was famous for arriving for concerts at the last second. Just as Roberto picked up his baton, Cenzo would swoop in for a front seat."

"I can imagine that." Time management was one of his smaller struggles. I wasn't sure whether he was too busy or too disorganized. It was easy, here, to get caught up in swirls of social events, promises to friends, commitments to relatives. The effect was both strangling and comforting.

A slew of older couples greeted Carmela before taking seats close to the center. One of the women waved at me. I didn't recognize her, but I smiled as I waved back. I'd probably met her somewhere around town. She probably hoped I would sell her my balmetto.

"Sofi!" Aunt Maria engulfed me in a hug. "Grazia is fine! She called this morning. The silly goose went down to Tuscany for a couple of nights without telling me."

Fine, was she? What kind of people had kidnapped her, nuns? But it wasn't my place to ruin my aunt's evening, so I played along. "Tuscany?"

"She has a school friend down there. I was worried for nothing!" She rushed off to find a seat with her friends.

I nudged Carmela. "I should get out my trumpet. It's almost nine."

"No rush."

"I thought the concert started at nine."

"That's only in theory!"

A few band members were in the stage area warming up, but most were on the sidelines talking to family and friends. They didn't seem concerned about our imminent performance.

"Do concerts always start late?" I asked.

"Yes, but tonight's concert will start later than usual. The drummer had to run back to the rehearsal room because he forgot to pack up the percussion folders."

"Whoops. Roberto must be furious."

"Not really. The longer he waits to begin the concert, the more people will hear it! There's no reason to hurry. Two years ago we had a terrible rainstorm instead of a band concert, but tonight the sky is clear, so we don't have to beat the raindrops. By the way, naturally we're having a big dinner after the concert."

"At your balmetto?"

"We wouldn't fit! We'll celebrate at the rehearsal room instead. Bring Cenzo with you."

Gerardo entered the piazza from the far end near the concession stand. The last thing I needed was to get stuck talking to him. I hid behind Carmela.

Liza approached us with a friendly hello. In her left hand she held her music folder. "I love listening to your solo!"

Indeed, the rehearsal had gone well. "Let's hope I can play it as well tonight!"

"Don't worry. Our fans don't know the music well enough to catch mistakes. Of course, they might have a better idea if they didn't get so drunk!" Carmela said. "Look, even Baruzzo is tipsy."

A few feet in front of us, Gerardo's parents headed for seats friends had saved for them. They greeted people right and left as they slowly made their way down the aisle. Baruzzo Senior wore tan shorts and a short-sleeved shirt while his wife wore a loose yellow dress. They easily matched the other villagers; the men dressed casually and the women took more care with their appearance.

"I thought the Baruzzi were rich enough that they wouldn't need to come to a free band concert," I said.

Carmela laughed. "That's why they're rich. They don't pay for entertainment! But honestly, they've been generous with the band. The balmetto where we go after rehearsals belongs to them. They've loaned it to the band indefinitely."

I was impressed. "I thought balmetti were too precious to be loaned out."

"That's why people like to own more than one!" cried Carmela.

"Every year the Baruzzi donate several hundred euros for new music," said Liza. "You might say they're the band's biggest patron."

Embarrassed by all the mean things I'd thought about Baruzzo and his wife, I slipped away as soon as Liza and Carmela shifted to other small-town gossip. Bands needed patrons. Desperately.

I headed to the makeshift stage so I could start warming up. My interview had eaten up any possible rehearsal time at home, and I wanted to review crucial passages. Even though I'd practice them over and over, one more review would give me confidence.

"Good evening," Gerardo said, crouching beside me.

I was so startled that I practically fell from my seat. "Glad you could make it, Gerardo. I hope you enjoy the concert."

Gerardo mumbled a reply, but I couldn't hear it. While I would have sworn that some of the musicians never practiced, now they were squawking so loudly I could barely hear my own notes, let alone Gerardo.

He shouted over the racket. "Sofi, could we talk in private?"

I'd survived one date with Gerardo. That was plenty. "I need to warm up."

"Look, Cuz, I need to talk to you."

How many times did I need to tell this man that we weren't really cousins? Grazia had to tolerate him on occasion, but I did not. "After the concert, Gerardo."

"It won't wait."

I turned to the music and continued practicing.

"Sofi!"

I started blowing a low note. As I turned my head, I blew into Gerardo's ear. He automatically shuffled backwards. He might have thought it was an accident. He hadn't spent three years in middle school band.

Roberto rapped his baton on the music stand and signaled the oboist to sound a concert B-flat so that we could tune. The final musicians took their places, and Gerardo slunk away.

On the opening march, I kept my eyes on the music, barely glancing at Roberto until the cue for the final measures. Gerardo was over to the side by the clarinets, already impatient for the concert to be over. What an opportunist! I scanned the crowd for something wrong, someone who seemed out of place, but between the other musicians and the growing dark, I couldn't see much. I could hear the growing rumble, though. As Carmela had predicted, people stumbled into the piazza by the minute. All the chairs were taken, so people walked along the sides, searching for the best place to stand.

The second piece was a medley of Broadway tunes sung by a local favorite. Tommasino didn't sing very well; his vibrato wasn't consistent, and he wavered in and out of tune, but he was a showman. His energetic gestures kept the crowd's attention, and the applause was so strong that I thought we'd have to play the whole number again. Instead we continued to the Copeland piece. I lost my concentration and played on a rest, but the tuba's croaking covered my mistake.

When we reached the Hernández tune, I forced myself to block out everything but the music. I cracked on a note in the second measure, but I played the lengthy solo well enough that Roberto made me stand for a round of applause when the piece was finished. The other trumpet players shouted their approval, mainly because they were glad the burden hadn't fallen on them.

I felt triumphant. I'd played more solidly during the rehearsal, but I'd performed competently enough to be satisfied.

At the beginning of the intermission, I huddled in the center of the stage amidst the other musicians. I felt a growing unease, but I didn't know what to do about it. Nobody looked wrong. No one acted suspiciously. The townspeople were concentrated on partying and nothing more. Yet somewhere lurked a troublemaker. The threatening phone message hadn't been a figment of my imagination. Cenzo had heard it too.

I told myself to buck up and stop letting my emotions run away with me. Who could be dangerous at an outdoor concert? I'd been imagining things. I was wrong. I didn't know enough about the community. I wasn't truly one of them.

When I saw Gerardo working his way towards the stage, I slipped off to join Carmela, who was busy greeting well-wishers.

"Your solo was perfect!" she said, hugging me.

"Thank goodness. Otherwise I would be uninvited from the party!"

Several other ladies chimed in about the music, chatting as they came between us, so it took me several minutes to get close enough to Carmela to speak to her privately.

"You have to rescue me from Gerardo."

"Is he following you around?"

"I agreed to have dinner with him the other night, and I'm sure he misunderstood."

Carmela's eyebrows rose. "Don't worry. I've known him since he was born, and he's harmless."

"Harmless except for boring people to death."

Carmela giggled. "Maybe that's his secret weapon!"

"I wouldn't want Cenzo to get the wrong idea."

Carmela put her hand on my shoulder. "I know that Italians have a terrible reputation for jealousy, but Cenzo is not like that. I don't think he's even here."

He would be, somewhere. I just hoped he could distinguish my playing from my companions.'

Suddenly Gerardo caught up to us.

"Baruzzo Junior! How are you doing this evening?" Carmela said graciously. "Enjoying the concert?"

Before I could hear his reply, I hurried off, keeping in motion until I heard the oboist sound the concert B-flat. Then I dashed to the stage to the cheers of my fellow trumpeters, who were happy to give me a hard time for nearly being late.

The second half of the concert was easier for me. I could relax while the flautists battled their way through a Mozart scherzo and the bassoon and oboist chased each other through Debussy. My solo notes in the Saint-Saëns could have been more confident, but they were on time and in tune. Roberto was in fine form, gesturing wildly, and the crowd's applause grew with each number. I looked for Cenzo, but I couldn't find him.

Near the end of the concert, Gerardo inched closer to the stage. I refused to look his way. Maybe I should have. I had barely stashed the trumpet in its case when he clamped his hand on my arm. "I need you to come with me," he said.

"There's a band party right now, and I'm invited to it."

"The celebration will have to wait."

I yelped when he took my arm and pulled me away from the stage. "What do you think you're doing?"

He grabbed my trumpet case, leaving me clutching the music folder. "Aren't you the one who should be thinking?"

"About what?"

"Your cousin, of course."

Gerardo a kidnapper? That was the stupidest idea I could think of. Boring, cuckolded Gerardo with too much time on his hands and too many useless facts in his head? His grim look suggested that he took himself seriously. I instantly relaxed because the situation was ridiculous. I played along, protesting mildly as he marched me towards the parking lot.

"I promised Carmela I'd help her set up for the party," I complained.

"Help me first, and you'll be back in no time."

"You're hurting my arm!"

He softened his hold. "It's urgent. That's all."

I surveyed the area for reinforcements but didn't see either Cenzo or Stefano. "During a balmetto festival, the only thing that's urgent is the party."

"I wish that were the case."

He tried to hurry me towards his car, but I refused to hobble any faster. "A, I can't walk fast. B, I can't walk off without helping put things away. We have to take all that equipment back to the rehearsal room."

"Let the others take care of it."

"That's not fair. Why would I leave everybody stranded?"

Abruptly he stopped walking and shook my shoulders. "Don't you listen to your phone messages? Your cousin needs your help."

I played dumb on purpose. "Something happened to Renato?"

"I'm talking about Grazia."

"That woman is completely self-sufficient. How could she need my help?"

In answer Gerardo unlocked his car with a push on the remote and threw my trumpet case on the backseat. He nudged me into the passenger side.

"Where are we going?"

As he walked around to the driver's side, I started to get out. Then I caught sight of Cenzo, who was crouched behind a nearby vehicle. When he motioned me to stay in the car, I did.

"Believe me, Sofi," said Gerardo. "Your little cousin needs you. Don't make this hard." He started the engine with a jerk because he was too slow on the clutch.

"You might as well tell me where we're going."

"The family baita. Picturesque spot. You'll love it."

"In the dark?"

He didn't answer.

I sat back as if I thought we were out for a normal drive. "Why are you so uptight tonight? You're usually in a better mood."

"I've been working too hard."

"Is your dad that much of a slave driver?"

"I drive myself."

He was delusional. He'd probably brainwashed himself into thinking that he was in control.

As we rumbled past the balmetti and onto the hard road that led away from Monteleone, I knew I was in for a long ride. I thought I might as well play soccer, so I kicked. "You didn't tell me what's wrong with Grazia."

"Your cousin had a disagreement with my father."

"Why are we leaving Monteleone if your parents are still back in the piazza?"

Gerardo gripped the steering wheel as if it might escape him. "Could you be quiet for a minute?"

"Sure. If that's what you want. No problem." He sounded more nervous than I did. A kidnapping indeed!

He took the same mountain turnoff that Cenzo and I had followed the other day but at a much slower speed. "This is a difficult road, especially at night."

"Right."

We drove in silence except for the rumble of the engine. Whenever I managed subtle looks at the side mirror, all I saw was black. If we'd lost Cenzo, he wouldn't be able to find us again.

My good angel said Gerardo wouldn't hurt anybody. My bad angel said I should be ready to leap from the car.

Chapter Thirty

We took several sharp curves. More than once Gerardo threw the brakes on harshly only to crunch the gears before getting back on track. Although I still couldn't imagine him as a dangerous criminal, I wasn't sure I would survive the drive. Since I didn't notice Cenzo behind us, I searched for landmarks. I wanted to remember the road, but all the tall trees looked alike.

For some twenty minutes, we bumbled uphill towards Biò until we reached a private road that stretched into the woods. After a hundred yards, Gerardo pulled up in front of a metal gate that blocked the path. The padlock shone in the headlights.

He started to reach for the ashtray, but I spotted the tiny keychain before he did and snatched it up. "I'll do it," I said.

"Don't get any ideas."

"Oh, right," I laughed as I slowly made my way to the gate. At least Gerardo knew my limping was real. "I have no idea where we are, and without you I would be on foot!"

He mumbled a response that I couldn't hear. I stalled to give Cenzo the chance to catch up. To waste more time, I pretended I couldn't see clearly enough to insert the key into the lock. Both were rusty, so I genuinely had to pull on the lock several times before it cooperated. If Gerardo thought I were a weakling, all the better.

"Be sure to lock the gate behind you," Gerardo said as he drove through. "Otherwise kids come around and squat on the property."

As I pretended to follow orders, I listened to the night, but I didn't hear any other cars. Then I made a show of checking the lock. From a distance, it looked secure.

"Come on!" Gerardo shouted. "I thought you were in a hurry to get to your party."

Where was Cenzo? "What's the rush?" I feigned nonchalance as I hobbled to the passenger door. "That crowd drinks all night."

We continued up the private one-lane road. Not a single baita was in sight. On either side of the road, overgrown branches scratched the car doors like fingernails on a chalkboard.

"Popular route," I said.

"We don't come up here very often. We're too busy working."

Gerardo held the steering wheel as if he were a little old lady who drove to church once a week on Sundays. I must have been his first abduction. "Why bother with a mountain house if you don't have time for it?"

"It's useful for private conferences such as this one." He left the road and bumped over the grass until we reached a two-story stone baita. The top windows were dark, but light shone out from the bottom panes. Another light illuminated the porch.

"Expecting a party?" I asked.

"You're party enough. Come on."

"I do like parties!"

From his frown, I assumed he bought my act. He waited for me to get out of the car. I bent down as I pretended to re-strap my sandal. Even though I strained to hear the sounds of another set of tires, all I heard were crickets. So much for Cenzo's master plan.

Gerardo strong-armed me into a living room with a vaulted ceiling divided by wooden ties. A sink and stove hugged the opposite wall. To the left, doors opened to two more rooms. To the right, open windows admitted a few breaths of air.

The biggest piece of furniture was a round, wooden table circled by chairs. My cousin sat at the far side.

Grazia hadn't been in Tuscany at all. She'd been too busy scheming in Piemonte.

"Grazia!" I said brightly. "So this is where you've been hiding out! What a good choice! This place is charming!"

Grazia didn't know me well enough to see through the act. I headed over to greet her with a traditional hug, but she didn't embrace me; her hands were roped around the back of the chair.

"Why, Grazia! You're tied up." I pretended to be amused by a joke I couldn't understand.

"*Scema.*"

Funny, by now I was getting used to my cousin calling me "stupid."

"I told you, your cousin needs your help," Gerardo said.

I plopped next to Grazia and grinned. "My help? Are we playing charades?"

"It's a long story," she said. "You won't want to hear all the details." Grazia might have been a principal speaking to a first grader. She was poised and controlled. If she'd been tied to a chair against her will, she would have been screaming so loudly I would have heard her during the band concert. Cenzo was right; she and Gerardo were in league.

"Which details don't I want to hear?" I asked.

Gerardo shook his head. "No time for history."

"I'm surprised at you, Gerardo. You know that tradition is important."

Grazia sighed as if in deep pain. "Sofi, I need you to do me a favor."

"Should I look for a pair of scissors? Your arms must be uncomfortable."

"Che scema!"

My cousin needed to expand her vocabulary. I reached over to pat her shoulder. "Whatever can I do for you, Cuz?"

"It's a long story that doesn't concern you, so I don't know where to start."

"At the rate you're going, you'd better start at the end," Gerardo said. "I don't have time to mess around with either of you."

"I'll make it simple," Grazia said. "A long time ago, I promised Gerardo's father I'd sell him the family balmetto."

The check for ten-thousand euros. Grazia's smug demeanor. The long absence on the part of my family. All the elements added up. She was unconscionable. She'd played me the whole summer with every espresso she made for me and every false compliment. I was ready to match wits. "You have a balmetto you never told me about?"

"No, I mean the other one."

I may have been furious, but I was also a teacher. That meant I could be furious and play dumb at exactly the same time. "What other one?"

"Yours, of course. Well, it's hardly yours. The one your parents own with your uncle."

Come to think of it, I had never explained the arrangement we had with Uncle Luigi.

I stood, strolling around the room dramatically until I neared the open windows. "That would hardly qualify as 'the family balmetto' even though Renato keeps putting all his junk wine in there."

"Get on with it!" Gerardo ordered Grazia.

She gave her cousin a fierce look before turning to me. "I promised to sell the balmetto to Gerardo's father. End of story."

I stalled as if I needed time to think things through. Where was Cenzo? "How could you plan to sell something you didn't own?"

"Don't be ridiculous. All those years went by, and none of the American cousins came around anymore. We knew you didn't care."

Didn't care? Every year we had long discussions about what to do. But what did she know? She'd never come to the States to visit us either.

"If we didn't care," I said, "why were we paying you to look after the place?"

"Why would you want a silly old balmetto anyway?"

"If it's so old and silly, what's the fuss about?"

"We care and you don't and that's that."

I crossed my arms over my chest. "You and Renato?"

She frowned; calling me stupid again was too much work. "He doesn't have a head for money."

"You didn't answer my question."

"I don't bother him with things he doesn't understand."

In other words, he didn't know. So I had one decent cousin after all. But why hadn't Cenzo barged in yet? If I had to, I could jump out the window, crawl into the woods, and grab a big stick.

I hoisted myself onto the window ledge, scraping the backs of my legs in the process. "Let me get this straight. You were planning to sell property that wasn't yours, and I wasn't supposed to notice. That's some plan."

Grazia held my eyes with hers. "You messed everything up by coming here this summer. All the things I had to do for you! All the million things about Monteleone that you didn't understand! The places Ivano and I took you to! But never mind. Overlook all those favors I did if you want to. But right now, sign over your balmetto, and we'll be even again."

I slapped my hand to my heart. "Imagine this: I'm not selling. Mom and Dad have already planned a huge reunion for June First of next year. All the American relatives are coming."

"It's not that easy," said Gerardo. "My family promised the balmetto to Alfredo Ignotto."

"That's Alfredo's problem, not mine."

"He's the biggest mafioso up here in the north!" Grazia exclaimed. "He might kill us!"

"Lay off with the mafia bullshit. The gangs around here are all Romanian, and they wouldn't put up with you for an eighth of a second."

"Sofi!"

"They might get a kick out of that underground passage though. Great place to trap enemies."

"You said she didn't know!" Gerardo hissed.

I hadn't been so pleased in days.

"I never told her anything!" Grazia shouted. "It's not my fault if she figured it out!"

"You're wasting time." Gerardo jabbed his index finger at me. "She promised my dad."

"He seems like a reasonable guy," I said. "He'll understand."

"No," Grazia said slowly. "You will sign the balmetto over to Gerardo. Now."

A couple of weeks earlier, I might have been naïve enough to go for it. "No sale!"

Gerardo addressed Grazia. "You're right. She's an idiot." Then he turned to me. "We're not paying you. It's not that kind of deal."

"Sign away my property? No. Sell it to you? After I triple the price!"

As he sighed, I noticed the circles under his eyes. Kidnapping did not sit well with him. Maybe he was tuckered out from putting up with my cousin. "Don't you understand? Grazia doesn't go free until you sign over your balmetto!"

Outside, soft footsteps rustled through the grass. Finally.

"Congratulations, Gerardo," I said. "First date, dinner, second date, kidnapping. You're not so boring after all. But do you know what I hate? You went to Ivano's funeral and pretended to be sorry he was dead. Not only is that rude, but it's really bad luck." I genuflected, punching my chest so hard it hurt.

"This is a small town, for Christ's sake. That's what people do."

The rustling grew louder. I nearly fell out of the windowsill trying to listen. I pointed at Grazia. "Ivano found out about the passageway, didn't he?" I spoke so quietly she had to strain to hear me. "That's when you realized you had to get rid of him. Who did the honors?"

"You don't know what you're talking about," Grazia said. "My husband is none of your business. The balmetto is a different matter. Now hurry up. My hands hurt, my head hurts, and I want to go home."

"Yes," said Gerardo. "Have pity on her poor little hands."

"Cousin, dear, you put those ropes around your wrist when you heard the car pull up," I said. "That's been how long, five minutes? Smart of you to fake a kidnapping. But how dare you worry your mother? She was beside herself."

"My mother shouldn't hover."

"It's her job to worry."

"That's no excuse."

289

Gerardo opened a briefcase that was on the floor near the table. He brought out a document that was several sheets thick. It was stapled together in the left-hand corner. He flipped to the last page where a blank line awaited a signature. "Shut up and come sign this."

Carefully I let myself down from the windowsill. I shoved the contract across the table so fast that it flew past Gerardo and sailed to the floor. "Think again."

Gerardo arm-wrestled his jacket until a small handgun shook loose. Then he strode over to Grazia and placed the barrel against her temple. "Either you sign or I shoot her. Or else I shoot her and then you sign."

Given Gerardo's poor driving, I hated seeing him with anything mechanical, but Grazia's eyes showed no fear, which meant she was calling the shots. No doubt she'd been planning for weeks and waiting until my final days in Monteleone. I felt my cheeks turning red. I wanted to kill both of them. "Go right ahead. According to her, I don't care."

"Sofi!" Grazia shouted.

Gerardo's arm wavered; he wasn't used to holding anything more lethal than a pen. "Why make me shoot your cousin when you can prevent it?"

Without warning, the door punched open. Cenzo marched in, holding a pistol with both hands. "Put it down, Gerardo!"

He was so surprised that he stumbled backwards. "What are you doing here?"

"Making house calls. Put it down!"

"You — you — you can't barge in like this!"

Cenzo shot the ceiling, and pieces of white drifted down. "Drop it!"

"I haven't done anything wrong! Your word against mine!"

"Stefano!" Cenzo shouted the name without turning around.

From outside the window, Stefano sent a bullet into the wall a few feet above Gerardo's head. As Gerardo dropped to his knees, the weapon flew from his hands and skidded along the floor until Cenzo clamped his foot on it.

"Great," Cenzo said. "Now we can talk."

"But—"

"You're right. This is a poor place for a discussion. We'll go down to the office. Stefano!"

Stefano hoisted himself in through the window. He handcuffed Gerardo before the silly man could think of another reply.

"Cuff her too?" Stefano asked.

"Not at the moment," Cenzo replied. He embraced me before planting a big kiss right on my lips. "How's that for teamwork?" he asked.

I hugged him tightly. I didn't need to say what I was thinking, that it was pretty darned good.

Chapter Thirty-One

I planted myself against the doorjamb to Cenzo's office as if punishing it. The tersely silent drive down from the mountain had given Grazia time to work on her story, and I wanted to remember every false word of it. Then I wanted to punch her.

Cenzo stared at my cousin from behind his desk. He seemed tranquil, as if everything were settled. I was the opposite, the genie inside a bottle of *frizzante* that had been shaken too many times. I was ready to explode. If Cenzo left the room, I might.

"When did Gerardo kidnap you?" Cenzo asked.

My cousin stared at the wall behind Cenzo. "I don't exactly remember."

"That's strange," said Cenzo. "Most victims have a perfect memory of when they were nabbed from their normal lives."

Grazia clasped and then reclasped her hands. "Tuesday," she finally said.

"Time?"

"I wasn't paying attention."

"No hurry. Think carefully." He leaned back and clammed up. I knew the trick from teaching. Pose a question and wait. Silence makes people uncomfortable.

"I simply can't remember," she finally said.

Cenzo sat as still as a rock.

Grazia didn't squirm for a full thirty seconds, but after that she couldn't stop herself. "It didn't start out as a kidnapping. Gerardo came by and asked if I wanted to go for an ice cream. I didn't want to go, but I agreed anyway."

"Why go if you didn't want to?" Cenzo asked.

"To get out of the house. I've been so upset since Ivano's death."

"Devastated."

Grazia ignored the sarcasm. She was too busy improvising now that things hadn't gone her way. "I needed a break."

"You went out with Gerardo, and then he abducted you," Cenzo said.

"He wouldn't even let me call my mother. It was outrageous."

Cenzo leaned back so far I worried he would fall over. He regained his balance at the last second. "Why does Baruzzo Senior want Sofi's balmetto?"

Grazia's eyes widened. She started several sentences before finishing one: "Not Baruzzo Senior. Gerardo wants it."

Cenzo shook his head. "That man doesn't eat breakfast unless his father tells him to. Why do they want the balmetto?"

She shrugged.

Cenzo planted both hands on the desk. "Why?"

He shouted so loudly that Grazia shrank back. "They didn't tell me!"

"Why was Ivano found dead there!"

"I don't know!" She hid crocodile tears in her hands.

"Tell us about the ten thousand," Cenzo demanded.

She didn't look up. "I don't know."

"That's funny. You signed for it."

"I don't care about any stupid wine cellar."

I suddenly remembered our trip to Dario's office. He'd wanted Daniella to sign rights to the riverfront. "If Grazia could get a down payment for my balmetto, she could give Dario money to invest in his power plant.

Then all she had to do was convince Ivano to give the go-ahead."

Cenzo made a notation. "Yes. That's a very likely scenario."

"You're a bully, Cenzo Bot! I hate you!"

He clasped his hands. "Hating me won't help you, especially after you're charged with making illegal grappa."

Her eyes widened. "I never made any!"

"You helped store illegal property. I can fine you by the bottle. Sofi, how many did we find down there? Four thousand?"

I counted on my fingers. "Four or five."

He pulled a calculator from his drawer and punched in a few numbers. "Ah. That's a big fine." He regarded the elements in his office. "Enough to buy way better furniture after I buy a new car. This is perfect, Sofi. It's a win-win situation, isn't it?"

"I had nothing to do with grappa!" Grazia shouted. "It was all Gerardo!"

Cenzo rummaged through his desk for a form and then shoved it at Grazia. "That's your story, is it? Put it all down in your report."

"What report?"

"Where you talk about the kidnapping."

Grazia stared blankly.

"Have you forgotten you were kidnapped?"

"Of course not!"

"So you have to write a report." He slapped a pen on top of the form.

For several seconds she stared at it.

"Need reading glasses?" Cenzo asked. "Getting old hurts, doesn't it?"

"I don't want to prosecute," she said softly.

Cenzo raised his eyebrows. "Gerardo threatened to kill you."

"I forgive him. We're related, after all."

"He held a gun to your head. Not a problem?"

"It's the strain of trying to please his father. Don't be hard on him." She crossed her legs slowly as if Cenzo were easily distracted. "May I go now?"

Cenzo pointed to the door. "I wish you would."

What? Let her walk away free?

She rose. "You have my purse."

Cenzo opened his top desk drawer and took out the large leather bag. He dumped the entire contents on his desk. They included lipstick, tissues, a pen, a tin of throat lozenges, a wallet, three books, a cell phone, a hairbrush, and a small, white plastic sack fastened with a twisty.

Cenzo started to peer into the sack.

"Don't open that."

He untied the twisty.

"I told you not to open that!"

She lunged towards him, but he held the sack out of her reach.

"You've done many things wrong tonight," he said calmly. "I have a whole list of complaints against you. Telling me what not to do is the most obnoxious, though not the most illegal. Stay back or I'll push you away, and you won't like that."

He opened the sack and quickly closed it again. "Underwear," he told me. "Probably three days' worth. If I ever get kidnapped, I hope they warn me ahead of time so that I bring the correct number of clean panties."

"No toothbrush?" I asked.

Cenzo unzipped the purse's side pockets one after another. In an inside pocket, he found a toothbrush and a small tube of toothpaste. He placed the items next to the books, which he examined one by one.

D.R. Ransdell

"Romances, I see. Something to help pass the time." He handed her the empty bag. "We already took pictures, so you might as well keep it."

"I need my cell phone," Grazia said softly.

"It's evidence."

"It's a cell phone!"

"With lots of numbers stored in the address book and a call history. You will tell me the code to open it."

"I will not."

"The lab can open it instead. I don't care."

She hesitated, unsure. She'd had so little practice in not getting her way that she didn't know how to handle it.

"You, you have no right," she said softly.

"You were part of a conspiracy," Cenzo said, "but since Gerardo was holding the weapon, he can take the blame. He's easy to convict even without false testimony about your pretend abduction. Also, his parents have more money than anyone in town. They can pay the fees. Come to think of it, I wonder how much we could get out of your mother." He turned to me. "Aunt Maria lives simply, but so do most of the elderly people around here. When they pass, we find they've been keeping a fortune under their mattresses. Piemontesi, you know. Always building nest eggs in case of hard times."

"You wouldn't take my mother's savings!"

"Don't try to outthink me, Grazia." He pointed to the door. "Go."

"I need a ride!"

"Not my problem."

"I'm supposed to walk home?"

Cenzo made notes as he spoke. "I don't care what you do. Not to worry. It's not more than three kilometers to Monteleone."

"I can't call a taxi this late!"

"Besides which, you don't have a phone," I pointed out.

"It's nearly three in the morning!"

Cenzo tapped his watch. "And I've been working overtime. But the only societal threat around here is in the other room, and he won't be leaving. You're perfectly safe. Great night for a stroll."

Grazia turned towards me. "Sofi?"

"After being locked up for three and a half days, you need the exercise."

She glared at me. "I need you to take me home."

I glared right back. "My car is over by the balmetti."

"Don't just stand there! Convince this monster to give me a ride!"

I pretended to size Cenzo up. "If he's a monster, I'm a bunny rabbit."

"Borrow Cenzo's car and take me home. You need to help me right now."

I switched to the other door jamb, pleased I hadn't lost control. "There's no help for you, Grazia. The laziest college students are better liars than you are."

"Sofi!"

I turned and left. Given a better ankle, I would have jogged around the building to let off steam. Instead I limped over to the riverbank and sat. As I listened to the angry river, I asked how a woman from a loving home could ruin her life so casually. Maybe I'd never understand.

"Are you all right?" Cenzo asked.

"You'd best stay back. I might be dangerous."

"I'd be angry too."

"Why did you let her go?"

"It's easier to let Gerardo incriminate her later. Watch and see. She won't run. She doesn't have anywhere to go."

"She played me for the biggest fool in town. She nearly succeeded."

"I know."

I grabbed the small tire around my stomach. "It hurts here! Inside! How could she betray me?"

"Boh."

As Cenzo came a few steps closer, I shook my head. "You don't know what it feels like."

He bent over and locked me in his arms. "I know exactly what it feels like. Never mind about my ex-wife. Some other time, ask me about my brother."

For several long moments I closed my eyes, listened to the river, and felt Cenzo's arms. Slowly bits of tension let loose from my neck, my shoulders, and finally my limbs.

"Betrayal is the worst of all," Cenzo said softly as he led me back inside the station. "Unfortunately, almost all of us go through it."

Stefano met us in the lobby. "Did you get anything useful out of Grazia?"

"Enough. We'll have to decide what to do with it." Cenzo indicated the detention room. "What did our little kidnapper say?"

"He won't talk," said Stefano. "Says he wants to consult his lawyer."

"Wise idea. In his case, I'd say the same."

"It's late and I'm tired," said Stefano. "What's the game plan?"

"Nothing for right now. We'll let Gerardo call his lawyer in the morning, but there's no reason to alarm good folk by calling them in the middle of the night. Who's his lawyer, Santini?"

"Paolo, I think, not Gustavo."

"Right. Tomorrow Paolo will be tied up in the balmetto parade. He has at least four horses. He'll probably be out of reach all day long."

Cenzo winked. "You'd be surprised how happy people are to cooperate if you give them the chance."

I knew someone I would never cooperate with no matter the circumstances: Grazia Ferreri Francese Visconti.

♠ ♥ ♠

An hour later I sat on the bed while watching Cenzo take off his shirt and then his jeans. Normally, I would have found the sight enticing. Tonight I was too distracted. I'd exchanged my black band clothes for gym shorts and a shapeless beige T-shirt whose motto might have been "Don't touch me."

"I'm sorry about your experience with Gerardo tonight," Cenzo said. "I know it was rough."

"What hurt was realizing that Grazia was in it with him. And then I saw the gun."

He sat beside me. "We were waiting for Gerardo to incriminate himself."

"I wasn't sure you were following his car."

"We were behind you from the time you left the piazza, but it's hard to follow somebody on a small mountain road and be discreet unless you turn off your headlights. When we reached the baita, we listened outside the door until Gerardo made a clear threat. Smart thinking to go over to the windowsill. Made it much easier to follow the conversation."

"Too bad you didn't record it."

"Why do you think I brought Stefano?"

I smiled; Cenzo was more prepared than I'd expected him to be. "The next time you have a murder case or a kidnapping case or any case at all, remind me to stay out of it."

"You knew what to do, which allowed us to take Gerardo by surprise."

"A ten-year-old could have staged a smarter kidnapping."

"Grazia convinced Gerardo that you would do anything to protect her."

"A couple of weeks ago, I would have. Instead I nearly gave Gerardo the slip in the piazza."

"It's good that you played along. Otherwise we'd still be searching for Grazia."

"I liked her better lost. Anyway, she's lost to me now."

Cenzo exhaled slowly. "Sofi, I do know how you feel. My first betrayer was my brother. The second was my wife, the woman I'd pledged my life to. People always surprise you."

I was surprised all right.

He gently put his hand on mine, but I masked any reaction.

"You don't have to stay. I'm terrible company."

Cenzo gave me a brief hug. "I'd be worried if you were jovial."

"I thought she was in love. So much for my powers of observation. I don't have any."

"Here's the silver lining. Ivano probably didn't realize she was using him."

"Maybe he caught on when he swallowed that bad wine."

Cenzo gently brushed strands of hair out of my face. "We still don't know the relationship between Ivano's death and your property. Maybe there isn't one."

"When I wrote Grazia that I wanted to work on the balmetto over the summer, she sent me a list of the most pressing repairs. At the time I thought she was encouraging me. Instead she was hoping I'd give up. She never expected that I would go through with it."

"When you arrived, she had to revise her scheme."

"Grazia cheated me emotionally as well as psychologically. If she'd managed to cheat me financially, it would have been a trifecta."

"Surely you had some nice times together."

"Ivano's murder cancels all that. Worse, I experienced Monteleone through the two of them. I'll have to go back and erase every image. Whatever I thought I knew about this town, I don't know at all. Any pleasant memories are based on false premises."

"You've made other friends."

"Yes." Carmela had embraced me in every way, and I knew she wasn't acting out of self-interest because she already had use of a balmetto. A nice big one.

"Monteleone isn't all bad," Cenzo said. "The band members are nice. And they like you."

"One good solo and you're in for life. I guess that's something."

"I like you."

I didn't answer.

"Would you feel more comfortable if I left?" Cenzo asked.

I squeezed his hand. "No, no. Stay. Please. It's just that I don't live here. I don't know where I'm going to be next week at this time. I don't—"

Cenzo lay back and pulled me to his chest. "For tonight, relax. You'll have to give yourself some time."

After a few false starts, I found a comfortable position at Cenzo's side. I listened to his heartbeat as I felt his warm skin against mine.

Moments later he fell asleep, and I was alone all over again.

Chapter Thirty-Two

By the time Cenzo woke up, I was standing at the window watching the rain. It peppered down so hard I was surprised he'd slept through it. "I guess they'll cancel the parade."

"How's your ankle?"

I was impressed he thought to ask. "Still swollen, but not as bad."

Cenzo joined me at the window. The rain was so heavy that we couldn't spot the house next door. "People can't take their horses and carriages out in this."

"Does that mean we might as well go back to bed?"

Cenzo laughed. "No. It means people will spend a whole lot more time drinking. If we want to talk to anyone who is still coherent, we'll have to do it soon."

"Nobody goes out in this heavy a rain."

"You don't know Monteleonesi."

I knew enough to coax one lone Monteleonese under the sheet, so it was over an hour before we hit balmetto row. By then the rain had reduced itself to a spit, and lots of other townspeople were heading for the balmetti at the same time we were.

Cenzo had exaggerated. Almost everyone was still coherent. The rain had delayed the festivities so much that the proprietors were barely arriving themselves. Some were visible inside their picnic areas as they rushed to prepare appetizers and open bottles of wine.

Carmela had assured me that not only would the balmetti be full of partiers from all the nearby communities, but that the more exuberant drinkers would croon old Piemontese tunes.

The children would be so stuffed with candy that they would be run around as if on speed, and the empty bottles would pile up faster than snowflakes during a blizzard. She'd invited me to stop by her balmetto but warned me that she couldn't take responsibility for anyone's outlandish behavior, especially not her husband's. She had done her part by baking several hundred pistachio *canestrelli* before losing count.

Cenzo and I had calculated that the balmetto with the passageway leading to my property was the fifth, sixth, or seventh. We started our investigation in the eighth balmetto, where so many people had gathered that we could barely fit in the yard. Cenzo maneuvered close enough to the cellar to peer inside, but he didn't recognize it.

The seventh balmetto held a more moderate gathering. We drifted inside the yard and sampled gorgonzola on crackers. While Cenzo talked to cohorts, I slipped down to the cellar where the owner promptly awarded me a plastic cupful of wine. I didn't need to spend time looking around. This cellar was completely different from the one we'd stumbled into.

The sixth balmetto was closed. We went up to the gate of the fifth and entered into the courtyard. Guests stood around a small a table trying to decide whether they preferred Prosciutto di San Daniele or Prosciutto di Modena.

"*Scusate,*" Cenzo said as unfamiliar faces politely smiled. "Sorry. I thought this balmetto belonged to my friend, Bruno Martinelli."

Several people pointed east at the same time.

"Right next door," said a white-haired man. "I'm surprised he hasn't come yet. Must have been scared off by the rain!"

"Try what I made last summer!" A man with an apron, presumably the property owner, approached with a big plastic jug and poured us two glasses of red wine.

"Gladly," Cenzo said. "My friend here is from the U.S., and she didn't believe me when I said that most of the locals made their own."

"I make the best around here!" exclaimed the white-haired man.

"You do not! I do!" claimed the owner, slapping his friend on the back and losing several drops of wine in the process.

"You're both wrong! Mine is the best!" shouted a tall man standing to one side.

"We have relatives in Chicago," said an elderly woman whose hand wavered as she spoke. "Do you know Sandra Petrelli?"

"No," I replied, "but I haven't been to Chicago."

The woman brushed her lips with a paper napkin and folded it in half. "She keeps inviting me to visit, but it's too far for an old lady."

"It's not that far," said the tall man, "but you're too old!"

The partiers guffawed, making wisecracks about the woman's age, which she accepted wholeheartedly.

"Would you mind if we peeked in your cellar?" Cenzo asked. "I've been trying to explain that the cellars keep a nice cool temperature all year round."

"Come on in!" The owner raced us down the steps. "I have the finest cellar on this whole street!"

He did. It contained neatly arranged rows of bottles, several rounds of cheeses, and carefully stacked glasses. The scene was so orderly that it was completely unfamiliar. In excruciating detail, the proprietor told us all about every vat he'd purchased for his wines and which years had been the best. He might have detailed us to death if his cousins hadn't arrived. We took the opportunity to scoot out while the man hugged his new arrivals and join the foot traffic.

"At least we've ruled out other possibilities," Cenzo said. "If we can get Bruno talking, we should be all set."

Cenzo and I entered the fourth establishment where several men sat with plates of mortadella and pecorino.

"*Salve*, Cenzo!" Bruno squeezed us into a shady corner after miraculously producing chairs. "What a surprise to see you out having fun for a change!"

"I wouldn't want to miss the balmetto festival."

"Drink up when you have the chance. Who's the lady?"

Bruno settled down next to me. The jolly man was a firefighter who looked more like a baker. Once he learned I was from the States, he talked my ears off. He assumed I was an expert about the whole country. He was fascinated with Arizona. Even though I'd never been, he asked about rattlesnakes and saguaros. He'd read lots of Westerns when he was a kid, and he was still in love with the Old West. A cowboy hat hung proudly on his wall; his daughter had bought it for him in New Mexico the summer before.

Bruno grilled me with such enthusiasm that I was afraid we'd never be allowed to leave his balmetto, but Cenzo seemed unhurried. He listened absentmindedly, helping out when I got stuck on the translation of specialized words.

"I notice you've been remodeling," Cenzo said when Bruno momentarily ran out of questions. "It must be a relief to have a new roof."

Bruno poured Cenzo more wine before refilling his glass; I hadn't touched mine. "Yes, now we have a strong roof, but we worked on it for over a month. A couple of friends were helping me, but they could only come on the weekends, and then it rained three Saturdays in a row."

"There are a lot of building restrictions," Cenzo explained as if I were a true tourist. "Even if your balmetto is almost falling to the ground, you have to rebuild the outside exactly the way it used to be, only stronger. You aren't allowed to make improvements over the original design."

"That's why it's so hard to get anything done," said Bruno. "Not many people know how to imitate the old style."

"Is that why your neighbors haven't done anything?" Cenzo asked.

"Which neighbors?" Bruno asked.

"Two doors down. The balmetto with the red door."

"I'm not sure. Some lady owns it, but since her husband died, she never comes around."

"What's the family name?"

"I can't remember."

"Emilia Visconti?"

"No."

"Samantia Nobochini?"

"No. But her name is on the tip of my tongue."

"I know who owns that balmetto," piped up a man. "It's the mother of that kid who used to be a mechanic for Torre Automobile."

"Antonella?" Cenzo and I exclaimed at the same time.

"That sounds right," said Bruno. "And the kid's name is—"

"Magru," Cenzo said flatly.

"Bravo!" said Bruno. "Here. Have another glass of wine."

"Magru!" Cenzo exclaimed after we returned to the street. "He produced grappa with your kidnapper."

I shook my head. "I can't imagine him working with Gerardo."

"Gerardo provided the capital. Magru did the work. You'd be surprised how amiable people become when there's a lot of money involved. Guess what we need to do now."

"Grill Gerardo about his little assistant."

"Exactly. Now that we know what to ask, it shouldn't be too hard."

♠ ♠ ♠

Minutes later Cenzo and I zipped through the lobby to the detention room.

"Where in the hell have you been?" Gerardo yelled.

Incarceration hadn't improved his appearance. His wrinkled pants had picked up dirt, and his hair stuck out in random directions as if he'd been pulling on it.

"We've been to the festival, of course," Cenzo said. "Where else do you think everyone would be today?"

"You have no right to hold me!"

"You wanted to speak to your lawyer. He hasn't returned your call. Think about that ahead of time for your next kidnapping."

"I took Sofi for a ride. She misunderstood my intentions."

Cenzo shook his head. "Stefano and I both saw you coerce her into your car."

"I was in a hurry, that's all."

"To reach your other victim," Cenzo said.

"Grazia wasn't being held against her will. I'm sure she explained that to you."

"So you're both guilty of kidnapping Sofi. This is getting better and better."

"You can't make it stick."

Cenzo grinned. "To tell you the truth, I don't much care about the kidnapping. In the scheme of things, it's minor."

"Exactly. So why have you kept me here so long?"

Cenzo scooted his chair closer to Gerardo's. "Why did you kill Ivano?"

"What?"

"He found your bootleg grappa. Isn't murder a bit harsh?"

"No!"

"You've had a key to Sofi's balmetto all along, haven't you? The same key probably opens both your door and hers. Did you kill Ivano and help Magru with the body, or was it the other way around?"

"I have no idea what you're talking about!"

"C'mon, Sofi," Cenzo said. "We might as well go back to the festival and have a few more drinks."

"You can't keep me here all day!" cried Gerardo. "It's inhumane!"

"You're right. We'll call for help."

We closed the door behind us, and Gerardo's shouting became muffled. Cenzo sped-dialed a number. "Stefano, are you still sober? Excellent. Any sign of Baruzzo? Great. Bring him here. Tell him that we're holding his son."

♠ ♦ ♠

I was stirring sugar into my espresso when Baruzzo marched into Cenzo's office wearing the same comfortable clothes from the night before.

"This is an outrage! This is the Balmetto Festival! The most beautiful day of the year! What could possibly be so important that you've dragged me away from it?" As he shouted, his moustache twitched.

"Arresting your son isn't reason enough?"

Baruzzo swirled to face Stefano, who towered over him. "I thought you were kidding."

Stefano shrugged.

"Not again! What has that idiot son of mine done this time? Two years ago he ruined my festival with a car accident!"

"This time it's worse."

Baruzzo paused. "I suppose he hasn't been involved in another accident or we'd be having this conversation at the hospital."

"Come on," Cenzo said. "It'll be easier if you talk to him in person."

Gerardo started yelling as soon as he heard people approaching. "It's about time you brought my lawyer! This is an outrage! I demand — "

When Gerardo saw his father, his expression changed from indignation to surprise to humility. He stepped back as his father advanced.

"Gerardo, what the hell is going on?"

"Nothing, Dad! A mix-up. A misunderstanding. I won't say anything else until Cenzo calls my lawyer. I told him that last night." He tried to act normal, but his lower lip trembled.

"You've been here since last night and Cenzo didn't call me?" Baruzzo shouted more loudly than his son had.

Cenzo held up his hand as if it were a stop sign. "I never make calls after two in the morning. People hear the phone and think their relatives have died. It's too much of a shock."

Baruzzo slowly nodded. "I appreciate your not ruining my sleep. The matter was not urgent. I suppose you have uncovered my son's grappa production."

"Dad!"

Baruzzo Senior pretended he hadn't heard. "Cenzo, I know grappa production is illegal without a license. We are prepared to pay the proper fines in connection with my son's immediate release."

"It's not that easy. Your son has turned to kidnapping."

"Kidnapping!" The man's body tensed. He stood back as if he were about to bolt.

"Your son held Grazia Francese Visconti for three days."

Gerardo waved his hands. He might have auditioned for an exercise tape. "No, I didn't! She volunteered! We said she was kidnapped for Sofi's benefit!"

Cenzo strolled back and forth slowly. "So she's an accomplice. We can deal with her later. But after the concert, your son dragged Sofi to your baita against her will. He threatened to shoot Grazia if Sofi didn't sign over her balmetto to him."

Baruzzo Senior made fists. "This is nonsense!"

"I'm afraid not," Cenzo said. "Sofi's balmetto is on the other side of your property, of course. The balmetti were originally built as one unit."

"Not my property at all! The Quacchia property belongs to my wife."

"But you wanted to acquire the other side of it."

"When I thought the Americans weren't going to claim it, yes, I did. I spoke to Grazia to let her know I was in the market. In fact I gave her a ten-thousand-euro retainer which, given the circumstances, she has promised to return." He turned to his son. "But you! What have you done behind my back in time to ruin my festival?"

Gerardo said nothing. He'd turned back into a five-year-old caught with his hand in the candy drawer.

Baruzzo's face was flushed. He rolled back and forth on the balls of his feet as if he couldn't get his balance. "All this trouble for a silly balmetto!"

"It wasn't completely silly," Cenzo said. "A passageway links Sofi's to the one owned by Antonella Pasquinaletto, which is on the bottom row."

Baruzzo waved his fists at his son. "And you've been bootlegging with that nincompoop mechanic!"

Gerardo backed into the corner. He was taller than his father, but somehow he'd shrunk in stature.

"It wasn't a bad plan," said Cenzo. "They found extra space to store the grappa."

"Gerardo!"

"Bottles and bottles," Cenzo said. "I'll have to confiscate them, but that's beside the point. Here's my problem. Kidnapping is a grave offense, but in this case, we could probably overlook that as well. Murder, however, we can't."

"Murder!" Baruzzo roared.

"I'm afraid so."

Baruzzo rushed to his son, grabbed him by the shoulders, and shook. "What have you done! And why!"

"Dad, he's lying! Don't let Cenzo trick you!" Gerardo's voice had risen five notches.

Baruzzo let go, but for several minutes father and son shouted at one another in Piemontese. I couldn't catch many words, but the hand gestures and exaggerated tones were more entertaining than the best TV sitcom. I was rather enjoying myself.

When they started swinging at one another, Cenzo stepped between them.

"Hear me out," Cenzo told Baruzzo Senior. "I find that your son has been doing everything possible to get possession of the very balmetto where the mayor met an untimely death. I'm sorry, Bernardo. Either your son murdered Ivano or his accomplice did. If Gerardo was an unwilling accomplice, he should confess now. Otherwise, I'm not sure when you'll be seeing him."

Baruzzo covered his eyes with his hands. "Gerardo!"

"Dad, it's not true! I know nothing about what happened to Ivano!"

Cenzo stood back and crossed his arms over his chest. "We'll link your fingerprints to the body. It won't be that difficult."

"I had no reason to kill Ivano!"

"Sure, you did," said Cenzo. "He found out about your tunnel. He was probably going through the files when he ran across the design of the original balmetti and noticed the link between them. When he mentioned it to you, he became a liability. Worse, Ivano realized some of the balmetto owners weren't paying taxes."

"I had no issues with Ivano! If you want to learn something, ask Antonella!"

Baruzzo pursed his lips. "Ask her what?"

"She and Ivano were lovers!"

Cenzo laughed. "I learned that days ago. How does it explain Ivano's death?"

Gerardo waved his hands. "How should I know?"

"I've heard enough!" Baruzzo shouted. He shook his fist at his son. "If you got into this much trouble, you're going to have to get yourself out! Cenzo, I'm deeply, deeply sorry. I will never find words to express myself."

Baruzzo abruptly left the room. We heard the door bang behind him as he left the building.

Leaving Gerardo behind, Stefano and I followed Cenzo back into his office.

"That went well," said Stefano softly. "It's always refreshing when parents admit their children are failures."

"Heartwarming," I said. "But we have to talk to Antonella. Should we go to her house?"

Cenzo leaned against his desk. "She won't be there. We'll have to go back to the festival."

Of course. In Piemonte, tradition came first. It even trumped murder.

Chapter Thirty-Three

By the time we returned to the festival, the balmetti swarmed. Now that the rain had stopped and rays of sun darted among the clouds, people had popped up like mushrooms. While the celebration had been delayed, it hadn't been cancelled, so the air was filled with a mixture of relief and merriment.

I scanned the parade of townspeople. "We're supposed to find Antonella in all this?"

"She's here somewhere," Stefano said. "Everyone is."

"Is it crucial we find her?"

Cenzo nodded. "Better today before Gerardo talks to a lawyer and has a chance to tip off Antonella's son. Also, if we can get some information out of her, maybe even accidentally, we might know how to play things."

I didn't like his answer. "So we're laying a necessary trap."

"Something like that," Cenzo said.

Stefano pointed to the highest row of balmetti. "I'll start at the top and work my way down. Should I ask for Antonella?"

"Be subtle," Cenzo said. "Lie if you have to, as in, 'We just saw Magru, who was looking for his mother.' Sofi and I will start at Roberto and Carmela's."

Stefano slid through the crowd while Cenzo and I joined it. Passersby offered wine from their flasks while balmetto owners beckoned us inside their courtyards. Singing broke out sporadically as individuals lost their inhibitions.

On another day, I would have loved every moment. Under better circumstances, I would have thrown open the door to my newly renovated party house and invited everyone to celebrate with me. Effortlessly, I would have unloaded lots of wine. Instead every passing moment reminded me of Ivano. He would have appreciated every villager he talked to, every balmetto, and every taste of wine.

"What's the matter?" Cenzo asked as he squeezed my hand. "Would you rather people didn't think we were together?"

"If I had a problem with that, I'd never have invited you to spend the night."

He squeezed my hand again. "Then why are you so unhappy? I know it was unpleasant being with Gerardo, but—"

"No. I keep thinking about Ivano."

"Right," Cenzo said. "This was his kind of scene."

"And now his wife has schemed against me. Maybe against him too."

Cenzo pulled me out of the flow of traffic and into a niche between balmetti. He stared at me with translucent eyes and gathered my hands in his. "You can't help feeling hurt."

"Hurt? She might have murdered Ivano herself!"

"She was in Aosta, remember?"

"She had the money. She could have paid someone."

Cenzo shook his head. "We're missing some pieces. That's why we need Magru."

I leaned against the stone wall, and crumbs of cement scattered. "I've been living a lie. These last few days have reversed my whole experience in Monteleone!"

Cenzo pulled me against his chest, enveloping me with his arms and his body. "I know."

"Up until now I always celebrated my heritage. I felt smug holding a dual passport and boring friends with stories about my cousins in the Old Country. Now what? For every angel in this town, a devil lurks right behind. I can't tell the difference."

Finally he broke the hold. "It's natural that you're angry. Worse, at such an emotional time, you have to decide whether or not to sell the balmetto, whether or not to stay in Italy—"

"I took the job in Lugano. I'll be so close we can spit at one another."

For a second he wavered. Disappointment? Relief? "Great! You hadn't mentioned the interview, so I didn't want to ask."

"It doesn't pay that much. It's probably not that great a job, but it turns out that they were desperate. Maybe I am too."

"Now you don't have to worry about whether or not to fly home next week."

"I'll go ahead and use the ticket. I need to clean out my apartment, put my furniture in storage, all that stuff. I don't have to be in Switzerland right away."

"I see."

"I'm sorry I didn't tell you last night."

He hugged me again, but since I couldn't see his eyes, I couldn't read his expression. "Now you're set. You can experience Italy from a distance. You can get out of town and forget Monteleone altogether."

"I don't want to forget everything. You, for example."

He softly stroked my cheeks. "I'll be close by."

"The fastest route by train is four hours. I already checked."

He smiled as we joined the stream of traffic. "It's only two hours by car. But never mind that. For today just concentrate on the festival. There's nothing more that can go wrong."

"Sure, there is. If we run into Grazia, I might kill her myself."

Cenzo laughed, but I was only partly kidding. We visited balmetti as a couple out to enjoy the afternoon, here accepting a glass of wine, there taking a canestrello or an almond cookie. Meanwhile my thoughts bounced between Ivano and his scheming wife.

I was so distracted that I couldn't keep track of where we were. We couldn't make steady progress because Cenzo had to greet everyone he knew, which was a surprising number of people. Every time we entered a balmetto we risked another twenty-minute delay.

As we headed towards the second tier of party houses, Cenzo stopped abruptly. "See the balmetto with the gray gate? It belongs to Laura's parents. Grazia might be there. Shall I check before we go in, or would you rather skip on by?"

"We need to find Antonella. We can't afford to skip anything."

"You're sure?"

My heart pounded. "I don't want to face Grazia, but I'd rather do so with you."

Cenzo whipped out his cell phone and dialed Stefano. "Nothing yet, and we'll be out of range for a while." Cenzo tucked the phone back into his pocket. "All right. Let's give it a whirl."

"We might as well."

"Hello, everyone!" Cenzo called loudly as we entered the courtyard.

I didn't recognize the elderly couple that rose from the table to greet us, but Renato's daughter ran to hug me, and Aunt Maria tottered out from the upstairs room.

"Sofi!" Aunt Maria went down the steps one by one, right leg first, clinging to the handrail. "Sit down. We've been wondering about you. Laura and Renato have gone for a stroll, but please join us. These are Laura's parents, Marco and Valentina Moretti."

The Morettis said they were thrilled to meet me; they'd heard so much about my renovations that they felt they knew me already.

"She's the one that ruined things, isn't she?" Sig. Moretti asked his wife in French.

She quieted him down without answering, but it was too late. I'd understood the question. Was I the one who ruined his poor little son-in-law's chances for a balmetto? Yes. That was me. Guilty as charged. Had Renato been more straightforward, I might have felt differently.

I caught Sig. Moretti's eyes and gave him my best fake smile. For half a second he met my gaze, but then he turned away and picked up a toothpick. I hoped he would stick himself.

In the meantime there was a chance Cenzo and I might be hungry, so Aunt Maria immediately took out extra plates, magically producing helpings of leftovers from lunch: stuffed tomatoes, veal scaloppini piccata, soppressata, and melon slices.

"I can boil some pasta," Aunt Maria said. "It'll only take a minute."

"Please don't," I protested. "We've been snacking all morning."

"What a day!" Sig. Moretti exclaimed. "We had all the food prepared, and then it started raining so hard that we couldn't leave the house. We didn't have lunch until two-thirty."

"He doesn't like his schedule messed up," Sra. Moretti explained. "Some days it can't be helped."

Maybe not. But he sure liked his wine. And I knew just what he wanted. Another place for it.

The Morettis continued to berate the rain as if it were a personal affront. The others chimed in with their own anecdotes and complaints. It wasn't until Sra. Moretti served us coffee that Cenzo asked about Grazia.

"Silly girl," said Aunt Maria. "Last night she drove home from Tuscany. She called this morning, but she was so tired that she had to take a nap. She's going to miss the whole festival!"

Tuscany. I wondered if Aunt Maria would ever find out differently and hoped she wouldn't. She shredded her paper napkin bit by bit. "I'm worried about her, but what can a mother do?"

"Hello, hello!" A group of women knocked at the open door, chirping greetings as they waltzed in.

Antonella was among them. She was dressed simply in a flattering lavender dress. She'd secured her black, wavy hair behind her head. She'd added such a small touch of makeup that I could only detect it when we embraced. As we did, I inhaled an odd but pleasant combination of grappa and perfume.

The women crowded around the table, turning down hearty food but accepting wine and biscotti. Conversations broke out all around. Antonella spoke to us in long, exaggerated outbursts, clearly influenced by the effect of fermented grapes.

Finally the conversation turned to children.

"Where's Magru?" Cenzo asked.

"The rain didn't faze him," Antonella said. "He started drinking last night."

I faked a laugh. "Did he make it home to sleep?"

"He struggled out of bed at noon and then tore out of the house!"

The adults shared tales of similar excesses as if showing reverence for a community of vineyards. Antonella didn't seem concerned. She was perfectly at ease, chatting and laughing with the rest of them.

I felt bad for her. She had no idea an earthquake was about to destroy her pleasant world.

When the ladies rose to leave, Cenzo and I followed suit, cheerfully waving goodbye as we left the courtyard.

"Antonella," Cenzo said softly.

She turned and smiled, but she caught something in Cenzo's expression. "What has Magru done?"

"Maybe nothing," Cenzo said.

"Tell me quickly."

"We need to ask some questions."

"He's done something terrible. I can feel it. A mother can tell." She made an excuse to her friends. Then she followed Cenzo and me out to the car.

♠ ♣ ♠

Cenzo sat behind his desk like a magistrate while Antonella sat before him. I stood to the side, hoping to catch a clue from Antonella's reaction.

The woman placed both hands on the desk. "For the third time, please tell me straight out. What did Magru do?"

Cenzo nodded. "Please understand that I don't give into gossip, but I represent a government law enforcement agency and have a mandate to act appropriately. Last night I had to detain a 'guest.' I am not inclined to believe his story, but he indicated that your son may be involved in some illegal activities."

"What kind?"

"Something to do with grappa."

"Oh, God! You don't have to tell me anything else. Magru's been caught selling grappa. I knew he would get into trouble for it! He probably can't afford to pay

Party Wine

the fine, can he?" She was tipsy enough that the words just tumbled out.

"Antonella—"

"I know it's wrong! I told him so a dozen times!"

"Antonella—"

"Don't blame him too much. I haven't been a good mother!"

"I hardly think that—"

She turned to me. "When Nico died, I fell apart. I didn't know how to put myself back together. It took me five years to stop feeling sorry for myself every minute of every day."

"You went through a hard time," Cenzo said softly.

"That's no excuse. Magru suffered too. Once I even smacked him. Can you imagine that?"

"Any parent can," Cenzo said. "That's no kind of crime."

"You don't understand. You don't know what he asked for."

Cenzo clasped his hands together. "Kids have unrealistic expectations."

"Magru said he wanted a little brother! And I slapped him." She cried into her hands. "I slapped my own son because I was so mad that Nico died and left me a widow and Magru an only child. What kind of mother reacts that way?"

"You did your best," I said. "You can't take the blame for everything."

"When I finally stopped feeling sorry for myself, it was worse. I let myself have some fun."

"Why should you have done differently?" I asked.

"Sofi, you're too young to understand. Rather, you're too American. I took up with a man for no good reason."

"There's nothing wrong with that," Cenzo said.

321

"There is in Monteleone. People talk here. They judge you. Everybody knows everybody. People are your friends right up to the time they start gossiping about you."

She'd summed up the situation exactly. I wish I'd consulted her earlier in the summer.

Cenzo tapped the desk with his index finger. "Antonella, you don't seem like the type to worry over gossip."

"Usually I wouldn't care. The problem was that I got caught, and the information leaked back to my son."

"He couldn't understand that you were lonely?"

"He couldn't understand why I wouldn't remarry."

Cenzo and I exchanged glances. Neither of us had expected such easy disclosures, and they came at us faster than bursts of color during fireworks. I made a mental note to never, ever to indulge in too much wine.

"Your friend had a wife?" Cenzo continued gently.

"I turned him down. That's why Magru became upset. He stopped talking to me."

"Maybe he stopped talking for some other reason," I said. Sullen jerk.

"So, Mom, sneaking next door again tonight?' he asked.

I stood back as the floodgates sprang open. So it was true after all. Antonella and Ivano. I shouldn't have been surprised. They were both nice people. They had deserved one another.

"Who told him, I don't know," Antonella continued. "We'd tried so hard to keep things secret. I don't mean we acted as if we didn't know each other. We went out to dinner and such, but we never showed a romantic moment. I don't know how he found out."

"Maybe one of the man's friends?" Cenzo suggested.

"Maybe one of mine even though I'd only confided in a couple of people. Anyway, never mind. And may he rest in peace."

"Ivano?" Cenzo asked quietly.

She genuflected. "We saw each other on and off for about five years. Maybe longer."

"What's the problem?" Cenzo asked. "That was before Grazia, right?"

She took a shy glance at me. "By then Ivano and I were just friends, but the damage was done. Magru started getting into trouble. One thing after another. Staying out late. Never keeping a schedule. Refusing to study. Disappearing with his friends. Worst of all, money schemes—anything to get rich without much work. But he's not motivated by money, not really. He's trying to find his way, and this is the only way he's found."

Cenzo's cell went off. It took him several seconds to extract the phone from his pocket. He listened for a few moments before barking a terse *sì* into the phone.

He stood. "Antonella, thanks for coming in and talking to us. Yes, your son has been involved in illegal grappa activities, and he'll have to pay a fine. But right now, we can't continue this interview. There's been an emergency."

"What happened?" I asked.

"It's pretty typical," said Cenzo as he headed towards the door. "There's been a brawl at one of the balmetti. Stefano doesn't think he can handle it by himself."

I grabbed my purse as Cenzo whisked Antonella outside. A real-life balmetto brawl? That wasn't the kind of thing I wanted to experience second-hand. I wanted to see it for myself.

We dropped Antonella at the turnoff to Monteleone and continued to the balmetti. By now it was early evening, and the crowds were starting to thin. As we followed Stefano's directions to climb to the east end of the top tier, we met other partiers gradually making their way down.

"There's a fight up there," said an old-timer. "I'd stay away if I was you."

Cenzo thanked him for the advice. We headed upwards, but as we reached the top, the narrow lane was so full that we couldn't get through.

"Keep working towards the middle," Cenzo told me. "I'll try the other side of the lane. If we get separated, meet me back at the car."

I continued forward, hampered by the confusion of hordes coming towards me.

"Sofi!" cried a voice.

I bristled when I saw Grazia. Her hair was neatly brushed and her makeup freshly applied. She wore a stylish green blouse she hadn't bought anywhere near Monteleone. Evidently she'd recovered from her late-night walk home. Once more I wondered why Cenzo hadn't locked her in the detention room and thrown the key into the Dora Bàltea so that it would have been flushed downstream.

"Grazia." Despite the cobblestones, my cousin wore three-inch heels. The leather matched the blouse, but one of the straps had worked itself loose and was hanging around her ankle. I hoped she would trip and fall on her nose or maybe bust a few front teeth.

"I'm so glad I found you!" she exclaimed. "I'm sorry there was a mix-up last night. Gerardo gets carried away, but he doesn't mean anything by it."

It was a record: four lies in a single breath. She wasn't glad, she wasn't sorry, it hadn't been a mix-up, and Gerardo had meant quite a few things. I wondered if she'd ever told me anything without a few lies thrown into the mix. Probably not.

"Get away." I couldn't promise to account for myself.

"You don't understand."

I turned towards the crowd, struggling forwards through the descending sea of tipsy villagers.

She tagged along beside me. "Why are you so angry?"

My good angel said to ignore her, but my bad angel put on boxing gloves. "*Porca Madonna!* You need a list?"

I marched away, but Grazia darted to keep up. "You don't get it!"

"Ivano did?" I asked.

"Don't bring my husband into this!"

As I stared into her lying eyes, I curled my right hand around my upper left arm and drew back my left forearm as I made a fist. Then I continued walking.

"Ivano wasn't concerned about what I did!" she yelled.

"He was when he got killed for it!"

"You American hussy! You need to drop the charges against Gerardo."

I was so surprised by her request that I stopped and faced her. "Do you even live on this planet?"

My cousin narrowed her eyes. I'm sure she was thinking *scema, scema, scema.* "It won't do you any good to press charges anyway. In court no one trusts a stupid foreigner."

That was it. The point of no return. The point where Cenzo himself wouldn't have been quick enough or strong enough to stop me. I punched Grazia in the cheek as hard as I could. Then I reeled because I'd really hurt my hand.

I couldn't believe I'd actually assaulted my cousin. I wasn't sure whether to celebrate or chide myself. Maybe both.

Grazia lost her footing and fell to the ground. She might have expected help from a passerby, but everyone turned towards the urgent cries coming from up the road. The stream of villages carried me towards the noise.

A short distance ahead, a man lay in a heap. Three feet away, Stefano questioned a fifty-something man with stained teeth. Further back, Cenzo fastened handcuffs on a squirming troublemaker wearing ripped gray jeans and a T-shirt dotted with wine. Antonio "Magru" Pasquinaletto was under control.

As Cenzo and Stefano strong-armed the youth down the hill, Luigi trailed along of his own accord, shouting that Magru was the guilty party. Neither Cenzo nor Stefano paid attention. They were too busy yelling *"permesso."* Asking for permission to pass by merely turned them into pied pipers. The townspeople followed us, all shouting at the same time.

♠ ♠ ♠

My ears didn't stop ringing until we reached the office. While Luigi wrote out his own account of what happened, Stefano and Cenzo and I crowded around Magru, who was slumped in a chair.

"Let's hear your whole story," Cenzo said. "Start with last night."

"My nights, none of your business," Magru sputtered. He could hardly sit up straight, but whenever he leaned too much to one side, Cenzo steadied him.

"Those nights become my business when crimes are committed."

"I can do what I want!"

"Perfect," said Stefano, searching for a pad of paper. "We can add disrespect to disorderly conduct."

"Too bad there's no crime against stupidity," Cenzo said. "Hurry up, Magru. Tell us what happened without wasting any more time."

I can do what I want.

That's when I put it together. Gray jeans. Fuzz ball. I fingered the scraps in my pocket. I tried to catch Cenzo's eye, but he was too concentrated.

"Tell us!" Cenzo yelled.

"Luigi hit me, and I hit him back." He reenacted the scene by punching the air.

"I thought you said Domenico started it," Cenzo said.

"Yeah! He hit me and I hit him back."

"You must have swung pretty hard. He's on his way to the hospital."

"Domenico's a douchebag."

"You beat him up for that?"

"None of your business," Magru said as he swayed.

"When Domenico leaves the hospital, we'll see how much of our business it is."

"Lemme go back to the party!"

Cenzo got in Magru's face until the latter shrank back. "Your antics broke up the party, but so what? Just a fight. Drunks beating each other up. I don't care. I'll be happy to get rid of you as soon as you explain about your little business deal with Gerardo."

"What?"

"How long have you been producing grappa, five, six years?"

"I never made grappa!

"Gerardo is under lock next door. All morning he's been singing his head off. So I know all about the liquor. Now tell me about the kidnapping."

Magru swayed. "Gerardo! Not me!"

"You might as well tell me," Cenzo said.

"No, no, no, no!"

"No what? No kidnapping or no grappa?"

"No anything!"

We went around in circles until Magru's chin dropped to his chest and his shoulders slumped. If Stefano hadn't grabbed his arm, the drunk would have fallen off the chair. Stefano lowered him to the floor.

"This is a celebration of wrongdoing," Stefano said. "We rarely need to use both detention rooms."

"You've used them both before?" I asked.

"Another balmetto festival. What was it—two years ago?"

"Maybe three," said Cenzo. "I can't remember back that far. Here," he told Stefano, "help me with his pockets."

Stefano methodically removed a ten-euro bill, several coins, and a set of car keys. "Something's stuck," he said, reaching into Magru's other pocket. Stefano had to struggle to extract a long metal object.

"Porca mattina!" shouted Cenzo.

"This means something to you?" Stefano asked.

Cenzo grimaced. "We'll soon see how much."

I was dumbfounded. Stefano held a key to my balmetto. I snatched it up to make sure, but the workmanship was unmistakable. Magru had a key to my property. If he hadn't passed out, I would have punched him as hard with my left hand as I had Grazia with my right. Then my hands could have hurt equally.

Luigi sauntered in from the outer office holding a piece of paper with unintelligible scratching. "Here's what happened," he said. "You got a bathroom?"

Stefano escorted him to the toilet while Cenzo scrutinized the report. I looked over his shoulder but gave up after several attempts to read the first line.

"Anything important?"

Cenzo shook his head. "A regular balmetto brawl. They don't usually get this bad. Normally we wouldn't file it, but if we call an ambulance, we have to make a report." He added the date and straightened the edges Luigi had inadvertently crumpled.

I pointed at the passed-out youth. "See those raggedy jeans?" Carefully, I pulled the pieces of fuzz out my pocket. "We can prove that Magru has been on the second floor of Grazia's house."

"Good job!" cried Stefano. He addressed Cenzo. "I'm warning you about her. Pretty soon she'll be the captain and we'll be in the unemployment line."

Cenzo winked. "We'll see about that. But tell me, Sofi, how did you like the festival?"

I was sorry I'd missed all the previous ones yet thankful I'd never have to attend another. One should have been enough for anybody. "Can hardly wait for next year."

My companions both laughed, but we turned as we heard a horrible sound. Magru was snoring.

Chapter Thirty-Four

Finally Magru opened his eyes. As soon as he realized he was on an unfamiliar floor, he scrambled to sit up. The first face he saw was mine. "Where am I?"

Cenzo and Stefano pulled the youth onto a chair. "We're asking the questions," Cenzo said. "How did you get the key to Sofi's balmetto?"

"I dunno."

Cenzo dangled the key before Magru. "Talk!"

"Found it on the ground."

"That's lame even for you."

Stefano turned to me. "Are you sure there aren't a few more copies?"

I'd always been told the romantic version of how one key was made for each of the offspring, but that version had never taken the Quacchia balmetto into account. "Maybe Magru's key opens the other side."

"Of course!" Cenzo said. "The keys look the same, but they might have small differences.

"Did Gerardo give you that key?" Stefano asked.

"Don't remember."

Stefano kicked the chair, nearly sending Magru to the floor again.

Cenzo kicked the chair from the other direction. "Why did you murder Ivano when you could have paid him off instead?"

Now that he was closer to sober, Magru had lost his earlier bravado. He looked from Stefano to Cenzo as a child caught between parents. "I never killed anyone!"

"Then you planted evidence," Cenzo said.

"You can't prove it!"

Cenzo winked at me. "No worries. The lab from Torino will match your fingerprints to the crime scene. They always do."

"Cenzo!" called a woman's voice at the front door.

"Now what?" Stefano asked.

Cenzo nodded him towards the door. He returned with a more sober and hence more distraught Antonella.

"Magru! What have you done? Half our neighbors called to say you got into a terrible fight. Are you all right?"

Magru refused to meet her eyes.

"Domenico's in the hospital," said Cenzo coldly. "Your son smashed his jaw to pieces. We're waiting for an update."

"No!"

"That's not too important to us right now. We're more concerned about the murder he committed a few days ago."

"Murder!" cried Antonella.

While Magru looked away, Cenzo pointed to him. "Your son has been working with Gerardo. They conspired to kidnap Sofi after they killed Ivano."

"Killed Ivano? No, no, no, NO!!!" She shrank back as if the words wouldn't hurt as much from a distance.

"Ivano was in their way. He found out about the grappa production and was going to stop them. Instead they silenced him permanently."

"I don't believe it. I can't!"

I clutched my chest. I couldn't believe it either.

"I found the murder weapon, so to speak, in Grazia's house. The container had been wiped clean, but there was a thumbprint along the bottom. So you see, it's rather easy for us now. Before we didn't know whom the prints belonged to. Now, we check Magru; we check Gerardo. We compare. It's easy. One person committed the murder. The other will be happy to cooperate."

Antonella waved her arms like a traffic cop about to get run over by a garbage truck. "Who would want to hurt Ivano?!"

"He hurt you when he married that whore," Magru growled.

Antonella stared at her son as her eyes grew wider. "What?!"

"That coward should have married you!"

For a dark moment Antonella couldn't respond, and neither could the rest of us. We froze in place. When Stefano's cell phone rang, he ignored it, so the loud *dings* ruled the room.

"Perhaps he should have married me, darling," Antonella finally said. "Perhaps he would have been better off. But you see, I never wanted to marry him."

"Sure you did!"

There was another dead pause, a longer one. I couldn't imagine what Antonella was thinking. I didn't want to be inside her head to find out.

"We were good friends," she continued slowly and carefully, "but I'm not sure my relationship with Ivano concerns you. You have no right to judge him, and I don't appreciate your doing so."

"I know what he made you do! Ask the Pope if that's not murder!"

Antonella stepped back as if she'd been struck by Pope Francis himself.

"That selfish wolf only cared about politics!" shouted Magru as he struggled to his feet. "That's why he made you kill my baby brother!"

"No!"

"But he paid! You should have heard him deny it! 'No, I never got your mother pregnant! I loved her!' That's what the bastard said when he started choking!"

Party Wine

"You didn't!" Antonella rushed her son, hitting him in the chest with awkward blows until Stefano yanked her away and held her back. "I loved Ivano!"

"I made him pay!" Magru yelled back.

As if a higher force had turned off a switch, Antonella went limp in Stefano's arms. After she slid to the floor, she punched it. Stefano straddled her, grabbing her arms so she couldn't hurt herself.

"What do we do?" Stefano shouted.

Cenzo whipped out his cell phone. "Call Dr. Tartoli."

Magru approached his mother. "I did you a favor!"

Cenzo pushed the youth into the nearest chair. "Shut up before I belt you."

I knelt on the floor beside Antonella. I wanted to put my hand on her shoulder, but I was afraid she might lash out at me.

"I did the right thing!" Magru yelled. "I got revenge!"

"Zitto!" hissed Cenzo. "Quiet!"

Magru kept shouting, but Antonella couldn't listen. She tried to wrestle free, but Stefano held her tightly.

"Stefano, take her home. Sofi, can you help?"

After three attempts, Stefano pulled the woman to her feet. I helped Stefano push-pull her outside, where she reeled in the remaining strands of sunlight. Then we stuffed her into the passenger seat of his car.

"Her purse," Stefano said.

I ran to the office, grabbed it, and sprinted back to the car. On the short drive, Antonella curled up into a ball and wailed while I fished out her keys. When we reached the house, Stefano and I had to combine forces to get her to the door.

"Bedroom," Stefano shouted.

To the left was a living room, but the staircase was directly in front of us. Stefano dragged her up the stairs while I followed behind, bracing myself to break the fall if they should start slipping back down.

We had a choice of four rooms. In the first, dirty gym clothes covered the bed. We continued past a bathroom to a master bedroom decorated in carefully matched blues. A mirror topped a double chest of drawers. An armoire took up one wall, a picture window the other. The corner held an easy chair that was draped by a nightgown. The room's biggest feature was the king-sized bed. Stefano awkwardly lay Antonella down but had to hold her arms to keep her there.

When the doorbell rang, I hurried to admit Dr. Tartoli, an elderly man with errant strands of hair. I ushered him to the bedroom where he quickly pulled equipment from his bag and gave Antonella a shot.

"Don't let up," he told Stefano. "The effect will take a few minutes."

The wait was excruciating, but Antonella gave up on her escape routine as her limbs slowly relaxed.

The doctor sat beside his patient. "Cenzo was right. She needed a heavy sedative."

"Is this behavior normal?"

"Big shock?"

I nodded. I wasn't sure how much we were supposed to say.

"It's fairly normal."

Dr. Tartoli stayed until Antonella's eyes fluttered. Then he struggled to his feet. "She should sleep deeply for several hours straight. She'll have a bad headache when she wakes, but she shouldn't notice other side effects. Which of you will stay with her?"

Stefano and I both stuttered.

"Work it out. Make sure she wakes up to a familiar face."

He saw himself out, promising to send the bill.

Soon Antonella was sleeping so soundly that she was faintly snoring. Stefano and I tried to make small talk, but we couldn't manage it.

"I should return to the office," Stefano said. "Would you mind if . . . . I mean, it's not exactly your job to stay with her."

"Go," I said, pulling the chair next to the bed. "I'll be fine."

I wasn't fine at all. As I watched over a drugged woman whose son had confessed to killing her lover, images slammed me: Magru spying on his mother, Magru jumping to conclusions, Magru envious another man captured his mother's attention. I might have landed in a Brazilian soap opera where I couldn't understand a single line of dialogue. The good angel on my shoulder said, "This can't have happened, this can't have happened, this can't have happened."

The bad angel snickered. Then he downed a shot of grappa.

Magru had developed a simple yet efficient plan. Poison the mayor, incriminate his wife, sit back and watch the fun. My cousin was an easy victim. She was careless with locking her door because she was confident no one would dare enter her palace uninvited. She hadn't counted on a weasel like the kid from next door.

I snapped my fingers. The bottle we'd found at Grazia's was small. The contents might have come from a larger batch.

Since Antonella was still sleeping deeply, I decided to explore. Antonella's bathroom held different kinds of makeup, but nothing unusual. Magru's held toothpaste and shaving cream, but nothing more. I looked through his room as well, but all I found were stinky clothes.

Antonella hadn't stirred, so I went down to the kitchen. The small square was decorated in orange and yellow with a low-hanging glass lamp and a wooden table covered with a lace tablecloth. As I searched through the cabinets, I detected the faint smell of ginger.

Nothing seemed unusual, so I continued out to the garage. The musty space resembled an abandoned tool store. Auto parts and gadgets covered every available ledge and shelf in no apparent order. I examined the area as carefully as if Ivano's life still depended on it. For over an hour I poked around, quickly identifying any bottle that looked suspicious. It wasn't until I searched through the recycling bin that I found a possible clue: a jar with generous traces of a colorless liquid. I took pictures on my cell. Then I texted Cenzo.

♠ ♦ ♠

I woke to the sound of crying. I'd been dozing on the floor beside the bed. I twisted around to see the alarm clock, which was on the nightstand above me: four a.m. I shuffled to my feet.

"Antonella?" I hadn't shut the curtains, so light from the streetlamp shone into the room.

The woman stopped sniffling. "Sofi! What are you doing here?"

I sat on the corner of the bed. "I was supposed to watch over you, but I fell asleep."

She peeked over the side. "On blankets?"

"I hope you don't mind. I found them in the linen closet."

"I'm so sorry!" She scrutinized my makeshift bed. "No pillow?"

"Doesn't matter."

"I had two pillows here!"

"You were sprawled over both of them. It's all right. I didn't mean to fall asleep."

"This dress is a mess." She pulled it off over her head and reached for her nightgown. "What a bother I've been!"

"You had a shock. Do you remember the doctor coming?"

"I remember everything. But it's the middle of the night. You should go to bed. There's a guest room at the end of the hall."

Her offer was tempting, but I didn't dare leave her alone. "I'll stay up a while. Can I get you something?"

She donned house slippers and led me down to the kitchen.

I sat at the table while she handed me a paper sack containing bread rolls.

"Help yourself. Yesterday I was so busy drinking I forgot to eat." She checked her refrigerator. "Leftover beef?"

"Come sit down."

She brought out a dish of beef slices and egg salad. "Here, try these."

"How's your head? Dr. Tartoli said it would hurt."

As she sat, she rubbed her temples. "My head is okay, but my life is a train wreck. I could be in a psychology book. My son killed my lover for the wrong reason. Then he had the stupidity to say so in front of all of you." She pulled apart a bread roll. "Yet here I am eating."

Only in Italy.

"You have to eat," I said.

"My poor boy! He's always been so bitter, at my husband for dying, and at me for not being a father to him. Now for this. Over and over I tried to talk to him about his attitude, but he locked me out. A jail sentence won't improve his mood. Or mine."

I didn't know how to console her. Had Magru been unlikeable by nature, or had the events of his life traumatized him? Either way Antonella might have been powerless to help.

D.R. Ransdell

To fill the silence, I spread a spoonful of egg salad onto a piece of bread. I was too numb to feel hungry. "People can't help their reactions." I didn't believe it, but Antonella needed to hear it.

"They can if they try to. But first they have to understand." She forked a strip of beef. "That's Magru's problem. He never once tried."

The words hung in the air. I could already imagine a courtroom full of crying women.

Antonella placed beef slices into a bread roll. "I had an inkling about the grappa production. All of a sudden Magru stopped asking for money. He quit a regular job as a mechanic's apprentice to work on his own. I assumed he didn't want to be told what to do. That's true, of course; he won't take orders. But he had a better money supply."

Antonella stopped to catch tears that trickled down her cheeks. "I'll learn to forgive him. Somehow."

How long would she need? A year? Twenty?

She bit into the roll as if she'd been on a three-day fast, gnashing at the bread as if punishing it.

She stopped half-way through. "Magru was right about the procedure," she whispered.

I glanced around the kitchen, noticing the open windows. "How could he have found out?" I whispered back.

"It's a small town. People gossip here. They don't have anything else to do."

Antonella finished her roll in another two bites. Then she went to the refrigerator and pulled out an unmarked bottle of red wine. She set it on the table and fetched two glasses. I didn't complain as she poured one for me. If I ever wanted to go back to sleep, I'd need several.

"The irony is that Ivano never knew." Antonella took a big slug. "I thought I was through the change.

Hadn't had a period for months." She dried tears with the sleeves of her nightgown. "Then I realized I was pregnant. Unbelievable."

And really rotten luck.

"Nature plays tricks," she continued. "That's why couples who adopt immediately get pregnant afterwards. I should have been more careful, but that wasn't the issue. I wasn't afraid to be a single mother. That part I could have handled."

Her children would have been nearly twenty years apart. People would have gossiped. She would have been the butt of every joke. "Surely Ivano would have married you?"

She clasped her hands. "That man proposed to me a dozen times. But imagine! An extrovert like Ivano with me? Parties and dinners every night? Dances? Concerts? Every social occasion? He loved those things. He thrived on public gatherings. I avoid them. I like a quiet, little life, and he didn't."

"Opposites attract."

"That's true. We laughed about our differences all the time. Here's the real irony. I refused to marry Ivano because I thought it would be too hard on Magru."

Porca Madonna.

Antonella stared blankly. She was in another world, another time period, another life. One that never happened. "I'll pay for that decision forever," she said softly.

"You made a logical choice."

She didn't answer. Then she spoke so softly I could barely hear her. "The fetus showed positive for Down's Syndrome. I know such babies are the gift of God, but it was a gift I wasn't prepared for. Otherwise I would have had the child whether Ivano wanted to be with me or not. I wouldn't have cared one way or the other."

I put down my roll and shut my eyes as a chill paralyzed my spine. I would have sworn that the devil himself was standing right behind me, laughing.

Chapter Thirty-Five

The next evening, I passed out plates while Carmela monitored the boiling water. Ostensibly, Cenzo and I had been invited to the balmetto to help finish up festival leftovers. Since the orecchiette were fresh, I knew the meal was an excuse for another get-together. Also, Cenzo and I had the best information about the recent crimes.

I didn't mind Carmela's deception. The pesto smelled like it was fresh out of a royal garden, and I was finally relaxed enough to anticipate a hearty meal.

Roberto poured the first glasses of wine but jumped right in. "How did you convince Magru to confess?"

Cenzo tasted the wine and smiled. "Through his accomplice. Once we proved that he'd bought rat poison with his own credit card, Gerardo sang like a pop star."

I patted myself on the back; I'd told Cenzo to check the man's bill.

Carmela added a pinch of salt, causing the water to dance. "He admitted that he was part of the set-up?"

"Oh, no. He claims that he told Magru he was going to the Carrefour, and Magru asked him to pick up some Rogar X."

"What does the little shrimp say?" asked Roberto.

"Magru claims he was playing a trick; he wanted to see if Ivano noticed anything was wrong with the wine."

I distributed the cutlery. "A flat lie."

Cenzo shrugged. "Rat poison is rarely fatal in humans unless you have a heart attack while you're consuming it, which may have been what happened."

D.R. Ransdell

Carmela monitored the boiling pasta. "I understand about Magru, but Gerardo's wife had several lovers. Why would Gerardo focus his revenge on Ivano?"

"Sofi?"

I pulled some papers from my purse. The first was the spreadsheet I'd found in Ivano's folder. The second was Margarita's plan for selling my property.

The handwriting matched exactly.

"Ivano bought Margarita a balmetto?" Roberto asked.

"Oh, no," I said. "We don't have every detail, but it looks like they were working together. These ten balmetti? All off the books."

Carmela nodded. "So that they could make a big profit?"

Cenzo shook his head. "Not necessarily. The balmetti were leverage. Ivano granted one to the plumbers, and voilà, they all went back to work. "

"That's well and good," I said, "but balmetti don't fall from the trees. There's a finite supply."

"That's true." Cenzo pointed to the list. "I'm not sure what plans he had for the others. Stefano and I will need some time to trace all the steps."

I regretted the blows to Ivano's reputation, but now the pieces fit into place. Gerardo was jealous not only because his ex-wife and Ivano had slept together, but because they'd made important business deals. Instead of taking revenge himself, Gerardo had planted the idea into the small brain of Magru. On the surface it was a low-risk plan.

Cenzo nodded as if reading my thoughts. "Magru simply waited for a golden opportunity. He saw Ivano put grocery sacks in his trunk and guessed where the man was heading. Magru followed along, pretended he'd run into Ivano by accident, and pulled out this 'great wine' from his friend's vineyard. Something like that."

It had been that simple. As simple as pretending to be friendly. As simple as pretending to share a glass of wine. All the more reason not to drink the stuff.

Carmela strained the pasta into her king-sized pot. "What about the car?"

I took a breadstick and broke it in half. "Magru drove Ivano's car back to the house. Mechanics are always driving other people's vehicles, so no one would have paid attention. Then he walked back to the balmetto to fetch his own."

"Did you find poisoned wine?" Carmela added a small jar of homemade pesto to her pot and stirred.

"We found Rogar X in the garage."

Roberto stopped mid-sip. "So Magru was clever enough to plant evidence to implicate Grazia?"

Cenzo shrugged. "It seems she was the backup plan."

"What happens to Gerardo?" Roberto asked.

"Boh," said Cenzo, unconcerned. "He's an accomplice. It's hard to say."

Not even a discussion about murder trumped the precise moment for enjoying pasta. As soon as Carmela passed the bowl, all four of us stopped talking and concentrated on her delicious combination of olive oil, basil, garlic, and pine nuts.

Yet I ate mechanically. My mind was on Gerardo. No matter his level of culpability, the man was slippery. His parents would provide the best lawyer in the region, if not in Italy. Wearing a business suit and looking like the perfect nerd, Gerardo would claim he was joking when he suggested Magru poison the mayor. "Are you kidding?" he would say on the stand. "Who would be stupid enough to think I was serious? I bought Rogar X because my cellar is full of rats." Then they would bring

Magru on the stand, and the idiot would seem more naïve than a five-year-old with learning issues. The jury would laugh about the testimony for the rest of the day, and Gerardo would earn their affection. He was bland enough that they wouldn't see the envy lurking behind his eyes.

♠ ♣ ♠

After dinner Carmela produced almond cookies that had miraculously survived the festival; she wasn't completely kidding about the leftovers after all. "What about the grappa production?" she asked.

"Gerardo and Magru started working together a few years ago," Cenzo said, devouring a cookie as he spoke. "Gerardo had the money to back the project, and Magru knew enough lowlifes to move all the grappa they could produce."

"They're an unlikely pair," Carmela said. "I wouldn't have guessed they could work together."

"When enough money is involved, you'd be amazed at people's levels of tolerance. The problem is that the partnership allowed Gerardo to plant seeds in Magru's head over time."

I imagined Gerardo patting himself on the back as he fed nonsense to Magru step by step by step. He was a master of patience. He'd played me too. Maybe he'd played the whole town.

Roberto noticed my wine glass was empty and refilled it; he hadn't seen me switch with Cenzo. "Come on, Sofi. Drink up. A little wine can't kill you."

"It sure as hell killed Ivano," I said.

For a moment, even my noisy friends fell silent. I had the sudden urge to pick up the wine bottle and throw it against the wall, but the sacrilege might have given Roberto a heart attack.

"Boh! Leave it to Sofi to point out a good irony," Cenzo said as if I'd been joking on purpose. "Around here everyone knows that wine means life." He held up his glass. "*Salute!*"

We all toasted. Even me.

"I suppose Ivano's death had nothing to do with grappa," Carmela said.

Cenzo took the fattest remaining cookie. "Not directly. I doubt that Gerardo chose Magru as a business partner so that he could eventually talk the man into harming his rival. He saw an opportunity and used it."

I broke the remaining breadstick into twos, then fours, then eighths. "Medical staff are sworn to secrecy. Patrizia's license should be torn into pieces."

Cenzo swallowed. "In theory."

Did everyone have to think practically except for me? "I could tear her into pieces myself."

Roberto shook a napkin at me. "Don't even think about it. She plays a strong second flute."

"She'd better not sit anywhere near me."

"No chance," Roberto said. "I never put the trumpets next to the flutes."

I smiled without wanting to. I wanted to darken the mood, but I was surrounded by Monteleonesi. They took life as it came no matter the ups, downs, or sideways spills. Our lives rolled forwards. Pasta and music and friendship and sex carried us through.

I gave the mood my last shot. "Magru had no reason to go ballistic."

Cenzo reached over me to get the water jug. Since I was the only one drinking water, it was nearly full. He refilled my glass, spilling water liberally on the table as if the action might cool me down. "My guess is that Ivano went around boasting that he and Grazia were planning a family. When Magru heard that, something snapped."

"Meanwhile Gerardo enjoys a coward's revenge," said Roberto. "Your wife has an affair, so you convince someone else to harm the man who cuckolds you."

Carmela slapped his arm with a clean spoon. "Don't get any smart ideas!"

I cut into the laughter. "How much time will Magru get?"

Roberto had filled Cenzo's glass so completely that the police officer had to slurp before picking it up. "Not much."

I slammed my first on the table, making the glasses shake. Droplets of wine went everywhere. "He killed someone!"

Cenzo held up his hand as if to ward off my blows. "The death will be considered accidental. The court won't consider Magru a threat to society."

"He murdered my cousin-in-law! He should be locked up! He should never get out again."

Cenzo placed his hand over my arm. "Had Magru used a knife or a gun, he'd be much easier to convict. But rat poison?"

Gently Carmela stretched her hand across the table and took mine. "You wouldn't want Antonella to lose her son on top of losing her lover, would you?"

"A son like that she's better off without."

"All this over a misunderstanding," Roberto said.

"A sexist one!" I added.

"Yes," said Carmela. "I might have made the same choice Antonella did."

Roberto looked down at his glass, embarrassed.

Several seconds passed before Carmela asked if anyone wanted coffee.

Meekly, we all said we did. No matter how bad the truth was, we had no choice but to wade right through.

It was midnight by the time I led Cenzo into my bedroom. Of one accord we kicked off our shoes and sat on the bed.

Cenzo took my hands in his. "If you'd rather be alone tonight, I'd understand."

"The last thing I want is to be alone." I placed my leg on top of his.

He lightly touched my ankle. "Still hurt?"

"It's better. What hurts is how I feel about Ivano. I thought that knowing the truth about his death would help, but it makes things worse."

He gently curved his fingers around the part that was still swollen. "It's a stupid waste of a life, but there's no use regretting it. None of us can bring him back."

"I liked Ivano." I spoke so softly that Cenzo had to lean in to catch each word. "I was thrilled for Grazia and envious of their relationship. They seemed like the perfect couple."

"You can forget about that idea. There's no such thing. Believe me."

I didn't have a reply. Instead I listened to the growing wind, which was blowing tree branches against the house.

"I'm sorry. I didn't mean that you weren't perfect or that—" Cenzo got lost in his apology.

"I understand what you mean." I wasn't being sarcastic. I knew well enough that I had plenty of shortcomings, but that wasn't the point. I thought Grazia and Ivano had a model marriage. Finding out how wrong I was gave me a dose of reality I wasn't ready for.

Cenzo took a deep breath. "Have you thought about whether or not to press charges for the kidnapping?" he asked.

"We both know it wasn't a real kidnapping."

I reached my arms around his waist, and Cenzo drew me closer as if he needed to hold me to the bed. "After all this, I'm not sure how I feel about Monteleone," I said.

"That's understandable."

"Or Italy."

"I understand that too."

I sighed. "The job in Lugano is ostensibly exactly what I'm looking for: full-time work at a reputable school."

"Jobs are hard to get."

I ran my thumb along his arm. "Meeting you makes it harder to leave."

"You won't be far away." He fingered strands of my hair. Usually I kept it above my shoulders, but over the summer it had grown. As soon as I got back to Boston, I'd cut it all off.

I sat back so that I could study his expression. "What about your future?"

"My life is chaos." He spoke sharply, as if I'd asked a pointless question. "I need to win custody of my kids. Until I can make that happen, I'll be in limbo."

"Right.

We'd skirted the subject before, but he hadn't wanted to talk about it then either. Maybe he was right to hold back. I wasn't a parent. I couldn't guess how he might feel, especially without meeting his ex. Maybe living in London wouldn't be bad for the kids, but one way or another, it would alter their world view. Cenzo was powerless to control the situation.

"What did you decide about the balmetto?" Cenzo asked. "I suppose Renato wants it as much as anyone else does."

I gently brushed away Cenzo's hand and stretched out on the bed. Cenzo mirrored my motions.

"I'm not giving up the property. My parents have already arranged a huge family function for next summer."

They'd called three times to explain more details. So far twenty-three East Coast relatives and in-laws had promised to come, all of whom wanted to bring along extra friends. My parents would need to hire a bus to travel from the airport to Monteleone. Part of me worried the party would be a disaster, but since it was a long way off, I didn't have to worry about it yet.

"So the balmetto sits empty?"

"For the time being, I'll loan it to Roberto Two."

Cenzo retreated a couple of inches. "Did you ask Carmela about this?"

"Absolutely. We had a long discussion about it. Then we had a long discussion with Roberto Two. The balmetto is his to use whenever I'm away, but he is not allowed to store loads of wine in it." I had a sudden sinking feeling. "You didn't want me to loan it to you?"

Cenzo's loud laughs reverberated through the room. "Oh, no. Remember? I've got one."

"That might be. But everyone needs five or six as far as I can tell."

Cenzo pulled me onto his chest and kissed the top of my head. "Not everyone. I'm glad if Roberto Two has some parties there. The property needs to build up happy memories. And I'll always feel invited."

Again we fell silent. When our breathing became so loud I couldn't think straight, I rose up so that I could look him in the eye and popped the question that I'd spent half the day rehearsing. "I realize you have a good job, but would you ever consider moving to Switzerland?"

He kissed each of my eyelids. "My job doesn't pay well considering that I'm on call 24/7, so I might consider moving. But how would I fit into your life?"

I'd spent the other half of the day hoping he wouldn't ask. "I don't know."

For one day, we'd both had plenty of honesty. Gently, I unbuttoned his shirt. Ever so slowly, he unbuttoned mine.

Chapter Thirty-Six

The night before my flight to the States, I used my renovated balmetto to throw a farewell party. Aunt Maria spent two days cooking a special Bolognese sauce, Laura prepared marinated peppers and stuffed mushrooms, and Carmela made tiramisu. We had a great turnout; people I didn't remember meeting stopped by to say goodbye. Roberto Two was one of several who brought presents of homemade red wine.

The dinner should have been a grand occasion: The food was delicious, the guests were in summer party mode, Grazia's connection to Gerardo had been hushed up, and the weather cooperated by giving us a fine night that was not too hot. We only had to spray for mosquitos a couple of times. Yet I couldn't enjoy myself. A nervous stomach halved my appetite. I felt guilty about yanking the balmetto away from Renato. I had to avoid sitting anywhere near Grazia, who had invited herself. I worried that Gerardo, who was out on bail, might wander by. Worse were the moments when I caught myself imagining how much Ivano would have enjoyed the party. On top of everything else, I had the regular worries of leaving a lover, however temporarily. Would Cenzo and I keep seeing each other? Would we want to?

No one noticed my discomfort. Sitting beside me, Cenzo told endless jokes in dialect. Roberto filled wine glasses. Carmela and Aunt Maria took turns re-offering extra portions of tiramisu. Daniella taunted her baby brother while Renato and Laura watched them lovingly.

Another night in Piemonte. Another night at a balmetto, where time stretched out immeasurably and everything seemed right with the world. Could I ever live in Monteleone permanently? Would I thrive in a tightknit community where the biggest news was that the owner of the grocery store had run off with his wife's second cousin or that the vineyards were producing exactly the right quality of grapes?

Occasionally I watched Grazia, who sat beside her mother with an easy smile and a full wine glass. She wore a tight black skirt I'd never seen before and a blouse cut so low she didn't need a hand fan. Since her husband's death hadn't fazed her, the clothing was perfect mourning attire. She was more lighthearted than she'd been all summer, yet whenever she caught my eye, she scowled.

I knew why. She hadn't come to the balmetto with me or Aunt Maria or any of the other relatives. Dario Sanalto had given her a ride but then refused every invitation to join us. Instead he stood at the gate saying goodbye to Grazia for half an hour while the rest of us pretended not to notice. I didn't have to question Grazia about what she would do with money she inherited from Ivano. She wanted to do business with her old boyfriend. And then? Dario would find a way to keep thanking her for it over and over.

From time to time, Cenzo put his arm around my shoulder or his hand on my leg, but I pretended not to notice. Even though we hadn't come close to making any promises to one another, I felt hesitant about moving to Switzerland even though Lugano wasn't far away. Why had I started something I couldn't finish? I too had succumbed to lust. I might have been twenty years old. Or simply a native.

Several glasses of wine finally caught up with Grazia. When she went outside to water the rocks, I

Party Wine

followed her. A party house without a bathroom! Quaint tradition, stupid idea. It reminded me of camping, which I wasn't fond of either.

I waited until she rose from her squat. "Got something to say, Cuz, or were you scowling for the fun of it?"

"Don't be hard on me."

"You didn't answer my question."

Grazia pouted. "Don't you dare start gossiping about me when you return to Boston."

Of all the stupid things to worry about, that was the stupidest. "You don't care about anyone in the States any more than you care about anyone here. And it's not gossip when it's true."

"You know nothing about the situation!"

"I know you wanted to steal my balmetto, never mind that your husband died there. You and Renato have been praying for years that you could claim it as your own. Guess you didn't pray hard enough. Honest to God. Selling a balmetto that wasn't even yours."

Grazia stomped on the ground as if claiming it. "I needed the money."

"You had what you needed."

"Not for me. For Ivano's campaign. He couldn't run for a higher office because he didn't have the funds."

"Ivano never wanted a higher office."

"He promised to try. You think I was satisfied being the wife of the mayor of Monteleone? Think again. You wouldn't have been satisfied either."

"Ivano had the money."

"He did not."

I recalled Cenzo's conversation with Ivano's lawyer. Evidently Ivano hadn't shared every last detail with his new bride. Three points for being cautious.

"Think what you want," I said. "You always do. But Ivano was a kind man. A fine mayor. Yet there you were, working with Dario behind his back."

"What's it to you?"

I was at the edge of an angry ocean balancing against a ten-foot wave. Had Ivano sensed something was wrong? "I hope Ivano never realized you didn't love him."

"Love is overrated," Grazia said evenly. "Think you love Cenzo? You don't. And he doesn't love you. You're having a cheap summer affair."

"We're both adults. Unmarried ones." Well, almost.

"What are you going to do, be a mother to his children? Hope you're ready for that."

"What I do doesn't concern you."

"All men betray women sooner or later. You wait and see." She held up her index finger and her little finger, the sign of being cuckolded. "You'll see what being Italian means then."

"Thanks for showing me the way."

"You dumb American slut! All those nights you sat in my kitchen. When you arrived in Monteleone, you couldn't even make an espresso."

As a teacher, I'd learned to monitor myself. I knew how to keep my cool and the students' respect. But I wasn't in the classroom. I was on summer vacation. While my good angel said to calm down, my bad angel embraced my breaking point. I lunged for Grazia, and we rolled on the dusty road as we went at each other. We reached for one another's hair and pulled as hard as we could, kicking and screaming. It took several minutes for strong arms to get between us and tear us apart.

The arms belonged to Cenzo, the man who would betray me.

"Being Italian is murder, all right," I shouted. Then I brushed myself off and marched back inside the

courtyard, where Carmela succeeded in handing me another piece of tiramisu and Roberto filled my glass with his finest dry red wine.

In the spirit of everything that was Piemontese, I even drank it. Meanwhile Grazia and I glared at one another while pretending we weren't thinking about one another. I'm not sure who was the better actor.

I was still glaring when I heard someone call for me at the gate.

Antonella waited for me patiently. "I wanted to say goodbye."

I tugged at her arm. "Come in for some wine."

"No, thanks. I don't want to see Grazia."

"Neither do I."

She managed a half smile. "I wanted to thank you."

"Thank me? Ivano's death was all my fault. If he hadn't gone to my balmetto that day—"

"Sofi, stop. You won't help yourself by analyzing it." She opened her purse and pulled out a round glass charm, a black dot circled by light blue, then white, then darker blue. She laid it gently in my hand. "This is to ward off the Evil Eye. Ivano brought it to me from Cyprus, but I want you to have it. You genuinely cared for him." She briefly looked up at the sky. "I'm sure he's smiling down on us."

"I don't deserve this."

"Don't misjudge yourself. He was fond of you as well. He loved that you appreciated your Italian roots."

"By now I'm not sure if I want to be Italian or not."

As our eyes filled with tears, she gave me a big hug. "We have to go on. You do, I do. There's no other way."

As Antonella headed back towards the piazza, I sank on a rock wall and let tears run down my face. Antonella had probably been the only sincere woman in Ivano's life, the one person who had loved him truly and who had put his needs before her own. She was the only woman true enough to love Ivano yet let him go. I prayed that if I ever needed to summon such courage, I'd be able to.

"Sofi?" Carmela asked.

I hadn't heard her come up behind me. "Antonella wouldn't come in."

"No, of course not. Not with Grazia here." Carmela sat next to me. "Are you all right?"

"Not yet."

"I know it's hard about Ivano."

"Cenzo wants me to press charges against Grazia and Gerardo. On principle."

Carmela took a deep breath of fresh night air. "And you?"

"I don't want to ruin Aunt Maria's life. I want to be able to come back to Monteleone."

Carmela patted me on the shoulder. "At my house you're always welcome. Remember that."

"Have any advice?"

She smiled sadly. "Ask Cenzo about his brother. Of course, Cenzo is a Pisces. He can't help when he was born."

"What do you mean?"

"He's conflicted. He thinks one way and then another without meeting himself in between."

"That can't be good."

She stood. "It makes his life more challenging."

"What happened with his brother?"

"Ask him sometime when you're alone. Come back inside?"

I nodded. "Give me a minute."

The air was heavy with betrayal. Magru and Gerardo were ordinary idiot-criminals, but my cousin was a winner. She had betrayed me, her husband, her family, and everyone around her. She had looked me in the eye and assured me that my new companion would undoubtedly betray me too.

Her pronouncement didn't give me a lot to look forward to. But maybe Cenzo and I wouldn't get that far. We'd alluded to visiting one another over long weekends, but we hadn't discussed our relationship. We were probably too scared.

I didn't want to think so, but maybe Cenzo and I were simply normal, half in a relationship, half out, the way I was half Italian, half American, half convinced, half confused. Like a cat straddling two balmetti. Maybe that in-between, undefined space was the only honest place to be.

At least I had my own party house. At some point I would enjoy using it.

Grazia stormed off, but I didn't bother to turn around. A few seconds later Roberto called for a corkscrew. Then I heard the sound of a cork being released into the night sky followed by the swoosh of wine being poured into one glass after another.

Moments later I heard laughter. Then guffaws. Then I heard Cenzo, whose voice boomed louder than the rest.

"Salute!" Someone cried. "Cheers!"

"Salute!" went another cry.

Cheers indeed.

I went inside and picked up my glass. "Is there any more wine?"

Cenzo and Roberto raced themselves to fill my glass. I raised it high, and a few drops splashed out. "To Ivano."

"To Ivano!" my friends all cheered.

I hoped, somehow, that he heard us.

Author's Note

When my cousin Giovanni was about to get married, my great aunt arranged a trip to the U.S. for him and his bride. In a month's time the Italian newlyweds stayed with relatives in Chicago, St. Louis, Clearwater, Washington D.C., and my hometown of Springfield, Illinois. I fell in love with Gabriella, my cousin-in-law, right away. She was cheerful and beautiful. Better yet, she extended warm invitations to all the relatives to visit the couple in Borgofranco, a small burg outside Ivrea.

Over the years I have accepted her generous offer repeatedly. I've made friends with other townspeople, particularly the Sonza families, and spent wonderful, calorie-rich nights at the very best balmetti where cellars keep their wines at a perfect sixty degrees. Eventually I acquired a boyfriend who had a balmetto of his own. I naturally envisioned using his balmettto as my office space for writing murder mysteries. The boyfriend didn't work out. The writing did.

In general I've depicted Monteleone (a vague version of Borgofranco) and the balmetti faithfully, but I have taken liberties. After all, this is a murder mystery in a town where murder is unthinkable. Instead, I invite you to check out the balmetto festival that is held on the third Sunday of every June; usually festivities last all weekend. You will be invited in, handed an unending glass of wine, and fed salami and cheese and bread until your pants don't fit.

But not to worry—there aren't really any underground passages. That I know of.

About the Author

Originally from Springfield, Illinois, D.R. Ransdell now resides in Tucson, Arizona. During the school year she teaches writing courses at the University of Arizona, but during the summers she heads abroad, often to Italy. D.R. celebrates being a quarter Italian, which gives her the excuse to wave her hands when she talks. She frequently hosts dinner parties, but she never cooks. Instead she's sure to provide her guests with plenty of wine that she doesn't drink herself. Please visit her online: http://www.dr-ransdell.com